THE
EYE
OF
SCALES

THE Eye OF SCALES

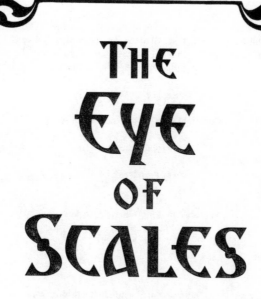

A SHROUD OF THE AVATAR NOVEL

TRACY HICKMAN AND RICHARD GARRIOTT

TOR

A TOM DOHERTY ASSOCIATES BOOK
NEW YORK

THE EYE OF SCALES

A Tor Book
Published by Tom Doherty Associates
120 Broadway
New York, NY 10271

www.tor-forge.com

Tor® is a registered trademark of Macmillan Publishing Group, LLC.

Library of Congress Cataloging-in-Publication Data

Names: Hickman, Tracy, author. | Garriott, Richard, author.
Title: The eye of scales / Tracy Hickman and Richard Garriott.
Description: First edition. | New York : Tor, 2022. |
Series: Blade of the avatar ; 2 | "A Tom Doherty Associates book."
Identifiers: LCCN 2022008339 (print) | LCCN 2022008340 (ebook) |
ISBN 9780765382320 (hardcover) | ISBN 9781466886810 (ebook)
Subjects: LCGFT: Novels. | Fantasy fiction.
Classification: LCC PS3558.I2297 E96 2022 (print) |
LCC PS3558.I2297 (ebook) | DDC 813'.54—dc23/eng/20220224
LC record available at https://lccn.loc.gov/2022008339
LC ebook record available at https://lccn.loc.gov/2022008340

Our books may be purchased in bulk for promotional, educational, or business use. Please contact your local bookseller or the Macmillan Corporate and Premium Sales Department at 1-800-221-7945, extension 5442, or by email at MacmillanSpecialMarkets@macmillan.com.

First Edition: 2022

Printed in the United States of America

0 9 8 7 6 5 4 3 2 1

CONTENTS

THE
EYE
OF
SCALES

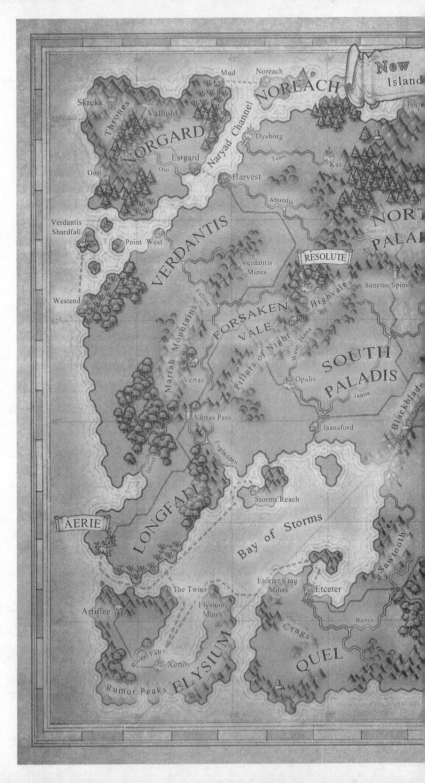

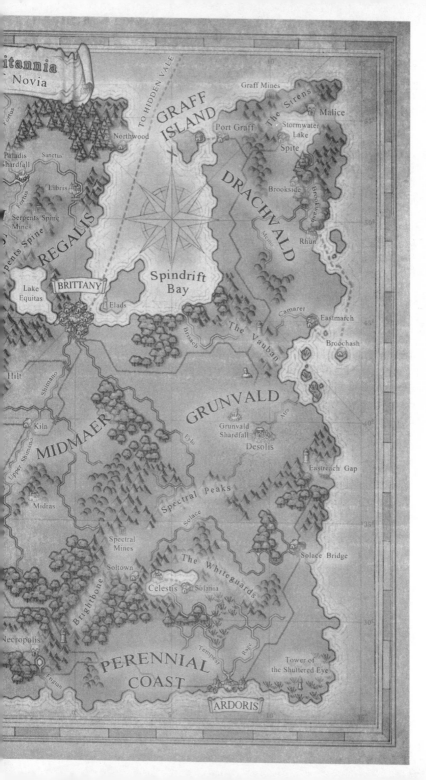

CHAPTER
1

The Guest of Opalis

Fires burned on the watchtowers flanking the ruined gate into the once proud city of Opalis. Normally such a great city would have cast a glow into the night sky, radiating its light into the darkness beyond. Now the twin fires on either side of the yawning opening were the only evidence the city was inhabited. They shone in the blackness like the reflected eyes of a cat, but weren't even bright enough to illuminate the churned and broken ground that had once been Opalis's grand thoroughfare.

Evard Dirae, craftmaster of the Obsidian Order, pulled up the hood of his heavy traveling cloak, lest any vestige of the watch fires illuminate his mostly white hair. It had been almost a month since the fall of Opalis and events had gone decidedly against him. The amount of magic he'd been forced to expend in an effort to simply learn what actually happened had been appalling, and still he did not know it all.

At least the guards aren't attentive, he thought as he passed the broken gate, well beyond the reach of the ineffective watch fires. Of course the guards had little need to be wary. Word of the fall of Opalis had gotten out and how it was now a ruined shell, a plundered corpse left to rot in the South Paladis sun.

Evard drew his cloak about his shoulders as a melancholy drizzle began to fall. The heat of the summer campaign season had given way to the first stirrings of autumn, and the air of the plains had turned chill. He cast a baleful glance into the sky as if the rain and the cold were some kind of personal affront and got a fat drop in one of his eyes for his trouble.

Cursing quietly, he turned left from the gate, passing between two buildings that had the look of warehouses, and found an alley that ran more or less west. The last time he'd been in Opalis, it had been teeming with life, with people moving here and there on purposes of their own. In such an environment it was easy to pass unnoticed. People bent on their own purposes had little time for strangers. Now, however, he would stand out like a candle in a dark room if anyone saw him, so he resolved to keep off the main streets.

As if to punctuate his reasoning, the ruddy light of a lantern sprang up at the far end of the alley where it met a main street. With nowhere to go, Evard pressed up against the side of the alley and held still. He watched as five legionnaires of the Norgard Empire passed by. They were relaxed, men with no fear of ambush or attack, yet one looked down the alley just the same.

Evard closed his eyes and focused his mind. He had enough magic left to deal with these soldiers if it came to that, but he'd rather it didn't. His reserves were perilously low and he was physically exhausted. The fewer problems he encountered, the better.

The legionnaire at the end of the alley paused and Evard's heart skipped a beat. He could clearly see the man's face in the torchlight. A ragged scar ran down the legionnaire's cheek splitting the stubble of a short beard as it disappeared under his jaw. The guard's eyes swept back and forth, passing over Evard's still form twice, then he turned away.

Evard waited a full minute after the light of the torch disappeared before he moved. When he reached the main thoroughfare there was no sign of the patrol. Breathing a sigh of relief, he pressed on.

Against the western wall of the city were the barracks of the city's former defenders, the Opalis Legion. Lights burned in the windows and Evard could see guardsmen leaning wearily on their spears as they stood watch by the gate and on the roof. Evard's attention lingered on the barracks and its dozing guards for a long moment, then he turned south, past the occupied buildings, to a squat, dark structure beyond, which housed the city jail. Under normal circumstances, it would house pickpockets, brawlers, drunks, and the odd malcontent. Today, it stood all but empty. There weren't even guards posted at the doors. If Evard's information was correct, however, the jail's sole occupant was the one man in the world that could tell him what he most wanted to know.

The whereabouts of Aren Bennis.

† † †

Evard pushed open the outer door of the jail and passed inside. The door creaked loudly as he pulled it closed behind him, but it wouldn't matter. He'd spent the last two hours watching the building and in all that time no one had come to check on the prisoner. He doubted anyone cared.

The inside of the jail was simple and utilitarian, much like the rest of the city. A guard area occupied the front with a hallway behind that had cells on either side. Evard summoned a sliver of his magic and raised his hand. A pulsating sphere of dim, silver light appeared over his open palm and he waited as his eyes adjusted to it before proceeding.

"Who's there," a raspy voice echoed from a cell in the very back.

Evard took great satisfaction at the miserable sound of it.

"Why General," he said, moving down the aisle, "I'm hurt you don't remember me. Has it been so long?"

As Evard reached the last cell, the faint light spilled over the man in the cell. General Milos Karpasic was huddled in a pile of straw for a bed and had a ragged blanket pulled about his shoulders to ward off the chill of the autumn night. This was a far cry from the haughty figure who had defied him and attacked Opalis before Evard's plans had been set in motion. It could be argued that all of Evard's current problems, the disappearance of Aren and the loss of the Avatar sword were directly attributable to that one act of defiance.

Karpasic's eyes narrowed as he recognized his visitor. Evard had expected the general would react with fear, but instead he seemed almost bored.

"Oh," he grunted, pulling his blanket around him more tightly. "It's just you. Come to gloat, or was this your plan all along?"

"My . . . ?" Evard stammered, dumbstruck. "How dare you lay this debacle at my feet," he growled, resisting the urge to shout. "Where is your army, General Karpasic? Where is the Avatar sword? Where is Aren Bennis?"

As Evard spoke, the silver light from his sphere grew brighter with his anger and he had to will it to dim again. Karpasic chuckled. It wasn't a mirthful sound, but rather one of mockery.

"So, he stuck the same knife in your back that he used on me, eh Sorcerer?"

Evard resisted the urge to summon enough magic to burn Karpasic to a cinder. Plenty of time for that later. Right now the man wasn't making sense, which meant Evard was still missing something—either that or the general's defeat had unhinged him.

"Who stuck a knife in my back?" he asked, forcing himself to be patient.

"Bennis!" Karpasic roared, surging to his feet. The blanket fell away, unnoticed, and Evard got his first good look at the man. He was noticeably thinner. It looked as if he'd lost near fifty pounds. Evard wondered if the Norgard soldiers were feeding him at all.

"What about Captain Bennis?"

Karpasic laughed again, but this time it *was* the sound of mirth.

"You don't get it," he said, slumping against the bars of his cell. "It was Bennis."

"He didn't deliver this city to you as we agreed?"

Karpasic stared through the bars, his wild eyes boring into Evard's.

"Of course he did," Karpasic giggled. "He marched out of here with his train of peasants and left the gate wide open."

"Then make yourself clear, General," Evard said, steel creeping back into his voice. "If you can."

"We took possession of the city without even drawing our weapons," Karpasic said. "But what did we find when we got here? What of the famed treasure of Opalis?"

The general seemed to be waiting for a response, so Evard shrugged.

"I give up, what did you find?"

"Nothing."

Evard raised an eyebrow at that. Everyone knew of the vast wealth of Opalis, even in faraway Desolis.

"Are you suggesting that Captain Bennis smuggled the treasure out of the city under your very nose?" Even as he said it, Evard knew that wasn't possible. A man possessed of as much greed as Karpasic wouldn't have allowed a copper penny out of the city.

"I don't know how he did it," Karpasic growled. "I only know that when we broke into their tower, there was nothing there." He took hold of the bars and pressed his face against them. His skin was loose because of the weight loss, and as he pushed against the bars, it stretched tight across his cheeks, leaving him with a feral grin. "And do you know what happened then, Sorcerer?"

Evard was firmly convinced that he didn't.

"The legions of Norgard surrounded the city," Karpasic went on. "Pinned us in here like rats in a trap."

Evard opened his mouth to scoff at that, but shut it almost immediately. He could see where Karpasic was going with this story.

"You think Captain Bennis tipped them off," he said. "You think he planned to betray the Empire."

Karpasic backed slowly away from the bars, but the manic smile on his face didn't move.

"Either that or the legionnaires of Norgard are the luckiest troops in all Paladis, coming upon us in exactly the right moment. That would be quite the coincidence, don't you think?"

Evard was young as sorcerers went, but he'd seen enough of life not to believe in coincidence. There were only three people who knew where and when Aren would surrender the city, and two of them were here in this jail.

"Ha!" Karpasic roared. He must have seen the realization in Evard's face. "He fooled you too, Craftmaster Dirae!"

"Lower your voice," Evard hissed, casting a nervous glance back up the aisle toward the front of the jail.

"That arrogant bastard fooled you," Karpasic said in a softer tone. "But you know who he didn't fool? Me. I knew he was an uppity little backstabber, always parading around like my victories were his, like I couldn't be trusted to put on my armor without his direction. I saw through all that. I put him in his place . . . until you intervened."

Karpasic threw back his head and laughed.

"That's right," he said, his flabby sides shaking with mirth. "You wanted him alive. If you'd just let me kill him like I wanted to, none of this would have happened. Look around, *Sorcerer,* this is all your fault."

"That's why you marched on Opalis," Evard snapped, putting the pieces together. "You wanted to make sure Aren was dead before I could find out how he came to be captured by the Council of Might."

"Of course I did," Karpasic said, his laughter subsiding. "And everything would have worked if you hadn't stepped in."

"You defied your orders," Evard pointed out. "You'd have had to answer for that in any case."

"Orders to march an entire army to the place where the Sanctus and Fortus Rivers cross?" Karpasic scoffed. "There's nothing there. It was a staging area, no one would care if we arrived a week or two late. And we would have, rich as kings to boot—if that traitor Bennis hadn't sold us all to the Norgards."

Evard ground his teeth. Karpasic was making sense, and worse, he didn't appear to be lying, which was the last thing the sorcerer had expected.

"Where is the Westreach Army, General?"

"Oh, your friend took care of them, too," Karpasic said. For the first time in their conversation his words sounded bitter. "I knew we only had one chance with the Norgard army pinning us in the city."

"You ordered your men to attack," Evard guessed.

Karpasic nodded.

"If we'd waited in the city, we'd have only grown weaker and more desperate," he said. "Our one chance was to break the Norgard lines and run for it."

"What happened?"

Karpasic shrugged then shook his head.

"We almost made it," he said. "Some of the men managed to escape, I think, but . . ." He shrugged as if what he was saying weren't really important. "The rest were cut down as they fled."

"Except you," Evard observed.

Karpasic snarled but the look on his face was one of shame.

"They had orders to take me alive," he admitted at last.

"So the rest of your army, a force of some thirty thousand men and Fomorians is—"

"Dead," Karpasic finished.

"Why do they want you?"

"I have no idea." He looked up the hall toward the door and the barracks beyond. "They haven't asked me any questions. It's like they don't know what to do." Karpasic chuckled. "The guards say they're going to chop off my head in a public execution but they can't decide if they're going to do it in Etceter or in Valhold."

"Then why not get on with it, General," Evard said. "There must be some reason they're keeping you alive."

He looked back at Evard again, the feral snarl back on his face.

"I'll be sure to ask them the next time they come in to mock me," he said, anger bubbling up in his voice. "Those pitiful excuses for soldiers have the gall to mock me, General Milos Karpasic, who's seen more conquest in the last year than they will in their entire worthless lives. Yet I must sit here and listen to them plan my execution."

Evard suddenly realized why, when he'd first appeared, Karpasic didn't fear him. Why he'd been taunting and baiting Evard the entire time.

"And you want me to end all that for you?" he guessed.

Karpasic lunged to the bars, reaching through as if he meant to strangle Evard.

"You owe me, Sorcerer," he spat as Evard stepped back. "If it wasn't for your close personal friend, Captain Bennis, I wouldn't be in here and my army would have another city for the glorious Obsidian Empire. But no, thanks to you and that traitor, the Westreach Army is lost. The Empire will never take me back, and it's your fault. The least you can do is end my suffering, you witless fraud."

Evard just stood, staring at Karpasic as the general clawed at him through the bars of his cell. He didn't want to believe that Aren could have betrayed the Empire so completely, but if Karpasic was right, the defeat of the Westreach Army had been brought about with a level of precision and planning that far exceeded the Norgard Legion. This was devious and precise, two traits that Aren Bennis had in abundance.

He shook his head. Whatever part Aren had played in this, Karpasic had brought his current predicament on himself.

"No," he said, fixing Karpasic with a cold stare.

"You can't leave me here," he snarled. "How would it look for a general of the Empire to be executed in a jerkwater place like Valhold. Do it, Sorcerer. Kill me."

Evard smiled at that. "I don't think I will."

"You owe me," Karpasic snarled.

Evard took another step back. "You seem to have given your pitiful circumstances a great deal of thought during your incarceration, General Karpasic," he said. "It's a pity that you haven't spared any of your valuable time on self-reflection. Self-reflection is good for a man. I wouldn't dream of depriving you of the opportunity to engage in it."

Karpasic pulled his arms back into his cell and grabbed the bars as if he meant to physically bend them open.

"You think you can deal with me like this, Sorcerer?" he shouted. "I'll bet the Norgards would much rather have a craftmaster of the Obsidian Cabal. It might even be worth the life of a general!" He turned and screamed up the hall toward the front of the jail, "Here! In here!"

Evard opened his palm and the silver ball of light he'd been holding leaped away. It streaked across the intervening space and slammed into Karpasic's gut. The air went out of the general's lungs with a whooshing sound and he dropped.

Even before he hit the ground, Karpasic was struggling for breath, gasping to fill his lungs again to shout some more. Evard could easily kill him. He wanted to kill him, but thought better of it.

"Enjoy your execution, General," he said, making his way quickly toward the front of the jail. "I wish I could be there to see it."

Evard opened the door to the jailhouse and peeked around it, but he needn't have bothered. No one had come in response to the general's summons. He left the building, shutting the door carefully behind him, then made his way back toward the backstreets and alleys that would conduct him to the broken gate.

It was a relief that he didn't see any more guards or patrols, but his mind wasn't easy. He'd expected the news to be bad once he'd learned that Karpasic had been taken by the Norgards, but the reality was worse even than he imagined. The Westreach Army lost, the Avatar sword in the hands of the enemy, and worst of all—Aren had done it.

It was unthinkable.

Evard and Aren had grown up together. He knew Aren as well as he knew himself, perhaps better. It was simply impossible that Aren had betrayed the Empire—betrayed him.

"Something else is at work here," he said out loud in an effort to convince himself.

The sword.

The cursed Avatar sword.

That had to be it. Karpasic had said it was cursed, that it had spoken to him when he touched it. And now the sword was speaking to Aren.

That explained everything. The sword knew the Obsidian Inner Circle meant to destroy it and has used that knowledge to poison Aren's mind. This probably convinced him that Evard himself meant him harm.

He clenched his fists, digging the nails of his hands into his palms as the realization washed over him. It's a good thing he hadn't found Aren yet. The sword would have tried to kill him, and he'd have been forced to kill Aren, never understanding why. Now, however, he knew what the sword had done. Now he had a chance to stop it, to save Aren.

"Hang on, Brother," Evard said to the dark, drizzling sky. "I'm coming for you."

CHAPTER 2

The Army of Might

The smell assaulted Mikas Trevan, captain of the Opalis Legion, long before the field came into view. A sickly mixture of putrefaction, offal, and the iron tinge of blood hung like a vapor in the humid air. He wrinkled his nose at the stench, pulling a kerchief tied around his neck up and over his nose and mouth.

"Whew," grunted the young man in plated armor riding alongside the captain as he reflexively put down the visor of his helmet.

"There's nothing like the stench of a battlefield, Sir Llewellyn," Trevan said. Unlike the young knight, Trevan was the veteran of many such fields. Opalis had been a peaceful city for generations, but any trading city will attract bandits, highwaymen, and thieves. In his younger days Trevan made quite a name for himself hunting down raider bands who would prey on the caravans traveling the Broken Road. It was that very reputation that had ultimately elevated him to the post of captain of the Opalis Legion.

"If you say so, sir," Llewellyn said.

A gagging noise came from inside the young knight's helmet, and Trevan was glad the kerchief hid his reflexive grin.

"Breathe through your mouth, son," he told Llewellyn. "Trust me, the air tastes much better than it smells."

"Thank you, sir," the knight said after a moment to recover himself.

"Captain Trevan," the overeager voice of Lorekeeper Wren called from behind.

Trevan stifled a groan and turned to watch the approach of a skinny woman on a dappled mare. She was tall and bony, all elbows and knees, with mud-brown hair and a long nose that reminded the captain of a weather vane. She had a near permanent squint to her eyes that Trevan attributed to too much staring at dusty books by candlelight, and she seemed to have been sent along on this expedition for the sole purpose of annoying him.

"How can I help you, Lorekeeper?" Trevan asked, managing to keep from sighing as he said it.

"I believe we're almost there," Lorekeeper Wren said, pulling a rolled map from a leather case at her side. "According to the reports, the location of the battle was just south of the northern edge of the Mariah Mountains near the Forsaken Vale." She unrolled the map and squinted at it, hunting for the location she'd described.

"Yes, Lorekeeper," Trevan said as patiently as he could manage. "I believe we've all apprehended that fact. Perhaps you've noticed the smell?"

Trevan was quite certain the lorekeeper hadn't. He was fairly sure she only noticed the going down of the sun because it made it harder to read.

"Oh," Wren said, her face wrinkling up in disgust. "That's very foul, isn't it?"

"Yes, Lorekeeper, it is."

"Well then," Wren said, her face brightening. "I was right, we're almost there. According to the message, Colonel Hendricks of the Aerie Army will be here somewhere to meet us."

"I remember," Trevan said. He could already see the thin smoke of a fire rising up above the plains to their right.

"That must be him there," Wren said, following Trevan's gaze. She turned her dappled mare but Trevan urged his own mount forward, blocking her path.

"If you don't mind, Lorekeeper, I'd like to survey the field of battle first."

Wren's face fell but then she shrugged.

"As you wish, I suppose."

Trevan didn't bother to explain that whatever kind of soldier Colonel Hendricks of Aerie was, he would probably want to explain his defeat in the most flattering terms. Terms that might have nothing to do with the truth. Battlefields, on the other hand, never lied.

"Lorekeeper!" Captain Artemis called as she came galloping up from the rear of their company. A dozen knights and a small baggage train with porters had accompanied Trevan on his mission to the Verdantis region. Artemis had been his choice to take charge of the troublesome lorekeeper, but while she was a competent archer and commander, she had precious little ability when it came to Wren.

Trevan gave her a flat stare as she approached, and she blushed. She reined her horse to a stop and her black hair swirled momentarily about her face. Artemis had been one of the legion captains assigned to the walls of Opalis, the leader of a company of archers. Now she, like Llewellyn and Trevan, was a soldier without a country. She still wore her battle dress: a blue tunic with the silver falcon of Opalis emblazoned on the back over a chain shirt. The only alteration was a scrap of black cloth tied around the bicep of her left arm. Trevan and Llewellyn each wore one, too, the outward symbol of their exile.

"There you are," Artemis said to Wren. "Captain Trevan charged me to make sure you were safe during our trip, you shouldn't wander off."

Wren gave the archer a contemptuous look down the long axis of her nose and sniffed.

"I'm in the middle of a group of soldiers," Wren protested. "I am not a child that needs minding."

Trevan was about to say something impolitic when young Llewellyn spoke up.

"With the Obsidian raiders on the loose, Lorekeeper, we would all do well to be on our guard."

This seemed to mollify the lorekeeper, which surprised Trevan. In his experience the woman was headstrong and had an opinion on everything. No doubt the reason the loremasters of the Atheneum sent her on a mission several hundred leagues from their new temporary home in Resolute. Still, she didn't seem inclined to argue with Sir Llewellyn.

Correction, Lorekeeper Wren doesn't seem inclined to argue with the handsome young knight, Sir Llewellyn.

Trevan smiled under his kerchief but the expression was short lived. As they topped a small rise, the site of the battle came into view. It was a wide flat bowl with the rocky foothills of the Mariah Ridge to the west and small woods to the south. It didn't seem very large, but the ground was strewn with slain horses, broken carts, and bloody warriors. Over a hundred corpses littered the ground, most stripped of their clothes and armor and left to bloat in the sun.

Trevan could see the occasional Obsidian monster among the dead. Most were obvious, as they had horns and a coat of short fur covering their bodies, but the ones with the pointed ears looked almost human.

"What are we to make of this?" Artemis said, reining in her mount next to him.

"A moment," Trevan said, then turned to the young knight on his other side.

"Sir Llewellyn," he said. "I have no doubt that Lorekeeper Wren will wish to survey the battlefield thoroughly so she can make an accurate report to her superiors. I want you to accompany her and make sure she has everything she needs."

"As you command, Captain," Llewellyn said, saluting smartly.

Wren opened her mouth to protest, but shut it again immediately.

"That will be fine, Captain," she said after a pause. "Thank you."

"This way, Lorekeeper," Llewellyn said, guiding his horse onto the field.

"Neatly done, Captain," Artemis said with a wry smile. "Though I don't envy Sir Llewellyn the responsibility."

Trevan wanted to agree, but the sight of the corpse-laden field drove any feelings of levity from his mind.

"The Obsidians lured our people here," he said. "They drew them onto the field, then ambushed them from those trees." Trevan pointed to the woods on the far edge of the field.

Artemis cast him a sidelong glance.

"How do you know that?"

Trevan pointed to the dead, lying where they fell.

"What do you see, Captain?"

Artemis straightened in her saddle, then stood up in the stirrups to get a better look.

"I can't tell friend from foe, apart from the obvious," she said.

"The enemy monster corpses down here are shot full of arrows," Trevan said. "You can see the shafts even from here. While these—" He pointed to a sort of goat man that lay in the grass near them as Artemis cast him a sidelong glance where they'd stopped. "These at this end of the field have pike wounds."

Artemis' gaze darkened slightly and she nodded.

"I see," she said. "The Obsidians rushed out of the woods, and some of them were cut down by Colonel Hendricks' archers."

"And?" Trevan prompted when Artemis paused.

"And Hendrick's archers were sent by Resolute," she said. "They're some of the best in the world, apart from my men. They would have cut down more if they'd been expecting a charge."

"That's the way I see it," Trevan said.

"How did the Obsidian raiders manage to ambush Hendricks?" Artemis asked. "Is he a fool?"

Trevan didn't know Hendricks, not even by reputation, but he doubted the Council of Might would turn over their new joint force to an incompetent commander.

"The Obsidians have been raiding towns and villages all over this area, so Hendricks thought of them as raiders," Trevan guessed. "He hunted them like raiders instead of like a disciplined army."

"What's the difference?" Artemis asked.

"Raiders are mostly cowards," Trevan said. "Once you get their scent, you run them to ground. They might put up a fight, but most will surrender if you offer quarter. Trained soldiers, on the other hand, they expect a fight, and Obsidians expect to win. I very much doubt if Hendricks is up to the task of hunting this kind of enemy."

If Artemis had an opinion on her captain's words, she didn't share it. After a few more minutes of silence, Trevan sighed.

"All right," he said, turning his mount toward the column of rising smoke to the west. "Let's go meet Hendricks and hear his side of things."

† † †

The encampment of the unified army of the Council of Might occupied a flat area right up against the mountains. There was a bored sentry at the edge of the camp who waved them through without listening to their names or their business.

"I didn't see any scouts," Artemis said.

"Hendricks isn't expecting trouble."

"That didn't work out very well for him before," Artemis said, looking back in the direction of the battlefield.

Trevan swept over the camp with his gaze. None of the soldiers seemed ready for a fight. Most weren't wearing their armor and some didn't even have weapons ready to hand. The ground was fairly defensible, especially with the mountain at their back, but if they were attacked now, most of these warriors would die before they could form up into ranks.

It was not encouraging.

Worse were the looks the soldiers gave him as he passed. They were curious, but none of them seemed to care who he was or what errand he might be on. They seemed resigned—numb. There was a spark of life in the Norgard soldiers, however. They saw the black armbands

Trevan and Artemis wore and wrinkled up their noses in disgust. Trevan ignored them and simply rode on.

"We're getting some hard looks from the Norgards," Artemis observed.

"Legate Argo lost more troops than he bargained for when they took Opalis from the Obsidians," Trevan explained. "They blame us for not softening up the Obsidians first."

Artemis's lip curled at that and her eyes narrowed.

"If their greed to take Opalis drove them into a fight they weren't prepared for that's no fault of mine," she said.

"Agreed," Trevan said. He was grateful that the Norgards managed to defeat Karpasic and his army, but it had still cost him his home to do it. He resolved not to think about that as they neared their meeting with Colonel Hendricks of Aerie.

Two pikemen in burnished breastplates stood outside the entrance to an enormous tent erected in the center of the camp. They saluted smartly as Trevan and Artemis approached. One was a senior soldier with bushy gray eyebrows and a stern, craggy face while the other was young with the stubble of a half-grown beard on his chin.

"Captain Trevan," the elder guardsman said, stepping forward to take the reins of Trevan's horse. "Colonel Hendricks is waiting for you inside."

Colonel Malcolm Hendricks, formerly of the Grand Army of Aerie, was a short, middle-aged man wearing an impressive dress uniform of red, with high boots, shined to perfection, and a decorative sword that could only be ceremonial at his side. He had a drooping gray mustache that gave his countenance a sorrowful, disapproving look.

Trevan took the measure of the man the moment he entered the overlarge tent. The colonel was clearly a career military man rather than some political stooge. He was fit, his uniform was immaculate, and he observed every rule of protocol when he greeted his guests.

"Captain Mikas Trevan of the Opalis Legion," he boomed when Trevan and Artemis were ushered in. "I am Colonel Malcolm Hendricks, commander of the unified army under the direction of the Council of Might. I greet you cordially and extend to you all the courtesies and hospitalities of my command."

He inclined his head and Trevan did as well. In Opalis he often had to engage in such formalities and he knew them by heart.

"I greet you cordially, Colonel Hendricks," he said. "And thank you for your welcome."

"Enough of that," Hendricks said, his voice terse. "You're here to find out who's responsible for this mess and report back to the council. Or did the council send you out here as my replacement?"

"Nothing like that," Trevan said, pasting on an easy smile. "They're naturally concerned after hearing your messenger's request for more troops, and they sent me to assess your needs."

Hendricks' mustache drooped even further, and Trevan could tell he didn't believe that explanation any more than Trevan did when he said it. Still, polite fiction was the heart and soul of diplomacy and Hendricks didn't challenge it.

"Tell me about the battle," Trevan said.

"Nothing to tell," the colonel said. "We picked up the raiders' trail and chased them all the way here. We would have taken them, too, but . . ." He rubbed his chin.

"But they suddenly got reinforcements," Trevan guessed.

"A bunch of those goat men and other abominations came right out of the woods at us. I got our pikemen turned to face them, but the archers were out of place. The Ardorin swordsmen charged and left them exposed." The colonel shook his head and sighed. "By the time I got everyone moving in the right direction, the archers had been wiped out."

"How many?" Artemis asked.

"We had eighty-two of Resolute's finest," Hendricks said. "Now we have seven. Of those, three are wounded and the healer tells me one of them won't live out the night."

"The warlords of Resolute aren't going to be happy about that," Artemis said.

"It's worse," Hendricks said. "They're refusing to send replacements. It's outrageous, this whole affair is outrageous."

"How so?" Trevan asked.

"From what I've heard, the raiders have split into two groups," Hendricks explained. "Together the two groups make up a regiment, at least twelve hundred men."

"That's not a raiding party, that's an army," Artemis said.

"Yes, and you don't have that many soldiers," Trevan observed. "Do you, Colonel?"

"No. Each member of the council sent a contingent, but each one would only send as many men as the others. Since Aerie is a small country and Etcher only has their guardsmen, they only sent a company each."

"That means you've got, what, eight hundred men?"

"Less after the fight with the Obsidians," Hendricks snarled. "And now Resolute won't send reinforcements, the cowardly bastards."

"Do you have any idea how long it takes to train a good archer?" Trevan asked.

Hendricks bit back an angry reply before admitting that he didn't.

"This is Captain Lynn Artemis." Trevan formally introduced his second. "She commands a company of archers and is responsible for their training."

"So how long does it take, Captain?" Hendricks asked the archer.

"If you want really good bowmen," Artemis said, "you start by training their grandfathers."

Hendricks considered that, then shook his head.

"Be that as it may, I still need archers. If your job is to tell the council what I need, then go back and tell them that."

Trevan smiled and put out his hand.

"I'll do that, Colonel," he said as the older man shook his hand. "With your permission, I'd like to look around the camp, then my men will need a place to set up."

"My aide will see to that," Hendricks said, turning back to a map table that stood to one side of the tent.

Trevan looked at Artemis and inclined his head toward the door.

"One more thing, Captain," Hendricks said as they started to leave. "How is it that you are a captain and Captain Artemis is a captain? I thought you were in charge of the Opalis Legion."

Trevan chuckled at that.

"I am," he explained. "Artemis is a captain *in* the legion, but I am captain *of* the legion. My official title is Grand Captain."

Hendricks turned from his table and actually looked surprised.

"That's confusing," he said. "If I failed to greet you properly, though, I meant no disrespect."

"No harm done," Trevan assured him, then Hendricks turned back to his maps and Trevan and Artemis left the tent.

"That was productive," Artemis said once they were outside. The tone of her voice clearly indicated that she thought the opposite. "Do you want me to find the colonel's aide and get our people situated?"

Trevan shook his head.

"No," he said. "We're heading back immediately."

To her credit, Artemis didn't act surprised.

"What about your duty to report the condition of the joint force to the council?" she asked. "They'll want to know why the raiders are still free to pillage Verdantis and South Paladis."

Trevan climbed back up on his horse and then pointed at the tents laid out around them.

"Take a good look, Captain," he told the archer. "A blind man could see it."

Artemis glanced around and then shrugged.

"They look like soldiers," she said. "Like any soldiers anywhere."

"Except the Norgards are there—" He pointed to the tents that flew their banner. "The Ardorin swordsmen are there, the Aerie pikemen are here—"

"And the contingent from Resolute is over there," Artemis finished. "Why does that matter?"

"Because most of these people's grandfathers were at war with each other at one point or another," Trevan explained. "Resolute and Norgard fought a war less than a score of years ago. None of these people trust each other."

"Oh," Artemis said, the look on her face clearly indicating that she understood the magnitude of her commander's statement. "How do we fix that?"

Trevan smiled at that question. It was one he actually had an answer for.

"These people need a commander they can put their faith in," he said. "Someone they can all trust."

"I nominate you," Artemis said with a sly grin. "Opalis doesn't have any soldiers here, so no one could accuse you of favoritism."

"I appreciate your confidence," Trevan said with a chuckle. "But we've been over this. The Norgards think we betrayed them, or at least deceived them when we left Opalis, and everyone knows we lost the city. Very few soldiers are eager to follow the lead of a commander who's failed that publicly."

Artemis's features had hardened during Trevan's explanation and her eyebrows now sat low over her eyes. She didn't like hearing her captain put down, even when he was doing it to himself. "Then who in the alliance, might I ask, could lead this rabble?"

"No one," Trevan admitted. "Everyone I can think of will have the same problem as Colonel Hendricks. None of them know how to think like an Obsidian."

"Then this joint army is doomed."

Trevan grinned at that.

"Maybe not," he said. "What this army needs is a leader who isn't from the alliance. Someone with no old grudges among the troops and someone who knows how the Obsidians fight and can counter them."

"Who fits that bill?" Artemis asked. "Someone from Midras?"

"No," Trevan said with a sigh. "I'm thinking it should be the man who so effectively defended against Karpasic's army, the Hero of Opalis, Captain Aren Bennis."

Chapter 3

Maradn

The Inner Circle of the Obsidian Cabal's council chamber was a round room adjacent to the throne platform of the Chamber of Souls. In a more civilized location, it would have been provided with the opulence and comfort that would befit the future ruler of the world. Since it was far underground in a chamber that had been cut out of solid rock, however, it was cold and damp with no way to properly heat it that didn't risk asphyxiating its occupants.

Maradn Norn shivered in the perpetual coolness of the room. She'd had a special fur-lined robe made for the occasions when she was required to attend meetings of the circle, but it could never fully repel the chill. It would have been child's play to use her magic to heat stones or bars of metal to heat the room, but that would weaken her, even if only slightly, and it would not do to show weakness of any kind in front of the other members of the circle. Clenching her jaw at the stupid, bullheadedness of it all, Maradn pulled her robe tighter around herself and tried to focus on the business at hand.

Tarvus Malakai currently had the floor, which alone irritated Maradn. Tarvus had been a soldier in his youth, part of an ill-fated program to use sorcerers as leaders in the Obsidian armies. Maradn had to admit that he had cut quite the heroic figure back then, all hard muscle and manly bluster. Now his muscle had slid into flab, giving him a distinct paunch around the middle. He had dark hair that pulled itself up in tight curls and a short cropped beard. The only real reminder of Tarvus' warrior past were the missing ring and little fingers on his left hand, the result of an enemy sword in the war to tame the lands of Grunvald.

"And why have we heard nothing from Hilt?" Tarvus asked, his voice booming in the stone chamber. As was his custom when speaking, he paced around the circular table in the center of the room like a carrion bird looking for a meal. "The Westreach Army moved on from Midras before the city was sufficiently pacified," he went on. "And now we receive reports of sabotage and subversion from our garrison there. I am given to understand, Lady Norn, that General Karpasic's orders to move before the job was done came from you."

Maradn repressed the desire to sneer at the preening fool. In retrospect, she wished that the sword that had deprived Lord Tarvus Malakai of his fingers had done a better job. Ever since the former Obsidian Eye, Malam Dirae, had died, Tarvus had been a thorn in Maradn's side. She'd thought when she arranged for the Eye to have a fatal accident, that the circle would promote her to the seventh throne, but then Tarvus revealed his own ambitions. Worse, Maradn had believed his soldier background left him without the wit for political machinations. It was a mistake she was still paying for.

"I demand you explain yourself, Maradn."

All eyes at the table turned to Maradn, and she kept her face expressionless for a long moment. Tarvus may have been an unexpected foe, but he was by no means her equal. No one on the council could match her in wit, power, or ruthless ambition; she just needed a little more time to prove it.

"Well?" Tarvus demanded when she didn't speak.

"Calm yourself, Tarvus," Maradn said, finally allowing a smirk to spread across her face. "I assure you that the movements of the Westreach Army were the results of careful consideration and need, not shortsighted whims."

"And those needs would be?"

The question came from Doran Valsond. Bald as an egg with a visage like a skull, Valsond was the eldest member of the circle. He was clever and, unlike Tarvus, tended to think many moves ahead when playing political games. Valsond was not one of Maradn's supporters, but neither was he an enemy. He tended to keep his own counsel and to only back decisions that would benefit his own power. Maradn respected that. Best of all, he seemed to have absolutely no aspirations to become the next Obsidian Eye. There were persistent rumors that he had once been Malam Dirae's lover, but those were only rumors. Besides, no one knew who had arranged for Malam's accident, and Maradn intended to keep it that way.

Maradn stood up slowly, giving herself time to think. Moving Karpasic's army had been her order. She didn't want to reveal the reason until she had confirmation Karpasic had completed his mission, but Tarvus was forcing her hand. She stopped herself from smiling wider at the thought of the triumph this would be for her. If all went well, she would be sitting on the seventh throne within the month.

"Fellow members of the Obsidian Circle," Maradn began. "I did order General Karpasic to move his force from Midras, and I admit, it was sooner than I would have liked. That said, the reason we have received no word from our forces at the Hilt is that Karpasic is no longer there."

A murmur of surprise and anger erupted around the table, and Maradn let it go on for a moment before she raised her hand.

"Rest assured I did not undertake these actions lightly."

"Nor did you undertake them with the approval of the circle," Lady Hurst interrupted.

Sirun Hurst was the youngest member of the circle and its only other woman. She was an adept schemer who looked at Maradn like an obstacle she would inevitably crush. Maradn hated her.

"General Karpasic is under my command, Lady Hurst," Maradn said with a scowl. "I realize the affairs of state have a tendency to elude you, but I'm surprised you have forgotten this."

Sirun blushed and looked down at the table.

"She's not wrong though," Tarvus said, ever the gallant. Little Sirun supported Tarvus for Obsidian Eye.

"You too, Tarvus?" She smirked. "In case you have forgotten as well, it was a vote of the circle that put me in charge of the Westreach Army. If, however, you'd like to change your minds, you may take another vote."

The threat hung in the air for a long moment while Tarvus and the other members of the circle tried to calculate what advantage they might gain from such a vote, and who might stand with them.

"I think," Valsond said in his drawling, nasal voice. "That before we take any such drastic action, that it might be worthwhile to hear your reasons for moving the army, Lady Norn."

Maradn almost pouted. Trust old Valsond to keep his head. It would have been fun to see if Tarvus could manage a vote of no confidence against her. It would have been even more fun to see his face when she played her trump card in the face of such a vote.

Oh well.

"Several months ago, I received information concerning a confluence of two rivers that could be vital to the strength of the cabal," she began, starting to pace around the table as Tarvus had done. "It is a place much like our home here in Desolis."

"What does that mean?" Fenric Castus asked politely. Fenric was Maradn's staunchest supporter among the circle.

"It means that this place, this . . . confluence, is a place of ancient magical power to rival Desolis itself."

The table erupted with everyone talking at once, but Maradn just kept pacing around the table. The power of the Obsidian Cabal sprang from the shardstone that fell from the sky, and nowhere was it more concentrated and potent than here in Desolis. Even if this confluence was only half as potent, it was a threat. If a rival group of sorcerers could take it and use it, they could wage an endless war upon the cabal until the lands of Novia were empty and barren.

If any such rival sorcerers existed, Maradn reminded herself.

"Why wasn't this presented to the circle immediately?" Tarvus asked once the noise had died down.

"Present what?" Maradn said with a subtle shrug of her shoulders. "I received a rumor, nothing more, but I judged it important enough to move Karpasic to seize and hold the area. I expect to hear word of his success any day now."

"And just where is this confluence?"

This came from the last member of the circle, Heldmar Pelk. He was young, still in his thirties with hair the color of trodden straw and a matching goatee. Heldmar was a thorn in Maradn's side, always looking for an opportunity to play Tarvus and her against each other. It was exactly what she did at his age, and he was good at it. Maradn had long ago resolved to keep a close watch on the young, ambitious sorcerer.

"At the intersection of the Sanctus and Fortus rivers in North Paladis," she explained.

Heldmar looked pensive, stroking his goatee with the long fingers of his hand. Something about that look communicated danger to Maradn.

"What troubles you, Lord Pelk?" she asked.

"Karpasic would have reached that area about a fortnight ago, perhaps sooner," Heldmar said. "Why have we not heard of his success yet?"

Maradn dug the long fingernails of her left hand into her palm, using the pain to keep any other expression off her face. Heldmar was right. Karpasic had been silent too long. The old glory hound should have announced his victory over an empty plain in the most grandiose manner possible by now.

"Are you," Sirun stuttered, her voice barely above a whisper. "Are you suggesting that Karpasic found this confluence occupied?"

"No," Heldmar said with a smile. "I have, however, heard from my spies in Etceter."

"Yes, what is the so-called Council of Might doing these days?" Fenric chuckled. "Have they agreed on where everyone will sit yet?"

Maradn chuckled at that along with the rest of the table. Ever since they first sent spies to watch the folly in Etceter it had provided an endless source of amusement. The fools couldn't manage to come together even to save their own skins, not that it would do any good against the might of the cabal.

"There are rumors that the old magics are returning," Heldmar continued.

"Those rumors run rampant ahead of our armies," Tarvus scoffed.

"Not like this," Heldmar said, his tone quite serious. "The Council of Might now know that an Avatar sword was found during the battle for Midras."

"This again," Fenric said with a raised eyebrow. "It sounds like more than a rumor. It might have some truth to it."

"Well, if that's true, the sword didn't do Midras much good," Valsond observed, his blue eyes shining out from his wizened face.

"It wasn't found by a soldier of Midras, but rather by one of Karpasic's captains," Maradn said.

"And," Heldmar continued, "according to the rumors, that officer was captured sometime later and taken to Opalis."

"Oh please," Tarvus said. "The Avatars are fairy stories for children. It's just nonsense."

He laughed, but no one at the table joined him, not even Sirun. Maradn felt a shiver run up her back under her fur-lined robe. Her mind had been occupied with thoughts of the vanished Avatars ever since she first heard of the sword. Something about the mention of it here, in the circle's council chamber, filled her with a nameless dread. The room radiated with a palpable fear.

"Surely you don't credit this Avatar nonsense?" Tarvus pressed.

"I'm not saying I believe it," Fenric said, his voice taut and strained. "But we know that the old magics ruled the world before the Shard Fall."

"And they stopped working when the shards fell," Sirun pointed out.

"And do you believe they will never return?" Maradn asked. "I wish I shared your surety, but I will not be so foolish."

"Nor I," Fenric said. "If this sword exists, real or not, we should make every effort to recover it."

"Recover it and destroy it," Sirun agreed.

"It seems General Karpasic is already doing just that," Heldmar said once silence reigned again. "I also have intelligence that the Westreach Army was seen traversing the Broken Road toward Opalis."

Silence filled the council chamber for a solid minute as the members of the circle mulled this information.

"If this really is an Avatar sword," Fenric said, "we shouldn't let it fall into the hands of the army."

"You doubt Karpasic's loyalty?" Valsond asked, steepling his fingers under his jaw.

Fenric shook his head.

"No," he said. "But if the legends are accurate, Avatar weapons were sources of great power. Artifacts of the old magic."

"Could Karpasic or one of his men wield that power?" Sirun asked, her eyes wide enough at the thought that Maradn could see the whites above and below.

"Not likely," Tarvus said, though he didn't sound confident in his assertion.

"I agree," Maradn said, seeing her opportunity to take back control of the conversation. "But if there is any chance that this sword could pose a threat to the cabal, we must send one of our own to recover it."

"You mean one of yours," Tarvus said, a low growl invading his voice.

That was exactly what Maradn meant. She opened her mouth to put Tarvus in his place but before she could speak, Doran Valsond stood.

"I am as concerned as we all are about the potential danger this supposed Avatar blade poses to the cabal," he said. "But I have news I trust will assuage some of those fears. I must confess that I learned about the possible existence of this sword some time ago."

He paused, casting his piercing blue eyes around the room in case anyone wanted to protest. No one did.

"I took it upon myself to send one of our order to Hilt to retrieve the sword. I had not heard that the sword had been lost, but this no doubt explains the actions of General Karpasic by moving to Opalis."

"And why are we hearing of this now?" Tarvus said, a hard edge in his voice.

Valsond shrugged his bony shoulders.

"Until now, I didn't believe there was anything to tell," he said. "It was only a rumor, after all."

"Of course," Maradn said. She resisted the urge to grind her teeth as the old fox used her own excuse back at her. Something in her gut told her that Valsond's involvement was a bad thing, but so far, she couldn't see why. "And whom did you send to recover this dangerous magic?"

Valsond smiled at her, his disturbingly blue eyes meeting hers.

"Why, the same person who brought me the news," he said. "Evard Dirae."

CHAPTER
4

Pet Projects

It took Maradn almost half an hour to get back to her rooms from the council chambers at the bottom of the Cave of Night. When she reached her heavy door she was tired and sweating from the walk, but she stopped to master herself before she went in. The chambers of the members of the Obsidian Circle had been hollowed out from the Temple Mound, named after the large, ornate space found at its center. Unlike the modest rooms of the craftmasters and the even smaller rooms of the acolytes, the quarters reserved for the Inner Circle were large and spacious. Better yet, a series of lava tubes connected the rooms in the Temple Mound to a natural steam vent, keeping them warm even in the early autumn chill.

Maradn loved everything about her enormous suite of rooms.

When she shut her heavy door, she walked slowly around her well-appointed parlor touching the elegant furniture and priceless decorations. Some of them had been taken from the halls of kings and other rulers conquered by the Empire.

Her Empire.

Maradn clenched her hands into fists and closed her eyes.

It was *her* Empire. She'd fought for it, she'd killed for it, and there was no way she would allow Malam Dirae's brat to prevent her from taking her rightful place as its leader.

She threw back her head and screamed, then blasted her favorite chair into firewood and scraps of batting. Magic surged through her body and she let it out with wild abandon, purging her fury until there was nothing left of her elegant parlor but singed walls and bits of furniture suitable only for kindling.

Her anger spent, Maradn took a deep, cleansing breath and brushed the remnants of an antique armoire from her robe. There wasn't any mirror left for her to check her hair in, but she knew a good bit of it had gone white. She was a master of magic, but it still extracted a price.

"You can handle this," she said out loud in the sudden silence of the ruined room. "There's always an advantage, you just have to find it."

The news that Evard Dirae had been the one to learn of the Avatar sword was disturbing. If the sword did indeed have power, then when Evard got hold of it, he would have that power, too. Would that be enough to elevate him to the Obsidian Circle? Could he use that power to elevate himself to the seventh throne? Make himself Obsidian Eye?

She clenched her fists and looked around for something else to break but mastered herself quickly. She'd had her temper tantrum and now it was time to think.

If Evard got the Avatar sword there was no guarantee that it had any power at all, even if long ago it might have. It was far more likely that the sword would serve the Empire's enemies as a symbol of hope. That would be an annoyance, but it wouldn't materially damage her plans.

On the other hand, if Evard failed to get hold of the sword and it fell into the hands of their enemies, that might work very nicely to Maradn's advantage. The ridiculous Council of Might would use the sword as a rallying cry, which might even bring them together. That would make conquering them that much harder and cost more in treasure and lives, but that could all be blamed on Evard.

It would finish him.

Maradn permitted a satisfied smile to creep onto her face.

"Yes," she said to the empty room. "If Evard brings the sword back, that's no great thing. He's just doing his duty. But should he fail . . ." She let the sentence trail off as her smile grew wider.

But what if the sword does have power?

The thought chilled her. From the moment the Avatar sword was first mentioned, some part of her mind had wanted to push the idea away, to bury it far away from her reality. Maradn hadn't put any stock in the old legends, she still didn't, but she couldn't deny the nameless dread that threatened to reach up out of the pit of her stomach and squeeze her heart.

The sword must be found. That much was certain. Power or no, it was far too dangerous to let loose in the world. It must be found, it must be destroyed, or failing that, buried in the deepest fissure below the Caves of Night.

"That means Evard must succeed," she growled.

It wasn't ideal, but she could see no way around it. She could downplay that accomplishment, but she would need something to push it out of the minds of her fellow members of the circle.

Maradn turned and marched through her broken and blasted parlor to a hallway beyond and then to her bedchamber. A service bell hung beside her bed and she jerked it smartly. Almost immediately a side door opened and a short, hunched creature entered. Its body resembled an alligator that had been twisted to walk upright with a short snout and no tail. Twisted rams horns sprouted from its head and its beady dark eyes glittered.

While the shapers had been busy turning captured humans into elves and satyrs, Maradn had turned her mind to different methods. The Kobolds are a reptilian race from the far northwestern region of Norgard, and though their physical attributes would make them the perfect troops, they are intelligent and defiant. The initial attempts to transform them into a compliant and useful asset were not successful. The shapers merged them with the minds of ants. The resultant creatures could be made quickly and easily and would function together with a hive mentality, and as their queen, Maradn held absolute sway over them.

The Kobolds were shorter than men, barely coming up to Maradn's chest, but they were strong enough to wield weapons. The infuriating problem was that even with her control over them, she couldn't make them warriors. Whatever instincts they needed to make them fight seemed utterly lacking in the modified creatures. It should have been a triumph, the greatest work of shaping in a generation, certainly better than the no-talent Tarvus and his fauns, but their minds were too simple. As such, the Kobolds were reduced to being porters and servants for the members of the circle. A different process would be required for their successful conversion into Fomorians: allowing the physical form to remain, removing their independent thinking, but still keeping the needed aggression.

The creature shuffled to a halt and bowed its head in a gesture of submission. It hissed at her submissively.

"I require my apprentice," she said. "Fetch him here at once."

The Kobold bowed again. "Yes, mistress," it rasped in its gravelly voice, then turned and scurried off through the service door.

Maradn turned to survey herself in the tall mirror mounted behind her dressing table. The use of her magic had left her long, blond locks streaked with white, and she scowled at the reflection.

Why can't magic be more orderly?

She drew a tiny fleck of power and formed a simple spell in her mind; when she released it, her mottled hair changed back to its usual gold. Only a single streak of white remained, representing the power she'd just used, but she'd chosen its placement, giving her a white forelock. This looked mysterious and appropriately magical as befit a member of the Obsidian Circle.

Satisfied that she had removed the ravages of her tirade, Maradn stripped off her fur-lined robe of office and changed into an elegant blue dress that had been expertly tailored. It clung to her in all the right places, while being loose in others to allow her easy motion. She had just finished accenting her attire with a sapphire necklace and tiara when there was a polite knock at her door.

"Right on time," she said to her reflection, then made her way back to the ruined parlor. "Enter," she said.

The door admitted a young man in his mid-twenties with dark curly hair and brown eyes in a pleasant enough face. He wore the black tunic of an Acolyte and his shoulders were slightly hunched, a side effect of all the reading magical training required. This was Maltius Tren, Maradn's apprentice.

"You summoned me, mistress," he said simply. If he was surprised to find his mistress' elegant parlor blasted to kindling, he gave no sign.

"Don't slouch," Maradn said out of habit.

Maltius straightened up, and Maradn favored him with a smile. The boy was one of her projects. Young, handsome, and from a deep magical bloodline, Maradn had worked him hard and trained him well, all the while whispering promises of power and prestige in his ear. When she judged him ready, he would exhibit his skill to the craftmasters and then join their ranks. All he needed to do, as Maradn reminded him often, was to trust her.

Eventually she would take him as a lover, further deepening his dependence on her. By the time she elevated him to the Obsidian Circle, he would be hers, body and soul. A willing ally for any project or proposal she wished. Until then, she would drive him and tempt him, challenge him with difficult tasks and reward him with power. Her form-fitting gown was one element in that plan. She had always been a handsome woman, and men were rather simple and easy to manipulate when it came to that.

"My plans for the new construct must be accelerated. Go to the shapers and see how they fare."

Maltius smiled at that and inclined his head.

"I anticipated your need, mistress," he said. "I have been down to the shaping pits this morning. The craftmaster informs me that their progress is slow. Your design requires a great deal of raw material and there is only so much available. The army has quite a sizable list of demands for the shapers' work."

Maradn's smile turned into a scowl.

"And does the craftmaster say how many slaves he needs for each trial?"

"At least twenty," Maltius replied. "Though thirty would be better."

It was not the news Maradn was hoping for. With the Empire's mission of justice and equity proceeding, the army was in constant need of Fomorians. Shaping was not as exact as regular spell casting; there was a certain element of trial and error in developing new constructs. Once the shapers got a Fomorian right, they could use it to make more of its kind, but getting that first one to work could take years and hundreds of tries. It typically required a great deal of slaves before the process was perfected.

"Perhaps the armies in the field could bring in more slaves," Maltius offered.

"No," Maradn said. "With the Westreach Army on the far side of the Blackblade Range, our forces are spread too thin. I'll have to think of something else."

"Is there some other way I can serve you, Mistress?"

Maradn put her smile back in place.

"Why, yes," she said. "I seem to be having some difficulty with the furniture in my parlor. Be a dear and show me how well you've learned your restoration spells. I want it all back, good as new, by supper."

Maltius' face blanched momentarily, but he recovered quickly. Maradn made a mental note to work on his facial control.

"It shall be as you say, mistress," he said.

Maradn turned and made her way to her library at the opposite end of the hall from her bedchamber. The work she'd given Maltius would keep him busy for hours and she had no desire to watch. She'd trained him well and he'd manage the task better without distraction.

A beautiful fresco of a field adorned the back wall of the library, flanked on either side by loaded shelves. Several comfortable chairs were scattered around the room with a writing desk on one side and a liquor cabinet on the other. Maradn made for the latter and poured herself a brandy. She meant to calm herself, but half a glass later and she was still pacing the room like a nervous cat.

There were just too many variables in play. Too much that was happening was out of her control. Maradn was a woman used to being in control and her current situation was making her skin itch.

The maddening part was that there wasn't any way to take control. *Not yet, at least.*

What she needed was information. If she knew what was happening at Opalis she'd be able to plan. Deciding at last, she drained her glass and set it on a table near her favorite reading chair.

The library was two stories high with a balcony that ran around the entire upper floor. Set into the upper wall at the far end of the room was an enormous brass birdcage that had been polished until it glowed. Maradn ascended the metal stairs leading up to the balcony and crossed to the cage.

At first glance the cage appeared to be unoccupied. Inside was a preserved tree branch that would give birds something to perch on. It was an unremarkable bit of a birch tree with two large bulbous protrusions in the twisted limb. It looked as if it might have been diseased at some point.

"Hello my darlings," Maradn said, opening the large door to the cage. "Wake up."

As she watched, the bulbous protrusions began to shift and change color. One turned blue and scaly with a gold streak passing along it, and the other was green with a red streak. Each creature uncoiled a long, scaly neck from around the branch. They looked like a bizarre combination of an iguana, a bat, and a snake all mashed together into one creature about the size of a large house cat.

They spread their wings and flew out of the cage, circling the library. These were her pseudodragons, a secret shaping project she had undertaken herself. Like the Kobolds, the dragons were linked to her mind, but with them, she had achieved a much more intimate link.

Jiri. Maradn called the blue one with a thought. It swooped down and came to rest on her shoulder, wrapping its long tail around her arm while its serpentine head rubbed her cheek.

Maradn took a bit of dried meat from a covered dish beside the cage and flipped it into the air. Jiri lunged after it, snapping it up before it hit the floor. Taking another bit of meat from the dish, Maradn called the green dragon to her. As it swooped in, she tossed the meat in the air and it snapped the morsel up with a flick of its long neck.

"You're a very strong flier, Lun," she said, scratching the creature's throat once it had settled on her shoulder. "I have a very special task for you."

The pseudodragons' minds were too primitive to think proper thoughts, but Maradn felt a burst of pride and eagerness from Lun. He was happy to be called on to serve his queen. She closed her eyes and visualized Evard Dirae, pushing the image into Lun's mind.

I want you to find this man, she thought. *I need to know what he is doing.*

Chapter 5

The Hero of Opalis

Aren had often heard healers and other liars say that a long sea voyage was good for the health. He wished he had one of them here so he could punch them in their ignorant face. Not that he was in any condition to engage in even a rudimentary physical confrontation at the moment.

The ship crested a wave and its bow dipped down over the backside of the swell, taking the deck along with it. Aren held on for dear life until the ship landed in the trough behind the wave and the rail he'd been clinging to suddenly rushed up and slammed him in the gut. If he'd eaten anything in the last three days he was sure it would have been violently expelled by the impact.

He turned, putting the rail to his back as the ship began its rise over the next wave in what seemed to be an unending parade. A young boy about nine or ten with a mop of curly blond hair scurried by him, carrying a basket filled with brown eggs he'd gathered from the ship's chicken coop. His name was Follis and he'd been the ship's boy on the *Orietta* for over a year. His mother worried about him being at sea, but with her husband gone, Follis' share of the *Orietta*'s cargo income was desperately needed. Aren envied the boy as he watched him turn and climb down the center hatch to deliver the eggs to the cook below. Like the other sailors aboard, he moved as if the ship were a rock, standing perfectly still, instead of what it was, a loose saddle atop a bucking stallion.

"It's all in the knees," Loremaster Zhal said, his voice surprisingly close.

Aren jumped, forcing him to tighten his grip on the rail. On land,

he had a warrior's sense of his surroundings. To his knowledge only
Syenna could approach him without being detected, although he
didn't mind that so much. The loremaster, however, was another matter entirely.

"What?" Aren growled, holding on as the boat dipped again.

The loremaster appeared beside him, standing on the pitching deck
as if he were out for a stroll in a pleasant garden. The frosty rime of
white hair that encircled the back of his head blew in the wind, making him look as if he had a glowing halo, and his blue eyes sparkled.

"Keeping your balance on deck," Zhal explained. "It's all in the
knees."

He bounced up and down, bending his knees to illustrate his point,
but the effect made Aren's stomach queasy.

"Don't do that," he said, turning back to the rail. "How did you
know that's what I was wondering?"

Zhal laughed at that.

"I often wonder something similar when I see the young folk scam-
pering about," Zhal said with a sigh. "Although in my case it has less
to do with the motion of ships and more to do with rheumatism."

Aren chuckled at that despite his churning gut.

"Look on the bright side," Zhal said when Aren didn't speak.
"You're doing much better than last time. I dare say after a dozen
more voyages, you'll have gotten used to it."

Aren wanted to tell the interfering old busybody exactly what he
could do with that thought, but the ship pitched down and he was
forced to hang on again.

"I'm glad you decided to join us on deck," Zhal went on, ignoring
Aren's plight. "It's good for the people to see you. You wouldn't believe
the rumors that were going around before the crew got a good look
at you."

Aren would and did. The savior of Etceter, that's what they were
calling him. He heard it whispered everywhere he went, from Resolute to Vertas and down to the Ash Coast. People said it with reverence, some said it with surprise, but all of them had an undertone
of devout faith. A desperate hope that Aren actually was a savior, a
miracle sent to protect them from the Obsidian Empire.

"Some folk were saying you were a fourth Titan," Zhal chuckled.
"Now that they see you're a man, like any other, they've settled on
believing you're an Avatar."

"I wish they wouldn't," Aren said, turning back to the deck.

"Why?" Zhal asked. His tone was that of a casual question but something in the old man's look told Aren it went far beyond that.

"I've seen the way they look at me," Aren said. He put his hand on the pommel of the sword belted round his waist. "I see it better than most."

The moment his hand made contact with the ornate pommel, a flood of emotions washed over him. On the front of the ship, a middle-aged man named Huel was repainting the figurehead, the image of a semi-nude woman clutching a trident. The sculpture reminded Huel of his wife, and he recalled her beauty and the years they'd been apart thanks to his life on the sea. As he painted the figurehead's hair red to match his love's, he wondered how much she had changed since he saw her last. It was a happy thought but laced with sadness for the time that had been lost between them.

Behind Aren on the quarterdeck, Marko, the ships navigator, was tracking the position of the sun with a delicate instrument made of brass. He knew that the *Orietta* would make landfall before dark if their course was right. Marko took pride in setting a good course. His father was an old friend of the *Orietta*'s captain and had gotten him the navigator job. Some of the crew disliked that and shunned him, though he'd won most of them over with his skill. More than anything, he wanted to captain his own ship, but to do that, he would have to impress his father, and that was much harder than setting an accurate course.

As Aren's gaze moved around the deck, his mind filled with similar stories. Some were tragic, some exultant, and others more mundane, but he knew them all. He knew the men and women of the *Orietta* better than he had known the soldiers in his own command. If he'd been a more devious man, he could have used that knowledge to his own advantage. The thought made him sick and terrified him at the same time.

Worse, however, where the things that came to his mind when one of the crew looked at him. All of them knew that the world balanced on a knife's edge, that war the likes of which they'd never seen was at their doorstep and they expected him to save them.

Aren knew he'd been lucky at Opalis. Fate handed him a trump card and he played it. Anyone could have done it. And yet these people looked at him as if he were some tactical mastermind, as if the victory were his and not fate's.

"What's wrong with the way they look at you?" Zhal asked.

Aren looked at the loremaster but found nothing in his eyes but idle curiosity. He wasn't immune to the sight granted by the sword, like Syenna seemed to be, but Aren never got much from him. The old fox seemed to know instinctively how to mask his intentions, to keep his desires so broad that Aren couldn't detect a pattern in them.

"They all want something from me," Aren said, taking his hand off the sword. "Some see me as the man who will save them from these uncertain times, others believe I'm some kind of herald of the Avatar's return."

"And that bothers you?"

"I don't owe these people anything," he growled. He hoped it sounded convincing.

Zhal smiled at that, but it was a look of kindness rather than mirth.

"Don't worry, Captain," the loremaster said. "They're only taking what you're freely giving them."

"What's that?"

"Hope."

Aren sighed and shook his head.

"In my experience, hope isn't worth very much."

"And that's why you need men of sense and years around," Zhal said, his voice changing to the one he used when he went on and on about some obscure point.

Aren resisted the urge to sigh.

"Fear and love are two of the strongest emotions that exist," Zhal explained. "Under their influence individuals can do amazing things. But hope . . . hope can motivate whole groups of people, from the crew of a ship"—he waved his hands at the men and women up in the rigging tending to the incomprehensible mass of ropes and sheets— "to entire nations. Like it or not, Captain, you are the hero of Opalis. No one there could have done what you did. No one believed it could be done, and that gives people hope."

Aren turned away from the loremaster to gaze out at the rolling sea. It made his stomach weak, but he preferred that to Zhal's insufferable cheerfulness.

"That was a fluke," he said. "Pure luck." He turned back to the deck and the crew moving about their tasks. "Now these people want me to somehow do it again. To keep the Obsidian Empire, my Empire I might add, at bay. One or two of them want me for king, ruler of the Council of Might."

"And what do *you* want?" Zhal asked.

Aren sighed.

"I just want some peace and quiet," he admitted. "I want people to stop trying to put the fate of the world on my shoulders."

His hand drifted back to the pommel of the Avatar sword. It was cold but warmed quickly to his hand. As he looked around the deck, a flood of information washed over him.

"I notice you do that a lot," Zhal said, indicating Aren's sword hand. "If the hopes of these good folk bother you so much, I suggest you cover up the sword. Or, better yet, leave it in your hammock below."

Aren jerked his hand away from the sword and the visions disappeared. He hadn't intended to touch it, but he had all the same. In that moment, he wondered how often his hand had held the sword's pommel, feeding him the lives, hopes, and fears of everyone around him. No wonder he was out of sorts. He resolved to do as Zhal suggested.

"That's a good idea, Loremaster," he said, taking a tentative step toward the hatch that led down into the *Orietta*'s hold. "Please excuse me."

† † †

Loremaster Zhal watched Aren make his way shakily across the deck and then disappear down the hatch into the bowels of the ship. He hoped the Obsidian captain hadn't been able to see his intentions, or at least not too clearly. Aren had been in a black mood since before the *Orietta* had departed for Etceter, and Zhal wanted to know why. Too much depended on Aren Bennis and his secondhand Avatar sword.

Zhal firmly believed that providence had put that sword into Aren's hands. That the same providence had allowed Aren and the sword to be captured by the Council of Might. The sight granted by the Avatar sword had boxed Aren in nicely in Opalis, made him care about the city and its treasure. The results were better even than Zhal could have hoped. Now, however, that same sight seemed to be a liability.

Baroness Baden-Fox had given Zhal an impossible task, find a way to save Novia from the inexorable advance of the Obsidians, and if Zhal wanted to have a chance, he needed Aren and the Avatar sword firmly in his camp. So far, Aren didn't seem to want to play along.

Zhal sighed, rubbing his chin.

It was a problem he didn't have much time to solve and he was fresh out of tricks. If Aren and his sword were to be of use to the baroness and her fledgling alliance, providence was going to have to provide more leverage.

"Where did Aren go?" Syenna's voice came from behind him. "Follis said he was actually up on deck and that's something I want to see."

She stepped up next to him clad in a loose-fitting shirt with a pair of calfskin breeches. Her long, honey colored hair had been undone from its usual braid and hung loose around her shoulders and down her back. She was large for a woman, standing taller than Zhal, with deeply tanned skin and dark almond-shaped eyes. She wasn't pretty, at least not in the ways of courtly ladies, but she had an exotic, mysterious beauty about her that was uniquely her own. Much like Syenna herself. Zhal had seen her intimidate many men with her rugged mystique.

Lesser men, he realized as he thought about it. *For the right man, she would present the perfect amount of challenge.*

A broad smile spread slowly across his face and he stroked his chin. After all, who was he to argue with providence?

"Aren went below for a moment," Zhal supplied helpfully. "I expect he'll return soon."

"I'm sorry I missed him," the shieldmaiden said with a grin and a shrug. She started to turn away, but Zhal put a hand on her arm.

"A moment, if you would."

She cocked an eyebrow at him and turned to face him fully.

"What do you want, old fox?" she asked, her voice full of suspicion.

"I've been talking with Aren, and I'm worried," Zhal said, ignoring her probing look. "His mind is in conflict about his current situation."

Syenna scoffed.

"You know better than that," she said. "The sword showed him what the Obsidians really are. I was there, remember?"

"So you've told me," Zhal said, nodding. He put his hand on Syenna's shoulder and led her to the rail, looking around as if he were afraid of being overheard.

"I'm sure you're right that Aren understands the Obsidian sorcerers," he said, his voice low and conspiratorial. "But I don't think he has renounced their cause."

"What do you—" Syenna began angrily then lowered her voice. "What do you mean, old man? You saw what he did at Opalis. He betrayed the Obsidians. No one forced him to do that, he did it because it was right."

As she spoke, Zhal saw fire in Syenna's eyes. She didn't just believe in the Avatar sword, she believed in the man who wielded it.

Providence indeed.

"You are right again," Zhal said. "But have you ever asked yourself why the sword chose Aren Bennis, above all others, to wield it?"

Her expression soured. Clearly she had asked herself that question and just as clearly she didn't have a satisfactory answer.

"Honestly, I don't know," she admitted. "But I'm glad that it did."

"I think you do know," Zhal said. "How would you describe Aren as a commander?"

Syenna thought about that for a moment before she spoke.

"Intelligent?" she said at last, though it was more of a question than a statement of fact. "Gifted maybe? He's the sort of leader who knows his soldiers and what they're capable of. He uses them to win but never throws their lives away on a hopeless objective."

"A practical man then?" Zhal supplied.

Syenna scowled at that.

"Isn't that what they call the kind of men who do anything to achieve their goals, even despicable things?"

Zhal laughed.

"You're not wrong," he admitted. "But those are people who have no basic morality to guide them. From what I've seen of Captain Bennis, he is a man driven by a fierce moral code, a belief that certain things, certain ideas are so pure that they are worth fighting for. Ideas worth killing and even dying for."

"That is certainly true," Syenna said.

"Such men view themselves as lesser than their mission," Zhal went on. "They exist to serve their cause, not the other way around. I believe that is why the sword chose him."

Syenna's brows furrowed and she shook her head.

"I don't understand."

"Do you remember how Captain Trevan described what happened when he touched the Avatar sword? He said it showed him the character of the people around him, but mostly it showed him himself. Now I've known Captain Trevan for many years and he is a good and decent man, but even he couldn't bear that scrutiny for long."

"Why?"

"Because we all lie to ourselves," Zhal explained. "We all tell ourselves that we're better than we are. We all fall short of the person we wish we could be. For most of us, confronting that is a painful experience."

"What are you saying? That Aren has no flaw, no faults?" Syenna's face split into grin that was half amusement, half derision.

"Not at all," he assured her. "The captain is just as human as the rest of us. What I'm saying is that a practical man knows he has flaws and simply chooses to get on with what he's doing."

Syenna cocked her head and furrowed her brows for a long moment. Zhal thought he might have to explain it even more simply, but she finally nodded.

"I guess I can see that," she said. "That's why General Karpasic could only hold the sword for a few moments."

Zhal tried to prevent his grin from becoming wolfish.

"Exactly," he said. "A man like that would never want to confront the truth of who he really is."

"So, what does all this have to do with why Aren betrayed the Obsidians and saved Opalis?"

"Did he?" Zhal asked. "Did he save Opalis from the Obsidians or did he save it from Karpasic?"

"Aren knows the corruption of the sorcerers and he knows the corruption of Karpasic," Syenna said with a shrug. "How is one different from the other?"

"They're not, but I don't think Aren has ever been loyal to either of them. Remember, Aren has a code, he believes in order and law. It is the Obsidian's stated goal to bring order and peace to the world. That is what Aren is loyal to, and I suspect he still is. As a practical man, he would understand that the sorcerers and Karpasic have become corrupt, but the goal is still perfect. The goal is still worth fighting for."

Syenna thought for a moment, then shrugged.

"If you're right, then he knows that backing the Obsidians won't serve his goal," she said. "He'll have to pursue that goal with us."

"Will he now?" Zhal said with exaggerated patience. "You've seen enough of the Council of Might to know that they are only united by the gravest of necessity. Norgard had an army within two days march of Opalis, yet still they wouldn't come to her aid. Aren knows that. Will he really reject the Empire for a collection of squabbling nations that will turn on each other as soon as the Obsidian threat is no more?"

Doubt washed across Syenna's face, clouding her dark eyes.

"And think about this," Zhal pressed on. "We'll reach Etceter soon. The last time we were there, Aren was an enemy soldier, a necessity to carry a cursed sword. Except for Ambassador Shepherd, the other members of the council completely ignored him. This time, however, he's coming as the hero of Opalis. How do you think the leaders and diplomats from the council nations will treat him now? What offers will they make him to entice him to ally with them or lead their armies?"

"Aren wouldn't accept those kinds of offers," Syenna said, hot anger filling her voice.

"Of course not," Zhal agreed. "But what will he think of the men and women who will make them?"

Syenna's eyes went wide as she finally understood.

"He'll despise them," she gasped. "He'll think they're just like General Karpasic, and he hated Karpasic."

"Exactly," Zhal said. He stepped closer so they were barely a foot apart and put his hand on her shoulder. "If we have any hope of winning Aren to our side, we have to keep him isolated from the individual members of the council, and not just them, any agents they might send in their stead."

"I can handle anyone the council might send," Syenna said. "But I can't watch him every minute."

"We'll trade off," Zhal assured her, "but the bulk of this task will fall on you."

"Why?"

"Because he trusts you," Zhal said simply. "Even when you were a spy in the Westreach Army, he relied on you. You were an anchor of decency in an indecent business. You must be his anchor in Etceter. You must keep him away from the council members outside of council meetings. If you fail, we'll lose him."

Syenna looked unsure.

"We need him, Syenna. Not just the sword he carries, but the man. It wasn't the sword that saved the accumulated knowledge of Opalis along with all her people, Aren did that. Right now, you are our only chance not just to hold on to him, but to win him to our side."

"Ahoy on deck," the voice of the lookout drifted down from far above them. "I've sighted Etceter off the starboard bow."

"Time's up," Zhal said. "We'll be ashore in a few hours. Are you in?"

Syenna gave him a sour look then nodded.

"Good," Zhal said, slapping her on the shoulder.

"I'll get my gear together," she said with a sigh. "Wouldn't want my new charge to go ashore before I'm ready." She started to turn away, but stopped and looked back at Zhal with a shrewd look.

"You know, Loremaster, it sounds like you're making me, alone, responsible for our success."

Zhal shrugged. She was right, of course, but if she weren't observant and clever, she wouldn't be the woman for the job.

"I have every confidence in you," he said, and meant it.

"I hope you're right," she said, then stalked away to make preparations for landfall.

"Me too," he said to the empty deck.

CHAPTER
6

The Report

Evard's breath steamed in the cold air as he surveyed the Broken Road down from the upper slopes of the Serpent's Spine Mountains. He could see the land at the foot of the mountains but there wasn't much detail in the fading light. Somewhere down there, in the gathering darkness, the Sanctus River crossed the Broken Road, flowing under an ancient bridge. He didn't know how far it was, but it would be impossible to miss. Once he found the bridge, he would follow the river until it met the Fortus. That was where General Karpasic had been ordered to go. As far as Evard knew there was nothing there, not even a town, but something must be there or the circle wouldn't have sent the entire Westreach Army.

You hope, he reminded himself.

So far his trip to the Paladis side of the Blackblade Mountains had been one disaster after another. First he somehow missed the Avatar sword subverting Aren and then using him to help the population of Opalis disappear right off the face of Novia. Then that fool Karpasic had managed to lose the entire Westreach Army. Evard knew he couldn't be blamed for that, but there were members of the circle who would jump at the chance if he gave it to them. He needed leverage to stave off any such accusations and he hoped whatever secret lay at the confluence of the Sanctus and Fortus Rivers would give it to him.

The setting sun finally slipped below the mountains to the west and shadow engulfed the Broken Road. Almost immediately the temperature dropped and Evard shivered. He wanted to keep going, to reach the bottom of the Sanctus Spine Pass, but he knew from experience that the temperature would only continue to drop. He needed to make camp.

When Evard traveled with the army, mundane tasks like making camp were much more pleasant affairs. There was always someone assigned to set up his tent, make his fire, and cook his dinner. A person traveling alone, even a powerful sorcerer, was a different matter entirely. Little things like making a fire could be dangerous. Cold camps were the norm for anyone traveling alone. Still, being a sorcerer did have its advantages.

With a sigh, Evard turned from the road and tracked into the trees to one side. He went a good way until he found a sizable stone on the ground, about the size of a man's head. Closing his eyes, he drew in his magic and then touched the stone. Power flowed out of him and a lock of his hair turned white. The spell taxed him physically and he dropped to one knee, suddenly dizzy.

Warmth began to flow over him as he knelt, waiting for his body to recover from the magic. The stone began to smoke as the spell heated it, burning away the grime and dirt from its surface. Evard reached out his hands to the rock, reveling in the warmth. The stone was already hot enough to cook on, but the smell of cooking food was almost as bad as the light from a fire when it came to attracting trouble. Evard was tired, footsore, and in no mood to deal with trouble, so he opened his traveling pack and took out a wrapped bundle of hard cheese and black bread. It wasn't elegant fare, but he'd gotten used to it.

He sat, putting himself close to the stone, and opened his cloak to better absorb the heat. As he ate his simple meal, he felt suddenly uneasy. He wondered if he'd forgotten something, but there wasn't anything for him to forget on the side of a mountain.

The uneasy feeling continued to build until Evard pulled his cloak back around his body to hide his hands. Pulling in power, he readied a spell in case he had to defend himself. He was quite sure now that he was being watched. Trying not to betray this knowledge, he let his eyes roam over his surroundings. The trees in this area were sparse and there was still enough light to see that no one had sneaked up on him unaware. Finally his eyes were drawn upward into a tree on the far side of his heat stone. There, about ten feet off the ground, crouched what looked like an enormous bat. It had large wings that were folded over its serpentine body with a long tail that coiled around the branch where it clung.

Evard allowed his eyes to go out of focus as he looked at the creature. It was a trick his mother had taught him, a way to see the constructs of magic. As his eyes adjusted to seeing in the magical spectrum, he saw the creature blazing with light. It was a construct all right, shaped from the bodies of lesser animals and bulked up with etherium. He was surprised by the creature. Monk was a construct of Evard's imagination, drawn entirely from his mind and his magic, but whoever had done this had taken existing animals as a base, the same way the shapers used slaves to make their Fomorian soldiers. As far as he knew, there was no reason to use an existing creature in such a construct, it would limit what could be done. The base creature's nature would assert itself somewhat in the resulting construct.

Someone had done it, though, and Evard wanted to know why. Did its shaper know something he didn't? He could clearly see the shapes of the base creatures inside the construct, a bat, a serpent, and some other kind of reptile. It was an odd mix but the construct creature seemed elegant with a long, lean body, large wings for swift flight, and powerful back legs. As he admired it, the creature's head turned to face him and Evard felt something pull at his consciousness.

He let the magical vision slip away as his mind made contact with another through the black eyes of the strange creature. There was a brief, unsettling feeling of being lifted away from his body, then he could see a room. It was a library, elegant and well-appointed with dark, mahogany bookshelves, brass lanterns and sconces, and comfortable furniture. Evard realized that he was looking out of the eyes of something small, no doubt a creature like the one before him. That meant that whoever was on the other end was probably looking back at him.

"Well, Evard," a familiar voice sounded in his mind. "Here you are at last, camping in the woods, how very rustic of you. I was told you were with General Karpasic and his army. What happened?"

Evard grimaced as he recognized the voice.

"Hello, Lady Maradn," he said aloud. A moment later he could see her in the vision of the library, semi-recumbent on a couch. "I didn't know my whereabouts were of interest to you."

It was true enough, his assignment hadn't come from her, so he wouldn't be expected to report to her. The fact that Maradn was searching for him was significant. She revealed this construct's existence to find him, something she would not have done for mundane reasons.

She knows the Council of Might has the sword, he guessed.

That was bad, but not unexpected. With tales about the Hero of

Opalis running rampant through South Paladis, it was only a matter of time before the circle learned of the sword's existence. Once that happened, Valsond would have revealed his knowledge of it and that Evard was attempting to recover it.

So, you want to know how successful I've been, he thought. *And to find a way to lay any failure at my feet, no doubt.*

"Normally the adventures of a simple craftmaster wouldn't interest me," Maradn said, her voice almost dripping with indifference. "But when he goes in search of an Avatar relic and then doesn't report back in weeks . . . well, the circle becomes concerned."

"You must offer the circle my heartfelt apologies," Evard said with the sincerest smile he could fake. "In this matter, I thought it best not to send regular communication lest they be intercepted and only to report once I had completed the task."

Maradn frowned, but her easy manner returned immediately. It was only a momentary slip, but Evard had seen it. She was worried. Obviously, the idea of the sword of an Avatar, found after all this time, disturbed her. The fact that it was not yet in the control of the Obsidian Cabal worried her more.

She's right to be worried.

"You have been away from Desolis for almost two months," she said. "Adequate time to recover a sword that was already in our possession."

Evard didn't smile at that. Maradn was pretending not to know that the sword had been lost. If he wasn't careful with his answer, she'd find a way to blame him for that.

"The sword you refer to has not been in our possession for some time," Evard said.

"You lost it?" she said after a brief pause. Her voice calm and easy but Evard knew that for the trap it was.

"I never had it," he admitted. "It was found by one of General Karpasic's officers in the aftermath of the taking of Midras."

"I don't recall hearing that particular detail from the general."

"Nor I," Evard said with a sad nod of the head. He wasn't about to take the blame for this debacle, and since it was all Karpasic's fault anyway, that's where he'd put the blame. The fact that Karpasic was well beyond Maradn's ability to question was an added bonus. "Unfortunately, the general allowed the officer who found the sword to be captured during an ill-advised scouting mission."

This time Maradn maintained her control but the pause before she spoke was longer this time.

"Where is the sword now?" she said at last.

"According to my information, it was taken to the Titans in Opalis."

"But you are not in Opalis, Craftmaster Dirae," Maradn said, her voice tight as if it were taking all her control to keep from screaming at him. "You are somewhere in the mountains, and there are no mountains near the city of the Titans."

So, she only knows what her creature can see. Interesting.

"When I caught up with the Westreach Army, General Karpasic was already on his way to Opalis to lay siege to the city and retrieve the sword," Evard explained.

"Then I'll ask again, why are you here instead of with the general?"

Evard couldn't help himself and chuckled.

"General Karpasic is at Opalis," he said. "That much is true, but I am rather glad not to be with him."

Maradn looked as if she would be angry as his mirth, but she wasn't the leader of the Obsidian Circle for no reason, she could tell that something was very wrong.

"Explain yourself," she said, her voice a low growl.

Evard did as he was instructed, laying out the events that had occurred at Opalis and keeping Aren's name out of it. When he reached the fate of the Westreach Army, Maradn gasped and leaped to her feet, her hands crackling with raw power. He was very glad he was not physically present in the room with her.

"Lost!" she nearly shrieked. "The entire army is lost?"

"I'm afraid so, my lady. In the past I have voiced my concerns about General Karpasic's fitness. Now he has proven himself not just foolish and greedy, but incompetent as well. In his haste to seize the fabled treasure of Opalis, he not only allowed the sword to be spirited away by our enemies, but he left his flanks open to attack."

"And what have you done about this, *Craftmaster* Dirae?" She emphasized the title with a sneer. "You are the only representative of the cabal in that region, what steps have you taken to rectify this?"

"As far as Karpasic is concerned"—he shrugged—"I have done nothing. I found him in the dungeons of Opalis awaiting the pleasure of the Norgard Legion or their new allies in the Council of Might." Maradn made a sour face at that but didn't interrupt. "There is nothing to be done about the Westreach Army," he continued. "Most of them are dead and their bodies lie moldering on the fields outside Opalis."

"And what of the sword?" she demanded.

"You asked why I was in the mountains," Evard said. "I have heard that the sword was taken west, toward Aerie, and I'm bound there to see if I can pick up its trail."

It was a calculated lie, but Evard didn't want to reveal his true location or destination. In truth, he had no idea where the sword had gone and none of the copies of Monk he'd sent out to look for Aren had returned with news.

"I see," Maradn said after a pause. "Yes, you must find the sword and retrieve it," she went on. "That is your first duty to the cabal."

"Indeed," Evard agreed.

The image of her and the library suddenly wavered in his mind and Maradn put a hand to her head.

"What's wrong?" Evard asked.

"It's nothing," Maradn said. "This form of communication is taxing and Lun grows tired. He needs to sleep." The image became dim and her voice receded from him. "We'll talk further in the morning."

Before he could answer, the connection broke and Evard found himself sitting cross-legged in front of his steaming rock. Above him in the tree the creature, Lun, looked at him with its dark eyes, then tucked its head beneath its wing and went to sleep.

Evard sat, studying the creature for the better part of an hour without moving. He hated Maradn, of course. She was always trying to undermine his position, and he guessed she had something to do with his mother's death. Still, Evard wasn't a man to allow his personal feelings to get in the way of power.

The creature Maradn had built was a marvel, unlike anything Evard had conceived before, and it was expertly made. If he could learn its secrets, he could remake Monk and send the creature to find Aren the same way it had found him. Evard was pretty sure Lun had located him by feeling out anyone using magic. That wouldn't work for Aren, but the sword would give off its own power and that could be tracked.

After an hour, Evard reluctantly stopped. He wanted to study the creature more, it really was quite a clever construct. He could probably spend days studying it. Unfortunately, he was out of time.

Reaching out to his enchanted rock, he touched it with his finger. Closing his eyes, he poured power into the stone, gently at first, seeking natural fissures in the rock. When he found the fault lines, he forced the magic into them, expanding the imperfections until the rock cracked into a dozen pieces. It wasn't a big use of magic, but Evard was tired from his long day of travel and he paused for a long moment before opening his eyes again.

"Come on," he said out loud, spurring himself to action.

He selected two of the pieces of broken stone that were more or less round and picked them up, slipping them into the inner pocket of his cloak. The rocks would stay warm most of the rest of the night, and he would need that warmth. When the creature Lun woke in the morning, Maradn would try to contact him. Evard intended to be miles away by then.

CHAPTER
7

New Resources

C haos erupted in the council chamber with all the members talking at once. Maradn sat at the head of the table, unmoving, with a confident smile plastered on her face. It wasn't that the loss of the Westreach Army, and worse still, the Avatar relic, didn't terrify her—she knew how bad this news was—but she had waited a day before reporting it to the circle. It was enough time for Evard to give Lun the slip, which irritated her to no end, but it also gave Maradn time to figure a way to turn these events to her advantage. Evard was trying to leave her holding the bag for this debacle and she'd deal with him in time. Right now, however, she had bigger problems.

"Our largest army is gone," Travis Malakai shouted over the din. His face bore a look of anger but Maradn could see him scheming behind his eyes. He waited a moment for the others to all stop talking at once. "The Westreach Army was twice the size of our other forces and you're telling us that it's been completely destroyed?"

"Yes," Maradn said simply.

"Worse," Heldmar Pelk said, his sand-colored eyebrows coming together on his forehead. "General Karpasic is in the hands of the Western Alliance and their Council of Might."

"To say nothing of the loss of the Avatar sword," Sirun Hurst added. She cast a furtive glance at Tarvus before meeting Maradn's gaze. "You were in charge of Karpasic and his force, clearly this mess is your fault."

A chorus of agreement arose around the table and Maradn let it go on without interrupting. Her smile didn't slip an inch. She knew the other circle members would smell blood at this news and she was the most likely target. Still, it galled her to her to hear it from that simpering fool, Sirun.

"I think it's quite clear," Maradn said once the noise died down, "that Craftmaster Dirae was correct. This mess is clearly of General Karpasic's making. He allowed the Avatar sword to fall into our enemy's hands, and when he realized his mistake he tried to recapture it without securing his own position."

She would have preferred to blame Evard for this, but he was just a lowly craftmaster. Her enemies would never accept his head over hers. By absolving him and backing his explanation, she also distanced herself from the entire affair. It would raise Evard's standing in the eyes of the circle, which was irksome but necessary.

"No matter whose fault this is, it is a disaster for us," Fenric Castus said, his flabby jowls shaking. "Without the Westreach Army to put pressure on them, the Alliance will have time to consolidate their defense, even build an army of their own."

Heldmar opened his mouth, presumably to point out that the so-called Council of Might was hopelessly fractured and had no real chance of unifying, but before he could get a word out, Sirun panicked.

"We must reinforce the garrison at Hilt," she gasped. "If an Alliance army takes that we'll lose the entire western side of the continent."

"How?" Doran Valsond asked. His voice was soft and he held his head slightly down so that he looked up at the circle from under his bushy brows. When silence greeted his question, he went on. "The Army of Night is engaged in the north and the rest of our forces are busy holding the territories we already control." He turned to Sirun and fixed his blue eyes on her. "Or are you suggesting that we muster out the Home Guard?"

Sirun's mouth dropped open but she said nothing. Maradn didn't take her eyes off her. She wanted to remember this moment.

"The Home Guard is needed here," Tarvus said, giving his idiot lover time to pull her foot out of her mouth. "Say what you like about the Council of Might, but they have far too many former pirates in their ranks. If we sent the Home Guard away from Desolis, they might try to sail an army around and attack us from the sea."

"Which leaves us back where we were," Heldmar said. "While I don't think the Council of Might will be able to muster an army sufficient enough to take the fortress at Hilt, I don't think them so inept that they will ignore this opportunity. When our armies threatened all of Paladis they were panicked, at each other's throats. Now they will see us as weak. They'll put their squabbles aside, and by the time we've rebuilt our forces, they'll be ready. This could delay the prophecy by decades."

Silence greeted his words, and Maradn let it stretch out. She knew someone would figure out their real peril if she let them go on long enough, and it impressed her how thoroughly Heldmar understood it. Mentioning the prophecy was a good touch, too. He was only in his thirties, the second-youngest member of the circle, but Maradn found him both sensible and cunning. She suspected he had his own designs on the seventh throne, so naturally she would have to crush him at some point.

"Which brings us back to where we started," Tarvus said, a self-satisfied smile spreading across his face. "I believe General Karpasic served at your pleasure, Maradn. You should have provided him more direct guidance. This setback is due to your lack of leadership."

"Our generals are supposed to operate under their own discretion," Fenric said, coming to her defense.

"Be that as it may," Sirun said, "do you have a way to fix this, Lady Maradn?"

All eyes at the table turned to look at her. Maradn counted to ten in her head before she answered, watching as Tarvus and Sirun became more and more sure of their victory.

"Of course I do, child," Maradn said in the most patronizing voice she could muster. "As Lord Heldmar has so succinctly pointed out, the most dangerous thing now is the perception that we are weak."

"A perception we will not be able to dispel without a reformed army," Heldmar said.

"Exactly." Maradn looked slowly around the table. "What we must do now is rebuild the Westreach Army as quickly as possible."

"And how do you propose we do that without leaving ourselves exposed?" Valsond asked, his voice even and neutral. "Most people of warrior age were already taken for our existing forces, and there aren't enough left to raise more than a small force."

"Send word to our forces occupying Midras," she answered. "And every other city up and down in Midmaer and Grunvald."

"Midras is not yet fully pacified," Heldmar pointed out. "If we withdraw our forces, we'd be giving the city back to them."

"We will instruct our forces to remove the civilian population," Maradn said. "All of them. They will escort them back here where those rebellious peasants can become Fomorians. If we can't recruit an army, then by the prophecy, we'll build one."

"That's liable to foment rebellion all across Midmaer," Fenric cautioned.

"Then we'll make sure that those who rebel are the first to be taken," Maradn said with a shrug. "That will keep most of the rest in line."

Silence greeted her. She allowed herself a satisfied smile at the sullen looks on Tarvus' and Sirun's faces.

"It could work," Valsond said, stroking the white stubble on his narrow chin. "If we start right away, we could field a new Westreach Army in just a few months."

"We'll need to promote some of the shaper acolytes to full shapers," Fenric said. "If we do that, we can keep the work going continuously."

"Are we in agreement then?" Maradn asked, smiling sweetly.

All around the table heads bobbed.

† † †

An hour later, Maradn swept into her quarters, exultant in her victory. When she reached her library, she poured herself a brandy and collapsed onto her favorite lounge. She raised the glass to her lips, but it trembled so violently she was forced to set it aside. The shakes that had dogged her since first hearing Evard's disastrous news threatened to overwhelm her, but she bit her lip and forced her fear back in check. She'd come too far, past bigger obstacles than some ancient sword; she would not be denied now. Focusing her breathing, she put the brandy to her lips again and drank.

In hindsight, it seemed like everything had gone her way, but she wasn't a fool. She knew that any unforeseen situation, any hesitation on her part, any hint of weakness and the circle would have eaten her alive. Even Fenric, her dedicated ally, would have abandoned her. Her quest for the seventh throne would have ended right there.

As it was, everything *had* gone her way. She'd been skilled, she'd been prepared . . . but she'd also been lucky.

"No," she said aloud, contradicting her own doubts. "I made my own luck."

She crossed to a bell pull and rang for a Kobold.

"Summon Maltius," she told the Kobold when it shuffled into the library.

"He awaits you in the parlor," the creature said in its growling voice.

Maradn raised an eyebrow at that. Word of what went on in the circle's meeting room couldn't have spread yet; the boy must have anticipated her needs.

"How very clever of him," she said. "Tell him to attend me here."

The Kobold hissed in response and went to fetch her apprentice. By the time he arrived, Maradn had perched herself on her lounge and managed another sip of her brandy.

"You summoned me, mistress?" Maltius said, bowing as he entered.

"It seems you knew that I would," Maradn said, not bothering to hide her pleasure.

"When I heard that the circle had been summoned into an unscheduled council, I suspected that I might be able to serve you," he said. "At least I hoped I could."

Maradn grinned at that. He'd flattered her and built himself up at the same time.

The boy is coming along well.

"Sit," she instructed, waving her hand at a chair opposite her lounge. She waited until he'd situated himself before giving him the details of her meeting with the circle.

"A very clever solution, mistress," he said once she had finished. "But what about Craftmaster Dirae? Surely he must be punished for his insolence."

Maradn laughed at that. After such a stressful day it felt good.

"Lun will find him the next time he uses his magic," she said. "Clearly he's doing something he doesn't want me to know. Once Lun finds him, you'll keep an eye on him until he does something I can use against him."

"Thank you, mistress," Maltius said with a pleased smile. "I will not fail you."

"I have no doubt of that. In the meantime, however, I want you to take a message to the master of the shapers."

"Of course."

"Tell him that I want him to proceed with my personal project," she said.

"If I may, mistress," Maltius interrupted. "He will object and claim that he doesn't have enough material to be successful."

Maradn sighed at that and allowed herself a satisfied smile.

"Tell him that he will have the resources he requires within the month," she said. "I will expect him to be ready."

Maltius rose and bowed.

"It shall be done, mistress."

Maradn nodded, then returned to her brandy. Karpasic's carelessness and stupidity had cost the cabal dearly, not to mention having the cursed Avatar sword loose in the world. Still, even with all that the day was turning out rather well. After all, Maradn wouldn't have gotten where she was if she couldn't turn adversity to her own advantage.

She sat for a while, letting her mind and body relax until she found her glass was empty. It was tempting to refill it, but there was work to be done, so she set the glass aside and rose. Crossing to the spiral stair that ran to the balcony, she climbed up and then opened the door to the elaborate birdcage.

"Come Jiri," she said to the sleeping pseudodragon.

It raised a sleepy head and looked at her through its dark eyes. It stretched, unfurling its wings in a lazy way, then flapped them once, taking flight. It swooped nimbly out of the cage, circled the room, then came to rest, lightly, on Maradn's shoulder.

"I hope you are well rested," she said, stroking the creature's scaly neck. "I need to communicate with your brother. It's time we found out where dear Evard has gone and what he so desperately wants to hide from me."

If she was lucky, he'd give her leverage she could use against him for years to come.

Yes, this was shaping up to be a good day, indeed.

CHAPTER
8

The Council
of Might

This was not shaping up to be a good day.

Aren sat on a hard bench on the left side of Baroness Baden-Fox's audience chamber. The room had a vaulted ceiling with rows of wooden benches facing the open floor along a wide, curved wall at the back. A raised dais ran along that wall with the baroness's throne in the center. Ranging out to either side along the dais were six large, important-looking chairs. They were arranged with three chairs on either side of the throne. These were for the various representatives of the baroness's alliance, the optimistically named Council of Might.

Aren had been sitting on one of the benches in the observer's gallery for most of the morning and he was stiff and sore. As a professional soldier, he was used to being uncomfortable, it was part of the job, but listening to a room of bickering diplomats was grating on his nerves.

The last time he'd been paying attention, which seemed like hours ago, Count Ekard of Aerie was complaining because the council used his country's ships to ferry the Titans and much of their books and scholars through the Straits of Elysium to Xenos. The representative from Resolute, an aging knight named Falcone had called the tall, spindly Ekard's manhood into question for whining about doing his nation's part when Resolute had absorbed most of the Opalis refugees without complaint. A rollicking argument had evolved from there featuring every council representative apart from Baroness Baden-Fox, who looked as irritated as Aren was, and Shogun Tsuneo of Ardoris. Aren hadn't yet heard the man speak more than one sentence in the week he'd been a mandatory guest of the council.

The shogun sat with his arms crossed over his brightly colored robe and a sour look on his face. Aren didn't need to touch the Avatar sword to know his mind: the man ruled a vast kingdom with no threatening neighbors. The Obsidian Empire was to the north of Ardoris, but the Spectral Peaks made any potential invasion difficult and would give the shogun ample time to prepare. His lands were not facing the immediate peril that hung over the rest of the council, but he wasn't a fool. He knew that if the other nations of the council fell, he would be left standing alone. Better to help his neighbors now and keep the brunt of the war far from his own lands. The threat to him, of course, was his autonomy. If the Council of Might managed to pull together, pressure would mount to make it permanent. If that happened, decisions would be made regarding Ardoris that were not exclusively Tsuneo's, and if Aren's assessment was right, the shogun would rather cut off his arm than allow that.

"Gentlemen!" Baroness Baden-Fox's voice cut through Aren's musings. Her ability to shout like a teamster was a surprise. As the echoes of her voice rang off the stone, she held her hands up for attention.

"I think we've exhausted the potential of this discussion," she said in a more refined voice. "I've just been informed that the Titan Sequana has returned."

"Have the raiders been dealt with then?" Tribune Tercius, Emperor of Norgard, asked.

"If your armies had done their job and destroyed them, the Obsidian leftovers wouldn't be terrorizing the lowlands of South Paladis," Arthur Falcone sneered.

"Enough!" The baroness shouted in her teamster voice. "As Sequana is still on her way to the council chamber, I suggest we take a short recess."

"Thank the Gods," Aren muttered, standing up. "I need some air."

"Sit down," Syenna said from beside him. Her voice sounded as taut and raw as his nerves.

"Why?" he demanded. "I've been watching this farce for a week. Why am I even here?"

"Because they want you here," Syenna said. It was the hundredth time she'd answered that question and she didn't bother to hide the sigh in her voice.

"For what?" he pressed. "Zhal and the Titans explained what happened at Opalis." He waved his hands at the raised chairs. "They didn't even ask me anything."

"They don't know what to ask you yet," Zhal said, appearing at his side.

"Speak of evil," Aren grumbled.

Zhal laughed at that.

"And I appear, eh?" He slapped Aren on the shoulder, his ever-present smile never wavering. Aren clenched his teeth and mentally counted to ten. He wondered if the baroness's guards would throw him in a nice quiet jail cell if he punched the loremaster in the face. The thought made him grin.

"You're supposed to wait until after I tell you the good news to smile," Zhal said.

His voice was easy and friendly, so Aren was immediately on guard.

"What good news?"

"While we wait for the Titan Sequana to arrive, the baroness has asked for you and Syenna to join her in her private chamber. I suspect she has some of those questions you so wanted to answer."

Aren resisted the urge to sigh.

"That isn't what I meant," he said.

"Oh dear," Zhal said with a look of shock that was far too exaggerated to be genuine. "I'd suggest that in the future, then, that you not tempt the gods like that."

Zhal turned and began to cross the floor to a small door on the far wall that led to a hallway behind the thrones. Aren knew the baroness had a room back there to retire to if the business of state ran long.

He hesitated for a moment as Zhal moved away. Despite his complaints, he knew his presence in the audience hall for the Council of Might meant some plan or other involving him was afoot. Now that the moment seemed to have presented itself, he wasn't sure he really wanted to know what the baroness and her allies had in store for him.

"Come on," Syenna said, stepping up and taking his arm. "Let's see what my lady wants."

Ever since they'd returned to Etceter, Syenna had been his shadow. She'd sat through every ridiculous council meeting right beside him, and her voice sounded almost as weary as he felt.

"I'm surprised," Aren said, allowing Syenna to lead him across the chamber.

"At what?"

"That your baroness left her prized shieldmaiden cooling her heels this long. Last time we were here, she seemed to rely on you rather heavily. I'm surprised she hasn't already found an assignment for . . ."

Aren let the sentence trail off as he realized the truth.

"I'm your assignment," he said. "Aren't I?"

Syenna smiled at that, with just a touch of mockery in her eyes.

"And people think you're clever," she said, patting his arm. "It only took you a week to figure that out."

"So, you want to tell me what this is all about?"

"I'm just supposed to make sure you don't wander off," Syenna said, though Aren was pretty sure that wasn't the whole truth. "I don't know what the baroness is going to say any more than you do."

Aren didn't know what he expected the baroness's private chamber to be, but he wasn't expecting the modest sitting room Zhal led them to. It was fairly narrow and long with two distinct areas. In the front, soft couches and overstuffed chairs sat facing each other while in the back stood a heavy writing desk along with a simple bed that was mostly concealed behind a folding screen.

The baroness was waiting for them, sitting cross-legged in a high-backed chair with a silver goblet in her hand. The dress she wore was an elaborate affair made of a blue satin with a corset that forced the baroness to sit up very straight in her chair. Aren thought he felt tired and worn from watching the proceedings of the council, but he hadn't really considered what it was like for the actual participants. Aren could see the exhausted slump of her shoulders and the dark circles around her bloodshot eyes that her makeup was not completely concealing.

"Captain Bennis," she said, as he entered. "Welcome back to Etceter. Captain Trevan tells me you had an eventful absence."

"Baroness," Aren said, bowing his head respectfully. "The captain is mistaken. I'm sure he exaggerated my involvement in the events at Opalis. No doubt for some mischievous reason of his own."

It wasn't much of a lie, but Aren felt he should at least make the attempt to dissuade the baroness from whatever course of action she had already chosen. Whatever it was, Aren felt sure it would put him in the most compromising position possible.

She looked up and held his eyes for a moment before she chuckled. She had a rich, contralto voice and her laugh was low and throaty.

"Don't be so modest, Captain," she said, sipping from her goblet. "Captain Trevan is a good man who knows his business. Do you know how I know that?"

His hand drifted toward the hilt of the Avatar sword, but he caught himself and clasped his hands behind his back instead. The sword would reveal the baroness's motives for bringing him here, but it would also show him everything else about her, and that had a way of making it hard to say no. Instead Aren resolved to find out about the baroness's motives the old-fashioned way.

And then say no.

"No, ma'am," he said. "I wasn't aware that you knew Captain Trevan."

"I know that the captain of the Opalis Legion is a good man because he freely admitted his failings when he told me the story of the sacking of Opalis. He said that if you hadn't taken charge, the Westreach Army would have had the city in less than a day."

"General Karpasic believed Opalis to be a city full of gold," Aren said with an easy shrug. "He was well motivated."

The baroness chuckled again, then nodded to the couch opposite her chair.

"Sit," she instructed, then motioned to a servant standing back by the desk. She hurried forward and offered Aren and Syenna silver goblets.

Aren took the offered cup and sipped at it. The wine had a fruity taste with a bit of a bite, so it wasn't new, but it hadn't aged very long.

"I appreciate your hospitality, Baroness," Aren said. "But, I'd like to know why I'm here."

The baroness looked for a moment as if she would put him off, but her face hardened and one of her dark eyebrows arched.

"What do you see when you're out there?" she asked, gesturing in the direction of the council chamber.

"Fear," Aren said. "Everyone's afraid. They're afraid of the Obsidians conquering their lands. They're afraid of committing to help their neighbors if they're attacked because it might leave them weak. Some of them are even afraid of this council."

"And why is that?"

"They all know the Council of Might is their only chance to stop the advance of the Obsidian Empire, but if the council is successful, they fear they will lose their individual nations to the rule of the council. It's like holding a tiger by the tail," Aren continued. "It's dangerous to hold on, but twice as dangerous to let go."

The baroness smiled. She had a look on her face that told Aren that he'd just confirmed something for her.

"Zhal spoke truly," she said. "That sword gives you remarkable insight into people. You're right, of course. While I don't have the advantage of an Avatar sword, I do have the benefit of experience. Our little alliance is balanced upon a knife's blade. The only question is which fear will doom us first, the fear that the council won't succeed—or the fear that it will."

"I'm afraid I can't tell you that, ma'am," Aren said. "The sword doesn't reveal the future; at least it hasn't up to now."

"You've heard about the raids that have been happening up and down South Paladis?" she said, suddenly changing the subject.

"I could hardly miss the last few days' discussion."

"What you don't know is that the council assembled an army to deal with the remnants of the Westreach Army," The baroness held up her goblet and the auburn-haired servant girl scrambled to refill it. "It was made up of units from each nation, and each contributed the barest minimum, just enough to claim they'd met their obligations."

Aren nodded. He hadn't known this, but it would have been easy to predict. None of the council nations wanted to weaken themselves lest it give an opportunity to their fellow members.

"Our forces were soundly defeated less than a fortnight ago," She lifted a sheet of paper off the little table beside her chair. "I have Captain Trevan's report right here." She tossed the paper on the floor with a contemptuous flick of her hand. "He says that the army is in disarray with low morale."

That made sense. Units from disparate forces weren't used to working together and tended not to trust commanders who weren't in their direct chain of command. A hodgepodge army like that was a recipe for disaster.

"You need a general who can unite your forces," Aren said.

The baroness smiled at him, but this time there was steel in her eyes and wolf in her smile.

"Our thoughts exactly," she said. It was crystal clear what she meant.

"Don't be absurd," Aren said, forgetting himself. Syenna elbowed him in the ribs but he ignored her. "I'm the enemy. No one in this Army of Might is going to follow me."

"Army of Might?" the baroness said with an amused look. "I like it. Seems you were made for this command."

Aren opened his mouth to object, but the baroness held up a hand, silencing him.

"You are the hero of Opalis," she said. "You saved that entire city from enslavement and ruin and everyone knows it. Besides, as you so

cleverly pointed out yourself, I can't put one of our leaders in charge."
She swept her hand in the direction of the council chamber. "Whatever nation the general came from would see it as an opportunity to control the army while the other nations would resist their new commander. The only person capable of uniting our forces is an outsider." She raised her hand up in mock salute. "And the only outsider here, my dear captain, is you."

It made sense—in an insane way. Anyone else the council put in charge would be undermined by parts of their own army. Aren would either be accepted for his defense of Opalis, treated as a ringer or a savior . . . or they'd mutiny and string him up.

"I'm sorry, Baroness," he said. "But I don't want the job."

She looked peeved at that, but hid it quickly.

"And why not? Do you harbor some dream of returning to the Obsidians?"

"No," he admitted. "But just because I didn't want to abandon the people of Opalis to the *tender* mercies of General Karpasic, it doesn't mean I want to join your Alliance. For all its faults, the Obsidian Empire has done some good."

"Law and order," the baroness said.

Aren looked at Syenna, but she met his gaze imperiously. He'd told her in confidence about his childhood and his reasons for joining the army, but she'd clearly passed it on.

"Yes," he admitted. "From what I've seen of these western lands, they're in as much chaos as your council. Several of those nations out there were at war with each other only a few years ago."

The baroness considered him for a long moment, boring into him with her brown eyes.

"Do you like my city?" she said, somewhat out of the blue.

Aren nodded. Etceter was an interesting mix of old and new buildings with clean, well ordered streets and a continual bustle of activity.

"I do," he said.

"Etceter is a wealthy city," she explained. "We make our money by commerce, Captain Bennis, by trade."

Aren didn't see the significance of that and said so.

"Trade requires order, Captain. Laws must be maintained, trade routes must be established and kept free of brigands. Taxes must be levied, but not so much that they discourage the very trade they exist to support. Treaties must be negotiated with partner nations. A trading nation is a nation of order."

"What about the others?"

The baroness's wolfish smile came back to her face.

"I have plans for them," she said.

"You want to use this council beyond the threat of the Obsidian Empire," Aren guessed. "You want to use it to establish those treaties you mentioned. To extend the order of Etceter across all of the west."

"Very good, Captain. I will use my position as the council's leader to—*encourage* the other members to secure their roads, open their cities, and above all, protect trade."

"I'm sure that will make Etceter very rich," Aren said. He could see that a woman as determined as the baroness would be able to do exactly as she said, though he doubted it would benefit her partners nearly as much.

"Of course we will," she admitted with no trace of shame. "But you are missing the by-product of all that trade."

"Order?" he said.

She nodded back at him.

"Once the treaties are in place, and the goods begin to flow, each nation will become dependent on their neighbors for the things they can't or won't produce. War will become a costly interruption to business."

Aren wasn't sure if this was genius or insanity.

"You can't think it's that simple," he said at last.

"Of course it's not. It will take decades of work to secure this alliance and the peace that will follow. Old hatreds will need time to cool and new generations will have to come up without them. I probably won't live to see its fruition, but if we play our cards right, you and I, we can set the western lands in motion toward that law and order you desire."

She stood, and Aren and Syenna hastily got to their feet.

"All I need to accomplish this vision, mine and yours, is for you to help me unite the members of the council." She held out her hand to him. "Accept my commission and take command of the Army of Might. Use your skill as a military commander to forge them into the weapon we will need to repel the Obsidians. Deal with the remnants of your former army, stop their raiding, and prove to the council that we are better off united than divided."

Aren felt his blood stirring at her words. There was no wondering why the woman was known as the Bloodsteel Baroness, she was a force of nature. Worse, her argument made sense. Still, something tugged at the edges of his consciousness, warning him to be wary.

"I can't argue with your logic," he said at last. "But this is a lot to consider. Will Your Grace allow me time to think it over?"

Aren saw the briefest moment of disappointment in her eyes, but then she smiled.

"Of course," she said, sounding quite sincere. "I understand this is a momentous decision, but I will need your answer by week's end."

Aren nodded and the baroness picked up a small silver bell from her side table. When she rang it, the door opened immediately and Zhal came in. Aren had the uncomfortable feeling that he'd been listening in the hall the whole time.

"I don't think the captain and dear Syenna need to remain for the rest of the council's proceedings today," she said to the loremaster. "Why don't you give him a tour of the city."

"An excellent idea, Your Grace," Zhal said with a delighted smile. "I'm sure the captain would like to visit tailor's row, perhaps acquire something a bit more appropriate to wear to dinner?"

Aren had no idea what Zhal was insinuating, but the baroness did. Her wolfish grin reappeared, and she nodded.

"An excellent idea, Zhal," she said. "I knew I could count on you."

CHAPTER
9

The Fomorian

ren fidgeted with the collar of the doublet Zhal had picked out for him. It was black with silver trim in an obvious homage to his Obsidian armor. It was also absurdly uncomfortable. He wondered if it was uncomfortable because it was new or because he hated dinner parties.

As an Obsidian officer, Aren had been to social functions before, but not often. He liked it that way.

"Don't fidget," Zhal said as Aren pulled on his collar again.

"Why am I doing this?" Aren asked as the carriage rumbled over a ditch that must have been a yard wide.

"Well," Zhal said in his philosopher's voice, "you did get those nice new clothes today; it would be a shame if you didn't have anywhere to go in them."

"You paid for those," he grumbled. "It wasn't my idea." The carriage turned off the road and passed between a massive pair of wrought iron gates. A grand-looking manor house stood beyond them along a cobbled lane, but Aren saw no signs of torches, footmen, or other arriving guests.

"This isn't our destination," Zhal said, reading Aren's expression.

Before Aren could ask what they were doing here, the carriage came to a stop in front of what appeared to be a solidly built stable, and Zhal opened the door. Two women in the ridiculous shieldmaiden armor—plumed helmets, pantaloons, and all—stood to either side of a heavy door. As Zhal dismounted the carriage, the door opened, and a woman emerged. She wore a deep blue gown that hugged her figure, tapering to her waist before flowing over her hips and down to a pair of open sandals. A belt of silver links encircled the woman's waist twice and matching bangles hung from her ears. Her blond hair flowed loosely behind her and over her shoulders to her mid back.

"You look lovely, my dear," Zhal said, taking the woman's hand.

"Thank you," she said, and Aren almost jumped.

The woman was Syenna.

He cocked his head as Zhal led her to the open door of the carriage. Aren tried to reconcile the sight before him with his experiences with the shieldmaiden. As far as he remembered, he'd never seen her wearing anything other than the tunic and breeches she wore as a scout and her ceremonial armor. Neither of those had been designed in any way to accent beauty and neither had prepared him for the sight before him.

Syenna seated herself across from Aren, then Zhal climbed aboard, shutting the door behind him.

"What?" Syenna said, giving Aren a hard look.

He must have been staring.

"You clean up well, Shieldmaiden," he said.

"Lieutenant," she said, her expression frosty. "I'm a lieutenant in the baroness's guard."

"My apologies, Lieutenant," Aren said. "Is this the guard's barracks?"

He didn't really care, but for some reason Syenna was angry at him and he wanted to change the subject.

"This is the baroness's estate," Syenna said, her frosty tone not thawing a degree. "The barracks of the shieldmaidens used to be a stable in the days when the manor was owned by a pirate. In those days, horse theft was common, so the stables were built of stone with guard houses attached. The baroness's family converted it when they acquired the manor."

Aren made a noncommittal noise and the carriage lapsed into silence. A quarter of an hour later the carriage stopped in front of a modest cottage. It was large, as cottages went, three stories with a low stone fence around it and clinging ivy crawling up the walls. Gleaming brass lamps glowing with soft light flanked the wrought iron gate while a matching pair illuminated a solid front door set with an enormous brass knocker in its center.

"Here we are," Zhal said.

Aren assumed they were here to pick up another guest. The home was neat and well situated, but it didn't seem like the kind of place to find a gathering of Etceter's important citizens.

Zhal opened the door and stepped out, then turned, offering his hand to Syenna. Aren was looking right at her as her eyes moved to the door. He'd seen those eyes in darkness and light, around campfires, on battlefields, and in camps full of soldiers. Aren had seen her eyes as she watched men die in the aftermath of combat, holding their hands as they gasped out their last. He knew those dark blue eyes—he knew them better even than he knew his own. The moment they moved to the loremaster's face, Syenna's eyes hardened into motes of solid ice.

Aren had assumed that her obvious displeasure was the result of being dragged off to some dinner party, but now he saw the error in that thinking. Syenna was a noblewoman's guard, she would have accompanied her mistress to many such functions. Whatever had roused the shieldmaiden's ire, it had been Zhal that had done it.

Something more than a dinner party is on for tonight.

Aren hated being on a battlefield without knowing the ground beforehand. You could never judge the direction an attack might come. He resolved to find a nice corner in the little cottage and keep his back to it.

And keep from between Zhal and Syenna.

"Whose home is this?" Aren asked as he exited the carriage. He thought at least that would be a safe topic for conversation, but Syenna's frosty gaze turned back to him.

"It's mine," she said. There was a note of challenge in her voice, as if daring him to comment on the cottage. As someone who had never owned so much as a barren patch of ground, Aren was at a loss to explain her challenge.

"It's very nice," he said, deciding to stay as neutral as possible.

Syenna's look softened, but she didn't respond. Zhal seized the moment and opened the gate, ushering them up the stone walk to the door.

A sturdy-looking older woman with dark, braided hair opened the door in response to Zhal's knock. She wore an elegant dress, but she looked uncomfortable; clearly it wasn't the way she usually dressed. When she saw Syenna, however, she smiled fondly.

"Sarah," Syenna said, stepping forward to embrace the woman.

"Welcome back," Sarah said, hugging the shieldmaiden tightly. "Why don't you all come in," she went on, stepping back from the door. "Amanda is so anxious to see you."

Now it made sense. Aren had forgotten about Syenna's sister, the one the Obsidians had tried and failed to change. He looked at Zhal, but the loremaster hurried past him into the foyer of the house. No wonder Syenna was angry at Zhal—he was blatantly using her sister as a pawn to bully Aren into heading the baroness's army.

He gave a fleeting thought to just turning around and walking away, but he'd be damned if he let the smug loremaster intimidate him with a crippled girl. Taking a deep breath, he stepped inside.

The house wasn't really designed for large groups. The door led directly into a decent-sized sitting room. Whatever furniture the room usually held had been removed aside from a few overstuffed chairs and a padded bench under a bay window. A fire blazed in a stone hearth, casting ruddy light out into the middle of the room. Several people were already there and Aren recognized Sequana and Captain Artemis of the Opalis Legion speaking with a diplomat that he didn't recognize.

To one side of the hearth sat a young woman in a red dress. Her white-blond hair flowed loose over her shoulders. She had her hands clasped in her lap, but even at this distance, Aren could see that she was kneading her fingers nervously. Her face erupted in a dazzling smile when Syenna crossed the floor to her.

The young woman put her hands on the arms of her chair as if she were about to stand, but Syenna quickened her pace and leaned over to hug her while she was still seated.

"You've haven't met Amanda yet, have you?" Zhal said, sounding for all the world as if her presence here were something he'd just remembered. "Come, I'll introduce you."

Aren rolled his eyes at that but Zhal didn't notice.

"Hello, Zhal," Amanda said when they approached. She sounded as if she were genuinely delighted to see the old fox.

She probably doesn't really know him, Aren thought.

"Did you bring me any new books?" she went on.

"Of course I did," Zhal replied with a wink and a grin. "I've got an entire trunk full in my quarters. "I'll send five of them over to you tomorrow. That should get you started."

Amanda beamed at the news, and Syenna's hard look melted away. It was clear that a large part of the shieldmaiden's life was devoted to making her sister happy. Aren remembered the deal she'd made with Evard, the deal that would have cost Amanda her life. He'd been shocked by how desperate Syenna had been, how devastated she was when he told her the truth.

Aren hadn't given much thought to his friend's motivations when he made the deal with Syenna. Now, standing here with the beautiful girl before him, he hated Evard in a way he'd never imagined possible.

"And this is Captain Aren Bennis," he heard Zhal saying, "the hero of Opalis. Captain Bennis, this is Amanda of Quel."

She looked up from her chair and somehow her smile got even wider. As her head turned, however, her hair draped away from her face, revealing the tip of a pointed ear.

"Captain," Amanda said, "I have so wanted to meet you. My sister has told me many things about you and I just had to see you for myself."

She put out her hand and Aren took it. He noticed that the fingers of the hand were longer than usual, more delicate. Whatever the Obsidian shapers had done to her had been subtle, but he'd been around enough of their work to spot it.

"Charmed," he said, kissing her hand. "I must confess you have the advantage of me. Syenna has told me precious little about you, an oversight no doubt. Now that I'm here, I look forward to rectifying that."

Amanda gave her sister a look of mock offense, and Aren was certain that had her sister not been there, the shieldmaiden would have punched him for saying that. Syenna's gown clung to her impressive physique very artfully, but Aren was certain there were a few places where a dagger could still be concealed. He resolved not to bait her so openly for the rest of the evening.

"Mistress Syenna," a young man in a formal tunic called, approaching from across the room. "Sarah requires your presence in the kitchen."

It was a transparent excuse designed to get Syenna away from Amanda so she could talk. Both she and Aren looked at Zhal, but he suddenly noticed the Titan Sequana motioning for him to approach and excused himself. Aren found it difficult to suppress a grin as Syenna mastered herself and accompanied the boy back to the kitchens.

"You noticed," Amanda said once they were alone.

"It was a rather transparent excuse to remove your sister," he said, looking after Syenna until she disappeared into a side hall.

"Not that," Amanda said.

Something in her voice pulled Aren's attention back to her. She raised her hand to the side of her head and pulled her hair back, revealing her pointed ear.

"This," she said.

"I knew," Aaron admitted.

"It hurts her," she said, looking away to where Syenna had gone. "Every time she sees me. She tries to hide it, but I know."

Aren squatted down so he was on the same level as the seated girl.

"I once saw her offer an Obsidian sorcerer whatever he wanted in order to reverse what they did to you," he said. "She loves you more than anything in the world."

Amanda blushed but shook her head.

"She blames herself." She reached down and pulled open the slit that ran up the side of her long skirt. The leg exposed beneath was withered and misshapen in stark contrast to the rest of her.

"I'm sorry," he said, feeling some of what Syenna must feel every day. He knew what had happened to her had nothing to do with him, but he couldn't help feeling somewhat responsible. How many Fomorians had he led in battle without wondering once where they had really come from?

"It isn't her fault," Amanda said, covering her leg with her dress. "Any more than it's my fault, or my parents . . . or yours." He looked up to meet her eyes. They were blue, like her sister's but where Syenna's eyes were the dark blue of sapphires, Amanda's were the pale blue of a summer sky.

"Thank you," Aren said, meaning it. "Though I suspect you're being too charitable. I knew what the sorcerers were doing, but I confess, I never really thought about it. I never met a Fomorian who still retained any of their past before."

"Fomorian?" Amanda asked, confusion spreading across her delicate features.

"That's what the Obsidians call their creations," he explained. "I shouldn't have called you that."

"I would prefer if you didn't," Amanda said, her smile returning. "There are some who remember, you know. They called us the Dross, their mistakes, those of us that survived anyway." A shadow crossed Amanda's face and Aren felt the sudden urge to find the shapers who had done this and slit their throats. "The ones that were still useful were put to work, the others . . ."

She didn't finish her thought, but she didn't have to. Aren had no illusions about what happened to a mistake that wasn't useful.

"They taught me to read and write," Amanda went on. "Then they put me to work copying books. I was there until Syenna came for me."

Her face lit up as it did each time she mentioned her sister.

Aren reached out and took her hand again.

"I'm sorry for what they did to you," he said. "For what they took from you and from your sister."

"I know it haunts Syenna," she said. "But it's just my life now. The only thing I really regret are the memories they took." When Aren looked confused, she explained. "Only part of me was left after they changed me. I remember some of my past, but much of it is a blank."

Aren remembered the Fomorians he'd seen with the aid of the Avatar sword, how they were simply empty blank slates that the Obsidians had scrawled on.

"Zhal told me that your sword lets you see people for who they really are," she said. Something in her voice told him she'd been wanting to talk about this since they met.

Aren nodded.

"And you want to know what it shows me about you?" he guessed.

She blushed again. Aren found her lack of guile adorable.

"I was wondering," she said, looking him square in the eyes, "if you'd let me hold it."

Aren looked down, breaking their eye contact.

"That wouldn't be a good idea," he said. "Everyone who touches this sword has had a bad reaction to it, everyone but me. I wouldn't want you to come to harm."

Amanda looked as though she might object, but after a moment she nodded.

"Very well, then tell me what the sword shows you about me."

Aren hesitated. He'd managed to go almost a week without touching the sword in public. He was starting to enjoy not being privy to the hopes, dreams, and foibles of everyone around him.

"Surely you wouldn't deny your host this one indulgence?" Amanda said. She still had the angelic smile on her lips, but her eyes had steel in them. Aren had seen that determined look before on Syenna. He knew it was useless to fight it.

"If that's what you want," he said, standing up straight. "I will do it, of course, but you need to understand that the sword will show me everything about you. Even things you'd probably wish I didn't know."

"Captain Bennis—"

"Aren," he interrupted.

"Aren, I have no youthful indiscretions or secret lovers hidden away. My past is as much a mystery to me as to anyone. I'll brave a little potential embarrassment for even an ounce of truth."

She put out a hand and took his.

"Please. Do this for me."

Aren put his other hand on top of hers and sighed.

"Of course," he said.

She released his hands and he took hold of the handle of the Avatar sword. As his fingers closed about the grip, his vision shifted and he saw everything. Like the other Fomorians he'd seen, much of her past was simply gone, wiped clean like a slate board to make room for the being the Obsidians wanted her to be. What remained were Amanda's thoughts and memories of her sister. If Aren had to guess, she'd clung to the thought of Syenna and that had anchored her against the Obsidian magic.

On the other hand, Aren could see what the Obsidians had intended, a tall, muscular warrior with dexterous hands and sharp eyes. They wanted an archer. Just another soldier to throw into their war effort.

Aren tried to release the sword, to stop the flood of information now that he knew what Amanda wanted. He wanted to turn it off before the rest came, but the sword seemed to resist his efforts, keeping his hand on its grip. Images of Amanda came to him, cold and alone in some dank underground complex where she was led around by armed men in the same armor Aren had worn for most of his life. He felt her despair and her loss as she struggled to remember her past. There were moments of happiness, as she learned to read and as she read the books the men in armor gave her to copy. Exaltation when Syenna came for her and pain at the look in her sister's eyes every time she looked at Amanda. Aren felt her loneliness as Syenna left her here, with little to do but read and stitch, and her fear at people's reaction when they discovered what she was.

Aren gasped and jerked his hand free of the sword. He had a moment of dizziness and knelt down on the soft rug that covered the floor.

"Was it really so bad?" Amanda said. Her voice was easy, but Aren knew she feared that the changes she'd undergone made her a monster.

He reached out and took her long-fingered hand, squeezing it gently.

"No," he assured her. "Sometimes the experience is . . . personal."

She smiled shyly.

"So what did you see?" She sounded both excited and fearful.

Aren took a breath, then faced her, looking her in the eyes.

"I didn't see anything in your past that you don't already know," he said. "The Obsidians wiped that away."

"Oh," she said, dropping her eyes to her lap.

"But I did see why they failed," Aren said. He waited until Amanda raised her eyes to meet his again before he went on. "When they took you, you believed that Syenna would come, that she would save you. That belief is what kept you from being changed into a monster, from losing your will and your identity. It anchored you to who you really are, it protected you from the Obsidians' magic."

Amanda smiled a sad smile at that as a single tear ran down her cheek.

"I hoped you could tell me more, but it is enough to know that Syenna saved me. She always saves me."

"She loves you very much," Aren agreed.

"Someday I would like to help her like she helps me," Amanda said, "but I'm not strong or brave like she is."

"You're braver than you think," Aren said, remembering the vague memories of the sorcerers twisting Amanda's body with their magic, trying to force it to serve them. She had only been a girl and yet she had resisted the full might of Obsidian magic. He suspected Amanda was far stronger than even she knew.

CHAPTER
10

Revelations

S yenna stood in the shadow of the doorway that separated the sitting room from the back hallway of her Etceter home. Behind her labored the dozen or so cooks and serving staff the baroness had contracted for the evening. The sounds of them setting up for the impending meal made enough noise that Syenna couldn't hear what was going on in the sitting room, but she didn't need to. Almost directly across from her sat her sister. She was listening intently to Aren Bennis, who stood facing her. Syenna was fairly proficient at reading lips, it was a skill that had served her well as a scout, but Aren's back was to her. What she could see, however, were the tears streaming down her sister's face as she listened.

"How's it going?" Zhal said, making Syenna jump. She'd been so focused on the conversation taking place across the sitting room that she hadn't noticed the loremaster's approach. She mentally cursed her inattention. That kind of thing could get a girl killed in the field.

"She's crying," Syenna said, her lips tight. It felt like every muscle in her back was stretched taut, like so many harpsichord wires.

"All part of the plan," Zhal said, peering around Syenna to look for himself.

"You should have told her what to expect."

Zhal shook his head and stepped back into the cover of the hallway.

"No," he said. "We need her reactions to be genuine for this to work."

"I served the Obsidian army as a scout for five years," she said, not taking her eyes off Amanda. "In that time, I learned just about every way it's possible to kill someone." She turned to look at the loremaster's wizened face. "If he hurts her, you'll be the one I'll make suffer for it."

"Now, now," Zhal said, patting her on the arm in the manner one might use to quiet an unruly child. "Your sister is made of sterner stuff than that, and besides, from the look of things, everything is going according to plan."

Syenna looked back to where her sister sat by the fire. Aren wasn't standing over her anymore, but had sat on the hearth beside her and they were talking quietly.

"I don't see how this is going to convince Aren to lead our makeshift army," she said, crossing her arms under her breasts. "He's one of the most stubborn men I've ever met."

Zhal chuckled and she turned to him. He had that annoying patronizing look she'd always seen as a child from her teachers.

"Don't worry," he said. "Amanda is just there to remind him what the Obsidians do when they need soldiers."

Before Syenna could ask what the rest of Zhal's plan might be, a gong sounded, announcing that the guests should make their way to the dining room.

"I'd better go get Amanda," Syenna said, but Zhal put a restraining hand on her arm.

"I think the good captain has that well in hand." He nodded to where Aren was lifting Amanda out of her chair. She had her arms around his neck for support and he cradled her against his chest. Syenna felt a hot flash of indignation.

"Hurry," Zhal said, tugging at her arm. "I want to double check the seating arrangements."

Syenna had no idea what game the loremaster was playing now, so she just followed along and stood behind the chair he appointed to her. By the time Aren arrived, carrying Amanda, there were only two seats left, the one at the head of the table and the one to its immediate left. Syenna sat on the opposite side from the second chair and the Titan Sequana sat next to it.

"Put her here," Syenna said to Aren, pulling out the chair at the head of the table. This would put Amanda next to her, and Syenna liked that. After all, she hadn't had a chance to really talk with her sister since she'd return to the city.

Aren set her down and then sat in the remaining empty chair between Amanda and Sequana. As he sat, Zhal stood and greeted everyone in the name of the baroness, who sent her regrets on being unable to attend. He went around the table introducing everyone, but Syenna paid this no heed. Instead she watched Aren. She knew his face, his moods, and that look he made when his mind was calculating the best way to attack a problem. At the moment, however, he just looked tired, like after a forced march tired. Syenna knew he'd been getting plenty of rest.

When Zhal announced the Hero of Opalis, there was a round of applause and Aren raised his glass to accept it, but there was no stirring of interest in his eyes. From where Syenna sat, it looked like whatever game Zhal was playing, the loremaster was currently losing.

When Zhal finished the introductions, food was brought in and the meal began. Small talk broke out around the table for a few minutes and Syenna took the opportunity to finally converse with her sister. Before she could direct the conversation around to what she and Aren had talked about, however, the young diplomat who served Sir Arthur Falcone of Resolute spoke up.

"My Lady Sequana," he said, speaking up above the din. "I understand you have just returned from my homeland. Can you give us news of the army and their pursuit of the raiders?"

"The army suffered a defeat at the hands of the raiders," she said. "They are currently in disarray."

Syenna already knew this, of course, and so did Aren. She looked across the table at him but he seemed not to be listening.

"That's terrible," the young diplomat said. His words expressed concern but the tone of his voice was anxious. "These are no common raiders, they cannot be allowed to pillage the lowlands."

Syenna rolled her eyes, clearly the man didn't learn his part in this drama very well, he sounded like he was reading his lines off a card.

"I'm sure the council will send support to the army soon," Zhal said. "But I understand you have other news."

Sequana paused until silence descended around the table and all eyes turned to her. Aren set aside his fork and turned toward the Titan, but he seemed even more weary than before.

He knows that what's coming is meant for him.

"The ship *Seabrease,* out of South Paladis, made a stop at the mouth of the Fang River," Sequana said, her voice slow and deliberate. "Her captain was there to pick up spies who had been keeping an eye on the Obsidians in Midras."

Aren looked up for the first time, interest blossoming in his eyes.

"According to them, the occupying force there is rounding up the citizens and marching them east toward Grunvald."

"Why would they do that?" the diplomat asked, finally sounding genuinely interested.

"Because of the loss of General Karpasic and the Westreach Army," Aren said, his voice cold and hard.

"The Empire will want to rebuild their army as quickly as possible," Sequana said in her slow voice.

Syenna kept her eyes on Aren to gauge his reaction, but at that moment Amanda gasped and seized her arm with a death grip.

"Yes," the Titan confirmed, turning to Amanda. "We believe they intend to transform the civilians into soldiers."

Amanda made a noise that sounded like a squeak and the grip on Syenna's arm went slack. She slumped in her chair with a stricken look on her face. Syenna jumped to her feet but Aren was there before her, lifting Amanda gently out of her chair.

"Please excuse us," he said, standing up with the girl. "Amanda is feeling unwell."

"This way," Syenna said, guiding him down the hall to a narrow stair that led to the upper floors. Amanda's room was to the left of the stairway and Syenna opened the door as Aren carried her sister in and set her gently on the bed.

"Thank you," Amanda gasped, rousing briefly. She looked pale and drawn. "I just need a minute."

"Of course," Aren said, stepping back out into the hall. He didn't return to the dinner, but instead took up a guard position outside the door.

Syenna helped Amanda lay down and covered her with a blanket before retiring to the hall.

"How is she?" Aren asked.

"Whenever she thinks about others suffering what she did, it disturbs her," Syenna said. "She'll be all right once she's had time to rest."

"I'm glad to hear that." Zhal's voice came from the stairs as he climbed up to join them in the hall. "Everyone is worried."

"You're not," Aren said, not bothering to hide the disdain in his voice. "Everything that happened tonight was your doing."

Zhal raised an eyebrow at that but made no response.

"Do you deny it?" Aren pressed.

"Of course not," Zhal said. "If you weren't smart enough to see through this, you wouldn't be the man we need."

Aren stabbed his finger in the direction of Amanda's room.

"You put that girl in danger," he accused.

"She is a bit upset right now," Zhal admitted. "But her feelings are genuine, and everything Sequana said was true. The Obsidians are rounding up everyone they can to rebuild their lost army, and if we give them time, they'll succeed. The only chance she has—" He pointed at Amanda's door. "The only chance any of us have, is if the council's army is ready."

Aren clenched his fists so tightly Syenna saw the blood drain from his knuckles. She expected him to explode at the loremaster but instead, he relaxed. The tired look he'd worn since he arrived melted away and his eyes became fierce and intense.

"I knew you were up to something when you brought me here," he said to Zhal. "I just underestimated you. You've boxed me in rather neatly."

"If you mean I've simply arranged for you to see things as they really are, then yes."

"You've made it impossible for me to stay out of this," Aren continued.

"You bear an Avatar sword," Zhal pointed out. "It wasn't *me* that chose you."

"Fine," Aren said after a pause. "Tell your baroness that I'll take command of her patchwork army." He turned to leave but stopped and turned back to Zhal. "And tell Her Grace that I'll be taking the lieutenant here with me." He nodded in Syenna's direction, then headed down the stairs.

"Well," Zhal said once Aren's footsteps faded away. "I think that went rather well."

"You used my sister for this plan of yours," Syenna growled, crossing her arms. "Played with her emotions to leverage Aren. You'd better be right."

"You know I am," Zhal said.

"What makes you think that?"

Zhal turned to face her. The character of the jovial pedagogue was gone and a haggard, desperate visage took its place.

"Because if I'm wrong, we're all doomed, and you're far too competent a soldier to doubt that."

CHAPTER
11

The Confluence

vard dunked his tin cup into the running water of the Sanctus
River then raised it to his lips. The mountains where the river
originated were already covered with snow and the water was
so cold it gave the sorcerer a headache as he drank. He finished the
cup, then tucked it back into his pack. The weather in the lowlands
was still mild, even warm, and Evard was sweating under his travel
cloak. It had been a week since he'd given Maradn's creation the slip
and he'd been pushing himself hard ever since. Now, as he sat on the
banks of the fast-flowing Sanctus, his goal was in sight.

He stood, slinging his pack onto his back and shifting its weight
between his shoulders. In the distance, an angled spire of rock thrust
up over the vast stretch of rolling hills, a lonely sentinel against an
otherwise empty sky. A faint sound hung in the air, hovering on the
edge of perception. To Evard, it sounded like the wind that constantly
blew through the tunnels at Desolis.

Evard couldn't see the base of the rock spire, but he felt sure when
he reached it, he would find whatever Karpasic had been sent out here
to find. He set off, following the river east, his steps quickening despite his bone deep weariness from a week of hard travel. Whatever
that spire was, Evard sensed it represented something profound.

Destiny maybe?

As he walked, tramping a path through the waist-high grass, the
sound grew louder until it was a thunderous roar. It reminded Evard
of a waterfall, but he couldn't see any water pouring from the spire of
rock and nothing else in the area was high enough to make that kind
of sound.

After another hour of travel, the base of the spire came into sight. It was shrouded in mist and Evard could feel the humidity in the air rise noticeably. As he drew near, he could see where the Sanctus and Fortis Rivers crossed. The spire of rock rose out of the exact center and the rivers swirled around it with enough force that he could see whitecaps and waves breaking against the stone. That was clearly the source of the roaring sound and the persistent mist that hung in the air.

An hour later, Evard could see a slender stone bridge reaching out of the mist to touch the ground on his side of the river. It seemed to hang in the air as if supported by the spray of water being kicked up against the spire's side.

When he reached it, Evard knew he'd found what the circle was looking for. The bridge was not constructed of cut stone or wooden planks but appeared to be one solid piece of rock. The sides and bottom looked utterly smooth but the top had grooves cut in it to drain water and provide a rough enough surface to prevent passers from slipping off. The grooves were each perfectly even in their width and spacing.

Too perfect.

Only magic could have created such a structure.

Evard took a deep breath. Even the air seemed to tingle with magic.

The bridge had no railings, and it was narrow enough to make him nervous, but no force on Novia would stop him from stepping out onto it. Gooseflesh raced along his arms and down his back as his foot touched the dark stone. Magic power radiated out from the spire in ways Evard hadn't felt since he left Desolis.

Carefully putting one foot in front of the other, he crossed the bridge. At the far end, the spray being kicked up from the fast swirling water below formed a physical barrier. Evard had no doubt that if he'd tried to force his way through the water, it would have sent him flying from the bridge into the churning vortex. The barrier would keep any mundane invader at bay, but Evard was not mundane.

Reaching into his reservoir of magic power, he extended his finger until it touched the water. Instantly ice formed around the spot, spreading up and down, flowing around into an arch and then a tunnel, pushing back away from Evard until it flowed up against the side of the spire. As the water drained away from the suddenly protected space, an opening was revealed with stairs that went up until they disappeared into darkness.

Evard stood for a moment, just staring at the open passage as the water surged around and over his ice dam. Since it took magic just to get inside, it was likely no one had tread those stairs in years, maybe not since the Shard Fall.

It was exciting, even for a powerful and revered sorcerer of the Obsidian Cabal.

He raised his hand and called a globe of pale bluish light to his palm, then raised it high and walked across the last few feet of the bridge and into the spire. The effort hit him physically and he had to take a moment and catch his breath. The light globe was simple enough but he'd expended a great deal of his stored power on the ice dam. He'd need to rest and replenish his power soon.

The steps ran up for a short distance, then the spire opened up, revealing a hollow core. A walkway that appeared to be made of metal ran around the inside of the space and Evard could see stairways running up and down from it, spiraling around the walls of the open chamber.

He also noticed that despite the humidity in the air, the metal showed no sign of rust or corrosion.

The interior of the spire reminded Evard of the Cavern of Night in Desolis. In the cavern, the place of power was down at the base of the vertical shaft in the Chamber of Souls. Not believing the similarity was a coincidence, Evard circled the walkway until he came to the spiral stair going down, then followed it.

From inside the spire, the rushing sound of the water was dulled to a distant vibration and the ring of Evard's boots on the metal stairs echoed off the walls. He passed several openings, and two more landings, but pressed downward, seeking the bottom. By the time he reached it, he was well below the level of the rivers outside.

A grate of the same incorruptible metal covered the bottom and Evard could see water reflecting his light from beneath it. A single opening yawned to his left and Evard quickened his steps, feeling that his journey's end was near.

Passing through the opening, he found himself in a round room with a domed ceiling. Veins of purple crystal wound through the dome like the roots of a tree, spreading out from the exact center where a shaft of the same crystal hung down a few feet. A flow of water ran down over the crystal, falling in an unbroken stream. It landed in a large stone bowl, held up from the center of the floor by a short pillar. The floor was the same metal grate as the previous room and the water falling from the ceiling overflowed the bowl, splashing down to disappear through the floor. Around the walls relief carvings were cut into the stone with the same perfect smoothness as the grooves on the bridge. They depicted scenes of men and women warring with one another in great battles, but none of the images seemed familiar.

Evard took in the room at a glance. It wasn't impressive or even particularly large, but the very air seemed permeated with magic. Crossing to the stone bowl in the center of the chamber, he reached out, putting his hand into the icy flow of water. Despite the cold, the water almost burned his hand with the raw magical energy it contained.

He closed his eyes and drew in the power, replacing the energies he'd spent to make the ice archway. Normally it would have taken a quarter hour of meditation to recover that power, but here it came to him in an instant.

"Now I know why the circle wants this place," he said to the empty room. "It's a shard chamber."

It wasn't as big as Desolis, but the magic here was more concentrated, probably because there wasn't a city of sorcerers above drawing away its power. This spire, here at the confluence of the two rivers, was an untapped source. A sorcerer standing in this room was arguably the most powerful sorcerer in the world.

The possibilities made Evard lightheaded.

Or is it the magic?

He pulled his hand out of the intoxicating flow of water and the feeling of power faded a bit. Temptation or no, his impulse had been right. With control of this confluence, he could do anything, maybe even challenge the circle itself. He could deal with Maradn and make himself Obsidian Eye.

"Assuming you could get her here, to this room," he cautioned himself. An unlikely possibility at best.

A smart man would use this power to weaken Maradn's position, while strengthening his own at the same time. Evard fancied himself a very smart man.

He put his hand back into the falling water, letting the magic flow through his body again. It was incredible. The power was his to control, all he needed to do was find the right vehicle for his ambition.

"The sword," he said aloud.

The Avatar sword that represented such a threat to the Empire, the cabal of sorcerers, and the Central Circle. With this much power at his command, he should be able to destroy the sword utterly, Avatar blade or no. Such a feat would secure him his seat in the circle, it might even secure him the support he'd need to take the seventh throne itself.

Evard smiled at the thought. If he played his cards right, he might be able to get Maradn to publicly oppose his efforts to destroy the sword. That would make his victory even more substantial and weaken Maradn's position in the bargain.

That was his play.

"Now all I need to do is find Aren and that blasted sword," Evard said.

Ever since he'd determined to free his friend from the thrall of the Avatar weapon, Evard had given considerable thought about how to find them. So far he'd made over one hundred versions of Monk and none of them had managed to locate Aren. He needed a new plan, a new way to suss out the sword's hiding place.

What he needed—was a squirrel.

† † †

I t took Evard two days to find and catch a squirrel. Magic was an incredible tool, certainly, but it was a tool of patience, not well suited to catching nimble rodents. He'd tried making a copy of Monk and setting the creature after his prey, but while the homunculus could catch a squirrel, its wings were far too weak to carry one. Every time Monk caught one of the wily creatures, it managed to escape before Monk could return to its master.

Eventually Evard was forced to bait one of the foul vermin into a snare. Even then it had taken almost a full day and he had to reset the snare a dozen times. It was maddening that such a simple task had taken so much time, but trapping was a skill he'd never really learned.

Evard carried his wiggling prize in a sack as he strode into the crystal chamber in the confluence. Ever since he'd seen Maradn's pseudodragon, he'd wanted one of his own. He'd thought long and hard about that creation during his journey here, trying to work out what she had done and how she had done it.

Monk was a creature made entirely of magic. The substance of his body was etherium, magical energy made physical. Using magic to construct Monk allowed Evard to make copies of him easily, but it had some very serious limitations. The homunculus' mind was simple, incapable of performing complex tasks or understanding detailed instructions, to say nothing of its obvious physical weaknesses. In contrast, Maradn had used a bat and a lizard to build her servants, and that gained her the creatures' instincts and the benefit of their brains, which made them much more capable than something made of magic.

The real limitation of Maradn's method was that only small amounts of etherium could be added to a living creature during transformation. That meant that if Evard wanted to make a large creature, he would have to catch more squirrels.

After catching the one, Evard had decided that he didn't need a large creature for the task he had in mind.

Reaching into his bag, Evard pulled out the small brown creature by its bushy tail, holding it up as it struggled to escape. He drew in his magic and summoned Monk, assembling the creature as he had done many times before. The homunculus chirped and fluttered its weak wings, landing on Evard's shoulder and clinging with its needle-like claws.

Evard cupped his left hand under the falling water from the crystal overhead, feeling the power wash over his body, spreading out from his palm. Focusing his mind, he poured power into the body of the squirrel, pulling it into a shape more closely resembling Monk. The animal's mind was simple, easily cleansed and prepared for the more detailed tasks Evard would give it.

Once the squirrel was changed to the form Evard wanted, he joined it to Monk, combining the two beings. Monk's form got the strength, dexterity, and more serviceable mind of the squirrel, along with its coat of short, brown fur. The new Monk flapped its now sturdier wings and swooped around the room before landing back on Evard's shoulder.

Once the creature was finished, Evard bent his magic on the creature's mind. It was easier than he thought to change it, to let Monk link with another mind the way Maradn's creation had.

His work finished, Evard dropped down to one knee, panting. Despite having access to a direct source of magic, the effort had exhausted him, both physically and mentally.

"Monk," he called as he sat down, heavily, on the metal floor.

The creature landed in front of him, looking up with its dark, now intelligent eyes.

"I have work for you," Evard went on. He looked the creature in the eyes and linked his mind to Monk's, sending an image of Aren and the Avatar sword. "Find this man," he said. "He'll probably be in the city of Etceter to the south." Evard pushed out an image of where the former pirate town was located in relation to the confluence. "When you find him, you must link to me and let me know."

The improved Monk bobbed its head and chirped, then spread its wings and leapt into the air. It circled the chamber twice, then flew out into the main shaft and disappeared.

Evard lay down on the floor, tired but well pleased with himself. Once Monk found Aren, he'd go retrieve his friend and the troublesome sword. With the power of the confluence, he would destroy the sword, restore his friend to himself, and take his rightful place on his mother's throne.

Unless Aren makes that difficult.

The thought irritated Evard. He wanted to revel in his triumph in remaking Monk; unfortunately, the more cautious side of his mind had a point. The avatar sword was a powerful relic. It wasn't likely to give up its host without a fight. He was going to have to prepare for that contingency.

Evard sighed wearily.

He would need an army if he had to extract Aren by force. Even if he could somehow trick Aren into using a transport stone, he might need the threat of an army. With Karpasic captured and his soldiers gone, the Empire was fresh out of available armies. Still, there was a small force at Hilt that he could command, maybe five hundred men. Not enough for his purposes, but maybe enough to start. Changing Monk had given him an idea.

Evard knew the craft of the shapers, he'd done the work himself many times. If he could get slaves brought here to the confluence, he could simply make his own army. Surely a force of five hundred men would be enough to capture any nearby towns or villages. That would give him the raw material he needed to make Fomorian soldiers. It would take time to build up sufficient forces, but he needed to give Monk time to find Aren anyway.

Yes, that would do nicely.

As soon as he'd rested a bit, Evard would create one of his original homunculi and send the creature to the garrison commander at Hilt. The homunculus would relay his order for the expeditionary force to join Evard here at the confluence. The homunculus's mind was enough for that simple task.

A thought suddenly occurred to Evard and he sat up.

When Monk found Aren, how would the creature link back to Evard? He needed to look the creature in the eyes to establish the mental link.

With a groan, Evard flopped back down on the floor.

He was going to need another squirrel.

CHAPTER 12

The General

Aren stood shuffling from foot to foot trying to get comfortable in his armor. The last time he'd had it on was when he led the refugees out of Opalis, months ago. He'd spent a good portion of the last decade practically living in armor and yet it felt strange on him now.

"I wish I could just pack this," he muttered.

"It would take three weeks to get there," Syenna said, standing beside him, clad in her own scout armor of leathers and a chain shirt. "Sequana can only take the three of us, so whatever we want, we have to carry."

Aren wanted to argue with her, mostly because he was still irritated at the entire situation. From the moment he'd picked up the Avatar blade, his world had been turned upside down. He had no one to blame but himself, of course. Syenna had practically begged him not to touch the Avatar sword, after all. Still, there wasn't any satisfaction in blaming himself, so he grumbled under his breath.

"Stop grousing," Syenna said. "General," she added, giving him a mocking smile.

He wanted to tell her off, but at that moment the door opened and Sequana entered with Zhal.

"I'm sorry to have kept you waiting," Sequana said in her mild, somewhat lilting voice. "The loremaster wanted a word."

"I'm sure," Aren grumbled, giving Zhal a sour look that the loremaster studiously ignored.

"Are you ready?" Sequana continued.

Aren and Syenna each bent down to pick up their gear.

"Do you have everything you need?" Sequana asked, stepping between them. "I've made too many trips in recent days and I won't be able to make another trip out to the Army of Might."

Aren nodded. He may have grown uncomfortable in his armor, but he knew how to pack for duty.

The Titan reached out and took his right hand in her left, then took Syenna's hand with her right.

"Join hands," she instructed.

Aren hesitated, then reached out for the shieldmaiden's free hand. For some reason it felt strange, standing there holding hands. He had been transported by the Titans many times before, but always in their home. In Opalis they could just summon him from wherever he was and then send him wherever they wanted. Sequana had made many trips like this since they left Opalis, conveying herself and occasionally others across great distances, usually in the name of expediency.

Aren hadn't been paying attention at Zhal's dinner party, but now that he held her hand, she looked bone tired. Her eyes were bloodshot and there were streaks of gray in her hair that he hadn't remembered. Whatever price this kind of travel exacted, it seemed to be weighing heavily on the Titan.

"Good luck, General," Zhal said.

Aren opened his mouth to respond, but the world around him seemed to turn sideways and suddenly he wasn't there anymore. His previous experiences with this kind of transportation were instant, but it felt as if he was spinning, weightless, for a long time. He could feel Sequana's hand firmly holding his hand and Syenna clinging desperately to the other.

After maybe a minute the world righted itself, snapping quickly into focus around him. He stood on a small hillock overlooking a grassy valley filled with tents, campfires, and soldiers. A sudden pain went through his head until he felt his ears pop. He knew the Army of Might was encamped somewhere in the Middle Downs, just south of Monk's Hood Pass, a significantly higher elevation than the sea-level city of Etceter.

Syenna let go of his hand and opened her mouth wide, working her jaw in an effort to get her ears to adjust to the pressure change. Sequana did not release his hand, but instead leaned, heavily on him.

"I'm sorry," she said, reaching out to steady herself by gripping Aren's shoulder with her free hand. "I'm going to need to rest before I return to Etceter."

"Who's in charge here?" Aren shouted toward the camp in his best command voice. Soldiers the world over were trained to respond to that tone.

"I guess you could say that I am," a familiar voice came from behind Aren.

He turned to find Captain Trevan of the Opalis Legion coming up the hill with a small cadre of warriors.

"Trevan," Aren said with a smile. He had to admit, it was nice to see a friendly face. "Lady Sequana needs to rest."

"I have a place already prepared . . . Sir Llewellyn." This last was addressed to a solidly built knight on Trevan's left. "Conduct our guest to her tent and ensure her needs are met and she is not disturbed."

The young knight saluted, clanging his mailed fist on his breastplate, then moved to support the Titan.

"This way, my lady."

Aren waited until the young knight had helped the Titan off toward a cluster of nearby tents before turning back to Captain Trevan.

"I read your report," he said, surveying the field. "It doesn't look like Commander Hendricks took your advice."

"Hendricks is a bit . . . old fashioned," Trevan said.

Aren had expected that. Putting Aren in charge of the combined force was a desperation move, a last resort. It was bound to face resistance. Fortunately, Aren had come prepared.

"Syenna, conduct a survey of the perimeter and bring me a report." He turned to Trevan. "Where's my tent?"

"I imagine you'll be moving into Hendricks' tent," he said. "It's that big one over there." Trevan pointed to a cluster of tents up against a stand of trees where a particularly large tent could be seen standing above the others.

Aren shook his head.

"I need somewhere to operate before I meet with Hendricks."

"In that case, you can use my tent," Trevan said, indicating a stand of three tents near the horse paddock. "It's down there."

Aren turned back to Syenna, and she nodded. She removed her cloak and traveling pack, pushing them into the hands of one of Trevan's knights.

"Hang on to this for me," she said, then looked to Aren. "I'll be back within the hour."

† † †

The tent belonging to Mikas Trevan, Captain of the Opalis Legion, wasn't large or luxurious. It had a fur-covered cot and a trunk to one side with a small writing table and chair opposite and an armor stand by the entrance flap. To Aren, it was exactly the kind of tent a commander needed without any of the ostentatious display that so many seemed to require. He guessed this tent and five like it would fit inside the one General Karpasic had used.

"I'll move my gear out," Trevan said as Aren unslung his duffel and set it down.

Aren shook his head.

"Don't bother," he said. "I only need it for a few hours, then it will be yours again."

He opened his bag and pulled out a round wooden case with caps at the ends, then set the bag aside. Removing one of the caps, he slid a stack of rolled documents into his hand.

"Is there something I can help with?" Trevan said as Aren moved to the writing table.

"Yes," Aren said, unrolling the papers and using a pair of flat rocks on the desk to hold them open. He leafed through them until he found the one he wanted. "I want you to be my second," he continued, extracting a page of neat writing that was stamped with both the seal of the Titans and the seal of Etceter. He handed the paper to Trevan for his perusal. "This has all the particulars. You've been released from your obligations to the Opalis Legion, as that army is now mostly defunct, and appointed to the rank of general in the Unified Army of the Alliance, now called the Army of Might."

"The Opalis Legion is not defunct," Trevan said indignantly. "It's being reformed in Xenos."

"Yes, Grannus explained that they were taking all that knowledge we saved to Xenos in an effort to secure it," Aren said. "He also told me that they won't be able to spare any of those forces at the moment, so you and your men are Opalis's contribution to the Army of Might."

"What happens once, Gods willing, this war is over?"

Aren waved at the paper.

"Your position will be held for you while you serve with the Army of Might, it's in here somewhere."

Trevan read through the document, holding it at arm's length as he did so.

"So if I'm a general, what does that make you?" he asked. "I thought you were in charge."

"I've been made commanding general," Aren said.

"That's going to get confusing. Why not just make me a colonel?"

Aren rifled through his stack of papers and pulled out a half dozen more commissions, each stamped with the seal of Etceter and one of the other Alliance members.

"I'm making all the current commanders from each nation my colonels," he explained. "But I'm going to need someone to keep them in line."

"Someone who outranks them to do your dirty work?" Trevan asked. His voice wasn't disapproving, but it held no enthusiasm.

"That's what I like about you, General Trevan, you see things clearly."

Trevan walked over so he stood in front of the writing desk and held up the commission paper.

"Before I accept this, I want to know what you plan to do," he said.

Aren smiled at that. Trevan wouldn't have been the right man for this job if he'd blindly accepted it. Aren had guessed that, but it was nice to have his instincts confirmed.

"I plan to follow the advice in your report," Aren said. "The only way to get this army functioning is to break up the factions and make them work together. I want the colonels commanding units with few, if any, of their own men, and I want the junior officers to be integrated as well."

Trevan chuckled mirthlessly.

"They won't like that," he said. "In fact I'll go so far to say that they'll fight you on it."

"That's why I need you for my second," Aren said, standing to face Trevan. "I need someone who understands what needs to be done and believes in it. You're right about how the others will see this, I won't be able to trust any of them to stand with me."

"What if the others unite against you?"

"That's what these are for," Aren said, patting the remaining documents under the rocks. "Any officer not accepting their new commission in the Army of Might is ordered to return to their homeland for reassignment."

"What will you do if they all go and take their men with them?"

"These orders are very specific. Only they are relieved, their troops stay. If I have to, I'll promote whoever I need to in order to fill the ranks."

Trevan put his hands behind his back and began to pace in little circles in the space between the cot and the writing table. Aren sat back and let him think.

"We're going to need more men for this to work," he said finally. "The raiders have half again as many men as we do."

"You're right, of course," Aren said. "But we're going to have to prove ourselves before the council will give us any more reinforcements. I did manage to secure us a company of knights and a platoon of archers."

Trevan snorted at that.

"We need a battalion at least," he said. He wasn't wrong, but Aren didn't see the need to comment. "Who did you con out of those troops?"

"You," Aren said with a grin. "They're from the Opalis Legion, all Boreus could spare. Captain Artemis is leading them here from the Ash Coast."

Trevan raised an eyebrow at that, then shook his head.

"I suppose I can put Sir Llewellyn in charge of the knights," he said. "And it will be good to see Artemis again." He sighed and shook his head. "All right," he said, sticking out his hand for Aren to clasp. "I'm your man. How do we start?"

✝ ✝ ✝

Prefect Claudius Aquila of the Fourth Cohort of the Estgard Third Legion was a relatively young man to hold such a position. He'd obtained his rank thanks to a combination of hard work, talent, political connections, and a fair amount of luck. He had been part of the Dysborg campaign and had comported himself and his men with distinction, causing him to be moved from the Eighth Cohort all the way up to the Fourth. At this rate, he would make legate before he turned forty and be in command of his own legion.

Claudius was not a man given to false pride or foolish ambition. He would be promoted in good time and would still be well ahead of his fellow prefects. It was eminently satisfactory . . . or rather it had been. For some reason he couldn't fathom, he and his cohort had been sent away from Norgard to chase bandits in Resolute.

Bandits that fool Legate Argo should have never let escape, he reminded himself. But Argo had let them get away and now Claudius's career was slipping through his fingers, assigned a hopeless task. It was clear that the Aerie commander of this fool's errand didn't understand the prey he was supposedly hunting and had managed to lose most of their archers already. Claudius had considered seizing control right then, but doubted anyone else would support his bid to depose their hapless leader. Also, his own orders strictly forbade him from making any such bid for control, and while he didn't believe those orders had come from the emperor himself, they certainly conveyed his authority. All Claudius could hope for now was to survive this debacle with his forces intact until he could arrange to be recalled home.

The entire situation irritated him, and so when he received a summons from a General Bennis, someone he didn't know but whose authority he didn't dare question, he put on his armor and made his way to a small tent near the edge of the camp. He allowed himself a faint hope that the fools in Etceter had sent someone competent to take over the army, but when he heard what that new commander proposed to do, he was outraged.

"You mean to destroy my forces," he said, trembling from the effort to keep from shouting.

"Not at all Prefect Aquila," the new general said, sitting behind a simple desk. "I mean to utilize them effectively, as is my responsibility."

"I won't allow it," Claudius declared.

The man behind the desk wore black armor of a mismatched design. Parts of it were clearly Obsidian in origin but where he'd gotten the other pieces was anybody's guess. He was a big man with big shoulders and hands, though Claudius couldn't tell his height while the man was seated. He'd heard stories of Aren Bennis, the man who'd found a magic sword and single-handedly rescued the populace of Opalis from an Obsidian siege. He'd been an Obsidian himself. Claudius had no reason to trust a former Obsidian, and that was before he'd proposed breaking up his cohort to form new, mixed units.

General Bennis didn't react to Claudius's declaration immediately, he just sat, looking at the man. Finally he picked up a rolled piece of parchment from the table and unrolled it.

"You recognize the seal?" Bennis asked.

Claudius did. At the bottom of the document was a wax stamp marked with the emperor's personal seal. Whatever Claudius thought of the orders that sent him here, he was absolutely sure these orders came from Tribune Marcus Tercius himself.

"These orders relieve you of your command, Prefect Aquila," Bennis went on. "Your men are released into my charge and you are directed to return home to Estgard for reassignment."

A crushing weight seemed to press down on Claudius's chest, making it difficult to breathe. No matter how the orders on the general's desk worded it, his being relieved of command would mean disgrace. The promised reassignment would be a demotion, even if he remained a prefect.

"Yes sir," he said, determined to salvage as much of his dignity as he could. For his part, the general simply sat with his hands folded on the table, looking at him. Claudius had the disturbing impression that the man could see right through him, and could tell what toll the loss of his career was taking. "If that's all, sir, I'll pack my things."

"Not yet, Prefect," the second man in the room said. Claudius had seen him around the camp, he was the former commander of the Opalis Legion. He didn't know what function the man served for this new general, but he'd stood quietly by the tent flap during Claudius's interview.

"I said that these orders relieved you of command," the general said, pulling Claudius's attention back to the table. Bennis reached into a satchel at his feet and pulled out another rolled parchment, spreading it out beside the first. "But these orders are quite different."

"What do they say?" Claudius asked, then hastily added, "Sir."

Bennis stood for the first time, regarding Claudius with his mild but penetrating gaze.

"Do you know what will happen if this army isn't successful in capturing or killing the raiders?"

The question took Claudius by surprise. In truth, he figured that since the raiders were in Resolute, they were Resolute's problem and he said so.

"You're right, of course," Bennis said, starting to pace around the table, the tent pole, and Claudius. "But I need you to think bigger, Prefect. Your forces scored a great victory against the Westreach Army of the Obsidian Empire, but do you think the empire will take that lying down?"

Claudius hadn't given it a great deal of thought, but he supposed not.

"No," Bennis answered for him. "At this very moment, they're stripping their lands of every person old enough to carry a sword they can get. The rest they're transforming into their monsters. Soon they'll have an even bigger army to send against the lands west of the Blackblade Range. What will happen then? Do you think the Council of Might will be able to stand against them then if we can't kill a few hundred raiders now?"

"You think it doesn't matter," the second man said. "I was there at

Opalis when the armies of Norgard stood by and watched, hoping to swoop in and take the city once her defenders and the Obsidians had exhausted themselves."

Claudius didn't answer that. He wasn't ashamed of being part of a smart military.

"I'll bet you believe that when the Obsidians come you'll just do the same thing," General Bennis said, still pacing. "That your emperor will pull you back to your island home and wait for the council and the Obsidians to destroy each other. Then, when they're done, you'll emerge, strong and rested, and roll over both, taking the western lands for yourselves."

It wasn't a bad plan at all, Claudius thought, and definitely more prudent than spending Norgard blood to keep other nations free from Obsidian control.

"I wouldn't presume to speak for the emperor," he said, somewhat stiffly.

"You don't have to," Bennis said, so close behind Claudius he could feel the man's breath. "I spoke to him before I came here. Like you, he believed that your island would keep you safe if the worst happened. But tell me, Prefect, what will happen to your island when the Obsidians capture Etceter?"

"Just because they capture their ships, doesn't mean they'll be able to sail them," Claudius said. It was true the former pirates of Etceter had some of the fastest, most maneuverable ships in the world. That fact kept anyone from seriously considering attacking the merchant city from the sea; troop ships would be sunk long before they could make landfall.

"The Obsidians won't need to sail them," Bennis said, coming around the table again to stand before him. "The captains of Etceter will do it for them."

Claudius resisted the urge to break out laughing.

"They're descended from pirates, they'd never serve the black ones."

"Yes they will," the other man said. "The Obsidians will round up all those captains and transform their children and their loved ones into monsters right before their eyes until one of them cracks. They'll serve the Obsidians as long as their families are in danger."

"When that happens," General Bennis said, giving Claudius a hard look. "No part of your island will be safe. The army of the Obsidian Empire will be able to land anywhere they wish, under the cover of darkness, and march on Valhold before you can move troops to stop them."

That weight on Claudius's chest was back. This new general was right. The Obsidians lived in a blasted desert. They were terrible sailors, but if they took Etceter, it would give them sea access to Aerie, Ardoris, and Norgard. One by one, they'd sweep them up, using their terrible magic to reinforce their armies with monsters. In a moment of terrible clarity, Claudius saw the answer to General Bennis's question.

"If this army isn't successful in stopping these raiders," Prefect Claudius Aquila said, coming to attention. "Then the nations of the council will never give it the forces it needs to be successful. And if that happens, we are all dead men."

Bennis's intense look didn't fade, but he nodded.

"If it's all the same to you, General," Claudius said. "I'd like to know what the other orders say."

General Bennis picked up the orders and handed them over.

"These give me permission from your emperor to conscript you and your men into the United Army of the West, now called the Army of Might. You will be under my command and will receive the rank of colonel, equal to the rank of legate in the Norgard Legion."

Claudius managed to keep his hands from shaking as he read the orders, written in the Emperor's own hand.

"Understand, Prefect Aquila, if you accept this commission, you will obey my orders without question and hesitation."

Claudius looked up into the general's eyes. Bennis's mild look was gone, replaced by a desperate, determined intensity as if weighing Claudius in the balance.

"In that case, General, I accept," he said, slamming his fist against his breastplate in the Norgard salute.

Bennis exchanged a brief look with the other man, who nodded subtly.

"Very well, Colonel Aquila," the general said. "The lives of everyone we know and love will depend on how well you do your job, so you need to understand. If you fail, I will kill you myself."

It was clearly meant as a threat, but Claudius was a soldier of Norgard, he would expect nothing less.

"If I fail, General, you will not have that pleasure," he said, only slightly indignantly. "Because my body will be left on the field."

Bennis held his gaze for a long moment, then nodded.

"This is General Mikas Trevan," he said, introducing the other man. "You will report to him and obey any orders he gives you."

Claudius turned and gave General Trevan a formal salute.

"Now take those orders and read them to your men," Bennis went on. "Do it personally, I don't want any misunderstandings, and be sure to—"

At that moment, the tent flap burst inward and a tall, muscular woman entered. She had broad shoulders and hips, with sun-bleached blond hair that was tightly braided into a thick cord. She wore simple clothes, tunic and breeches, but Claudius could see a chain shirt hanging below the hem of her mud-spattered tunic. Now that Claudius noticed, her entire appearance was a bit disheveled, her hands were dirty and her trousers and boots were covered in dried mud. Not at all the way a subordinate should appear before their commander.

"I thought you said you'd be back within the hour," General Bennis said. His brooding intensity was gone and he even smiled in response to the woman's sudden appearance.

The woman didn't smile in return. Instead she overturned a pouch she carried onto the writing desk. A half dozen bloody ears thudded onto the table. Most of them were covered with fur and the ones that weren't were decidedly pointed.

"I was a little busy," she said.

Chapter 13

Command Performance

Aren stared at the bloody ears on his table for a moment while his mind raced down multiple lines of possibilities. He spared a glance for Syenna. She was dirty and there was blood on the sleeve of her tunic that didn't appear to be hers.

"Report," he said.

"There weren't any scouts on our perimeter," she said, disgust registering plainly on her face. "So I found a couple of rangers from the Resolute contingent and we did a sweep."

"I see you found someone."

She nodded.

"An elf scout and five satyrs were watching the camp from the woods to the south. They had a cold camp. Looks like they'd been there for a while."

"It's good that you found them," Trevan said.

Syenna nodded, but she wasn't smiling.

"What else?" he asked.

"When we found the camp all their gear was packed up," she said.

"They're spies," Trevan said with a shrug. "Aren't they always ready to move?"

"If you've been somewhere for more than a day or two, you leave your bedroll out," Syenna said.

"So why is it important that they packed theirs?" Claudius Aquila asked.

"It means they're done watching," Aren said, turning to the Norgard officer. "Colonel Aquila, how quickly can your men be ready for action."

"You don't think the raiders intend to attack the camp," Trevan said. "We've got woods to the south, and mountains to the west and north. The only way to bring an army in is to the east, and that's grassland for miles. We'd see them coming."

Aren's new general had a point. If the raiders tried attacking through the Monk's Hood Pass, their forces would get bottled up on the narrow road. If they tried attacking through the woods, the trees would slow them down, making it impossible to charge. In either case they wouldn't be able to utilize their superior numbers, and no commander worth his salt would choose a battle where he couldn't press his advantage. Not unless he was desperate.

"Do you have someone watching the eastern approach?" he asked Syenna.

"Yes," she said. "If they see anything, they'll send a runner here."

"Maybe the spies were getting ready to report back," Aquila suggested.

"That *would* explain everything," Trevan agreed.

He was correct, but something about the whole situation still bothered Aren. The Army of Might had been camped in this spot for a week, and if Syenna was right, and she usually was, the spies had been here most of that time. The army wasn't preparing to leave, so why were the spies? Had they decided the Army of Might was too ineffective to be worth their time? Maybe the raiders were moving on to better hunting grounds?

Aren turned to General Trevan.

"Have the raiders attacked any towns recently?" he asked.

"A place called Miskhallen," Trevan said. "But they didn't get much. The town elders burned a silo full of grain rather than let them have it."

Aren nodded as the disparate pieces of this puzzle began to fit together in his mind.

"How long did you say it would take your men to get ready," he said, turning back to Aquila.

"I didn't," Aquila said. "But they can be ready in fifteen minutes," he went on without hesitation. "Ten if they leave off their bracers and greaves."

"Do it, but be quiet about it. No alarms, no running, no yelling," Aren said. "Once you're ready, move your force to the south, facing the woods. Have them form up behind the last group of tents. Keep a lookout and as soon as anyone sees a raider, move your men out and form a shield wall just beyond the camp."

"I don't think—" Trevan began but Aren waved him silent.

"Go," he told Aquila.

"Yes, sir," the colonel said with a quick salute, then he turned and pushed through the tent flap.

"I'm sorry, General," Trevan said once Aquila was gone. "I shouldn't have disagreed with you in front of Aquila, but you and I both know the raiders aren't going to attack through the woods. They wouldn't be able to attack in force if they did that."

Aren ignored him, looking instead to Syenna.

"How long until dark?"

The shieldmaiden pushed the tent flap open and stuck her head out for a moment.

"The sun's already behind the mountains," she said. "I guess it'll be twilight in about an hour or so, with full dark in two."

"They'll hit us at twilight," Aren said. "They'll need some light to see by."

"Isn't Trevan right?" Syenna asked as Aren hurriedly dug through a stack of rolled up documents in his bag. "Even if the raiders took us completely by surprise, the woods will slow down their forces and spread them out. We'd have time to form up and counterattack. They're professional soldiers, they know that, why would they risk it?"

"Because as far as this action is concerned, they're not soldiers. They're raiders," Aren said. "What do raiders want?"

"Money?" Syenna said.

"Usually," Aren agreed, finally locating the paper he sought. "But these raiders are alone, far from home. What do they want?"

"Food," Trevan interjected. "And we just got a supply caravan this morning."

"The raiders will attack with a small force from the trees," Aren said, leading the way out of the tent.

"And when we rush to respond," Trevan said, falling into step beside him. "They'll steal our supply wagons. It's not an attack, it's a diversion."

"They must have a small force hiding among the hills," Syenna said, looking south to the open plains. "They'd only need fifty men or so to steal wagons."

"Take your scouts and watch," Aren said. "I'm going to send the Ardorins to protect the wagons, make sure they know when the raiders are coming."

Syenna grinned and nodded, then turned to go.

"And stay out of the fight," Aren called after her. "I'm going to need you and those scouts later."

Syenna waved but didn't answer. Aren wasn't sure she would obey that order, but he'd done all he could to keep her out of trouble. Now he needed to get the supply wagons out of trouble.

"Llewelyn!" he bellowed at the little cluster of tents around Trevan's.

"Here," a call came back from a nearby campfire. A moment later the big knight appeared at a run. He was dressed for camp in his breeches and a blue surcoat with the insignia of Opalis on it. Aren would have preferred he be in full armor, but at least he had his sword.

"Sir," the knight said, raising his open palm in salute.

"Round up your fellow knights," Aren said. "I want you to go to the teamster's camp and locate the supply wagons. Tell them you've got orders from the commander. I want you to get those wagons moving, take them up the canyon, away from the camp. Take whoever you need, push them if you have to, I don't care, just get them up there. Most importantly, do it quietly."

"Uh," Sir Llewelyn said, clearly not sure he'd heard that right.

"Now, Knight," Aren said, his voice low but forceful. "And if anyone gives you any trouble you have my permission to force the issue. Get it done."

"Yes, sir," he said, then dashed back toward the campfire to muster his fellow knights.

Aren turned, taking a moment to orient himself before remembering he hadn't set up this camp.

"Where's the Ardorin contingent?" he asked, noting for the first time that most of the tents in camp were monotonously uniform.

"That way," Trevan said, pointing up by the mouth of the canyon. "Shouldn't you go to Colonel Hendricks now?"

Aren set off in the direction Trevan indicated.

"Hendricks will take too long," Aren said. "He's from Aerie, he'll want everything in triplicate." He held up a roll of vellum that had been tied with a purple ribbon and sealed with wax. "These orders are for the leader of the Ardorin contingent, a man named Koshiban."

"Koshiba," Trevan corrected. "Samurai Tanobu Koshiba."

Aren was sure he would never remember that. Ardorin names sounded strange in his ears.

"Anyway, these orders put me in command and they're signed by their shogun himself. Once Koshina—"

"Koshiba."

Aren clenched his teeth.

"Once the samurai reads these, he'll obey without question."

"You have to love Ardorin military discipline," Trevan agreed.

† † †

Samurai Tanobu Koshiba was younger than Aren expected. He looked to be in his early twenties, with coal black hair and dark eyes that reminded Aren of Syenna's. His tent was modest in size, but hung with all manner of colorful banners and decorations inside. The man himself was similarly adorned, wearing a red-and-gold robe over what looked like a quilted gambeson. A short version of the long, curved swords favored by his people was thrust through a blue sash tied about the man's waist and he wore simple sandals on his feet.

A man in full Ardorin armor attended him, standing respectfully to one side as the samurai sat cross-legged on an enormous embroidered cushion. The soldier's armor, like the tent and the samurai, was elaborate. The breastplate was made of laminated and studded wooden bands that overlapped each other and included a back plate. Reinforced spaulders covered the shoulders and upper arms. Bracers of leather, reinforced with wooden strips, protected the forearms and hands. A kilt of similarly laminated plates hung down to the man's knees with fitted leather greaves on the lower legs. An elaborate helmet with winged arms on either side of the face completed the protection. The entire armor had been dyed a deep red, like the color of drying blood, and Aren wasn't sure if its intimidating look made up for its being mostly made of wood and cloth.

The young soldier who had conducted them into the samurai's tent stopped and bowed at the waist to Koshiba. He wore less elaborate armor than the samurai's guard, just the breastplate and kilt.

"My Lord Koshiba," he said, formally. "Captain Trevan of the Opalis Legion and Aren Bennis, ambassador from the Council of Might, beg an audience."

Koshiba looked up from the book he was reading. The move was slow, deliberate, and Aren sensed a tone of theatrical formality to the gesture. He laid the book aside and closed it with a flick of his fingers, then looked up at the soldier.

"Present them," he said.

The soldier turned and bowed to Aren and Trevan, then withdrew.

As soon as the flap of the tent was closed, Koshiba smiled and stood, extending his hand to Trevan.

"Good to see you again, Captain," he said. His manner was easy, even friendly as he clasped Trevan's hand. "Who's your friend?"

"This is Aren Bennis," Trevan said, even though the soldier had already introduced him. "The hero of Opalis."

Koshiba looked at Aren with curious, inquisitive eyes.

"The Obsidian?" He stuck out his hand for Aren to shake. "I must confess, I've never met an Obsidian officer before. Come in, sit." He gestured to the cushions spread around the interior of the tent.

Aren was a bit taken aback by the young man's demeanor. What he'd heard about Ardorins was that they were stiff and formal, with elaborate social rules. His meeting with Shogun Tsuneo had only re-inforced that, yet this young man seemed completely at ease. Aren suspected that was the reason he'd been given this command in the first place. It spoke well of the Shogun that he understood what this combined army would need from a commander.

"No time for that, I'm afraid," Aren said, handing Koshiba the sealed scroll.

The young man took it with a questioning look that turned to as-tonishment when he saw the signet stamped in the wax. Being careful not to destroy the seal, Koshiba peeled it away then unrolled the doc-ument to read it. Aren knew what it said, he'd been there when the shogun had written it. A moment later, Samurai Koshiba dropped to one knee. A surprised second after that, the guard in the blood armor followed suit.

"Forgive me for not receiving you properly just now, my Lord Gen-eral," he said. "Lord Tsuneo wishes me to convey his compliments to you and to place myself and my warriors at your disposal. How may I serve you?"

"You can stop that," Aren said, offering the young man a hand up. "I don't mean to disrespect your traditions but time is short. This camp will be attacked in less than an hour and I need you and your warriors to protect the supply wagons."

A cloud seemed to pass in front of Koshiba's face but he recovered quickly. Aren guessed that protecting wagons was not the glorious first assignment the samurai had been hoping for. He quickly out-lined what he suspected the raiders had in mind.

"The Norgard legionnaires will repel the diversionary attack," he concluded. "But their real target are the supplies. I've got men moving the wagons up toward the north end of camp, but I need your warriors to keep the raiders off them while they work."

By this time Koshiba was smiling and nodded.

"I understand," he said, then called the soldier outside his tent. "Pass the word for the samurai to assemble their warriors," he said. "We move in ten minutes."

The soldier bowed and left but two more came in once he'd gone. They moved to the back of the tent and uncovered an armor stand with an even more elaborate suit of Ardorin armor than the guard wore on it. Like the guard's armor, it was blood red, but with accents of painted gold and a green sash. Koshiba set aside his short sword and discarded his robe. The two soldiers dressed the samurai in his armor, which went on much quicker than Aren would have guessed. Finally the red-clad guard handed the samurai a long, curved sword in a black sheath which he slipped into a sash as his waist.

Aren felt a little underdressed in his mostly mismatched black armor as they exited Koshiba's tent. Outside, soldiers were already assembling. They wore simpler versions of the samurai armor and all carried swords like Koshiba's. They knelt when their commander emerged from his tent, waiting for his pleasure. For his part, Koshiba just stood, not moving, obviously waiting for the rest of his men to assemble. Each group of soldiers was led by a samurai in the red armor, and when all the Samurai were assembled, Koshiba held up the letter from Shogun Tsuneo.

"I have received a communication from Lord Tsuneo," he announced. "We are now in service to the Army of Might, led by Lord General Aren Bennis." Koshiba indicated Aren. "You will obey his commands as if they were from my own mouth. It is the will of Lord Tsuneo. All hail Lord General Bennis."

"Hail, Lord General Bennis," the assembled soldiers said in unison, dropping their heads as they rested on one knee. Clearly they'd done this before, but it was a new experience for Aren. He got a chill.

Koshiba turned to Aren and bowed. It was clear he expected Aren to speak to the soldiers and give them their orders. Cursing all this formality, he addressed the assembled warriors.

"Raiders will attack the supply wagons soon," he said. "You will prevent that."

It wasn't much of a speech, but he wasn't prepared and they were running out of time. He turned back to Koshiba.

"Move your men out," he said. "Stay with the wagons until I send someone to relieve you."

"Yes, my Lord General," Koshiba said, bowing, then he turned to the soldiers, gave a short whistle and walked away toward the south. As he passed, the samurai and then the soldiers fell in line behind him.

"Neatly done," Trevan said at Aren's elbow.

"It took too long," Aren said, turning toward the large tent in the center of camp. "If the attack starts before we tell Colonel Hendricks what's going on, he might start issuing orders and bungle everything."

† † †

There was already a commotion at Hendricks tent when Aren and Trevan arrived. From inside the tent, Aren could hear someone complaining loudly that the supply wagons were being moved and when he'd objected a soldier had punched him.

"Did we order the wagons moved?" someone Aren presumed to be Hendricks asked.

"No, sir," came the reply.

"Well, take a squad and sort it out, Captain," Hendricks said. "Those wagons are not to be moved. I want you to arrest whoever's interfering. I'll deal with them tomorrow."

Several people were milling about outside the tent, talking nervously in low voices. Two armed soldiers in Aerie armor glared at them, as if daring them to interrupt Hendricks.

"Halt," one of them called as Aren and Trevan came marching up.

Aren definitely didn't have time for long explanations.

"Out of the way," he barked in his best commander's voice. Startled, the guard took a step back and Aren simply walked into the tent before the man could recover. Inside were two more Aerie guards and three officers. The aging man with the drooping gray mustache had to be Hendricks. Aren had expected an Aerie bureaucrat but this man at least had the look of a professional soldier.

A professional who doesn't bother to post scouts around his camp, Aren reminded himself.

"What is the meaning of this, Trevan?" Hendricks said, surprised at the interruption. "I'm rather busy at the moment."

He waved at one of the officers and the man saluted before turning to leave.

"Stand down, Captain," Aren said, still with his commander voice.

The officer gave him a quizzical look and stopped when Aren wouldn't move out of the entrance.

"How dare you give my men orders," Hendricks said. "Who do you think you are?"

Aren pulled his last rolled scroll from his belt and handed it to Trevan.

"Colonel Hendricks of Aerie," Trevan said, walking forward until he could pass the older man the document. "May I present General Aren Bennis, appointed commander of the Army of Might by unanimous vote of the council."

Hendricks mustache drooped even further, and he snatched the scroll out of Trevan's hand.

"I take it you're the one that's been ordering people around behind my back?" Hendricks growled as he read. "Someone reported that the Norgards are arming up for battle."

"They are," Aren said.

"Damned irregular time to be running drills," Hendricks said. "And I'm going to have to verify this document, so don't go giving any more orders. I'm still in command here until—"

"There's no time for that, Colonel," Aren said. "This camp is about to come under attack from the Obsidian raiders."

The other officer scoffed at that and Hendricks nodded in approval.

"Nonsense," he said. "I've got people watching the approach from the east, they reported in just an hour ago. If an army was moving up that way, we'd have seen them before noon."

"They aren't coming that way," Aren said. "They'll attack from the woods to the south, which you'd know if you had bothered to send out scouts when you encamped here."

Hendricks puffed up like a bullfrog and his bushy eyebrows came together across his forehead.

"That's the most ridiculous thing I ever—"

Before Hendricks finished, a cry of alarm rose up in the distance. It was quickly picked up, moving through the camp like wildfire before it was joined by the sounds of battle and the clash of arms.

Chapter
14

The Ambush

Syenna sat atop a loaded wagon, her eyes relentlessly sweeping the rolling grassland to the east. The light was almost completely gone, leaving the shifting grass a black, undulating mass, making it virtually impossible to detect any movement. Still, she had a job to do, at least until the Ardorin swordsmen arrived.

"Get down from there you," one of the teamsters yelled up at her. "I've got to move this wagon."

She glanced down at the man from her perch. His clothes were ragged and dirty and he clearly hadn't shaved in days. The only distinguishing thing about him was the bright red kerchief he had tied around his arm. It reminded Syenna of the black bands worn by the relatively few members of the Opalis Legion in camp.

"This wagon isn't essential," she told the man. It was the reason she'd picked it for her vantage point. According to the master of the supply yard, this particular wagon held furniture and table silver for some fancy officer who hadn't even arrived yet. It reminded her of something General Karpasic would do. She almost smiled at the thought of Aren even considering such things, much less using them.

"Go see that man, he will tell you what wagons to move first." She pointed to where Sir Llewelyn was helping to push one of the wagons into a line of them heading for the canyon. Around him other ragged men were busy hitching horses to wagons, getting ready to move. Most looked like the man below her on the ground, many even wore the same red kerchiefs on their arm, no doubt as some symbol of rank among the teamsters. So far, of the fifty or so wagons in the supply yard, less than twenty were moving.

"I just came from him," the teamster persisted. "He said this wagon was next."

Syenna opened her mouth to argue, but a sudden light at the far end of camp caught her eye. From the south, dozens of flaming arrows rose into the sky and arced down among the tents. Fires sprang up immediately along with cries of alarm.

The rasp of a sword being drawn from a sheath pulled her attention back. Below her, the teamster had pulled a short sword from under his stained tunic. He wasn't looking at her any more, but had his attention focused on the other wagons. Syenna turned just in time to see another of the red kerchief men drive a dagger into Sir Llewelyn's back.

The man on the ground dashed around the front of the wagon, heading for where the Opalis knights were under attack from his fellows. Without thinking, Syenna leaped off the wagon, landing hard on the running man and driving her elbow into him as her weight bore him to the ground. Shock from the impact ran up her arm and into her shoulder and she heard one of the man's ribs crack beneath her.

The fake teamster howled and tried to throw Syenna off, but she was already moving. With a broken rib or two, he was no longer the primary threat. To her left, the man who had knifed Sir Llewelyn was slashing at one of the real teamsters, who was holding him at bay with an empty bucket. Syenna rolled, coming to her feet and dashed into the fray, drawing her own sword as she went. With a casual ease she drove the tip of her weapon into the back of the teamster the same way he'd attacked Sir Llewelyn.

The man screamed and collapsed. As she jerked her sword free of him, Syenna noticed that he was young, probably just over a score of years. She noted his youth, but spared him no compassion because of it. He was a raider and an Obsidian and it had been far too long since she'd been able to actually fight her enemies.

A sound behind her made Syenna turn, far too late to stop the man with the broken rib. Ignoring his obvious pain he rushed at her, sword held low like a spear. Syenna tried to parry it, but she was off balance. In a moment of terrible clarity, she realized that nothing she could do would prevent the enraged man from driving his weapon straight through her chest. Before he could land the blow, however, a foot lashed out and kicked the man in the knee, pushing it to the side with a sickening crack.

The man howled and went down in a heap, and Syenna stepped

forward, driving the tip of her bloody sword into his neck. Leaving the sword in place she released it and offered her hand to her savior, Sir Llewelyn.

"Thanks," she said, helping the young knight get to his feet. "I thought you were dead."

"So did he," Llewelyn said, pulling up his surcoat to reveal a chain shirt underneath.

Syenna jerked her sword out of the dead man as Llewelyn drew his own.

"The men with the red kerchiefs on their arms are impostors," she said heading off to where several of the real teamsters lay dead. "The Obsidians must have snuck them into camp a few at a time." A group of the impostors were trying to turn one of the heavy wagons toward the east.

Realizing that these men weren't enough to accomplish the theft they intended, she stopped and looked east. Even in the dark she could see dozens of shapes rushing forward through the grass. The wagon with the impostors rattled by her and Syenna had to step back to avoid a sword slash from the driver as he passed.

She hesitated, not knowing if she should pursue the wagon or help Llewelyn and the teamsters fight off the impostors. Remembering Aren's order not to get involved, she elected to chase down the wagon. As she ran to catch it, however, a shadow suddenly reared up on the far side of the driver and Syenna saw the long curved edge of a sword gleam in the dim moonlight. A moment later the sword fell and she had to jump to avoid tripping on the driver's head as it rolled across the grass.

The warrior leapt off the moving wagon, landing in front of Syenna. She could see the distinctive Ardorin armor and knew him to be a friend but he had no such advantage when seeing her.

"Wait!" Syenna called as he raised his blade again. "I'm with you."

The man hesitated but before she could explain a shadow appeared in the darkness.

"Behind you!"

Something in Syenna's voice told the Ardorin that she was serious and he swept his sword around in a glittering arc. He struck the satyr under the arm, cutting a vicious slash into the Fomorian's side. It bellowed but brought down the club it had raised above its head, smashing the Ardorin warrior to the ground in a bloody heap.

Syenna darted in, but the creature swung its club up from the ground one-handed and she had to throw herself down to avoid it. The satyr stepped over her, raising its club again to bash her to a pulp. She pushed up with her hips and lashed out, kicking the hilt of the Ardorin's sword, still stuck in the beast-man's side. It howled and dropped to one knee, shuddering in pain. Seizing the opportunity, Syenna rolled onto her left side and stabbed upward, driving the tip of her sword under the satyr's ribs and into its heart.

It fell down on top of her, its now dead weight pressing her to the ground. Syenna took a moment to recover her breath, then heaved the monster off of her. As she got to her feet, the sounds of armed combat erupted around her. Ardorin soldiers slammed into the oncoming wave of raiders, their long blades severing limbs as easily as reapers cutting wheat. Raiders wielding clubs, swords, and spears came on into the deadly wall, exacting revenge for their fallen comrades.

The wagon Syenna had been chasing continued on to the east, pulled by horses spooked by the smell of blood. Even as she looked, she knew it had gone too far, the raiders would cut her down if she went after it. Giving it up for lost, she turned back to the supply yard. Sir Llewelyn and his fellow knights were locked in a desperate struggle with the red-kerchiefed raiders. Most of the teamsters were dead or wounded and already the raiders who weren't keeping the knights at bay were struggling to get several supply wagons turned around.

With the bulk of the wagons still heading toward the canyon, the raiders had concentrated on the ones at the end of the line, but there wasn't a lot of space to turn them around. Syenna dashed to the wagon she'd used as a perch. Sheathing her sword, she grabbed an axe from the toolbox under the driver's bench. She wasn't worried about being seen in the chaos of the fight, but she circled around the embattled knights anyway, coming up behind the wagon the raiders were struggling to turn.

If she'd had more time, she would have tried to disguise herself by taking one of the red kerchiefs off a dead raider and wearing it herself.

But she was out of time.

Sir Llewelyn and his knights were holding out, but there wasn't anything they could do to stop the raiders, and the Ardorins had their hands full with the charging Fomorians. If the raiders got the first wagon turned around and moved out, it would create room to turn the next. They'd easily make off with half a dozen then.

Gripping the axe in both hands, Syenna darted forward toward the struggling raiders. Three of them pulled the team of horses through the brush, trying to get them facing the right way, while four more struggled to push the wheels. She brought the axe around her body in a sweeping arc but not aimed at the raider straining to turn the rear wheel.

The axe hit the spokes of the wheel, shattering two. With a curse, the raider leaped back. Syenna raised the axe and chopped away another spoke. The raider jerked a dagger from his belt and slashed at her, driving her back. She tried to sweep the axe back into the wheel, but the raider stabbed at her and she felt the blade skate across her ribs. Hot pain bloomed in her side, but she ignored it. Reversing the axe, she drove the handle into the raider's leering face, snapping his head back and shattering some of his teeth. Howling in pain he stumbled back.

Seizing the opportunity, Syenna raised the axe over her head and, ignoring her shrieking side, brought it down with all the force she had. The heavy blade slammed into the spokes, snapping them like twigs, and the entire wagon sagged as the wheel came free from the axle.

The raider trying to drive the wagon swore a string of curses that could only have come from an actual teamster, or maybe a sailor. He jumped up on the seat, glaring down at Syenna.

"Cut the horses loose," he yelled to men Syenna couldn't see. "And turn this wagon over, get it out of the way."

Someone grabbed Syenna's hair, trying to jerk her backward and off her feet. Lashing out with her elbow, she caught the raider in the jaw and he went down, losing his grip. Another loomed up in front of her, and she jammed the axe handle into his gut. Air whooshed out of his lungs as he staggered back.

Syenna knew more were coming and she decided it was time to leave this fight to people in proper armor. Darting to the side, she headed west toward the canyon where the other wagons were making their way to safety. Two steps later something heavy slammed into her and the world turned on its end.

She knew she should roll, that a crushing, killing blow would follow the first, but her body didn't respond. A dark shape loomed over her, but her eyes focused beyond it where the wagon driver stood looking down from atop the wagon. As she waited for death, she was a bit surprised when a sword blade suddenly emerged from the man's chest.

The shadow above her wavered and turned as voices erupted into noise Syenna wasn't able to understand. The raider on the wagon pitched forward, falling down into the dirt. He was so close to Syenna's face that she could see his eyes. They were blue.

Incoherent sounds erupted around her but all she could do about it was stare into the empty eyes of the dead raider. She was aware of time passing, but it seemed more like a dream than reality, as if nothing existed in the real world.

". . . alive," a voice said, quite close to her ear. It sounded like someone she'd heard before, but she couldn't manage to make her brain put a face to the voice.

Hands lifted her, and she could hear herself groan as the wound in her side was pulled open. Light suddenly bathed over her and her eyes snapped into focus. Aren walked beside her, helping to carry the blanket they were using as a litter. The light came from the Avatar sword, slung at his side, and it shone out as if the scabbard weren't there at all. As she looked, however, the light changed, coming from behind Aren.

That's when the woman appeared.

She was shorter than Aren, and thin, with dark, curly hair. She stepped up from somewhere behind Aren and put her hand on his shoulder. The move was intimate on her part, but Aren didn't seem to notice at all. That wasn't the strangest thing, though, the strangest thing was that the woman was glowing. Light seemed to emanate from beneath her skin, shimmering over Aren's neck and back as she pressed against him. As Syenna watched, the woman looked down at her, right into her eyes. A smile spread across her face that made Syenna's flesh crawl, then the woman leaned forward, her lips almost touching Aren's ear, and she whispered.

Aren turned immediately, looking down. His expression was one of concern but he smiled when he saw her eyes open. The look of relief and pleasure at her being awake faded almost instantly, hardening into one of anger.

"I thought I told you to stay out of the fight," he said. His voice seemed to come from far away, but at least she understood it.

"Did my best," she said, slurring the words.

"Yeah," he said in a voice that clearly indicated that he didn't believe her. "Sir Llewelyn told me about the wagon wheel. Very subtle."

"They didn't get that wagon," Syenna said.

"They only got one," Aren said, his tone still one of irritation. "And if it had been two or even five, that would have been fine. I can afford to lose a few wagons, I cannot afford to lose my best scout."

"So we won?" she said, attempting to change the subject.

"I'm sure Colonel Hendricks will see it that way," Aren said. "But it's a pyrrhic victory at best. We lost too many soldiers for too little gain."

He went on, but Syenna couldn't hear. The ringing in her ears that had started when she got hit in the head was back and suddenly her eyesight was fuzzy. The only thing still in sharp focus was the glowing woman, who gazed down at her with a disapproving, condescending look, complete with a mocking pout.

Bitch, Syenna thought, then she passed out.

Chapter
15

Aftermath

The morning after the supply raid found the encampment of the Army of Might in disarray. The attack from the southern woods had been the expected diversion, but the raiders had started their attack by launching flaming arrows into the camp. The ensuing fires had created chaos and destroyed a good many tents and some gear.

Aren tried to look stoic as he surveyed the damage. Many of the tent fires had been put out quickly, but there were also burnt-out husks that represented total losses. More troubling were the soldiers wounded in the attack. As he moved through the camp, Aren saw quite a few men and women with arrow wounds, and there was no telling how many lay dead in the field beyond the medical tent. Outnumbered as his army was by the raiders, even one was too many.

Colonel Hendricks walked beside Aren, a look of naked calculation on his face. The camp had almost been taken by surprise and that was on him for not putting out scouts. Still, Aren had given him the letter relieving him of command before the attack. Hendricks hadn't accepted it on its face, but he could say that he did and then the aftermath of the raider attack would be laid at Aren's feet.

Officially anyway.

Aren almost wished the colonel would try to pawn off his failure, at least then Hendricks would have to relinquish command without a fight. It would all come down to which decision the colonel thought would let him save the most face.

With my luck he'll fight me until the baroness herself comes out here and orders him home.

"General," a familiar voice called.

Aren looked around to find Sir Llewelyn coming through the disorganized maze of tents. The young man had a bandage wrapped around his left forearm and his knuckles were bruised, but those were the only mementos of his defense of the supply wagons.

"Report," Aren said once the knight reached him.

"I've just come from the medical tent," Llewelyn said, snapping a salute. "There are twenty-two wounded, five seriously, and eight dead."

"What about the enemy?"

"They weren't expecting any resistance, so they suffered more serious losses," he said. "We've collected thirty-two bodies, mostly monsters, and we have six wounded prisoners, all under guard."

"Reliable guards?" Aren asked, resisting the urge to look at Hendricks.

"My brother knights," Sir Llewelyn said with a nod.

"Good. I'll be along shortly to interrogate the prisoners."

"They're not in very good shape," the knight cautioned. "You might want to wait until they've healed up a bit."

"Nothing like that, Sir Llewelyn," Aren said. "I just want to ask them some questions."

The knight shrugged.

"I doubt they'll answer."

Aren's hand dropped onto the hilt of the Avatar blade. Talkative or not, he had other ways to extract information from the Obsidian captives.

"I doubt they have anything useful to say," Colonel Hendricks interjected. "They are only raiders, after all."

"You're wrong about that, Colonel," Aren said, remembering to be somewhat diplomatic and keeping his voice neutral. "They're soldiers. Formerly soldiers of one of the most successful armies in history. Thinking of them as simple bandits and thugs is what caused you to let your guard down when you camped here. No simple raider band would have dared a supply theft against an army so well situated, but trained soldiers?" He shrugged. "They almost managed it."

Hendricks didn't seem impressed by Aren's line of thought.

"Feel free to waste your time," he said. "I've seen enough of this." He waved his hand at the burned tents and the broken and overturned wagons in the supply yard. "I've got reports to write and I need to validate that letter of yours."

With that, the colonel turned and headed up the hill back toward his massive command tent. Aren watched him go until he disappeared between two rows of tents.

"Walk with me," he said to Sir Llewelyn as he turned toward the camp of the Opalis contingent.

"Is there something else, sir?" Llewelyn asked.

"Yes," Aren nodded. "I don't trust Hendricks. I want you to put on your armor, the whole kit. Get some of your knights and have them gear up as well, then relieve the guards watching the prisoners. I want you looking formidable and dangerous if anyone shows up. Under no circumstances is anyone to question the prisoners without me being there."

"Yes, General," the knight said.

"I have something I need to do first, but I'll be along within the hour," Aren said.

"I understand, sir," Llewelyn replied.

† † †

There were three women among Sir Llewelyn's knights, and Aren made straight for the tent they shared. The flap had been pulled back and tied open to allow air to flow through the canvas structure. Inside, Aren could see four sleeping pallets. Only one was occupied.

Syenna looked up from where she lay as Aren stepped inside. She had on a simple brown nightdress and there was a bandage bound around her head. Aren mouthed the words, *How's your hearing,* though he didn't make any actual sounds. A flash of confusion played across Syenna's face, then her eyes narrowed.

"You're not funny," she said, sitting up slowly, her hand gripping her side where the sword had cut her. "And my hearing is fine."

"Are your ears still ringing?"

She hesitated before answering. When she observed Aren noticing her hesitation, she grimaced. "Only a little," she said defensively. "Here, help me up."

She reached out, but Aren folded his arms over his chest.

"You are not supposed to get up," he said. "You are supposed to be resting while your wounds heal."

She reached up to the neckline of her dress and pulled it down far enough for Aren to see the bandages wrapped around her chest.

"Laying here isn't accomplishing anything," she argued. "The healer's got me bundled up tight, so it'll be fine for me to walk around a bit. Besides, you'll need all the help you can get whipping this army into shape."

"I've sent out pickets and scouts," Aren said. "I do not, in fact, need your help. Until Hendricks formally accepts his orders, I doubt he'll let me do anything too drastic anyway. So, your orders are to lie in that bunk and get better, Captain."

"It's lieutenant, remember?" she corrected him. "You didn't get hit in the head by a shovel, too, did you?"

"No," Aren said. "I managed to follow my own orders and stayed out of the fight. I also don't argue with my commanding officer when he issues me a field promotion."

Syenna blushed briefly at the rebuke. "What do you mean a field promotion? Do you have a letter from the baroness about me?"

"No," Aren chuckled. "But the baroness did put you, specifically, under my command, and I'm making you the leader of the scouts for the Army of Might. You'll have the rank of captain and, as soon as the healers say you can get back on your feet, I want you to assemble a full platoon of scouts."

"And where am I supposed to get the men for this platoon?"

"Anywhere you find someone with the skills you need," Aren said. "I'll give you official orders that will allow you to draw from anywhere in the army. You'll be in charge of the scouts, and I'll expect you to handle deploying them and making sure this army has eyes."

She hesitated for a moment, probably running everything over in her mind, then shot him a suspicious look.

"Is this just your way of keeping me in camp?" she asked with only the hint of a smirk.

"You will be in charge," Aren said with a shrug. "That means you'll need to be around to brief me and to consult on any potential action."

"It also means I'll need to be in the field from time to time," she countered. "Both to keep my skills sharp and to make sure my scouts are properly trained."

Aren hesitated, then grudgingly nodded his assent.

Finally Syenna smiled.

"I won't let you down," she said, sticking out her hand again for him to help her up. "I guess I'd better get started."

Aren shook his head.

"Later," he said. "You may remember that Hendricks isn't going to let me move the army anytime soon. The scouts I have out right now will report to me if they find anything, so until that changes, you lie there and heal."

"All right," Syenna said, withdrawing her hand. She looked up at him from her pallet with an exasperated expression. She didn't like being cooped up any more than he did. After a moment, however, her gaze turned quizzical, and she tilted her head to look behind Aren. He turned, expecting someone to be waiting there, one of the knights who used this tent perhaps, but the space was empty.

"What are you looking at?"

"Are you feeling okay?" she asked, ignoring his question.

Aren thought about the question for a moment before nodding.

"Yes, I'm fine. Why do you ask?"

"In the ruins of the temple, at Midras," she went on, seeming to change the subject again, "you said you saw a woman."

"And again in Opalis," Aren said with a shrug. "I never managed to catch up to her. What of it?"

"In Midras, she led you to the Avatar sword, didn't she?"

Aren hadn't really thought about it that way. He'd been following her in Midras because she looked like she knew where she was going and he was being chased at the time.

"I guess she kind of did," he said. "In a roundabout way."

"What did she look like?" Syenna asked.

Aren thought back to the two times he'd seen the strange woman. Both instances were burned, indelibly, into his mind.

"She's a bit shorter than you," he said, conjuring up a mental image. "With pale skin, blue eyes, and curly black hair. She has a way of looking desperate and confident at the same time, too." He grasped for a better description but it eluded him. "Why do you ask?"

"It's nothing," she said, but something in her eyes told Aren it wasn't nothing. Still, he'd seen that look before and he knew Syenna was done talking.

"Get some rest, Captain," he said. "And if I see you out of that bunk before the healer gives his okay, I'll have you tied to it."

She flashed him a look that clearly indicated that not only would she be out of her bunk by the end of the day, but that Aren would not see her. Deciding not to argue, Aren wished her a speedy recovery and left the tent.

† † †

Aren was surprised to find Sir Llewelyn and five of his fellow knights guarding the Obsidian prisoners when he arrived. As elaborate as the knights' metal armor was, he figured it would take them longer to put it on. The knights stood in a rough circle around a small fire where six pallets had been laid out like the spokes of a wagon wheel.

Of the wounded prisoners, four were humans, the teamster impostors from the looks of them, and the other two were elves. All of them had bandages wrapped around their limbs or torsos where they'd received wounds, and most of the wrappings were stained red as blood seeped through from the wounds beneath. The elves had their hands tied together and one foot tied to a stake in the ground, though neither the elves nor the men looked like they were in any condition to walk, much less make a run for it.

Aren dropped his right hand down onto the pommel of the Avatar sword. Instantly his vision shifted, and he could see the knights and the prisoners superimposed over pulsing motes of light. Aren decided that the light was somehow a representation of a person's soul, of who they really were. Some of the lights were golden and bright, while others faded to a sickly green that pulsed with a sullen malevolence. The worst, however, were the empty ones—the Fomorians.

As Aren looked at the elves, he could see them, or rather the lack of them. They had no past, they had no hopes or goals. All that existed within them was a nameless hunger: a desire to serve their sorcerer masters.

He knew he'd get nothing useful from them, so Aren shifted his gaze to the men. All of them had been soldiers in the Westreach Army, though none had ever served with him. He was surprised to see that they were almost as empty as the Fomorians, but for different reasons. They'd lost all hope. Their single, overarching passion seemed to be to simply stay alive, to exist.

"What do you want?" one of the men asked when he noticed Aren staring.

His name was Omar Gluac and his father was a butcher. He'd been conscripted into the Obsidian army, much to his mother's distress, but that had been over a decade ago. Now Omar was a sergeant, a career man, or he had been until his army had inexplicably been ambushed outside of Opalis.

"I'm General Bennis," Aren said, meeting Omar's challenging gaze. "I have some questions for you."

"We have nothing to say," Omar said, though his voice wasn't as steady as he might have liked it to be.

"Bennis?" the man to Omar's left said. His name was Michul Sulin and he came from a farming village in Grunvald. Unlike Omar, he'd run away to join the army when he'd gotten two different local girls pregnant. He'd served in the Obsidian army, doing as little as possible, for almost two years now.

"Not Aren Bennis?" Michul asked, his voice hot with anger.

"So, you're the traitor," Omar said. "The so-called Hero of Opalis. You're the one who sold us out. You took all the people out and said you'd leave the gold for us, but there wasn't any gold, was there?"

"Then you left us for the Norgards," Michul snarled. "Got all our friends killed, and then left us in this Gods-forsaken country to rot."

For his part, Aren just listened. The sword was telling him far more than the prisoners words so he let them vent. They had been elated at the prospect of sacking a treasure city, even more so when they found out that the people in the city would give up and leave without a fight. But the city held no treasure, no gold or jewels, and common soldiers like Omar and Michul had been devastated to learn that. Not as devastated as they had been when they found themselves surrounded by the Norgard Legions. They'd made a desperate charge to escape and they'd succeeded, though they didn't consider themselves lucky. There was no way the Obsidians would take them back now, and even if they did, it would only be to turn them into Fomorian soldiers, ones whose loyalty was above question. Worst of all, word had reached the raiders that the Obsidians were emptying Midras and surrounding towns and villages, taking the civilians back to become monsters in service of the Obsidian cause. Each man among the prisoners held an intense fear that the sorcerers would come for their families and loved ones eventually.

And it was all the fault of the traitor, Aren Bennis.

That bothered him. Not because of the hardship being endured by his former brothers in arms; he'd understood the consequences of that decision when he'd made it. What bothered him was that the soldiers knew him. They knew he'd sold out the Westreach Army. He supposed that someone might have heard that from Karpasic, but they'd called him the Hero of Opalis, a name Karpasic couldn't have known. A name no one in the Westreach Army would know.

"Where did you hear me called the Hero of Opalis?" Aren asked.

None of the men answered, but Aren read their answers through the sword. They'd heard that name from their commander, the man who now led the Obsidian raiders. The only thing Aren couldn't see was his name.

"Thank you," he told the men. "You've been a great help."

With that he turned on his heel and made his way back across the camp to the tent he was sharing with General Trevan. The sturdy man was there, behind his desk, going over inventory reports from the master of the supply yard and making notes.

"How's Syenna?" he asked as Aren entered.

"Ornery," Aren said. "Less so than Colonel Hendricks, though."

"Is he going to be trouble?"

Aren nodded. "Probably."

"What are we going to do about that?"

Aren had given that some thought, and he still didn't have a good answer.

"I've already got the Norgards and the Ardorin contingents," he said, sitting down on the opposite side of the table from Trevan. "I still need to meet with the Resolute commander—"

"Major Lucinda Tibbs," Trevan interjected.

"What's she like?"

"Tough as nails, and bullheaded to boot," Trevan said with a grin, then his expression grew serious. "She's also the daughter of one of their warlords, so she has a certain amount of political pull. It makes dealing with her . . . tricky."

"I'll take that under advisement."

Trevan chuckled at that and went back to his reports.

"Can you get a message to Highvale?" Aren asked after a moment.

"Sure, it's actually not that far away. Should take a week to get a reply back." Trevan looked up from his writing with a grin. "Why, do you want to try an end run around the major?"

"No," Aren said, leaning back in his chair. "When I spoke to the prisoners just now, they knew who I was."

"Well, you were one of Karpasic's captains, it's not surprising that the regular soldiers would know you."

Aren shook his head.

"That's not what I mean. They called me the Hero of Opalis. How would they know about that? No one started using that absurd title until after we got to Resolute."

Trevan shrugged and set his pen aside.

"They have been raiding in the area," he suggested. "They might have picked it up that way."

"Seems like a strange thing for random townspeople and villagers to tell raiders."

Trevan made a noncommittal sound and shrugged.

"So how will writing to Resolute help with that?"

"Send a letter to whoever's in charge of their prisons," Aren said. "I need to know what became of my former lieutenant, Nik Halik."

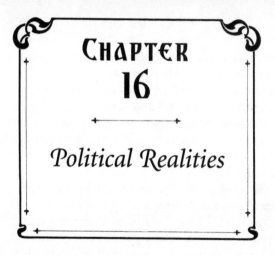

CHAPTER
16

Political Realities

Major Lucinda Tibbs reined in her horse at the top of a small hill just east of the Unified Army encampment. She'd been taking this ride every day but, thanks to yesterday's ill-fated attack on the camp, today she had two members of her personal guard with her. If her second had had his way it would have been an entire squad.

She grimaced at the thought. Hawkes was just doing his duty to protect his commander, but she hardly needed it. Lightning was faster than any goat-man or Obsidian soldier. She leaned down and patted her partner on the side of his long neck, getting her a whinny of appreciation in return.

It would be a cold day in hell before some Obsidian ambusher got the drop on her.

"Anything wrong ma'am," the smaller of her nursemaids asked. Lancer Morgani was a young woman just out of her training period, but she handled her mount with a grace and skill that still eluded some of her fellow lancers. She had brown hair the color of acorns framing a plain face with scars on her forehead from an unfortunate case of youthful acne.

"Nothing wrong, Lancer," Tibbs said. "This is a pleasure ride, not a drill. From time to time I like to stop and admire the scenery."

She looked up at the sky and marked the position of the sun.

Speaking of scenery.

Nudging Lightning with her knees, Tibbs sent him trotting forward, south toward the woods that bordered the camp. She knew from experience that the Ardorins liked to train there once the sun moved behind the trees and granted them some shade. A ring of trampled ground marked the spot where every day the Ardorin commander would lead a dozen or so of his warriors out of camp.

Tibbs crested a nearby hill and brought Lightning to a stop. The warriors of Ardoris were already there and she sat watching as the young man stripped to the waist and began apply pitch from a bucket to the sides of wooden training swords. His fellow warriors did the same and when they were done, the commander stepped into the ring. The others lined up in two rows and he led them through a slow, deliberate series of sword forms with the wooden weapons.

"What's all that?" Lancer Tyrie asked. Tyrie was a man in his thirties and the veteran of several campaigns. His face needed a shave and his chain tunic was slightly rusty, but the man was sharp where it counted.

"Those are the Ardorin Samurai," Tibbs said, watching as the commander squared off with a rather small-looking woman who wielded two short swords rather than one long one. If the woman felt intimidated by her larger opponent, she gave no sign. When the call to fight was given, she rushed at her commander, trying to knock his single blade aside to strike him with her off-hand weapon. The commander evaded her, cutting low with his sword in a blow the woman barely managed to block.

Tibbs had watched this every day, and she knew that any hit would leave a pitch stain on the opponent. Three marks meant a loss. Tibbs had met the Ardorin commander when they'd first reported to Colonel Hendricks. He was young with an infectious smile and an unpronounceable name. Tibbs thought him far too pretty to be an actual warrior. It was quite common for officers to gain their commands through political influence or favors rather than skill. Watching the young man fight, however, she had to admit that he had earned his command. In all the times she'd watched he'd only been beaten twice.

"They train like this for two hours every day," Tibbs continued her explanation.

"I see what you mean, Major," Lancer Morgani said with a sly smile. "Excellent scenery."

The young commander finished the bout, beating the woman three hits to one. As two new combatants took to the circle, he took the young woman aside and gave her a few pointers before sending her back to join her fellows.

"Rider coming," Tyrie said, snapping Tibbs out of her reverie. She instantly became aware of approaching hoofbeats, sounds that she should have heard before. Maybe it was a good thing Hawkes made her bring her bodyguards after all.

The rider was one of her own, though she didn't know his name. He reined in as he approached, trotting to a stop before her with his open hand up in salute.

"Begging your pardon, Major, but your presence is requested in the Opalis camp." He handed her a rolled bit of parchment that turned out to be an invitation to call upon Captain Trevan of the Opalis Legion at her earliest convenience. The language was cordial, couched as a request, but Tibbs knew an order when she saw one. She'd heard, of course, that there was a new leader for the army, someone sent by the Council of Might and being conducted around by Trevan. As of yet, she hadn't met him, but it looked like that was about to change.

"The new general?" Tyrie asked with a grin. "Maybe we'll finally get some action, since they left us out of that scrap last night."

"Did you receive a message from Colonel Hendricks?" Tibbs asked the messenger.

"No ma'am," he said.

"Well then, I guess we'd better go meet the general," Tibbs said, reluctantly turning her horse away from the Ardorin training ring.

† † †

General Aren Bennis sat on his side of the writing table he shared with Mikas Trevan. Ostensibly, he was going over troop assessments for the Army of Might and determining what units he wanted to form and who would command them. In reality, he spent most of his time trying to keep his knees from bumping Trevan's under the narrow expanse of the table. Never in his life had Aren wanted a grand command tent, but he was coming precariously close to having that exact thought.

Syenna would laugh at you, he reminded himself. He could always count on her to keep him grounded.

As he tried to put his mind back on the task at hand, the sound of several approaching horses pulled him away again. Only a cavalry officer would bother riding a horse through the congested camp.

She's dedicated, I'll give her that.

A moment later the tent flap was pulled back and the young Opalis guardsman who stood outside stuck his head in.

"Begging the general's pardon, but there's a Major Tibbs of Resolute here to see you."

"Show her in," Aren said, setting his pen aside.

He and Trevan both stood as a short woman with tightly braided red hair entered. She had on a chain-mail tunic that reached down to her mid-thigh with a blue surcoat over it emblazoned with a silver dragon. A long, curved scimitar hung in a sheath from a belt at her waist, and she carried a simple metal helmet with a leather coif under her arm. It looked to Aren like she was of middle years. She had a shrewd face, clever eyes, and freckles on her nose.

"Captain Trevan," she said with a smile. "To what do I owe the pleasure of your gracious invitation?"

Trevan inclined his head to her.

"I'm sure you've heard by now that the council has sent a new commander for this army," he said.

Major Tibbs smile grew sly.

"I had heard something like that," she admitted.

Aren wondered if she'd guessed the reason for her summons. It would explain her horse and her armor, two things most went without while in camp.

"May I present General Bennis," Trevan said, pointing to Aren. "He has been given command of this army by unanimous order of the Council of Might."

"Bennis?" Tibbs said, one of her red eyebrows arcing. "Not Aren Bennis, the former Obsidian? The Hero of Opalis?"

"The same," Trevan confirmed.

The major turned to Aren and smiled a smile of genuine pleasure.

"I doubt you remember, but we met in Highvale at a reception given by Marshal Nimbus."

Aren wasn't surprised that he didn't remember meeting the major; he'd met at least a hundred people that night, probably more.

"Well it's nice to meet you again," Aren said, returning her smile. He picked up the orders for her from the table and handed them over. Unlike the Norgard and Ardoris contingents, Aren didn't have two sets of orders for Tibbs. The previous orders had been written by each country's leader for their respective commander and brooked no dissent; these orders, unfortunately, had been written by Ambassador Falcone. They carried the weight of the council behind them, of course, but they were not, strictly speaking, binding on a Resolute officer here in the kingdom of Resolute.

Tibbs unrolled the orders and read them through twice before looking up.

"Well, General," she said to Aren. "You've put me in a very awkward position."

Aren had been warned about this possibility, so he kept his expression friendly.

"How so?"

"My family is important in Resolute," she explained. "I don't mean that to brag, but as a simple statement of fact. My father is in the marshal's extended family. This means that if I were to refuse this commission you've offered me, I'd have to resign from my post. If I did that, for any reason, my family's enemies could use it to make trouble for the marshal."

"And why would you be tempted to resign?" Aren asked.

Her smile grew cunning and she set her helmet down on the writing desk.

"That has to do with the other side of my family. You see, we have extensive business dealings with Aerie. When I was younger, my father took me there many times."

"And those deals would be threatened if you appeared to offend Colonel Hendricks by accepting my offer?" Aren guessed.

"No," she said, shaking her head. "The problem is that my aunt is Colonel Hendricks' sister."

Aren resisted the urge to swear. He didn't have time for this.

Tibbs held up her orders.

"This says that I'm being offered the position of colonel in your army, a position that I would happily accept under normal circumstances. Unfortunately, if I do that before the colonel has officially turned command over to you . . ."

"You cause strife in your family and give your enemies in both nations something to use against you."

Tibbs nodded, fixing him with an appraising eye.

"Maybe you are the right man for this job," she admitted. "You seem to have a good grasp of politics and, begging the general's pardon, this job is going to be rife with politics. That said, I'm interested to know how good you are at tactics."

"What do you mean, Major?" Trevan cut in, the tone of his voice a warning.

"She wants to know what I'm going to have her doing in my army," Aren said. This was the kind of political maneuvering he was familiar with. Almost every decision he'd made in the Westreach Army had to consider how it would be received by the temperamental General

Karpasic, after all. "As it says in your offer, Major, you'd be promoted to colonel. You'd report to me or General Trevan here."

"Good so far," she said.

"As for what you'll be doing, you'll be in charge of all cavalry units."

"So the same thing I'm doing now?"

"Not quite. You'll have your own light cavalry, plus the Opalis Knights."

She smirked.

"What will I do with them? On those massive war horses with their metal armor they can't maneuver, not like my riders can."

"Your riders are a dagger," Aren said. "The Opalis Knights are a war hammer. Your force makes quick, slashing attacks and then retreats out of range. Fully armored knights simply ride over everything in their path, and their heavy lances can kill an ogre."

"A what?"

"Giant unit," Trevan supplied. "Big as a house." In response to the major's disbelieving look, he added, "Really."

"A commander of your experience should be able to find many uses for that kind of power," Aren said

Major Tibbs stroked one of her long braids, twirling it absently in her fingers as she thought over what she'd heard.

"I'll have to give it some thought," was all she'd say, but Aren could tell that she was already considering the possibilities. "What about my hasars and my longbowmen?"

"Your archers will be transferred to the command of Colonel Artemis of Opalis," Aren said. "She's coming up from Aerie with a force from the Opalis Legion and some more knights. She should arrive within the month."

"And the hasars?" Tibbs asked again.

Aren glanced at Trevan.

"Horse archers," he supplied.

Aren wasn't familiar with that. It seemed to him like shooting from horseback wouldn't be very effective.

"The term comes from the word 'harassers,'" Tibbs explained. "We use them to rake enemy formations or defenses from a distance, then quickly retreat."

"They sound like cavalry to me," Aren said. "That makes them your responsibility." Tibbs seemed to like that answer. "You'll also be responsible for all the horses except for the ones belonging to the teamsters."

She shrugged at that. "Goes with the territory. Besides, I don't trust my mount to anyone but me."

"So, what do you think?" Aren said. "Should I call you 'colonel.'"

The major's smile faded and she shook her head.

"Not yet, I'm afraid. I can't do anything until Colonel Hendricks makes his move, whatever that will be. I can say that I look forward to serving in this new army of yours, should that time come."

It wasn't a no, so Aren decided to count it a win. Tibbs saluted and turned to go, but Aren decided to push his luck just a bit more.

"Would your uncle object if you decided to picket the horses somewhere else, like say the south end of camp?"

The major thought about that for a moment.

"I don't see why he would. As far as I know, he didn't give any specific orders about setting up."

"Good," Aren said. "Do it. Please," he added, remembering that officially anyway, this was a request. He turned to Trevan. "I want to see Koshiba and Aquila as soon as possible, find someone to sound officer's call."

Trevan just stared back at him.

"Sir?"

"A signalman," Aren explained. "How do you communicate with your troops in battle?"

"We use the bells on the city tower and the ones over each gate," Trevan said. "I've heard the Ardorins use drums."

Aren felt what he was sure was the first of many headaches coming on.

"So no trumpeters."

"We use bugles," Tibbs offered.

"Okay, what's that?"

"It's like a trumpet but kind of rolled up around itself so it can be played from horseback."

Aren was starting to wonder if there was anything the soldiers of Resolute didn't do from horseback.

"Can you hear this bugle over distance?" he asked.

Tibbs nodded with a grin. "They're quite loud."

"Good. Send me one along with a man to play it. Unless you think your uncle would object?"

"I don't think that would cause any problems," Tibbs said, then she picked up her helmet and withdrew.

"If that's true," Trevan said after she'd gone. "It'll be the first thing in this army that didn't cause problems."

Aren agreed.

"You realize that you'll have to work out a whole new set of signals once that bugler gets here," Trevan pointed out.

Aren sighed and sat back down at the writing table.

"I know," he said.

CHAPTER
17

Insufficient Forces

The spire of rock that overlooked the confluence of the Fortus and Sanctus rivers had several rooms at the very top. One was obviously there to house the person in charge, which at this point was Evard Dirae. The little suite had two rooms, the larger with a balcony that had been formed out of the stone itself. Evard sat in a comfortable chair overlooking the prairie far below. The carpet of green stretched out to the east until it vanished against the Vaughban Mountains in the extreme distance.

The sound of someone approaching, climbing up the incorruptible metal stairway, reached his ears. Evard knew from experience that it would take his visitor several minutes to arrive, so he closed his eyes and enjoyed his chair for a few moments more. The chair itself was excessively comfortable, just the right height and firmness. It had the advantage of being a construct, an object created by Evard's magic and crafted from pure etherium.

Normally Evard wouldn't engage in such a frivolous waste of power. In this place, however, Evard had replenished his magical energies mere moments after he'd made the chair. Since it was made from etherium, it was far from permanent, he'd have to remake it in a month or so, but that meant nothing to him here.

Standing, he left the balcony, entering into a large room he'd made his personal quarters. A conjured bed, just like the chair outside, occupied the back wall along with a wardrobe and a writing desk. He could do more, of course, but those few things were all he needed. He was a sorcerer of the Obsidian Cabal, soon to be a member of the circle. Such a man had no need for ostentatious display, his power and position spoke for him.

Crossing to the wardrobe, Evard retrieved his black robe with the embroidered silver symbols and slipped it on over his more practical clothing.

"Craftmaster Dirae?" A tentative voice came from the outer room.

"A moment," Evard called, buckling a belt of silver plates around his waist. He thought about conjuring a mirror so he could check his appearance, but decided not to waste the power. Hours ago, Homer, his new homunculus, had brought word that the soldiers from Hilt were close. Evard might waste power on a comfortable chair, but not to impress some junior officer.

Crossing the room, he opened the door and passed into the outer room. This chamber was bare of decoration and empty except for a somewhat bedraggled-looking man in black Obsidian armor who saluted smartly. He was younger than Evard, by the look of him, but only just, with brown hair, blue eyes, and a face that hadn't seen a razor in several days.

"I am Captain Geran Torgus of the Hilt Reserve Company," he said, formally. "Reporting as ordered."

Evard resisted the urge to make a face at that. His first message to the commander at Hilt had gone unheeded. In the end, Evard had to use Homer to make some very pointed threats in order to get the commander to send any soldiers at all.

"How many soldiers do you bring with you, Captain?"

"I have a full company, comprised of men and Fomorians."

Evard suppressed another grimace.

"I'm afraid I'm not familiar with military designations, Captain," he explained. "I need to know how many soldiers you have."

"Sorry, Craftmaster," Captain Torgus said. He didn't look offended by the questions, but his voice was a bit hard. "I have two hundred warriors, seventy-five men, and one hundred twenty-five Fomorians."

Evard did make a face this time. That was far less than he'd hoped for. To challenge the Council of Might he would need an army of at least ten thousand, perhaps more. There were many small settlements in the area where he could get slaves to feed that army, but he doubted that would amount to more than a couple thousand men.

It was an irritating problem, but he would solve it.

"If I may ask, sir," Torgus said, "what do you want my men to do?"

Evard raised an eyebrow. What indeed?

"I had hoped, Captain, that your force would be enough to secure this place."

"From what, Craftmaster? There isn't a hostile force for hundreds of leagues in any direction."

Evard gave Torgus a hard look.

"The cabal's reasons for wanting this place secured are not your concern, Captain," he said. "Your concern is to secure this spire."

"I meant no offense, Craftmaster," the captain said, though he didn't sound as contrite as Evard would have liked. "I just mean that with the men I've got, the best I could do is blockade the bridge that leads into the spire."

Evard held his gaze for a long moment.

"And how many soldiers would you need to secure this place properly?"

"At least two thousand, for a start," Torgus said. "That would let me build a defensive wall and put up guard towers. To hold against a proper assault, it would take five thousand."

"That's about what I figured," Evard began, but the captain cut him off.

"That's just the soldiers," he said. "We'll need bridges across the rivers, and that takes engineers, to say nothing of the supply lines we'll need to feed everyone."

"Speaking of that, how long will your current supplies last?"

"I have two weeks of food in our supply train, and I've already ordered hunting parties to see if we can find any deer or bison in the area."

"I have an easier method in mind," Evard said. "There are several farming villages within a day's travel. It's harvest season, so take your men and relieve them of their stores. Once you've done that, round up the people and bring them here."

"W-why, sir?" Torgus looked surprised. "The Fomorians work better than any plough boy, and having civilians here will mean more mouths to feed."

"What it will mean is more Fomorians for you to command," Evard said. "I will take the people you bring me and transform them."

"No," Torgus said.

"What do you mean, no?" Evard made an effort to put just the right amount of malice in his voice.

"I mean that if a few little villages get raided and some food goes missing, no one cares," Torgus said. If he was intimidated by Evard's withering stare, he hid it very well. "If villages vanish without a trace, however, someone is going to come looking. We're in Resolute's territory here, and my soldiers wouldn't last five minutes against their cavalry."

"I'm giving you a direct order, Captain," Evard growled through his teeth. "You will take your men and you will bring me those civilians and their supplies."

"With all due respect, Craftmaster, you don't have the authority to give that order."

Evard took a breath to argue, but Torgus rushed on.

"My chain of command is very clear," he said. "In enemy lands I am only accountable to a superior officer in the Obsidian Military Command. My orders from Colonel Warren at Hilt are to lend you whatever aid I can and to preserve my soldiers for the glory of the Obsidian cause. Provoking the armies of Resolute will violate both of those instructions. And before you ask, only a member of the Obsidian Circle can override those orders."

Evard had visions of making this upstart Captain his first new Fomorian, but the more rational part of his mind pointed out that any lieutenants under Torgus probably had the same orders. He could transform them all, but if he did, the soldiers might mutiny or desert leaving him only the Fomorians, and they were fairly useless without officers to command them.

"Then I suggest you get your soldiers deployed by the bridge, Captain," he said, keeping his voice easy. "I'll communicate with the circle and see about getting you more soldiers."

"Yes, Craftmaster," the captain said, then he saluted and left.

Evard listened to the sound of the man's feet as he retreated down the metal stairs. His hands clenched into fists and he choked down a profanity. Under no circumstances could he let the idiot captain hear his frustration. He hadn't counted on anyone in the army giving him trouble. Karpasic had been easy enough to manipulate, but he'd been the man at the top of the hierarchy. Captain Torgus was a nobody and that very anonymity gave him protection. No one would blame him for following the orders of the circle to the letter, it's what was expected of a good soldier. If Evard had actually been on an errand for the circle, he could have new orders for the captain in a matter of days, but he was still actively hiding from Maradn's flying lizard, so that was out.

There must be a way to get the captain to do what Evard wanted without violating his orders. Unfortunately, Evard had no idea what that particular loophole might be.

He'd have to give the matter some thought.

† † †

Hours later, Evard sat on his balcony looking out at the darkening sky. The sounds of soldiers setting up camp drifted aloft, but at this height, it was just so much background noise. The distracting part was the occasional wafting aroma of cooking. Evard's rations had long ago run out and he'd been eating whatever he could forage. On the prairie he'd managed to catch rabbits using snares, and now that he was at the confluence he caught fish. Still, he wasn't much of a forager and he often went hungry.

His stomach rumbled and he ignored it. He'd go down to eat with the men tomorrow. It would hurt his mystique of being a powerful and dangerous master of magic to appear too familiar—or hungry.

Sipping a cup of cold water, he contented himself with the stars and his comfortable chair. Unfortunately they were the only things he could take contentment from. He hadn't yet come up with a way to get Captain Torgus on his side, and that gnawed at him the way a dog gnawed a bone. If he was going to have any hope of finding Aren and destroying the cursed Avatar sword, he had to have an army. Whatever Westland nation was hiding his friend wasn't likely to give him up without a fight, and with the magic of the sword controlling Aren's mind, he wasn't going to come willingly.

Evard took another drink, wishing he could trick his senses into believing the water was something stronger. Anything stronger. As he sat wishing for a vintage wine, something brushed against his consciousness. The experience was like hearing a familiar sound over and over and then finally noticing it.

"Homer," he said.

From above the balcony, the sound of claws scrabbling on stone drifted down. A moment later the homunculus gilded down and landed on the stone railing that surrounded the balcony. It hunched down into a squatting position, pulling its wings about its body like a cloak.

Evard looked straight ahead, right into the twin dark pits of the creature's eyes. In a moment he felt the connection between Homer and Monk-the-second. He'd sent Monk south to the city of Etceter weeks ago in the hope of turning up Aren's location. So far the creature hadn't been able to learn anything. Last night, however, his spy stumbled upon something interesting. A large woman, large even for a man, had arrived in the city by ship. Evard had never seen one of the famed Titans of Opalis, but he knew one of them was a woman.

Some other women dressed in burnished breastplates and plumed helmets had met the Titan at the docks and called her Sequana, confirming her identity. From that moment on, Evard had ordered Monk-the-second to follow her and to connect with him if she mentioned his missing friend.

"Let's see what you have for me, Monk," he said as his mind linked to Homer's and then across the impossible miles of intervening space to Monk.

Evard's mind seemed to drift in a sea of colors and light until finally his vision returned. Rather than the starlit sky outside his balcony, however, he found himself looking through a wavy pane of glass. His perspective was high up, as if looking through the top of a tall window. Beyond the glass was a snug sitting room with comfortable overstuffed chairs, couches, reading tables, shelves full of books and curios, and a sideboard with bottles of liquor and a tray of fruit, meat, and cheese on it. Fire glowed from an enormous stone hearth, and the room was bathed in the winking light of oil lamps that were polished to a shine.

The room was homey and well appointed, but certainly not rich or fancy. It was a strange place to find one of the rulers of the fallen city of Opalis, yet there she was, standing before the hearth warming her long fingers.

"What news do you bring me of my sister?" said someone Evard couldn't see. He made a mental note to work on Monk's ears when he got the creature back. While its hearing was sharp enough, voices sounded off key and tinny by the time they reached Evard.

"You could at least ask me about my trip," the Titan said with a smile and a wink.

The first speaker sighed, and Evard directed Monk to look around. A woman he hadn't noticed before sat in a high, wing-backed chair on the far side of the hearth from where Monk watched. She had a blanket over her stomach and legs and her hands held an embroidery hoop.

"Fine," she said, setting the hoop aside and clasping her hands together. "My dear Sequana," she said in an exaggerated, ingratiating voice, "it's so good to see you again. Pray, sit, tell me all about your journeys in the western lands and regale me with tales of adventure and forbidden love."

The Titan burst out laughing, then went to sit on a couch opposite the girl's chair. She was strange to look at for some reason, the girl not the Titan. Her hair was so blond as to be almost white and her features were both delicate and sharp, with high, prominent cheekbones. Something about her seemed familiar, but Evard was at a loss to explain why.

"All right," the Titan said. "Have it your way. I left Syenna and Captain Bennis three weeks ago near the Middle Downs."

Evard sat up in his chair, not daring to blink lest that break the connection between himself, Homer, and Monk. The Middle Downs wasn't exactly close to him, but if Aren was hiding there, Evard might be able to capture him with the men he had on hand.

"Why did you take a ship back?" the girl asked.

"The transportation matrix is convenient, but it takes a lot out of me to use it, and it does need to recharge," Sequana said. "It will be some time before I can use it reliably again."

Evard clenched his fists, wishing he could yell at them to get back to Aren Bennis and the Middle Downs.

"So how did it go?" the girl asked. "Did the army accept them?"
Army?

"When I left, the colonel from Aerie hadn't yet accepted the transition, but the Aerie are a stubborn people when it comes to contracts and official documents. I imagine Aren and Syenna will have got it worked out by now."

The girl shook her head, absently picking up her embroidery hoop again.

"I can't believe the council put Aren in charge of their army," she said.

Evard felt his chest tighten as if the air were being squeezed out of him. Aren? In charge of an army made up of the nations of the Council of Might. He didn't doubt the sense of it—Evard knew that Aren was a capable commander—he just couldn't wrap his head around it. How could the Avatar sword have dominated him so completely?

"Zhal was correct," Sequana said. "He's the only one all the nations would trust to command."

Evard could understand that. One of the reasons the cabal didn't take the Council of Might seriously was that its member nations were always squabbling amongst themselves.

"And what of my sister?"

"Aren put her in charge of the scouts."

Evard's eyes snapped back to the girl. She was Syenna's sister, the Dross girl. Now that he knew it, he could see the unmistakable signs, her long fingers and the tips of pointed ears protruding slightly from her hair. That also explained the blanket covering her legs, the legs some shaper or other had failed to perfect.

"Have they fought any raiders yet?"

"The remaining Obsidians tried to steal the supply wagons, but Syenna found their scouts and Aren managed to organize a defense in time," Sequana said. "Syenna was wounded in the fight, but it was only minor. She's fine now."

While the Titan spoke, the elf girl's face clouded over with worry, but she relaxed when she learned that her sister was okay.

"I'm just concerned," she said. "Zhal told me that the council nations haven't sent enough soldiers to deal with the Obsidian raiders."

"I'm sure Aren and your sister will make due," Sequana said.

From there, the conversation turned to the ins and outs of ship travel across the Bay of Storms, which all sounded thoroughly terrifying. Evard hated boats. As the women talked, his mind drifted back to their conversation about this council army. From the sound of it, it was small, but Evard guessed it was still far too large for his meager force to overcome.

He would need more men. Fortunately, he knew exactly where to get them.

Apparently some part of General Karpasic's army had managed to escape the battle with the Norgard Legions and they were now raiding the countryside somewhere near the Middle Downs. If he could find them, that would give him the army he needed, at least in the short term.

Unless they've got the same orders as Captain Torgus, he reminded himself.

If he wanted to command the armies of the Obsidian Empire, Evard was going to need official sanction from the circle.

He grimaced at that thought.

As soon as Maradn learned of his plan, she would make it hers, therefore any success he had would be hers as well. To achieve his goals, the circle must be kept in the dark.

Evard sighed, rubbing his chin. There had to be another way to accomplish the same goal. If he couldn't get sanction with the circle, maybe he could find a high-ranking officer willing to do his bidding. He laughed as the thought struck him. He should have seen the solution to his problem earlier. He knew right where to find a high-ranking Obsidian officer and exactly what to offer him to buy his loyalty—well, his obedience at least.

"Monk," Evard said aloud. "You're done there, I need you to come to me at once."

"Who said that?" the girl said. She and the Titan had continued their conversation during Evard's musings, but he'd ignored them. Now the girl's voice was loud and much clearer, as if he were suddenly in the room listening with his own ears and not Monk's.

Evard focused his mind back on the scene through the window. It was exactly as he had last seen it with one notable exception: the Dross girl was looking right at him, or rather right at Monk.

"What a strange creature," her voice said again, though Evard noticed that her lips weren't moving. "Is he yours?"

With a shock, Evard realized that Syenna's sister was addressing him. That shouldn't even be possible, but then he remembered how he could see and hear Maradn when he locked eyes with her pseudodragon.

"Can you see me?" He projected his thoughts through Homer to Monk.

"Yes," her voice came back, colder than before. "You're one of them, aren't you?"

"One of whom?"

"A sorcerer," she said. "Like the ones who hurt me."

A wave of pain, anger, fear, and loss washed over Evard, clearly coming from the girl. The emotions weren't unfamiliar, but Evard wasn't prepared for the assault and he shrank back from them.

"You're him," the voice came again. "Aren's friend. The one who tried to kill me."

That last came with a flash of anger that burned Evard, and he had to shut his eyes to dull the connection.

"She wanted you free of the effects of our failure," Evard said, recovering himself. "Unfortunately, death is the only release."

"But you didn't tell her that, did you? DID YOU?"

This last came at him like a thunderclap, and Evard reeled. How was this girl, this failure of magic, able to link back to him, much less browbeat him through the connection? It shouldn't be possible.

"You hurt my sister," the voice came again, mild, almost conciliatory this time.

Evard opened his eyes and found the girl struggling to stand from her chair. The Titan tried to stop her, but she waved the bigger woman away with such energy that the Titan relented.

"You are a cruel and vile man," she said, her withered legs trembling with the effort to stand. "I want you out of my house, and out of my city, but I'm going to keep your pet. He deserves better than the likes of you."

Before Evard could respond, to laugh at her feeble attempt to stand and her absurd demands, the connection between Monk and Homer broke. Evard had severed the connection many times before and it had just faded away. This time, however, it shattered and the impact hit the sorcerer like a physical blow, knocking his chair over backward and sending him sprawling to the floor.

"Monk," he gasped, struggling to his feet. He reached out with his mind, searching for the elusive touch of the homunculus's consciousness, but there was nothing there for him to find.

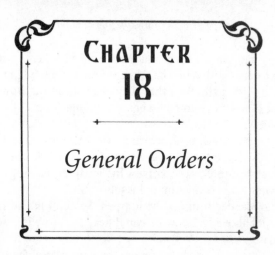

Chapter 18

General Orders

eneral Milos Karpasic shivered under his blanket as the last rays of the warming autumn sun vanished behind the walls of Opalis. The nights had gotten progressively colder, and yet his keepers hadn't seen fit to give him a better blanket than the ragged, stained bit of fabric he had. When the night finally came, he would lie down on the moldering straw pile and pull as much of the stuff on top of him as he could, all the while trying to leave enough beneath to keep him off the freezing floor.

To make matters worse, the Norgards who watched him hadn't exactly been overfeeding him. He had no idea how much weight he'd lost, but his skin hung around him now in wrinkles and rolls, like a child in his father's cloak. Being a fat man had its advantages; he'd never really been cold before, he was too well insulated for that. Now he was cold all the time, even when the sun shone down on the slate roof of the prison, radiating its warmth down into the cells below.

Despite the sun being gone, Karpasic didn't leave his post by the barred window. He knew that his keepers would be tending their horses soon. It was a precipitously boring thing to watch, but the guards had a bad habit of gossiping while they worked. From what Karpasic had overheard, they believed they would soon be withdrawn from Opalis. Apparently some of his vanquished army had, indeed, escaped. Now they were raiding towns and villages up and down the countryside and the Council of Might needed soldiers to put a stop to it.

Initially that thought had made him smile. The idea that the Norgards didn't have the manpower to hold Opalis delighted him. But what would become of him when they pulled out? Would they take him with them, or slit his throat and leave him here, just another corpse in a dead city? When he'd begged for more food in the beginning, the guards had joked that they were slimming him down so that his head wouldn't pop off when they hanged him.

Maybe it wasn't a joke.

Whatever the truth of it, his time was likely running short. The guards guessed that they'd receive new orders within the week. The general kept standing by the window in the rapidly cooling air, straining to hear any news, any hint of his fate.

A sound startled him and he jumped. Something had landed on the slate roof above and now he could hear a scrambling, scratching noise moving closer.

Stepping back from the window, the general watched it closely until a tiny horned head appeared at the top, hanging upside down. It looked remarkably human, with two eyes, a nose, and mouth, the latter lined with needle-like teeth. The creature dropped down, turning over as it fell, to land on the windowsill. Its body was short and humanoid with a large, barrel chest tapering to narrow hips and muscular legs that ended in clawed feet. It had wings like a bat emerging from its back, but also arms and clawed hands that it crossed over its chest as it squatted down on the sill. The creature wore no clothing but was covered with short, red fur and had a leather pouch on a string hung round its neck.

Now that Karpasic could see it clearly, he knew what it was—a monster, a creation of an Obsidian sorcerer.

He didn't know whether to be elated or terrified, so he just stood and waited for the thing to speak. He'd seen similar monsters before and he knew they could carry short, simple messages.

The thing hissed at him, and Karpasic's eyes darted up to its leering face. The second he met those dark, soulless eyes, he felt the world twist around him, as if he was falling. Instead of hitting the ground, however, he seemed to float in an indistinct sea of light and color.

Finally his feet hit solid floor and the nothingness faded away, leaving him standing in a room that appeared to have been expertly carved out of stone. It reminded him of the excavations at Desolis, though this stone was not black. A large bed stood against the far wall of the room, along with a wardrobe. In the foreground was an ornate desk, occupied by a familiar face.

"General Karpasic," Sorcerer Evard Dirae said, sitting back in his chair and looking the general up and down. "I can't say it's a pleasure to see you again."

Then why do it? Karpasic thought. He almost said it aloud, but stopped himself.

That was a strange thing to say after going through such obvious effort to arrange this meeting. If the sorcerer had come to gloat, he would have led with that.

He needs something from me.

Karpasic had to spare real effort to keep the smile off his face. The sorcerer had slipped up with the first words out of his mouth. He'd given away the game and, more importantly, he'd given Karpasic leverage. If the general played his cards right, he might be able to get out of the mess he was currently in.

"Craftmaster Dirae," he said in a sarcastic, mocking tone. "What brings you to my humble abode? Slumming?"

Karpasic had to be careful here. The last time they'd met, he'd mocked and derided Evard in an effort to anger the sorcerer into killing him. He couldn't let on that he'd guessed the game by being too ingratiating.

"I see you're still alive," Evard said with a sneer. "What have you been telling the Norgards to keep them from chopping off your head?"

Karpasic laughed at that. He didn't even have to force it. Evard Dirae must be preoccupied if this was the best insult he could concoct. No doubt that preoccupation was the reason for this visit.

"I don't have to tell them anything, Sorcerer," he said. "Your friend Captain Bennis has no doubt told them everything they wish to know."

Evard's face tightened as if he wanted to yell, but he appeared to master himself.

"Yes," he said in a hard voice. "And lucky for you, the circle doesn't know about that."

"Why is that lucky for me? Won't they just assume that I have been talking then?" He gave Evard a quizzical look. "That sounds like it has the potential to be much worse for me."

"It's lucky for you because there are certain elements among the cabal who want you back. Or dead," he added with a wolfish grin. "Which one is up to me."

Karpasic didn't react; he just stood there, waiting expectantly. Now they were getting down to what the sorcerer actually wanted.

The death threat might be genuine, but Evard would only use it if Karpasic forced him to.

"As you may imagine," the sorcerer continued, "with the loss of the Westreach Army, the Empire finds itself lacking in skilled military commanders."

"You just got through reminding me of my failings in that regard," Karpasic said. "What would the Empire trust me to do, arrange the shifts in the officer's mess?"

"The Empire needs to build up a new army, General," Evard said. "To do that, we need slaves to transform. I have a small force at my disposal, just two hundred men, I need someone to take command and direct them to raid nearby towns."

"I doubt you need a general for that. A good lieutenant would do."

"Yes," Evard said, his tone becoming evasive. "But this force will grow as I add Fomorian soldiers to it. There are also remnants of your army raiding in Resolute. I need someone they'll listen to in order to bring them back to the Empire."

That much was certainly true. Those soldiers would believe that what awaited them in the Empire was transformation or death.

Still, that didn't explain why the sorcerer would need anyone to lead a simple raiding party, especially not a general. Whatever company Dirae had access to would already have a captain capable of raiding and slaving.

Unless the captain refuses to do it.

That was it. It had to be. But why would the captain refuse an order from Dirae? No sorcerer worth his salt would have trouble with an Obsidian officer unless what he was ordering was outside the chain of command.

He's working against the cabal! Or without their knowledge.

Now this was something Karpasic could use. He'd take command of the craftmaster's little band and help him build it into an army. When he was done, if whatever Dirae had planned worked, he could take credit as well as the conquering general. He'd be accepted back, his failures forgiven and forgotten.

On the other hand, if the craftmaster's plans failed, or if they looked like they were about to fail, Karpasic would sell him out to his superiors and lay the defeat at Opalis and the loss of the Westreach Army right at Evard's feet. Of course he would be believed, he was just a good soldier following orders that he believed to be from the cabal, not from some upstart traitor.

Yes, this would work out very well indeed.

"Well, it does sound like you could use a high-ranking Obsidian officer," Karpasic said, stroking his chin sagely. "I'm sure I could help you," he went on. "But I'm not exactly free to leave my current residence."

"Fear not, General," Dirae said, leaning forward in his chair. He picked up a small stone from his desk, a polished orb of pure obsidian. "I've taken steps to ensure your departure."

"If . . . ?" Karpasic asked, stitching the sound out.

"You will report to me, General, and only me, or I'll demote you to Fomorian scout. You will follow my instructions to the letter. No improvising or personal side trips."

"If you are going to be running the army," Karpasic said, "what do you need me for?"

Evard's jaw tightened and Karpasic tried not to smile. He was pushing, but the sorcerer clearly needed him, so he felt justified in claiming a few pounds of flesh. Besides, Evard might let something else slip.

"I will only be checking in on you the same way we're speaking now," he explained. "How you accomplish the objectives I give you will be up to you."

Better and better.

"All right," Karpasic said, nodding sagely as if he'd made some momentous decision rather than the only one he could make. "I'm happy to accept your terms. Now about my release?"

"As soon as I break the link that connects us, Eugene will give you a black stone like this one." He held up the stone in his hand.

"Eugene?"

"The construct," Evard said, clearly irritated at being interrupted. "Take the stone, then Eugene will hold up a second one. Touch yours to the one he has. That's all you have to do. Can you handle that?"

"I'll manage," Karpasic said, doing a credible job of hiding his excitement.

Evard waved his hand and the room vanished. Karpasic had a moment of vertigo, then the prison reappeared around him. He reached out and grabbed the bars behind him until the room stopped spinning.

The little creature reached into the leather bag around its neck and withdrew a polished black stone, holding it out so Karpasic could take it. Crossing his cell, he only hesitated a moment before reaching out to take the obsidian sphere from the little beast.

It felt cold in his hand, like a stone plucked from a mountain river. As Karpasic rolled it around in his palm, he could feel the hair on the back of his hand standing on end.

Eugene chirped and held out a second stone, fished from its bag. Karpasic wasn't sure what to expect, but since the Norgards would be pulling out soon, he didn't want to stay and see what they had in store for him. Holding the black sphere between his fingers and thumb, he touched it to its twin, held out by the creature. There was a popping noise, like a coal in a wood fire, and the cell, the guards, and the entire city of Opalis simply vanished.

† † †

The obsidian sphere on Evard's desk rose up a few inches, hovering in the air. The sorcerer could feel it resonating with its sister spheres far across the world, pulsating with the magic it was about to release. He could hear it thrumming, a sonorous note that began to rise in pitch. An immaterial shockwave erupted from it, traveling through the room and out of the spire into the dark, empty night. Of everything it passed through, only Evard felt its passing.

Light flared up suddenly, and the sorcerer shielded his eyes. When he lowered his hand, Karpasic and Eugene had appeared in his room, the former standing in his ragged clothes and ratty blanket, the latter scrambling to unfurl its wings as whatever it had perched on suddenly vanished beneath it.

"Welcome, General," Evard said, standing up to greet his guests. "Welcome to the Great Confluence."

Karpasic looked around, then tossed the black stone in the air, catching it with a self-satisfied grin.

"And what is the Great Confluence?" he said, dropping the stone on Evard's desk.

"It is a source of magic," Evard explained, "and the author of your salvation. From here I can create the army you will lead on your path back to glory."

"And why do you need an army, Dirae? What's this really about?"

Apparently the general was feeling peevish now that he was free. Evard had spent far too much energy recharging the transport stones. Even this close to a font of power, it would take him weeks to recover all the magic he'd used. That had the unfortunate side effect of turning half his hair white and making it impossible to send the upstart general back to his cell for another day or two to discourage his insolence.

"The circle is very upset with you, General," he said, choosing his words carefully. "Losing the Avatar sword was very stupid of you. They want it back and they've tasked me to get it. I, in turn, have selected you to lead my army and retrieve the sword."

"You're going to need a very big army if you want to assault Norgard," he said. "Assuming that's where that cursed thing ended up."

The general shivered at the mention of the sword, and Evard wondered what it had done to him when he had touched it. Why had it chosen to subvert Aren and not Karpasic?

It obviously needed someone with talent and skill.

Evard started to smile at the thought, but since he was stuck using Karpasic as a result of the sword's choice, he stopped.

"The sword is not in Norgard," Evard said. "In fact an army of a few thousand men will be all you'll need to retrieve it."

"And how many do I have now?"

"Two hundred."

Karpasic rolled his eyes and Evard hurried on.

"From the confluence, I can make as many Fomorian soldiers as you need."

Karpasic just stared at that.

"Where am I supposed to find two thousand or more slaves for you to make into soldiers?" he demanded.

"Take the soldiers you do have and raid the countryside," Evard said. "There are plenty of towns and villages—"

"Are you out of your mind?" he interrupted. "I could raid a hundred dung-heap farming towns and not have enough slaves to make an army, not to mention the fact it would take months."

"I don't have months," Evard said, a hard edge in his voice. "And you have even less time."

Much to Evard's chagrin, Karpasic smiled at that.

"It sounds like both our necks are on the block then," he said. "So why don't you tell me where the Avatar sword is, and what's guarding it, and I'll go get it for you."

Evard hesitated for a moment. He didn't want to give Karpasic too much information, but if the general was right, there might not be enough villagers in the vicinity to supply his army.

"The Council of Might has formed a joint army," Evard said, choosing his words carefully.

"And that has taken forces away from wherever the sword is being kept?" Karpasic asked when Evard didn't immediately continue.

"And they put Aren Bennis in charge of it."

Karpasic snorted, derisively.

"You want me to face an army made up of elite units from the nations of the west that's led by a man with intimate knowledge of my strategy and tactics?" he said, an incredulous look on his face. "Send me back to my cell. My chances of survival were better there."

"I'm not a fool, General," Evard said, sitting back in his chair. "I've been spying on the council, and as things stand now, their so-called army is a little over a thousand men. Just the minimum each member could send."

Karpasic's face split into a cunning grin.

"That means they're not elites," he guessed. "More than likely they're whatever soldiers their nations thought they could spare."

"So if we can muster a force of at least two thousand soldiers, you should be able to destroy the council army, retrieve the Avatar blade, and capture Aren Bennis," Evard said. "Alive."

A defiant sparkle bloomed in the general's eyes, but he nodded in spite of it.

"That still leaves us needing at least two thousand men," he said. "Three would be better, if you really want Bennis taken alive."

"I can transform as many slaves as you can bring me," Evard said.

"I doubt there are enough people in this area to matter," Karpasic said. "A few hundred at most."

"What about the raiders?" Evard said. "The remnants of the Westreach Army."

"Do you know where they are?" Karpasic asked, the old scheming look Evard knew suddenly back on his gaunt face.

Evard shrugged, noncommittally.

"Homer can find them," he said. "But finding them won't do us any good if they won't follow you."

Karpasic smiled at that, a wide grin that showed his teeth.

"Oh, they'll follow," he assured Evard.

"The last time they did that, it didn't work out very well for them."

Karpasic scoffed.

"They have the same chance you gave me," he said with a dismissive wave of his hand. "They can either stay raiding, in which case the

Council of Might will eventually catch them and kill them, or go back to the Empire and become Fomorians. We represent their only hope of redemption, Sorcerer. They'll follow."

Evard held the general's gaze for a long moment, then nodded.

"So be it," he said.

CHAPTER
19

Guests

The afternoon sun streamed in through the large bay window of the little cottage on the hill. Amanda laid aside her embroidery and gazed longingly out at the ships bobbing in the harbor below. She could see the sailors climbing in the riggings and moving about on the decks as the ships were loaded and unloaded during their brief stay in Etceter. She knew that when the tide went out, most of the ships would go, too.

She sighed and picked up her work, but just as quickly laid it aside again.

Amanda had never been on a ship of any kind, not even something small like a rowboat. Syenna had carried her across a few rivers during their escape from the Obsidian lands, but that was as close as she had ever come. The idea of traveling by ship fascinated her, like living in a house that went places.

She had listened with rapt attention as her new friend Sequana described her trip across the Sea of Storms on her way back from dropping Aren Bennis and her sister in Resolute.

The thought of Syenna made Amanda focus on the long dock reserved for the baroness and official Etceter business. How many times had she watched that dock, waiting for her sister to return? How many times had Syenna walked along it in her armor with her gear bag, waiting to leave on another errand for the baroness?

Someday, Amanda told herself, she would be down there, waiting for a ship to come for her. Waiting to do something important.

She sighed again and picked up her work. Who was she kidding? Syenna had her skills, she was a trained warrior and a scout without peer. The baroness and the council would always have tasks for her; important, necessary tasks. Amanda looked at the cloth she'd been embroidering. It was a complex image of a lighthouse rising up from rock with the foamy sea crashing against its base. Golden beams of light radiated out from the top of the lighthouse, and she'd done the whole thing on a light gray fabric so the colors would stand out. She meant it to hang over the top of the baroness's throne in the council chamber so when the baroness was seated the light rays would form a sort of halo behind her head. The baroness would love it, of course, and display it proudly, but it was hardly important.

She ran her hand along the smooth edge of the wooden hoop that kept the fabric pulled tight.

"We all have our talents," she said out loud.

Some are just more useful than others.

With a final, longing look at the dock and its bobbing ships bustling with activity, Amanda returned to her needlework. By the time her fingers began to ache and her eyes felt strained, the lamplighters were out in the city below. As some point, Sarah had come in, leaving a tray of grapes and cheese with a bit of dark bread and some wine.

Setting her work aside, Amanda rubbed her eyes until they didn't feel about to fall out of her head. She selected a bit of cheese and popped it into her mouth, savoring it as she sat back in her chair. Gazing out the window, she stared absently at the docks and the now lit lane that connected them to the city proper.

As she watched, three people suddenly appeared in the glow of one of the streetlamps. She thought that the man of the group must be excessively tall based on his companions. He was clearly older but still fit, his muscular arms and broad shoulders visible above a blue-and-gold toga that hung draped over his left side. He had a dark salt-and-pepper beard that was cropped close to his face and he carried a tall metal staff that glowed from the inside as if it held magical fire in its core.

Amanda knew the women who accompanied the tall man. They had both been to her humble cottage before and they were welcome guests.

"Sarah," she called as she watched the trio's approach. "Get out the good wine, we're about to have guests."

The words had barely escaped her lips before Sarah was there, removing Amanda's piles of fabric, thread, and needles from the sideboard and storing them in a cupboard. She covered the mahogany and marble top of the sideboard with a purple cloth and got out the liquor decanters and the leaded crystal glasses, arranging them in a circle.

"The baroness sent word that she was coming," Sarah explained in answer to Amanda's raised eyebrow.

"Sarah," she protested, raising her hands to push back her white-blond hair. "I've been working all afternoon, I must look a fright."

Sarah rolled her eyes at that, but before she could comment there was a knock at the door.

"I'll get it," Sarah said, sweeping out of the room.

Now it was Amanda's turn to roll her eyes since she was clearly in no condition to get the door. Still, just because she couldn't walk didn't mean she couldn't exercise basic courtesy. She set aside the decorative blanket she used to cover her withered legs and gripped the arms of her chair. With great effort and quite a bit of pain, she forced herself into a standing position and plastered a smile on her face.

"Amanda, dear," the baroness's voice came from the foyer, "I wanted to come by and see . . ." Her voice trailed off as she entered the sitting room and found Amanda standing to greet her. "Sit down at once," she barked.

Amanda's smile didn't slip. She and the baroness had done this particular dance before, and it pleased Amanda to defy her, and Sarah, and everyone else who frowned upon her pushing herself.

"I didn't know you could do that." The voice of Sequana, the Titan, came through the archway from the foyer. "Well done."

Amanda actually blushed at that. The only other person who had praised her for all her hard work defying her withered limbs had been the Obsidian soldier, Aren Bennis. Of course that was the moment her legs chose to give out and she collapsed back to her chair.

"I've told you before, Amanda," the baroness said, sounding just like a fussy ladies maid, "you shouldn't do that. No one expects you to stand, and the last time you tried, you fell and hurt yourself."

Amanda glared at Sarah, but she was studiously examining a spot on the wall where the paint had chipped. She made a mental note to discuss Sarah's loose tongue later.

"Just trying to improve myself, Your Grace," she said with an innocent smile. It was a look she'd spent considerable time perfecting in a mirror and had the effect of disarming almost anyone.

"Do not make that face at me, young lady," the baroness said, her brows furrowing as she moved to stand in front of Amanda's chair. "I absolutely forbid you to hurt yourself. Your sister would never forgive me and I have great need of her services."

Of course. Syenna has skills that are useful.

"Is this what you're working on?" the baroness continued, reaching past Amanda to pick up the banner from the window seat. She held it up to the lamp and ran her hand over the delicate work. "It's exquisite," she said, her voice awed.

"Thank you," Amanda said. She appreciated the compliment, but it was just her usual work, nothing special.

"My mother tried to teach me embroidery," the baroness said, not taking her eyes off the chair banner. She chuckled in a mirthless way and looked down at Amanda. "My father had other ideas. He taught me commerce and sailing and how to navigate by the stars." She handed the banner back. "Things my mother didn't approve of."

Amanda thought those things sounded quite wonderful.

"What brings you to my home, Your Grace?" she said instead.

"The sudden visit is my fault, I'm afraid," Sequana said. "This is my brother, Grannus." She indicated the tall man with the beard who nodded to her. "I told him the story about your . . . uh, pet . . . he so wanted to meet you."

Amanda looked up at Grannus in apprehension. To be honest, she'd expected this conversation sooner—dreaded it in fact—but Sequana's brother looked at her with kind eyes; eyes free of judgment or censure, just bright with curiosity.

"I'd stand up," she said, giving the baroness a sly look, "but I've recently been reminded that it's bad for my health." She held out her hand, and the Titan took it, dropping to one knee to kiss it.

"Lovely to meet you, my dear," he said in a sonorous basso voice. "When my sister told me what happened when she was here the other day, I simply had to meet you." He looked up at Sequana and winked at her before turning back to Amanda. "Would it be okay if I asked you to tell me about you new friend? Could I see him?"

Amanda nodded, then closed her eyes. Reaching out with her mind, she found Monk. The creature was asleep on her room's balcony. She didn't know how she knew, how she could sense him, she just could.

Wake up, Monk. I have some guests and they'd like to meet you.

The creature stirred and chirped, fluttering its wings and then swooping off the balcony. She felt his flight as he dropped down to the sitting room window.

"Open the window, please," she said.

Sarah crossed to the back window and pulled it open, stepping away quickly as Monk hopped in. Amanda resisted the urge to grin. Sarah hadn't exactly warmed up to the little creature.

Monk jumped up into the air, flapping its wings, and flew to Amanda, landing on the arm of her chair. It chirped and leaned its horned head back so she could stroke its head and neck. Amanda obliged him, then offered him a grape, which he took with his swift hands and ate with gusto.

"Fascinating," Grannus said. He hadn't moved from where he stood, but the lights inside his staff were shifting and pulsating, something they had not done when he entered. "How did you make this creature's acquaintance?"

"Monk," Amanda said. "His name is Monk."

"You called him that when you first met him," Sequana said. "Why did you pick that?"

"I didn't," Amanda said, stroking the space between Monk's horns on the top of his head. "He told me. It's his name."

"So how did you and Monk meet?" Grannus asked again.

"Monk was spying on your sister and I," Amanda said. "I didn't notice him until the sorcerer controlling him spoke."

"He spoke through Monk?"

"No," Amanda said. "It was like he spoke in my mind. I don't think he meant for me to hear him, but I could."

"Go on," Grannus urged.

"Well, as soon as he realized I could hear him, the sorcerer started talking to me. I realized he's the same one who tried to poison me, and I got mad."

"Poison you?" the baroness said.

But Sequana shook her head. "Later."

"What happened then?" Grannus said.

"I told him off."

"Is he still watching?"

Amanda shook her head.

"No. I . . . I sort of felt his connection to Monk and I . . . I made it go away."

She looked up at Grannus apprehensively, but there was no worry or fear in his face.

"He's tried a few times to contact Monk since then," she went on. "Or maybe he's trying to contact me, I don't know, but Monk won't listen to him anymore."

"Because you told him not to?" Grannus said.

"Because I asked him not to."

"Do you think you could contact this sorcerer if you wanted?"

Gooseflesh ran up Amanda's arms at the thought. She'd seen him. Sitting in some nearly empty room in filthy clothes and in desperate need of a shave. He didn't look much like an all-powerful sorcerer, but then the only ones Amanda had ever seen were the junior shapers, the ones who had failed so miserably with her.

"I don't know," she admitted. "I could try if you wanted."

The baroness looked alarmed at that, but Grannus' calm, smiling face never wavered.

"It might be useful at some point, but not right now," he said.

Amanda felt a wave of relief flow through her. She wasn't too worried about a disheveled sorcerer half a world away being any real threat through whatever magical channel Monk carried inside him, but he was still a sorcerer. Only a fool would think dealing with one of them carried no risk.

"Thank you, Amanda," Grannus said. "I appreciate your telling me about Monk."

It sounded like a dismissal, and Amanda desperately wanted to know what this interview had really been about.

"What do you think of him?" she asked, stroking Monk's short fur.

"I think he will be an excellent companion for you," he said. "Be sure to take very good care of him."

"I will," she said. "He and I are alike, cousins in a very unusual family. Both of us were something else once, until the Obsidians changed us to serve their ends. Now we're both free. As far as I know, we're the only ones of our kind in the world."

"May I ask you a personal question?" Sequana said.

"Of course," Amanda said, surprised that the Titan would ask permission.

"Why did the Obsidians spare you? I mean, when they couldn't make you one of their soldiers, why didn't they . . ."

"Sequana!" the baroness objected.

"Why didn't they kill me?" Amanda prodded. "It's all right, it's actually one of the few things about my past that I remember clearly. You see I was no good as a soldier, but my mother taught me to read. When the Obsidians found out, they put me to work copying books for them. There were lots of other Dross there."

"Dross?" Sequana asked.

"It's what they call their failed transformations," Amanda said. "The ones they still think are useful, anyway. The rest they destroy."

"So that's what you were doing when Syenna came for you?" the baroness asked.

Amanda nodded, a faint smile ghosting her face. She remembered the moment like it was yesterday. She was at her table copying a book about the first Avatar war when her sister had melted out of the shadows of a hallway and literally carried her out of Desolis. Amanda would never forget the look in her big sister's eyes when she'd first seen what her kid sister had become.

Shock, horror, and revulsion.

It had only taken an instant, and Syenna covered it just as quickly, but Amanda knew in her heart what her big sister saw when she looked at her. It wasn't any wonder Syenna stayed away for long periods. She blamed herself. She wasn't strong enough or brave enough or fast enough to stop the Obsidians from pulling Amanda to pieces and putting her back together all wrong.

Amanda wondered when Syenna would finally feel that she was enough to stop others from suffering the same fate? How far would she push herself? She'd spent two years as a spy in the Obsidian army. Two years where Amanda woke up every day wondering if that would be the day she'd learn that Syenna had been captured and executed. How much further would she push her luck?

"I'm sorry," she said, realizing she had spent the last few moments lost in her own thoughts. "I'm not being a very good host. Can I offer you some refreshment?"

Grannus grinned at her. His face was friendly and open, utterly without guile.

"Talking with you has already been most refreshing," he said. "But alas, we have more calls to make tonight. It was lovely meeting you, Amanda." He knelt down and kissed her hand again. "I now see why my sister enjoys your company."

Sequana and the baroness made their goodbyes as well, and the trio left. Amanda just sat, absently scratching the fur on Monk's shoulders for a long time. She couldn't shake the feeling that something momentous had just happened, but she'd be damned if she could figure out what it had been. After almost an hour of sitting and thinking, she picked up her embroidery hoop and went back to work.

CHAPTER 20

High Councils

Baroness Gianna Baden-Fox sat in silence as her carriage conveyed her home. Beside her, the Titan Sequana sat staring out the window at the darkened streets as they passed. Grannus, her brother, sat on the far seat, sideways on account of his size. He hadn't spoken a word since they left Amanda's home and that concerned the baroness.

It was bad enough that the Obsidians were spying on the Titans, and presumably the council itself.

Bad, but not unexpected.

More concerning was the creature, Monk. Amanda believed that she had somehow broken its link with the man who created it. Far more likely was that the sorcerer had taken control of Amanda's mind through Monk. If the Obsidian sorcerers could do that, what was to stop them from dominating her guards, her soldiers, or even the council itself? Perhaps Amanda's being a failed transformation made her susceptible to such things, but the baroness couldn't take that chance.

The carriage rattled off the dirt lane onto the cobbled drive of the baroness's estate. When it drew up before her grand entryway, she led her guests into the foyer, through the great hall, and into a narrow spiral stairway that led down to the wine cellar. It wasn't the sort of place she usually conducted business, but Grannus had insisted they speak only in a stone room below ground level. When she reached the cool, damp room, her majordomo had already laid out several padded chairs and a table with an assortment of alcoholic beverages and fruits on it. All the lamps had been lit and the floor swept so that, apart from the damp, it was quite comfortable.

"All right, Grannus," she said once she'd dismissed her servants and the door had been shut. "Why are we meeting in my cellar and why couldn't we speak before?"

The Titan held up his staff and the light that seemed to constantly move up and down its length rushed up to the top, flaring out into blinding brightness. The baroness covered her face, but as quickly as the light had appeared it vanished, leaving her with spots swimming before her eyes.

"We are alone," Grannus said.

"It is easier to secure an underground room," Sequana explained as the baroness blinked her eyes in an effort to restore her vision. "We've seen the kind of little creatures the Obsidians can conjure to spy, and walls in manor houses have many secret places inside them." She gestured to the racks of wine bottles and the stone walls. "Here, there is only dirt behind the walls."

"Fine," the baroness said, deliberately trying not to think about hidden spaces inside the walls of her boudoir. "What did you discover? Is Amanda in the thrall of some Obsidian sorcerer?" She spoke calmly and deliberately, but she didn't feel it. Quite apart from her affection for Amanda and her desire not to see the girl abused, she worried what Syenna would suffer if her sister fell victim to the Obsidians again.

"A moment first, Baroness," Grannus said. He held out his staff with the tip resting on the stone floor, then released it. Instead of falling, it hung there as if suspended from the ceiling by a string. A moment later tiny motes of light shimmered out from it, coalescing into the figure of a man. He wasn't so tall as Grannus, and he appeared younger, but the family resemblance was unmistakable.

"May I present my brother, Boreus," Grannus said.

The image of the younger Titan was transparent, and the baroness could see the wine casks and bottle racks behind him. Still, he seemed perfectly aware of them, inclining his head to her.

"I must confess that my brother is better at biology that I am," Grannus continued, "so I've asked him to review my scans."

"A pleasure to make your acquaintance, Baroness," Boreus said. His voice sounded small, as if he were terribly far away, yet it was loud enough to be heard.

"Have you had a chance to go over the data?" Grannus asked the image.

Boreus nodded. "The creature was clearly made from some other being, much like the girl in question," he said. "I suspect it was a squirrel or a chipmunk. Perhaps that is where the name Monk comes from?"

"That's all fascinating," the baroness said, working hard to keep a frustrated edge out of her voice. Half the time when she talked with the Titans their minds seemed to be far away, occupied with other matters. "But I'm more concerned with Amanda and what has happened to her?"

"As far as I can tell from the data Grannus sent me," Boreus said, "the girl is perfectly fine."

"Was there any trace of a mind-link?" Sequana asked.

"Yes," Boreus admitted. "But the link exists between the girl and the construct. The creature Monk is certainly capable of communicating mentally, but no other link was present."

"And what does that mean?" the baroness asked.

"It means that Amanda is fine," Sequana said with a relieved smile.

The baroness sighed as her worry lifted off her.

"I think it means quite a bit more," Grannus said, stroking his beard thoughtfully.

"I know that look," Sequana said, with a bit of an edge in her voice. "What are you up to?"

Grannus gave his sister a serious look, then shrugged.

"Think about it," he said. "Miss Amanda and the creature Monk were both made by magic from existing beings."

"We knew that already," the baroness said. "How is it important?"

"Because," Grannus said with a raised eyebrow. "She was able to free Monk from the control of a full-blown sorcerer, and she did it so completely that nothing of that link remains."

Boreus's image nodded.

"I see where you're going with this, big brother," he said. "You think that if she did it with Monk, she might be able to do it with other Obsidian creations."

"You mean their monster armies," Sequana guessed. "You think she can free them from Obsidian control as well."

Grannus nodded sagely.

"She seems to be able to control Monk directly," he said. "What if she has that kind of influence over the monsters?"

"Let me get this straight," the baroness interjected. "You think that because Amanda was able to free Monk from the control of some sorcerer, she might be able to do the same with the transformed soldiers that make up the Obsidian army?"

"Yes," Sequana said. "That is exactly what my brother means."

"And how would she do that?" The baroness asked. "She'd have to be on the battlefield to even attempt it. She'd be killed."

"Obviously, precautions would have to be taken," the image of Boreus said.

"Precautions!" the baroness shouted, her temper finally getting the better of her. "Exactly how do you propose to keep a crippled girl with no military training or experience safe in the middle of a battle? One mistake and she'd be killed. I refuse to allow that."

"With all due respect, Baroness," Grannus said, "I think you're letting your sentiment for the girl override your intellect."

The baroness drew in a breath to tell the officious Titan just what he could do with his suggestion, but Sequana put a restraining hand on her arm.

"I think what my brother meant to say is that we may have no choice in the matter," she said, her face a mask of trepidation.

"Our sister is correct," Boreus said. "We are all aware that the Obsidians are desperately trying to rebuild their lost army. If they succeed within the next year, we will not have an army sufficient to stop them—even if General Bennis is successful with the Army of Might."

"General Karpasic's army was some thirty thousand soldiers," Grannus pointed out. "The Army of Might is barely one thousand. If General Bennis is successful in stopping the Obsidian raiders, we should be able to petition the council nations to send more troops, but that will take time."

"If the Obsidians move before we are ready, their victory will be as inevitable as the tides," Sequana finished. "Our only hope of keeping them at bay might be the threat of stealing away their transformed soldiers. That might be the only thing that will buy us the time we need to fortify ourselves."

The baroness wanted to say something profane, to tell these arrogant Titans to hang their notion of using Amanda as a weapon. Unfortunately, they were right. The growing Obsidian threat would eventually compel the member nations of the council to work together, but they were a long way from that at this point and the baroness knew it.

"We don't even know what Amanda did to Monk that broke whatever control that sorcerer had over it," she protested. "How can we know if she can do the same thing with one of their monster soldiers?"

"We can't," Boreus admitted.

"The only thing we can do is let her try," Grannus finished.

"How?"

"There are transformed soldiers in the raider forces," Sequana said. "We must take Amanda to the Army of Might immediately and let her try."

"You are forgetting that she's a cripple," the baroness said. "With your transportation abilities still recovering, how is she going to make that journey? You'll go by ship to the Ash Coast, that's simple enough, but I guarantee Amanda's never been on horseback. The only way to make the trip is by wagon, and the supply caravans leave from Aerie."

"None of that is difficult," Grannus said. "Just time consuming."

"And I have a few ideas to help her get around," Sequana said with a mysterious look in her eyes.

The baroness took a deep breath and let it out slowly. She knew the Titans were right, damn them. She knew that if Amanda really could break the Obsidian control of their monsters, it might be the only chance the nations of Paladis had to survive. Worse, she knew Amanda would jump at the chance; literally, if the baroness wasn't there to stop her.

"All right," she said at last. "I suppose it must be attempted. I'll speak to her in the morning."

The Titans didn't say anything, just nodded their agreement. Grannus reached out and took his staff and the image of Boreus vanished.

"Don't worry," Sequana said, putting a comforting hand on the baroness's arm. "I'll go with Amanda and keep her safe."

"You'd better," she growled. "Her sister is the best shieldmaiden I've got, and she won't be pleased by this little stunt."

She spoke the truth, of course. Syenna would be in a towering fury when Amanda showed up at the camp of the Army of Might. Still, that wasn't the only reason for the baroness's reluctance. As ruler of Etceter, people were always trying to take advantage, to curry favor, or to leverage their relationships with her. Of all the folk of her acquaintance, Amanda was one of the only people she actually considered a friend. She would never admit it, of course, the Bonesteel Baroness didn't have friends, only business partners. That said, she had a knot of worry in her gut at the thought of sending her innocent friend into a war.

She knew it was a feeling that would not go away soon.

CHAPTER 21

The Raider

C aptain Nik Halik of the Westreach Army ground his teeth as he paced back and forth inside the monstrosity that passed for his command tent. It had been liberated from a merchant caravan they had raided several weeks back and was made of a canvas patchwork of varying bright colors.

He felt like some filthy transient.

Of course, in a real sense that's what he was, a vagabond without home or heritage adrift in a garish canvas boat in the nearly infinite grassy sea of South Paladis.

"You're certain it isn't worth raiding?" he asked Lieutenant Tam Vurgil. The lieutenant was a mountain of a man with a bristling black beard broken by a thick scar that ran across the left side of his face. He sat hunched over, as if he were trying to fold in on himself like a turtle retreating into its shell. The lieutenant was the kind of man who was comfortable with violence, just not with making decisions.

"No, sir," he said. "The scouts say their grain is still in the fields."

Halik swore, but that was all he could do. In the last month he'd had to move farther and farther north to raid for food to feed his warriors. Worse, he had to dart from one forested area to another like a rabbit hiding from a hungry hawk. If he and his men were caught out on the open plains by Resolute cavalry or by the suddenly effective Army of Might, they were as good as dead.

"All right," he said at last. "Tell the men to break camp."

"And where, exactly are we going?" a snide voice asked. This belonged to Lieutenant Ari Kilmer, a Drachvald woman with bronze skin and red hair. She wasn't large or intimidating to look at, but everyone in her command treated her with the utmost respect. As Halik heard it, she had a wicked temper and a fondness for a hooked fighting knife, a weapon she was reputed to be quite skilled with. Unlike Lieutenant Vurgil, Ari Kilmer had no problem with being an officer. She had been leading the raiders herself until Halik had arrived, and she made no bones about the fact that if Halik messed up, she would be leading them again.

"The scouts reported that there aren't many settlements to the north," Kilmer continued.

If this had been the Westreach Army, Halik would have had her stripped naked, tied to a pole, and publicly flogged for daring such insubordination. Those times, unfortunately, were long gone. He needed Kilmer and the stability she represented. With only three officers, including himself, he needed both her and Vurgil to keep the troops in line. The other side of that coin was that one slipup on his part, and he'd be the one tied to a pole and Kilmer would have the whip hand, literally.

He smiled as if her snide tone didn't bother him in the least.

"I've just had a report that there is a town two days journey to the north called Turi's Anvil," he said. "Their fields are bare, which means their stores will be brimming with grain."

"They also have a palisade around the town," Kilmer said. "We should pick an easier target."

Vurgil scoffed at that.

"They'll surrender if we give them terms quickly," he said, and Kilmer gave him a sour look.

Vurgil meant that if the raiders promised not to kill anyone and not take all the grain stores, the town would surrender, and he was right. It was a bargain Halik would have to keep, of course. If word got out that they'd offered terms and then hadn't honored them, every other town they came across would fight them to the last man. Halik wasn't worried that his force couldn't deal with a bunch of farmers armed with pitchforks, but he'd lose soldiers with each such encounter. It would be the death of a thousand cuts.

"Since I doubt we have enough wagons to take their entire harvest," Halik said. "I think offering them terms would be fine."

"And what do we do after that?" Vurgil asked, quietly.

"That's what I'd like to know, too," Kilmer seconded the big man's question.

"One thing at a time," Halik said, unwilling to admit that he had no idea. "First let's secure the food. Pass the word to break camp, I want to move before noon."

The lieutenants saluted, banging their fists against their breast-plates, then left, barking orders to the men almost as soon as they were out of the ludicrous tent. Halik sighed and slumped down in the uncomfortable chair that had come with the tent. He had no idea where they were going. They'd been following the foothills north raiding whatever towns they came across, but already they could see the tops of the Serpent's Spine Range in the distance. Soon they would have to cross into North Paladis or the Army of Might was going to grind them right up against those mountains.

So far, they'd been lucky. With the harvest season well underway, most of the towns and villages they raided had plenty of food for the taking. It couldn't last though. Halik had to find a place for his men to winter, a place where they could hunt enough food to feed an army, and he had to do it in an unfamiliar land. At that moment he would have cut off a finger for a decent map.

A scrabbling noise snapped Halik out of his thoughts. Some animal was tearing at the canvas side of the patchwork tent, trying to crawl under it.

"Get out," he yelled, throwing a convenient boot at the spot.

The boot missed and hit the side of the tent, pulling the canvas up off the ground and allowing the animal in. Or rather creature, for it was no animal but a smallish, furred man with horns and leathery wings.

Halik's breath caught in his throat. He'd seen things like this before. Obsidian sorcerers made them and used them to carry messages to their armies in the field. It meant that the Obsidians had finally found them, a day he'd been dreading since his escape from the Norgards.

The little monstrosity hopped up onto the writing table in the center of the tent and just sat, staring at him. Halik had heard these things speak before, but this one said nothing. Finally he forced himself to look at the thing, and when he met its beady eyes, his ridiculous tent vanished.

"Captain Halik," the black robed Obsidian who appeared before him said with an ingratiating smile. He looked about Halik's age, maybe a bit older, with unkempt sand-colored hair and light eyes. He stood behind a small desk, which looked remarkably like the one in Halik's tent, in what appeared to be a mid-sized bedroom.

"Who are you?" Halik asked, not bothering to be ingratiating or polite.

"I am Craftmaster Evard Dirae, member in good standing of the Obsidian Cabal of Sorcerers," he said with a polite incline of his head. "And I've been looking for you."

Halik wondered that the man had bothered, and he said so.

"You seem to think that you are in some kind of trouble, Captain," Evard said with a friendly smile that gave Halik the shivers.

"My soldiers and I remember what happened to the Knife's Edge Army when they lost almost half their force," he answered. "All of them were made Fomorians as punishment for their failure."

The sorcerer's smile didn't slip one bit, he simply nodded, sagely, as if he'd expected this explanation.

"I can assure you, Captain, that I am not here as the voice of judgment, but rather the voice of opportunity." The congenial smile suddenly turned conspiratorial and the hair on Halik's arms stood on end.

He paused before he spoke, choosing his words closely.

"I'm listening," he said finally.

Half of an hour later, Halik emerged from his tent and yelled for his guard.

"Find lieutenants Vurgil and Kilmer," he said. "Have them report to me at once."

† † †

Syenna shifted in her perch, high in an elm tree, trying to work a kink out of her back. From her vantage point, she could see the raider camp clearly. She'd been following them for three days now.

Of course they made it easy by always camping in the woods where treetop perches were plentiful. She didn't blame them, of course. If they'd made camp on the open plains it would have been child's play for Aren's cavalry to ravage the camp before they could mount any kind of a defense.

They needn't have bothered. Aren and his cavalry weren't anywhere nearby.

The noise of activity from the camp tugged at Syenna's waning attention. Being careful not to move quickly, she pushed a leaf-covered limb aside with her foot to get a better look. Below, soldiers, both human and Fomorian, were moving, rolling up bedrolls and striking tents.

Syenna wanted to drop down to the ground to get a bit closer in the hopes of learning their plans, but she didn't dare. Since the raiders were made up of the remnants of the Westreach Army, there was a chance she might be recognized if she tried to slip into camp. She'd already seen one or two raiders that she knew well, to say nothing of their leader, Captain Halik. Her status as a spy was known by Halik, and she had no illusions about what the raiders would do to her if she were captured. If they found her, she would make sure that she died fighting.

"All right," a man's voice said, closer than Syenna expected. Her tree was far enough outside the camp that none of the soldiers had come out that far when relieving themselves.

She looked down and found two soldiers moving beneath her tree. They glanced around as if they were afraid of being seen, but they didn't think to look up. Nevertheless, Syenna wrapped her hand around the hilt of her dagger in case she needed to jump down and fight.

"Now can you tell me what this is about?" the man said once they'd stopped. He was large, with big shoulders, big hands, and a big bushy beard, and he had to lean down to speak with his companion. She was small and lithe, but despite her size, she was clearly the dominant one of the pair. Both wore officers' armor, though it had seen better days.

"I don't like this," the red-haired woman hissed. "The captain isn't just putting our lives on the line this time. You know what happened to the Knife's Edge."

"Halik said the cabal has agreed to take us back," the man said. "You know what that means? It means we won't be wandering around this gods forsaken grassland waiting for the Resolute riders to find us and hack us into bloody lumps."

"Are you going yellow on me?" the woman hissed, grabbing the front of his breastplate and pulling him down, nose to nose.

Syenna was impressed. The man could have broken her in half if he'd wanted to, but he just shrugged.

"You know I'm no coward," he said. "But there's no glory in painting some field with your guts, or would you rather starve?"

The woman bit back whatever she was about to say, and released his breastplate.

"What happens if the sorcerers are lying?" she asked. "What happens if they change us anyway?" Her voice trembled when she said it.

"The captain would be the first one to go," the man said. "He knows that. He wouldn't be doing this if he thought the cabal's offer wasn't real."

"So we just march up to the fortress at Hilt and expect a hero's welcome? Are you really buying that?"

"I don't expect a parade," the man said with a shrug. "But if the Empire really is scrambling to build a new army, they're going to need experienced officers." He reached out and grabbed the woman by the shoulders with his massive hands. "Think about it, Ari. They'll make us captains, give us our own companies to command."

She fixed him with a hard stare.

"We've got more troops than that here."

"They'll also give us supply lines full of food," the man went on. "All we have to do is go to Hilt."

"You say that like it's easy. Here we've got protection, but there's no trees between us and the Broken Road. You know what happens if the Army of Might catches up to us out there."

The big man shrugged.

"Then we surrender," he said.

The woman took a quick step away from him, her face filled with anger. Before she could speak the man held up his hand.

"Think about it," he said. "We outnumber them but they've got cavalry. Even if we beat them, there won't be more than a few hundred of us left. What do you think the colonel at Hilt will do if we're all that show up?"

The woman nodded.

"He'll lock the gates and laugh at us as we starve to death," she said.

"We know for a fact that Resolute feeds their prisoners," the man said. "If it comes to that, I'll spend the rest of the war with a full stomach."

"What happens when the Empire finally takes Resolute?" she said.

"They won't know I surrendered," he said with a shrug. "They'll just take me back like any other liberated prisoner."

The woman suddenly lashed out, punching the man on his arm.

"I hate when you're right," she snarled.

The man leaned in and gave her a playful bump with his shoulder that made her stagger back. Surprised, she jerked a crooked fighting knife from her belt and lunged back at him, pressing the naked blade against his throat.

"Just because I let you into my bed, it doesn't mean you shouldn't fear me," she said. The action was violent but her voice was playful.

"Perish the thought," the man said with a grin. He leaned down, forcing the woman to withdraw the knife from his throat, and kissed her.

"Enough of that," she said, pushing him away after a long moment. "If we're going to do this we'd best get about it."

"What odds would you give us?" the man said as they turned and headed back toward the camp.

"We'll have to stop and forage along the way," she said. "It'll take two weeks to get to Hilt at that rate. If the Army of Might figures out where we've gone, we've got no chance at all."

Syenna smiled to herself as she watched them go. The woman, Ari, was right. Once the Army of Might knew where they were headed, they'd have no chance to reach the safety of Hilt.

No chance at all.

Chapter 22

The Lure

The parlor in Maradn's quarters under Old Market mound had been fully restored and showed no signs that she had utterly destroyed it some months prior. Still, as she paced around, circling the chairs and lounges that had been artfully placed to encourage elegant conversation, she couldn't help the feeling that something wasn't right.

"I'll have Maltius in here," she muttered to herself. "Have him do it all again."

The thought brought a smile to her lips. Her apprentice had been getting a bit too full of himself lately and Maradn would have to put him back in his place. She knew from experience that as soon as an apprentice began feeling their oats, rebellion would inevitably follow. Maltius would have to be brought to heel before any thoughts of disobedience or independence took root. She would need someone in the circle to watch her back once she ascended to the seventh throne. Acolyte Maltius Tren had to be hers, body and soul, before he could be trusted with such an important task.

She raised her hand, intending to blast her favorite couch to splinters, but hesitated. It wasn't Maltius who was the source of her irritation, he was only a convenient symptom. Maradn would have to deal with him, but there were more important matters that required her attention.

"Where is Evard Dirae?" she shouted to the empty room.

The fact that Lun had been unable to find the missing sorcerer and thorn in Maradn's side had driven her beyond frustration into a towering rage. If the filthy lizard didn't do his job and find that upstart soon, she had half a mind to have him cooked and served over rice.

As if on cue, an excited chirp sounded behind Maradn. She turned to find Jiri, Lun's twin, sitting on her perch. The little dragon dipped its head, showing its long serpentine neck. It was a conciliatory gesture, and Maradn could see the scales of Jiri's neck shifting slightly green, a sign that it was nervous.

"Never fear, my pet," Maradn said, some of her irritation vanishing. "I would never eat you."

She held out her hand, and the creature leaped off the perch, flapped its leathery wings, and landed on her arm. Jiri made a trilling sound in its throat and rubbed its jaw against Maradn's hand. Opening her fingers, Maradn scratched the soft spot beneath the dragon's jaw.

"And what news do you bring me, my pet," she said. "Has your brother finally redeemed himself?"

Jiri cooed again, giving Maradn's hand a final nuzzle before it spread its wings and flapped back to the brass stand that served as its perch. Once it was settled, Jiri turned its head to Maradn and their eyes met.

Maradn felt the link take hold of her mind. She knew that there was no sense of distance involved in the connection, but she always fancied herself flying across the intervening miles as the link between Jiri and Lun grew to include her. As her vision cleared, Maradn saw a small farming town from high above. Several of the houses were aflame, and Obsidian soldiers were piling sacks of grain and barrels of meal into wagons. The surviving inhabitants of the town had been rounded up in the central square and were being watched by bowmen.

"This does not look like my missing sorcerer," Maradn said. She felt Lun's consciousness shrink away from hers as if he'd been slapped. "Still," Maradn went on, "who are these Obsidians and what are they doing in North Paladis?"

She felt a surge of excitement from Lun as the pseudodragon dipped down, dropping into a tree on the outskirts of the village. Several soldiers stood apart from the raid, watching. The one in the center looked familiar, but Maradn couldn't place him and his armor seemed to be a mismatched collection of whatever had been available. Still, the dark-haired man in the armor of an Obsidian lieutenant was deferring to him, so he must be in command.

Lun came to rest in a tree near the group.

"Good," the familiar man was saying to the lieutenant. "Have everyone ready to move within the hour. Have the wounded ride, we need to reach the confluence by tomorrow."

"Yes, General," the lieutenant said, banging his fist on his breast-plate in salute before turning away.

Maradn smiled as she recognized the man in the mismatched armor. She pushed out a thought to Lun and the creature let out a cry causing the man to turn.

"Hello, General Karpasic," she said when the startled man's image appeared before her. "You're not quite the man I remember, but then I had heard you'd been captured by the Norgards and executed."

Karpasic's surprise turned to chagrin, but he covered that almost instantly with the haughty look common to military men of high rank.

"Lady Norn," he said in a voice that sounded confident and even. "It's been some time. Any rumors of my demise were simple enemy propaganda. As you can see, I am alive and well and serving the Empire."

"By sacking villages?" Maradn said with a smirk. "Seems too base a task for a general. And if your goal was to serve the Empire," she went on, her voice turning chilly, "you should have obeyed your orders instead of attempting to line your purse with the wealth of Opalis."

Karpasic put on a wounded expression.

"I assure you, Lady Norn," he began, "in marching on Opalis I *was* following orders. One of my officers found an ancient sword when we took the city of Midras. It was believed to be an Avatar blade."

Maradn had to work to keep the disgust off her own face as that cursed sword came back to her mind. She had been fairly successful in ignoring its existence, thus far. She didn't like the feeling she got in her gut when she thought about it.

"I know about the sword," she said. "How is that relevant to your disobeying your orders to march into North Paladis?"

"While we were resupplying at Hilt, the man who carried the blade went missing along with the patrol he was leading. I assumed they'd all been killed in a rockslide or something like that, but was later informed that he'd been captured and taken to Opalis."

Maradn nodded gravely. She was certain that Karpasic wasn't telling her everything.

"So you rushed out to reclaim your lost officer?" she asked, not bothering to hide the mockery in her tone.

"Not at all," Karpasic said, unfazed by her words. "The loss of men, even officers, is the cost of any campaign. That said, I knew that if the sword he carried really was an ancient and powerful Avatar blade, it must not remain in the hands of the Empire's enemies."

That hadn't been the reason and Maradn knew it. Opalis was reputed to be a city stuffed with gold, jewels, and all manner of riches; the presence of the sword and Karpasic's wayward officer were a mere pretense.

"And yet you stoked your troops with stories of Opalis's wealth," she accused him. "Got them to betray the Empire with tales of their share of the prize money from such a rich conquest."

"Of course," Karpasic said easily, without any trace of denial. "Opalis was a city that had never been taken. I needed my troops to be well motivated."

"And yet you still failed."

Karpasic's expression changed; just for an instant a look of white-hot hatred overtook him. He mastered himself quickly, but Maradn had seen it. She expected him to say something, to attempt to explain himself, but he just shrugged.

"The sword was lost on that day," he said after a long moment. "But I will have it back for you soon."

A nagging thought tickled Maradn's mind. Karpasic had to know his life was forfeit for losing his entire army. Why was he bothering to be seen serving the Empire? Why not disappear into the wilds of western Novia?

The thought had barely taken shape in her mind when she realized the answer. She'd seen the reports; Karpasic had been captured during the defeat of his army. The portly general wasn't the type to mound a single-handed jailbreak. He hadn't escaped his captors, someone had freed him.

Evard Dirae.

Dear Evard was working to get the sword back, and if he did, he would be granted his seat in the circle, maybe even his mother's vacant throne.

Maradn clenched her fists, digging her fingernails into her palms hard enough to draw blood. She'd worked too hard and too long to allow the whelp of that bitch Malam Dirae to usurp her. Action was called for.

She took a deep breath and mastered her anger. Now was the time for careful action, thoughtful action. Karpasic believed the sword would soon be his, and with it, he could regain his place in the Empire. If he believed it, Evard believed it. Karpasic might be an optimistic fool, but Evard was not.

That meant the sword was close.

If she could reach it before Evard, she could snatch away his victory. She would get the glory of saving the Empire, and her ascendance to the seventh throne would be assured. At long last, she would be Obsidian Eye.

And Evard would take the blame for the loss of the sword in the first place, she reminded herself. It had been his responsibility to retrieve it, after all. He would never be allowed into the circle and the line of Dirae would be broken, supplanted by the line of Norn.

Maradn smiled. She could see it all so clearly. All she had to do now was beat Evard to the sword—and she knew just how to do that.

"Tell me, General Karpasic," she said in an easy, offhand manner. "What has Evard promised you in return for your service? Has he told you that when he gets the sword, he'll be elevated, that he'll take his mother's place in the Obsidian Circle?"

Karpasic didn't answer, but he didn't need to, the look of naked calculation on his face told Maradn everything.

"I want that sword, Milos," she said, calling him by his first name. "The person who secures it for the Empire will gain great status. For Evard, it means he will be elevated to the circle. From there, he will be in a position to speak for you—to obtain the circle's forgiveness for you and put you back at the head of our army of conquest."

"And what if you are the one who obtains the sword?" Karpasic asked. His voice was casual, as if the question were merely a point of curiosity, but Maradn knew that she had his utmost attention.

"If I secure the sword for the Empire," she said with a smile she simply couldn't hide. "Then I will become Obsidian Eye. I will rule the circle. None will oppose me when I restore your rank, expunge your record, and set you at the head of the largest army the world has ever known."

To his credit, Karpasic didn't react, just stood listening. He might be a self-absorbed fool, but one didn't become a general in any army without understanding how to play politics. Evard had rescued him, probably from the headsman's axe, but that was in the past. It was the future that concerned Karpasic now, and he knew which of the two masters desiring his allegiance had the best chance of securing that future for him.

He inclined his head and touched his fist to his chest.

"And how may I assist you in obtaining the sword, Lady Norn?"

"Tell me how Evard plans to get the sword," she said. "Where is it now?"

The general explained briefly about the Army of Might and how his former captain was leading it, still in possession of the sword.

"Evard has set a trap for the Army of Might," Karpasic went on. "He allowed one of their spies to learn that the remnants of my army under the command of Captain Halik are moving toward Hilt. Bennis will try to catch them in the open where he can employ his cavalry."

"How is this a trap for anyone other than your man Halik?"

"Because," Karpasic said, "when Halik and his raiders reach the Broken Road, I will be waiting with supplies and men. Without the need to stop and forage, we will continue south to Blackblade Fork. Once there we will move past the fork and hide our force until the Army of Might enters the canyon."

"Then you'll flank them," Maradn said as the plan became clear to her. "In the pass they won't be able to use the cavalry and they'll have nowhere to go. You'll grind them up against the fortress at Hilt and retake the Avatar sword."

"That is the plan, my lady."

Maradn almost swooned. It was perfect. All she had to do was reach Hilt in time and then she and not Evard would recover the troublesome sword.

"Very good, General," she said. "I will contact you again soon, but until then continue with Evard's plan."

"There is one more thing, my lady," Karpasic said. "The man who carries the sword, Captain Bennis."

"What of him?"

"I want the privilege of killing him, myself."

Maradn shrugged. She didn't care what happened to the traitor Bennis, and if this made Karpasic happy, so much the better.

"He's yours to do with as you like," she said. "Just make sure you get that sword before you indulge yourself, General."

Karpasic saluted again.

"It shall be as you command, my lady."

The image faded and Maradn let the link between Jiri and Lun lapse. As it broke, she sent a warm thought of praise to Lun. He hadn't found Evard, but now he didn't have to, and better still now Maradn had a way to ensure her ascension.

It all hinged on her reaching Hilt within a fortnight.

Or did it?

"Maltius!" she yelled at the top of her lungs, causing Jiri to jump off its perch and go swooping around the room, chirping irritably. A few moments later, her apprentice came running up the stairs that led to the workshop below her apartments.

"You . . ." he panted. "You called, mistress?"

"Have you been down to the shapers today?" she asked, putting an irritated edge in her voice. She was still angry with him, after all.

"Yes, mistress," he said. "They report success, but they can't seem to make it fly."

"And what have they tried?" she demanded, knowing full well that Maltius would have no idea.

He shook his head, a helpless look on his face.

"I'm starting to think that you are as useless as the rest of the fool acolytes," she said, advancing on him in the slow manor of a stalking cat. "I chose you from among the others all because I believed I saw something more in you." She reached him and jabbed her fingernail under his chin, lifting his head until he looked her in the eyes. "Was I wrong?"

"N-no, mistress."

"Good," she said, holding his gaze. "Then go back down to those idiots and tell them that if they don't get them flying within the week, I'll be using them as bait to capture the next one. Do you understand?"

"Y-yes, mistress," Maltius said.

Maradn let her eyes soften and allowed a sensual smile to creep across her face.

"Good," she said. "Now go."

Maltius turned to go, but she reached out and caught his shoulder.

"Wait," she said. She'd been so preoccupied with her anger that she'd forgotten her own struggles. Her first attempts to create Jiri were marred by a similar problem. The constructs she made had wings, but lacked the instincts to fly. She'd solved the problem by adding a bat into the mix, bringing with it the knowledge of how to fly and the unfortunate habit of sleeping while hanging upside down. It hadn't been quite that simple, of course, she'd gone through many generations before she made Jiri. If the shapers started with bats, it would take too long.

She looked at where Jiri had settled back on the brass perch. A pang of white-hot agony tore through her, and she let herself feel it before she reached out to her creation.

"Come," she said. Jiri roused itself, flapping over to Maradn's outstretched arm. "Go with Maltius," she told the creature as she passed it to her apprentice. "Tell the shapers that they need a creature with flying instincts," she said, not allowing the tears that were blossoming in her eyes to fall. "Jiri has the knowledge that they need."

Maltius took the pseudodragon, then turned and fled. Clearly, he'd seen the tears in Maradn's eyes and wanted to be well clear when they broke loose. Maradn waited until he was gone before letting out the pent up scream of primal agony she'd been keeping bottled up. She spent the next half hour destroying her parlor. It vented her rage and would give Maltius something to do as penance for his poor attitude. When she was done, her rage had abated, but it was replaced with an emptiness and loss that threatened to squeeze the air from her lungs.

Maradn fled to her room, where she threw herself on her bed and wept.

CHAPTER 23

The Reinforcements

Aren Bennis shifted in the saddle for the umpteenth time. He missed his old saddle, he'd managed to break it in perfectly. Unfortunately it was probably now in the possession of some soldier of Norgard, taken as a prize when Opalis was sacked. He'd been given a fancy new saddle, one of Norgard design that was supposed to befit his station as a general. It was impressive enough to look at, glossy black with silver embellishments, but it felt like he was sitting on rocks.

"You're fidgeting again," Syenna said as she rode next to him.

He made a face but didn't respond. She seemed to be at home on any mount with any saddle, and in that moment he envied her.

"You're not still upset about Turi's Anvil?" she pressed.

He was, but that had nothing to do with his impending saddle sores.

"That wasn't my fault," Syenna said, her voice slightly annoyed. She gave him an apologetic look. "It really was a good plan."

"Yes," he said. "It was."

It was a great plan, one Aren had spent weeks implementing perfectly. He'd systematically removed all potential targets from Halik and his raiders, moving harvests out of towns and villages while keeping those who hadn't harvested yet from doing so. The result was that Halik had been driven north in search of ready food, and the only place for him to get it was the town of Turi's Anvil.

That was where Aren had set his trap.

The town had been emptied weeks ago and an inner palisade wall had been installed. When Halik's raiders showed up to attack it, Aren's forces would put up token resistance, then fall back as the raiders forced their way inside. That was when Aren and the cavalry of the Army of Might would charge, pinning the raiders against the outer wall. It really was a great plan.

But then the Empire had to go and spoil it.

Syenna had returned from one of her scouting parties to report that the raiders were pressing east, making for the safety of the fortress at Hilt. The only saving grace was that they would have to stop and forage for food along the way, and that would give Aren time to overtake them.

If he hurried.

He turned to look at the army behind him, strung out in a long line that rolled over the prairie grasslands like a long, black snake.

A very slow-moving snake.

He had cavalry, of course, but most of them were walking their mounts at the moment. An army could only travel as fast as the slowest supply wagon.

"There's time," Syenna said, reading his look.

"I hope you're right," he said, shifting again. "Damn saddle."

Syenna laughed at that, the sound coming out with a very unladylike snort.

Aren opened his mouth to say something he would doubtless have to apologize for later, but the sound of approaching hoofbeats interrupted him. A soldier was galloping up along the rear column, riding hard. He wore the armor of Resolute and moved with the grace of an expert horsemen.

"General," he said, saluting once he'd reined in alongside Aren and Syenna. "Colonel Tibbs sends her compliments and asks me to inform you that our outriders have sighted riders to the west."

Aren returned the rider's salute, then looked over to where General Trevan rode, surrounded by the various functionaries that kept an army moving. Aren, by virtue of his status, rode apart with only Syenna for company, an arrangement he found eminently acceptable. Nudging his horse, Aren approached the knot of riders.

"Are we expecting company?" he asked Trevan, then explained about the approaching riders.

Trevan looked pained, then turned to a horse-faced woman with mouse-brown hair that rode in his group.

"Lorekeeper Wren," he addressed her. "When is the next supply caravan expected?"

The woman reached into her saddlebag and proceeded to extract a disorganized stack of papers that she rifled through, dropping at least two that had to be retrieved by Sir Llewelyn.

"Here it is," she said in a nasal voice that set Aren's teeth on edge. "The next supply wagon should rendezvous with us in ten days time."

Aren thanked her as Sir Llewelyn handed the lorekeeper back her missing pages. He turned back to the Resolute rider.

"Tell the colonel to have a patrol go and escort them in," he said. "And have them be careful. I don't want any surprises."

The rider saluted, turning his horse, but Syenna moved her own mount into his path and leaned in to speak to him. After a moment, the young man nodded and rode away.

Aren wanted to ask Syenna what she had told the man, but now that he'd joined Trevan's knot of functionaries, they each seemed to have a dozen questions they needed answers to that very minute. Worst of all was Lorekeeper Wren, who seemed to have an insatiable desire to know about every facet of command and scribbled furiously in a dog-eared notebook whenever Aren spoke to her.

He sighed and tried again to get comfortable in his saddle. It was going to be a long afternoon.

† † †

The sky was just turning from blue to the pale pink of evening when Aren at last called a halt to the day's march. He'd pushed his men, he knew that, but he had to catch Halik and his raiders before they reached the pass that led up to Hilt. If the raiders reached that, they would be beyond the power of Aren's smaller force, having both numbers and terrain on their side.

"Any idea where we are?" he asked Trevan as a team of men finished erecting his tent.

Trevan shook his head.

"Once I hear from the counters, I should be able to pin it down to within a few miles," he said.

The counters were two men who walked beside the supply wagons and counted how many times the wheels went around. It was a boring but important job as it gave a fairly good estimate of the distance the army made in a given day.

"We'll be at the Broken Road tomorrow sometime," Syenna said from close behind him.

Aren jumped. His scout captain had gone off to get her people organized and set up pickets and patrols for the night. He hadn't heard her return.

"You sure about that?" Trevan asked, grinning at Aren's reaction.

Syenna nodded.

"The Serpent's Spine Mountains have a high peak just before the pass to North Paladis," she said. "You can't see it now, but there's one just off to the east with snow on it."

"Good," Aren said. "If your information is right about the raiders having to stop and forage as they go, we should overtake them day after tomorrow. As soon as everyone's eaten, I want an officers' meeting in my tent. We'll need to be ready for—"

"Riders coming," someone called, and a moment later Sir Llewelyn appeared.

"Colonel Tibbs is approaching with a patrol, sir," he said. "She's escorting several persons."

"The riders our scouts saw," Syenna reminded Aren.

"Very good," Aren said to the young knight. "Direct them here."

Llewelyn saluted and withdrew, climbing on his massive warhorse and heading out the way the army had come.

"I wonder who it could be?" Trevan said as they watched the knight gallop away.

It wasn't prisoners, Aren knew. Tibbs would have simply kept them at the edge of camp under guard and sent word about what she found. If it was a messenger, she should have sent him on with only a pair of guards. The fact that she was bringing whomever it was in herself meant that it was someone important.

That thought made him nervous.

An important visitor could be someone from the council with new orders for him. He was too close to the raiders to give up now. Of course, if the messenger, whoever they were, wasn't able to meet with him for a few days, then he wouldn't have to disobey any orders in his quest to catch Halik. If he were conveniently out of camp with his scout captain observing the enemy, then Trevan could deal with the messenger, and if it was nothing, he could signal for Aren's return.

Aren turned to Trevan, but before he could put his plan into action Syenna spoke.

"It's Sequana," she said, brightly.

Aren felt hope leave him. The Titan wouldn't put up with such a flimsy reason for being put off. He would have to see her and receive any orders from the council she might have for him.

The rumbling of trotting horses reached Aren's ears, and he looked back to see three riders at the head of a short column. The one in the center appeared diminutive compared to the riders who flanked her. Colonel Tibbs sat on her horse, Lightning. Her mount wasn't small, but she barely came up to the flanks of Sir Llewelyn's massive war-horse. On the far side rode the Titan; taller than Sir Llewelyn, she required a warhorse as well, a massive beast as black as the dregs of midnight.

Behind them came two other riders, though Aren couldn't see them very well past Sequana and Sir Llewelyn. A dozen of Tibbs best lancers escorted the riders, resplendent in their armor.

As they approached, Aren caught a glimpse of wispy white hair behind the Titan and groaned as he recognized Gerard Zhal, Lore-master to the court of Baroness Baden-Fox of Etceter. Zhal had a way of talking too much that made Aren weary just thinking about it.

He stifled a groan. Aren had been smiling behind his hand at Trevan's dealings with the insatiable curiosity of the loquacious Lo-rekeeper Wren. Now he would have his own personal busybody to deal with.

Beside him, Syenna suddenly let out a strangled cry and stood up in her tiptoes. Her face was ashen and her eyes were wide with shock. She stood there, speechless and gasping for air for a long moment, then slowly dropped back down to her feet. As she did, her eyes hard-ened into two dark points, her face flushed, and her hand gripped the hilt of her sword until the knuckles were white.

Alarmed, Aren quickly followed her gaze back to the incoming riders. There was a third person in the group that didn't belong to the Resolute cavalry, but Aren couldn't see her very well. She rode beside the Titan with her long platinum hair flying behind her in the wind. Aren was sure he knew her, but couldn't quite place her. Clearly Syenna knew her and—

Aren turned back to Syenna as he made the connection, not sure what to expect from his scout captain. Her face had gone from flushed to somewhat green and she wore a worried, stricken look. Clearly her initial anger had been overridden by concern and that was good.

Aren could work with concern.

"Let me do the talking," he said in his most stern, command voice. She looked away from the approaching riders, the spell broken, and her brows furrowed so deeply they joined in the center of her forehead.

"I mean it," Aren said, lowering his voice. "Not a word."

The red flush returned to her cheeks and her jaw muscles flexed as she bit back whatever she'd been about to say.

"Fine," she muttered at last.

"There'll be plenty of time for whatever you want to say later. For now, let's greet your sister with a smile."

Aren turned away just as the honor guard led by Colonel Tibbs trotted up. She dismounted, then pulled off her helmet and cradled it under her arm before raising her hand in salute.

"I found some strays following our dust, General," the little woman said with a wry grin. "Thought we'd give them a proper escort. May I present, the Titan Sequana, Loremaster Zhal of Etceter, and the Lady Amanda."

Syenna made a gurgling sound in her throat as Amanda's name was announced, and Aren almost grinned as he imagined the sheer volume of profanities she was choking back. If Amanda noticed, she didn't show it. She sat on what looked like a specially constructed saddle, designed to keep her withered legs in place while she rode. Aren wondered how well that would work, since Amanda couldn't use her knees to direct the animal, but now wasn't the time to ask. For her part, Amanda wore a smile of pride that was absolutely beaming and her blue eyes sparkled in the afternoon sun.

"Thank you, Colonel," Aren said to Tibbs. "I appreciate your diligence."

Tibbs saluted, then whistled to her riders, and as one they turned and withdrew. She then strode forward and took hold of Sequana's reins while the Titan dismounted.

"Lady Sequana," Aren said, moving to stand beside Tibbs while Sir Llewelyn took Amanda's reins. "To what do I owe this rather unexpected pleasure?"

"I'm given to understand that you have found the raiders and are currently in pursuit?" she answered.

Aren nodded and related Syenna's discovery of the raider's plans.

"Do they still have a large contingent of Fomorians?" Zhal asked, swinging down from his horse with a grace that belied his advanced years.

"About a third of their force is our guess," Aren said. "Is that important?"

Sequana gave him an enigmatic look.

"It might be," she said. "We need to speak privately."

Aren turned to his command tent and found it ready and lit.

"Right this way," he said, holding out his arm to escort the Titan. "Sir Llewelyn, would you assist the Lady Amanda off her horse and bring her to my tent?"

The knight moved to comply, but Amanda waved him away.

"Thank you," she said, "but I don't require any assistance." Then she pulled a strap on her strange saddle and the restraints that appeared to hold her legs came free. That done, she stood, swinging her back leg, still encased in the metal restraints, over the saddle and stepped down onto the ground.

Now that she was free of the saddle, Aren could see that what he'd thought were restraints were actually some sort of mechanical device that encircled the young woman's hips and ran down each leg, giving them support. He recognized the machinery, it was the kind the Titans had used in Opalis.

A gasp to his left pulled Aren's attention away from Amanda. Syenna stood with her mouth agape, her face a mask of warring emotions. After a long moment of shock, tears filled the scout's eyes and she rushed forward to hug her sister.

"Lets give them time to catch up," Sequana said, tugging gently on Aren's arm and leading him toward the command tent.

"Stay with them, Sir Llewelyn," Trevan said, then turned to follow Aren and the Titan.

† † †

Aren paced back and forth behind his tent in the dim twilight of the almost vanished day. What he'd heard was fantastical, unbelievable, and ridiculous. If he'd heard it from Zhal he wouldn't have believed it, but with Sequana explaining their plan, he had to take it seriously.

Which didn't make the plan any less absurd, he reminded himself.

"There you are!" Syenna exclaimed, rounding the side of the tent. Her expression clearly indicated she knew of the plan and the part Amanda was supposed to play in it. Aren had a sudden impression of a coiled rattlesnake shaking its tail. The warning wasn't lost on him.

"Order her to go home," Syenna demanded, marching up to him. "Send her home right now."

"You know I can't do that," Aren said.

"Liar," she spat. "You are in command of this army, if you forbid her from taking part in this madness then that's it."

"Yes," he admitted. "I could do that. I could tell Zhal and Sequana 'no' and send them packing along with your sister."

"Then do it!"

"No," Aren said, raising his voice for the first time. "If I do that, they'll only be back, but next time they'll have orders from the council for me to follow their plan, and that's if we're lucky. They might have orders to put someone else in command."

Syenna's jaw dropped open at that.

"You're worried about your command?" she gasped. "You didn't even want to do this and now you're willing to sacrifice my sister to keep it."

To her credit, Syenna kept her voice under control, but Aren could tell she wanted to shriek to the heavens.

"I *don't* care about that," Aren said. "But if I'm the one in charge of implementing this plan, I can do my best to keep Amanda safe. Someone else might not bother."

Tears rolled down Syenna's face and she grabbed the top of Aren's breastplate.

"She's my sister," she pleaded. "She's all I have, don't take her away from me."

"I didn't make that decision," Aren said. "Amanda isn't a little girl anymore, she's a grown woman. She can own a business, inherit property, even marry if she wants, and this is what she wants to do. She has the blessing of the council. There's nothing I can do."

A look of sick horror crawled its way across Syenna's face, and she released Aren, backing away slowly.

"If you permit this," she gasped as if the words hurt her to say, "then I'm finished. I'll quit right now."

Aren took a deep breath and steeled himself. He didn't want to do what he was going to do, but Syenna needed it nonetheless.

"No, Captain," he said in his commander voice. "You will not. You are a shieldmaiden in service to Baroness Baden-Fox of Etceter, to whom you've taken an oath of allegiance. The baroness has graciously agreed to grant me your services for as long as I require them, and you will fulfill that oath until I say you are done. Is that clear?"

Syenna looked as if she'd been slapped. Her jaw clenched but, to her credit, she didn't reach for her sword. She closed her eyes and mastered herself, taking several heaving breaths until finally she looked up at Aren with hard, cold eyes.

"Crystal clear, General," she said at last. "Is there anything you need from me at this time?"

Aren held her gaze for a long moment.

"No," he said finally. "You're dismissed."

Syenna turned and stalked away without a word. Aren watched her go, remembering fondly the times they had worked and served together. No one knew him, or understood him, like she did. If he was honest with himself, she was his only real friend, and he had just wounded her in an intimate, personal way. The kind of wound only a friend *can* inflict. One close to the bone.

"Damn it," he swore once he was sure she was gone.

CHAPTER 24

The Offer

Amanda sighed as she stood watching some of General Trevan's men make space for her in Syenna's tent. She'd spent the previous hour convincing Aren that she wasn't crazy; of course Sequana and Zhal did most of it. All she wanted was to talk to her sister, whom she'd barely seen since she got here, and as soon as she got free, Syenna stalked off somewhere in a towering fury.

"We're done, ma'am," the soldier told her. He was handsome with an angular face, dark eyes, and a dimple in his chin. Amanda smiled at him, feeling suddenly self conscious.

"Thank you," she said.

He looked like he was about to respond but his eyes shifted from hers to the side of her head and his face blanched. Amanda felt herself blush as she pulled her hair forward and over the tips of her pointed ears as the young soldier hurried away.

She cursed under her breath, trying to force the color from her cheeks. Sequana and Zhal were used to her, they understood, but she hated the looks others gave her. Most simply stared, shocked that she was a monster. It was the ones who didn't stare who really got to her, though. The ones who feared her, who loathed her, they were the ones who made her hide. They were the reason the baroness ordered her confined to her own home, cut off from the few friends she had managed to make.

She hated them. Almost as much as she hated the Obsidians for making her a monster.

A tentative chirp made her look up. Monk clung to the center pole sticking out of the top of the tent. She smiled with relief. Monk had followed her since they left Etceter, flying along behind them and showing up whenever he arrived. Amanda worried about him when he was gone and was always relieved when he reappeared.

Monk's dark little eyes fixed on Amanda, and he spread his wings, swooping down to her, landing on her arm. He nuzzled her shoulder, being careful not to poke her with his horns, and made a soft trilling sound in the back of his throat.

He could always tell when she felt low.

She smiled and stroked his favorite spot between his wings.

"I guess we do take some getting used to," she said, looking after the retreating soldier. She sighed and turned to her tent.

She was just about to duck under the canvas when she heard the sound of swearing. She knew the words by heart.

"Calm down sister," she said as Syenna stormed into view. Her face was flushed and her jaw was clenched so tightly that Amanda could see the tendons in her neck.

"Don't you dare tell me to calm down," Syenna said, forcing her voice to stay low. She reached out to grab Amanda by the shoulder but recoiled when she saw Monk. "What the hell is that?"

Amanda grinned, and stroked Monk under his chin.

"This is my friend, Monk," she said. "He's the reason I'm here."

Syenna grabbed Amanda's arm and pulled her into the tent.

"You can take him with you when you go," she said. "I want you out of this camp, right now."

Her face was angry, but Amanda knew that look. She'd seen it many times during the long days and nights when Syenna had carried and dragged her from the Obsidian lands. Her big sister masked her fear with anger. She did it well, but she couldn't hide her feelings from Amanda.

"I know what I'm doing, sister," she said. "I'm not a scared little girl anymore, and I'm not a cripple anymore, either."

She stepped away from Syenna and walked around her, revealing the metal legs the Titan, Grannus, had made for her. The frame ran alongside her withered limbs, starting at her waist where a thick band rested just above her hips like a belt, and went down to wide, flat plates under her feet that gave her balance. It had taken her a few weeks to get used to them, but now she could stand and walk as easily as when she was a child. Her legs would hurt if she used the support machine too long, but it was a worthwhile trade in her opinion, and she didn't have to share that detail with Syenna.

Her sister's face softened and she took a deep breath.

"I'm happy you can walk," she said, taking Amanda's hands. "But what Sequana and Zhal are suggesting is madness. It's going to get you killed."

Amanda stepped forward quickly and hugged her sister.

"It's going to be all right," she said, holding Syenna tight. "You'll be there to protect me. You and Aren and everyone." She released her sister but held her at arm's length.

"Don't talk to me about Aren," she spat.

That made Amanda laugh and Monk chirped loudly in response.

"He wouldn't send me home, I take it?"

Syenna didn't answer but shot Amanda a dark look.

"It will be all right," she said, hugging her sister again. "Trust me."

Monk flapped his wings and trilled, louder this time.

Amanda looked at the little creature and its mind touched hers. Something Syenna had said made him very agitated.

"What's his problem?" Syenna asked.

Amanda tried to make sense of the disjointed images coming from the creature's mind. As she sorted it out, one image kept coming back to the forefront.

"I think that he wants to talk to Aren," she said at last.

"**G**eneral?" The voice of Sir Llewelyn came from outside the command tent.

Aren set aside the map he'd been studying and turned just as the young knight opened the tent flap and stepped inside.

"Aren't you supposed to be keeping an eye on the Lady Amanda?" Trevan said before Llewelyn could speak.

"Yes, sir," the knight replied. "That's why I'm here. The Lady Amanda would like to speak to General Bennis."

Aren took a breath but didn't sigh. After Syenna's reaction, he'd expected one of the sisters to show up before long. No doubt Syenna had been bullying the young woman mercilessly since Aren had refused to send her home. He felt guilty about that, even though it wasn't really his fault. The least he could do was hear Amanda out.

"Show her in," he said.

Sir Llewelyn held the flap up and Amanda ducked under it. The mechanical legs she wore hissed as she moved, lending her withered legs strength. Aren wondered how much of the Titan's waning power they had spent to make them? His eyes shifted to her face. She wore a look of determination on her perfect face, but she smiled when their eyes met. Aren had forgotten how pretty she was. He absently wondered how much of that was her own natural beauty and how much had been done by the Obsidian shapers. No sooner had the thought crossed his mind that he cursed himself for thinking it.

"Hello Amanda," he said, standing and offering her his chair. It was the only one in the tent, after all.

"No thank you," she said, a shadow of worry crossing her face. "There's something I need to show you."

Aren raised an eyebrow, then nodded. Amanda whistled and Sir Llewelyn held open the flap of the tent and something large flew in through the opening. Aren thought it might be a bird of prey, but when it landed, he recognized it.

"Monk?" he said. "What happened to you?"

It looked like his old homunculus, but much larger and covered in short, reddish fur. Monk had been made by Evard as a way for them to keep in touch.

"Where did you get him?" he asked. "Did he have a message for you?"

Monk hopped from the grass floor of the tent onto the map table and scrambled up Aren's arm and then onto his shoulder. Trevan grabbed his sword hilt, but Aren waved him off, pulling Monk down to rest on his forearm where he could get a better look at him.

"He was spying on me," Amanda said. "Well, really, he was looking for you."

"This is the Fomorian you turned?" Aren said, remembering Zhal's explanation of the girl's presence.

"I wouldn't put it that way," she said as Monk began nuzzling Aren's arm. "Some Obsidian sorcerer was bullying him to find you, and I just told him he could stay with me if he wanted to."

"And he did?" Trevan said, looking at Monk with a mixture of fascination and disgust.

"What sorcerer?" Aren asked, though he knew the answer.

"Your friend," Amanda said, somewhat pointedly. "The one who tried to poison me."

Aren nodded.

"His name is Evard Dirae. We were friends, once upon a time. How did you know that Monk was looking for me?"

"Your friend told me," Amanda said, reaching out to stroke the top of Monk's head, between his horns.

"Do you have a message for me?" Aren asked Monk. The creature ignored him.

"He doesn't speak," Amanda said. "Not with his mouth anyway. The sorcerer talks through his mind."

That was new. As far as Aren knew, Monk had a very limited mind that could only store a few words. Still, this Monk was bigger than the one he knew. Its mind might be different as well. Of course there was only one way Amanda could have known that.

"You spoke to him? To Evard, I mean." He felt a bit queasy at the thought of Amanda's reaction to that. Evard was a sorcerer of the Obsidian Cabal; if he could really project his mind through this new Monk, he might be able to dominate or control whoever Monk linked to.

"Briefly," Amanda said. "He was very upset when I banished him from Monk's mind."

Aren allowed himself a moment of relief. Still, it could be a trick. Evard was both clever and cunning, he could have simply convinced Amanda that she had managed to exile him.

"Has he tried to contact you again?"

Amanda nodded.

"His mind is always seeking to contact Monk, but Monk doesn't answer. I could contact him if I wanted to, though." She looked up into Aren's eyes. "I could if *you* wanted me to."

Trevan looked sharply at Aren, but Aren ignored him. If Amanda was under Evard's control, this soft request was just the kind of play he would make.

There was only one way to be sure.

Aren set Monk back down on the map table and dropped his hand to where the hilt of the Avatar sword hung. He'd managed to break himself of the habit of holding the hilt. It had taken longer than he liked to admit. The sword revealed everything about people, not just their strengths or their desires, but their weaknesses, too, every shameful thing they had ever done. In the beginning it made him feel closer to his fellow men, but the more he relied on it, the darker everyone seemed. It would have been easy to use that knowledge to strong-arm others, to play on their weaknesses.

The temptation had been almost overwhelming.

Aren hesitated, then let his hand rest on the pommel of the Avatar blade. The presence of the sword rushed into his mind and the world around him became brighter and sharper. He looked at Monk as the creature sat, grooming itself on the map table. It had no sentient mind to speak of, maybe slightly more than an animal's intelligence. A nimbus of white light encircled the creature's head with a tether of gossamer energy that reached out across the tent to Amanda. She was surrounded by a similar light, but this seemed to radiate outward from her. Aren could tell that the connection to Monk came from Amanda, not through her from Evard or some other outside influence. In the moment he looked at her he also saw her passion, the raw desire to prove to her sister and herself that she could make a difference, that she could play a part in important things, too. Layered deeper within her were innocence, goodness, and a surprising strength. That was what had allowed her to survive the Obsidians and all the pain they had inflicted on her. He could see that, too, of course, the dark stain that wove over and around her, twisting her form and obliterating much of who and what she had been.

Aren let go of the sword and the world grew dimmer and muddier. He had a sudden impulse to take hold of it again, but he pushed the thought away. Based on what he'd seen, Evard had no hold over Amanda or Monk.

So what then should he do about Amanda's offer? There was a time when Evard had been his brother, in every sense but blood. The Avatar sword had warned him that Evard and the Obsidians would seek to destroy him, but what if it was wrong? He'd never actually seen Evard while holding the sword. He had no deep insights into Evard's soul. Was he willing to go to war against his brother without at least making the attempt to recover him?

"Your sure you can contact the sorcerer?" he asked her.

"Yes," she responded, an eager light in her eyes.

Aren looked at Trevan, who wore a worried look but shrugged noncommittally in spite of it.

"All right," he said. "Do it."

CHAPTER
25

The Sorcerer

Evard felt the energies of the confluence course through him.
They made him light, threatening to lift his body off the ground
and into the air. The feeling was heady, like being drunk. It almost drowned out the screaming of the slave bound to the wooden
table.

He looked to be in his mid forties, but there was still plenty of
strength left in him. Evard closed his eyes and went over the spell
in his mind. He'd only served as a shaper for a few years, but he knew
how to make satyrs and elves, and that would be enough. Sure of his
intent, Evard opened his eyes and released the pent-up energy within
him through the spell.

The symbols formed in the air above the table where the slave was
bound. They glowed with power, and the slave shrieked as his limbs
began to flow like a muddy river, lengthening and growing thicker.
Fur sprouted all over the body and horns erupted on the head, curling
around like those of a ram.

The energy of the spell faded and Evard collapsed to the floor. The
expenditure of the magic left him feeling light-headed and woozy,
and it took him a moment to recover himself enough to stand. When
he managed it, the satyr looked at him calmly with its large, dark
eyes. No vestige of the panic and fear of the slave remained.

The bands that restrained the slave hung slack on the longer, leaner
body of the Fomorian, but the creature hadn't moved or attempted to
get off the table.

"Who are you?" Evard asked.

"A loyal soldier in the Obsidian cause," the satyr said, its voice rasping and raw.

"What do you want?"

"Only to serve, my lord."

Evard pulled one of the slack ropes over the hook that held it in place and bade the Fomorian stand.

"Go through there," he said, pointing to the chamber's only door. "A soldier will tell you what to do."

The satyr stood, wobbling for a moment on its hooves, then headed out through the door. Evard waited until it was gone before staggering over to where the shardstone hung down from the ceiling. He dipped his hands into the bowl that stood just under the shard. The icy water burned him, but the power trapped in it flowed into his body, giving him strength. Back in Desolis, Fomorians were made by a team of shapers working together. Only the presence of the shardstone made it possible for Evard to do it alone.

He heard someone enter the chamber behind him.

"I'm not ready for the next one yet," he snapped.

"And I'm not here to bring you a slave, Craftmaster."

It was General Karpasic's voice, and Evard sighed. Reluctantly, he pulled his hands from the invigorating bowl and turned to face his visitor.

"What is it, General?"

"The sun is fully down," Karpasic said. "If your pet is right, then Captain Halik and his men will reach the bottom of the Serpent's Spine pass in two days. If we don't leave in the next hour or so, we'll be late reinforcing him."

"I know," Evard snapped. He closed his eyes and took a deep breath, forcing himself to calm down.

"You asked me to tell you," Karpasic said with an edge in his voice. "If Halik and the raiders have to wait for us, there's a good chance the Army of Might will catch up to them with their cavalry. If that happens, Sorcerer, our chances of recovering the sword will vanish."

"I know," Evard said, mastering himself. An errant insect buzzed past his ear and he waved it away. Another annoyance to further fray his raw nerves.

"How many remain?" he asked.

"About a dozen," Karpasic said.

"I should be able to finish in an hour," Evard said. He would have to push himself to do it, but he'd have several days on the road to recover. It was worth the risk. "Get everyone ready to move so we can leave as soon as I'm done."

"Already done," Karpasic said. "I'll have a wagon ready for you as soon as you're done."

Evard scowled at him.

"I'm not a child," he snapped.

"You can barely stand now," Karpasic scoffed. "I need you to plead my case to the circle, and you can't do that if you fall off your horse and break your neck."

Evard almost laughed at the thought of Karpasic having to keep him safe. The general hated him almost as much as Evard hated Karpasic. Still this stand-off of mutual self-interest was one he could live with.

"Fine," he said, acquiescing to the ride in the wagon. He doubted he'd be able to sleep, but he could at least rest. He turned his back on the general and plunged his hands into the icy water of the bowl again.

"Have them bring in the next slave on your way out," he said as the buzzing in his ears sounded again. It was too cold to be an insect as he'd first thought, so it must have been a side effect of pushing himself so far. "And have them gag the next one," he added. "I'm starting to get a headache."

The general muttered something vaguely acknowledging and left, his heavy boots booming across the stone floor. Evard put a hand to his temple in an effort to stop the buzzing, but it only seemed to intensify. The odd thing was that his head didn't actually hurt. The only actual symptom of his headache was the sound. Closing his eyes, he focused his mind on the noise. It was both alien and familiar at the same time.

"Homer," he called as the sensation continued to tickle his mind.

The homunculus appeared a moment later, soaring in through the open door and dropping down onto the edge of the stone bowl. Evard looked the creature in its beady eyes and felt his mind connect to it.

"It's about time you paid attention," a woman's voice suddenly entered his mind. He recognized the touch of Monk's simple intelligence and he understood. The blond woman was trying to contact him.

The urge to lash out at her almost overwhelmed him, but Evard quashed it quickly. He didn't know how she had managed to sever his link to Monk, and that was something he desperately desired to understand. Perhaps if he could keep her talking, he could find out.

"I was under the impression you didn't want to talk to me," he said. He chose his words carefully, wanting to appear reasonable and friendly. Anything he could learn could be useful.

Now that he focused on the link, an image of the woman began to form around him. She stood in a large tent that clearly wasn't hers. An armor stand behind her held a serviceable-looking breastplate and helmet of a style Evard didn't know. The woman was dressed in simple traveling clothes with her platinum hair flowing over her shoulders. As the image solidified, Evard realized something was wrong. The sister had withered legs, a result of incompetence on the part of the shapers who had tried to bend her form to the Obsidian cause. His eyes darted to her legs and found them bound in a metal frame. It looked uncomfortable, but appeared to let her stand without pain. Hinges and joints at the hips and knees of the frame presumably allowed her to walk, but Evard couldn't see how that could work without some form of magic to give it life.

"You sent Monk to look for Aren Bennis," the woman said. Her voice was calm, self-assured even.

Her mistake.

"Yes," Evard said in his most pleasant voice. "Did you want to talk about him?"

She shook her head, sending her hair flying.

"No," she said. "He wanted to talk to you."

As she said it, Aren suddenly appeared, standing beside her. He looked rough and tired and his eyes were guarded. Evard felt the urge to smile and decided not to resist it.

"Hello, Brother," he said.

"Brother?" Aren said, his face and voice stiff. "The last time we spoke, you called me brother. All while you planned to kill me."

"What?" Evard was genuinely shocked. At no time had he ever wanted Aren dead.

"You said we'd take the sword back to Desolis," Aren said. "That I would present it to the Obsidian Circle and be rewarded, but that's not what would have happened, is it? Once the circle had the sword, they'd drop it and me into the deepest hole they could find and fill it in with lava rock."

Evard opened his mouth to refute that claim, but something in his mind tickled his memory. Maradn was definitely afraid of the sword, so afraid that she was willing to work with Evard to pursue it. If she were willing to take the risk of his succeeding and gaining membership in the circle, then she, and the circle, must be very afraid of that sword.

No, he realized in a flash of insight. They're not afraid of the sword, they're afraid of what it represents—the Avatars. According to legend, the Avatars came from some other world or place, but what if they didn't? What if the sword transformed its wielder into an Avatar. It wasn't likely, but if the circle thought it even remotely possible, they'd do exactly as Aren suggested, though they'd probably cut him into little pieces first.

"I hadn't thought of that possibility," Evard said, finally. "But it doesn't matter, Brother. I now have the power to destroy the sword without going to Desolis."

"And what would that gain?" Aren asked. "The Avatar sword isn't a threat to the lives and families of the people of the west, the Empire is."

Evard's jaw clenched at that. This wasn't Aren talking, it was the sword.

"The Empire brings order," he said. "It forges peace out of chaos and lawlessness. Aren Bennis knew that, he believed it."

"Now I know better," he said. "Do you know what's happening in the east right now?"

Evard shook his head. "I've been here, looking for you, since Opalis."

"The circle is emptying Midras, as well as towns and villages up and down Midmaer and Grunvald. They're taking those people to Desolis to turn them into Fomorians." He pulled out the sword at his side. It didn't look like much, a simple blade decorated with strange writing and symbols. "They're afraid of this," he said, holding it up. "And they're willing to empty the eastern lands to destroy it. Is that the lawful order you propose? To have your fellow men twisted into monstrous forces without mind or will? Tools fit for nothing but service and war?"

"You asked what good it would do to destroy the sword," Evard answered. "Don't you see that the sword is what's forcing the circle's hand? If it were gone, if you were back in the fold, with me, they'd have no need to take such drastic action. The work could continue without such distasteful methods."

"And what happens when the council nations resist?" Aren said. "What happens if they defeat the next army the Empire sends. What then? Will they stay their hand then, or will they make Fomorians of every man, woman, and youth they can get their hands on?"

"You give the council too much credit," Evard said. "But even if they could oppose the Empire, there is a way to prevent the circle from acting rashly."

He held Aren's gaze for a long moment, then went on when no response was forthcoming.

"If I recover the sword and destroy it," he said, "then my elevation to the circle will be assured. I will take my mother's place on the seventh throne as the Obsidian Eye. The circle will be mine to control, and I will put you in charge of our army of conquest. You know the nations of the Council of Might. You will know how to bring them into the Empire, by diplomacy or by force. The methods will be up to you. Together we will wipe away the stains of chaos, we will build a society of peace and order that will stand for a thousand years."

"And how much blood will we have to spill to make that happen?" Aren asked.

"That's not fair," Evard protested. "You of all people know that chaos is the natural state of men. Order is an act of will. Order must be imposed, and there are always people who will resist such an imposition. That is human nature and nothing you or I do will change that. What you have to ask yourself is how much blood will spill if the Empire were not a threat? The bickering nations of the Council of Might have been warring and killing each other since the days of the Shard Fall."

Aren actually smiled at that.

"Well, on that front, the Empire has already brought a semblance of order to the west. The loss of Opalis shocked the council into action. They're actually working together now."

"I suspect that's more due to you," Evard said. "I've been watching the pitiful army they gave you. You've done marvelous work turning them into a fighting force. Just imagine what you could do with the circle behind you, with the whole Empire behind you."

"I don't want to lead an army of conquerors in an orgy of blood and destruction across the continent," Aren said.

"No," Evard said. "You never did. But you do want the children of the continent to live in a world where their fathers and mothers aren't raped and killed by whatever raider gang happens to claim the land they live on. That's what my friend Aren Bennis wants. I don't know what the Avatar sword wants, but you need to ask yourself what will happen if the Empire is stopped? The council might work together for a few years, a decade at most, and then they'll be right back to raiding and killing each other."

"You may be right," Aren said after a brief pause. "But I'm not willing to make war on farmers and merchants to stop something that might happen. Far better to spend my energy helping the council to get stronger, to get them working together so that their little conflicts become less important."

Evard felt sick to his stomach. This is the kind of thing the Avatars of old were known to say and do, the result of their ridiculous and outmoded virtues. For the first time Evard felt real fear that his friend might actually be lost.

"I don't know what's happened to you, Aren," he said at last. "I suspect that sword is poisoning your mind. I swear to you that I will find you, and when I do I will take that sword and I will destroy it. I only hope that breaks whatever hold it has on you, Brother."

Aren chuckled mirthlessly at that.

"The only thing the sword has done is to show me some uncomfortable truths," he said. "I thought it was a curse. No, that's not true. I know it's a curse, but it's not one that controls me."

"I guess we'll find out when we meet."

"I guess so," Aren said, holding up an open hand in salute. "Farewell . . . Brother."

The girl raised a hand to her lips and blew him a kiss, then she, Aren, and the tent vanished.

Evard jerked his numb hands out of the icy water. They burned with cold, and he summoned a small magic to warm himself. He didn't want to waste any of the magic he'd recovered, but he needed to be able to feel his fingers. He had work to do and precious little time left to do it.

Behind him came the muffled grunting of a gagged and bound slave. Evard knew that what he was doing would further alienate Aren from him, but what choice did he have? What choice did anyone have in the face of the Obsidian Prophecy? The world needed order, and the Obsidians were charged with bringing it. Evard knew the Prophecy by heart, his own ancestor had received it from the mouth of the first Obsidian Eye and written it with his own hand.

The Prophecy was undeniable, and Evard would do whatever he must to follow it.

"Hold on, Brother," he said to himself again. This time the words weren't the former confident declaration but rather a desperate plea. He spoke against the darkness of his own thoughts. Thoughts that his oldest friend might, in fact, be beyond saving, and that he, Evard, would have to kill him.

Thrusting that thought from his mind with a curse, Evard pushed up the sleeves of his robe and turned back to the table and its cowering slave. There was work to be done, and he would do whatever it took, pay whatever price the Prophecy demanded to achieve his goals. If that price included the life of Aren Bennis, then he would pay that, too, but not before he did everything in his power to prevent it.

CHAPTER 26

The Path of the Sword

Aren felt the connection between himself and Evard break, and the image of his friend disappeared. On the map table, Monk went back to grooming himself, oblivious to the conversation that had just taken place. He looked over to Amanda and found her twisting uncomfortably in the metal girdle that supported her weight and connected her to the leg braces.

"It hurts if I stand for too long," she answered his unasked question.

"Zhal and Sequana think sending you into the thick of a battle is a good idea," he said.

"And you don't." It was a statement, not a question. "You and my sister."

"War is a place for soldiers," Aren said. "Not civilians."

"No one is born a soldier, General," she said with a slightly mocking smile. "Just like no one is born a general."

Aren chuckled at that. She had a point, but it was a perspective only a civilian could have.

"One thing that generals understand is that when they send men and women out onto the field of battle, they're sending many of them to their deaths. It is a simple reality that no amount of hope or desire can change."

A cloud of doubt covered Amanda's face, but she held his gaze and slowly nodded.

"I understand that," she said. "But I've been around the baroness and her advisors, a bit more than I think they realize, and I've heard them talking. The Obsidians are building an entire army of monsters."

Her breath caught in her throat, and she closed her eyes for a moment. "They're going to take innocent people and do to them what they did to me, except it will be worse. At least I'm still me. I remember most of my past, I remember my parents, I remember Syenna." She paused to take another shuddering breath. "The people the Obsidians transform into soldiers will just be mindless slaves, everything they were will be gone."

Tears were sparkling in her eyes now, but her voice was steady. Aren put a gentle hand on her shoulder.

"Joining us on the battlefield isn't going to change any of that," he said.

"I know." She wiped away the tears with her sleeve, then looked back a him with determination. "But the Obsidians are counting on that army to win. If I can rob them of their victims, even if I can just break the sorcerer's hold on them, like I did for Monk, then we might have a chance to win. We might live. Syenna might live."

She grasped Aren's hand on her shoulder and squeezed it tight.

"If I have to die for that, it's a price I'm willing to pay."

Aren didn't have to take hold of the Avatar sword to see the truth of Amanda's words. Her passion rang from every syllable like a bell. He'd had his doubts when the loremaster and the Titan had presented their plan, but he knew they'd just override him if he refused. He still had doubts, sending an untrained young woman into battle with the Obsidians was likely to get her killed. But, she'd been right. If the Obsidians succeeded in building their Fomorian army, no amount of cooperation between the council nations would save them. Amanda was his best chance.

"All right," he said, squeezing her shoulder. "I guess I have a new soldier."

She smiled but didn't respond.

"Go get some rest," he ordered. "I don't want you to get injured by using those legs too much."

Amanda gave a clumsy salute.

"Yes, General," she said, only half joking, then turned and left the tent.

Aren watched her go, then stood, staring at the tent flap for a long time after. He wasn't happy about putting Amanda in harm's way, to say nothing of what it would do to Syenna. That wasn't what bothered him, though. Reaching down, he drew out the Avatar sword and held it flat on his palms. The silver script that ran down the blade shimmered and changed even as he watched it. The triune sword symbol on the pommel glowed softly when the writing shifted, something he hadn't noticed before.

The three-sword design appeared on the pommel, the cross guard, and the blade itself. The ones on the pommel were arranged in a triangular pattern, each seeming to follow the other, round and round to infinity. The cross guard, however, had one blade on each arm of the guard and one on the langet that ran up over the blade. Since his escape from Opalis, the three swords on the pommel had changed from black to silver. Now one of the blades on the cross guard was silver as well.

Aren didn't know when the sword symbol had changed, and that bothered him. That and something Evard had said.

I don't know what the Avatar Sword wants, he had said, implying that Aren was being controlled by it. Aren knew that wasn't true; the sword showed him truth, but as far as he'd been able to verify, it didn't color that truth. But what if it didn't have to? What if the sword only showed him the truth it wanted him to see? After all, it still stubbornly refused to show him anything when he looked at Syenna. What if it had its own agenda.

"What is it you want?" he asked aloud.

It had shown him Amanda's strength and determination. Was it really his decision to let her take the field of battle, or was the sword leading him around by the nose?

"No," he said out loud again. He'd made that decision not because of what the sword showed him, but because it was right. "Amanda deserves the chance to fight to protect the people she loves, just like anyone else. Even if it costs her life. It's only just."

Aren suddenly felt the sword tingle in his hands, as if he'd tapped the blade on something hard. As he watched, the black coloring on the second sword symbol on the cross guard seemed to drain away, revealing bright silver beneath.

If Aren hadn't been looking right at it when it happened, he might not have believed it.

"So, are you telling me I made the right decision?" he asked the sword. "Or the one you wanted."

If the sword heard him, indeed if it were even capable of hearing him, it made no response.

"Fine," Aren said, tossing the whole thing onto the map table. "Keep your secrets."

He paced around the tent for the better part of an hour, going over everything in his mind, but he could make nothing more of it than he already knew. What he was sure of was that the Army of Might would have to be up early and on the hunt if they wanted to catch Halik. With that thought firmly in mind, he put out the lamps and retired to his pallet.

† † †

The moon was up when Aren awoke, and it illuminated the walls and roof of his tent with enough light to see by. He wasn't sure what woke him, but he had the impression it was a sound. Dropping his hand to the side of his sleeping pallet, he found his scabbard, right where he always put it. When Aren lifted it, however, it was far too light.

His sword was on the map table, right where he'd left it.

Movement caught his eye, and he clutched the empty scabbard, ready to use it as a club if necessary.

A figure emerged from the shadows on the far side of the tent's center pole. Aren felt his muscles tense, ready to spring as soon as the figure drew close enough, but whoever it was didn't approach. As they moved, Aren caught the silhouette of a womanly figure. Long, curly hair spilled down over her shoulders, obscuring her identity in the dim light.

"Who goes there?" Aren asked, sitting up.

The woman turned to look at him; as she did so, Aren caught the flash of blue eyes in a pale face. She raised her finger to her lips in a silencing gesture, then turned to the map table.

"Wait," Aren cautioned as she wrapped her hand around the hilt of the Avatar sword. Up to now, he was the only one who could bear its touch, but the woman picked it up easily. She traced her finger along the engraving that had turned silver earlier, then set the sword back down. Unsatisfied, she moved the sword a bit to the left, then let it go.

"Who are you?"

The woman didn't answer, but moved instead to the tent flap. She pulled it open, and bright moonlight streamed into the tent from outside, revealing her fully. Aren knew that face, he'd seen it before, just never this close.

The first time he'd seen her, she'd looked afraid and ragged. Dressed in the robes of a Midras priestess, he'd followed her through the ruins of the temple in a desperate race to escape the Midras Guardians. That was right before he'd found the Avatar blade.

The next time he saw her was on the walls of Opalis. She'd led him around the walls to the place where the Obsidians would mount their assault. If he hadn't been there, the Opalis Legion would never have been ready for the Westreach Army's rush.

"What are you trying to tell me this time?" he asked her.

The woman didn't answer. She smiled, her teeth almost iridescent in the moonlight, and nodded at the sword. Aren glanced at the sword, then back, but the woman had vanished and the tent flap fell back in place, plunging the tent into darkness.

"Wait," Aren called, leaping to his feet. He took a step, but his feet tangled in his blanket and he fell in a heap.

When he managed, with a great deal of cursing, to free himself, Aren darted to the tent flap and threw it aside. The brightness of the moonlight in contrast to the darkness of his tent blinded him for a moment, and when his vision cleared his visitor was nowhere to be seen. The only sign of life was a young soldier warming his hands over a small fire. He looked up when Aren stepped out of the tent, then straightened to stand at attention.

"Is everything all right, General?" he asked.

Aren almost asked him if he'd seen the woman leave his tent. Based on previous experience, he knew what the answer would be.

"What's your name, son?"

"Armsman Barish, sir."

"Go back to your fire, Armsman Barish," Aren said, turning back to his tent. "It's cold out tonight."

Heeding his own words, Aren crossed to his tent and threw his blanket over his shoulders. He lit the lamp hanging on the center pole of the tent, then turned to the map table. The sword lay there where the woman had left it.

"So it wasn't a dream," he said, more to convince himself than anything else.

He reached for the sword, but hesitated. The woman had made a fuss about putting it in just the right position. Aren doubted that was an accident. Walking around the table, he noted the sword from every angle. Nothing seemed to have changed and he knew from experience that the symbols were the same on both sides. When the sword on the cross guard changed, its twin on the back would have changed as well.

Ignoring the sword for the moment, Aren examined the rest of the table. Several of his maps were still out from when he and General Trevan had been planning earlier. The sword rested across them, but its point lay on a map of Hilt and its environs. Careful not to disrupt the sword or the map of Hilt, Aren removed the others and returned them to the round cases that protected them.

The area where the sword point rested didn't look like anything, just a nameless bit of mountain well north of the pass and the fortress at Hilt. Still, Aren doubted his mysterious benefactor made the trip for nothing, and just because he didn't know what might be in that remote stretch of mountain range didn't mean that nobody did.

"Armsman Barish," he called out. A moment later the young man appeared at the tent flap. "Go and fetch Captain Syenna," he said. "You'll find her."

"At once, General," Armsman Barish said, then he was off like a shot.

† † †

Let me see if I understand this," Loremaster Zhal said, rubbing the sleep from his eyes. "You had a dream that a young woman came to your tent and played with your sword?"

Syenna snickered, hiding a grin behind her hand.

"That's not exactly how I would summarize it," Aren said, casting his chief scout a withering look. "But accurate."

"And you've seen this young woman before," Sequana said. "In Midras and again in Opalis."

"That's right," Aren confirmed. "I don't know who, or even what she is, but she seemed tied up with me and the sword."

"I've seen her, too," Syenna said.

Aren looked at her sharply. This was the first he'd heard of that; in fact, she vehemently denied having seen her when they were in Midras.

"It was after the raider attack," she explained. "I thought I saw her standing behind you when you came to visit me."

Aren remembered her asking about the woman during that conversation, but Syenna didn't say anything about having seen her.

"She had her hand on your shoulder," Syenna went on, then shrugged. "I thought it was strange, but when I looked directly at her, she was gone."

Aren knew that feeling.

"So," Zhal said, standing in his nightrobe and beginning to pace around the tent. "This woman is what? Directing you from behind the scenes?"

Aren shrugged. He didn't feel like he'd been influenced in any way.

"I don't think it's quite to that extent," he said. "In every interaction I've had with her so far, all she's done is to help me get to the right place at the right time."

Sequana moved over to the map table and looked down at the spot Aren had marked with a colored pebble. Unlike Zhal, who had answered his summons in his nightrobe, Sequana wore a loose-fitting shirt and riding breeches.

"So, this is the right place, then?" she asked.

"I don't know," Aren admitted.

"Yes," Syenna said at the same moment.

Aren rolled his eyes at her, which she ignored. She crossed to the map and indicated the spot.

"When I escorted General Bennis from Hilt—" she began.

"You mean when you brained me, drugged me, and abducted me," Aren corrected her.

Syenna shot him an amused look and continued, ignoring his comment. "This is where the secret road through the Blackblade Mountains comes out. Since Aren was drugged at the time"—she smirked at him—"he couldn't possibly know that."

"So," Zhal said, still pacing. "Whoever this young woman is, and whatever powers she represents, she or they want you to go to Hilt through a secret pass."

"The Sulfurous Road," Syenna said. "That's what it's called."

"Sounds lovely," Aren said. "And yes," he continued, turning to Zhal, "that's exactly what she's telling us."

"And if you refuse?" Sequana asked.

Aren just shook his head. He had no idea what refusing this particular message might involve.

"I couldn't even guess," he said.

"The future is always unknowable," Zhal said, coming over to join the group around the map table. "But we can take a few clues from the past. If you hadn't followed this woman in Midras, what would have happened?"

"We'd probably be dead," Syenna said. "We were being chased by Midras Guardians at the time."

Aren nodded his agreement.

"Even if we had survived, I would have been with General Karpasic when he attacked Opalis. They'd have broken through the Storm Gate and sacked the city."

"And when they discovered Opalis had no treasure," Syenna added, "they'd have murdered everyone."

"Yes," Sequana agreed darkly. "So far, I'd say it's a very good thing you saw this woman, whoever she is."

"That's my reading of the facts," Zhal said, stroking his bearded chin. "Do you suppose she's the ghost of an Avatar?" he asked, his voice full of wonder. "Maybe the last person to carry the sword?"

"It doesn't matter," Aren said. "What does matter is this." He indicated the colored stone. "Do we take the Army of Might here or do we keep following Halik and the raiders?"

"The Sulfurous Road is a narrow walkway up the side of a cliff," Syenna said, shaking her head. "We couldn't take an army through there."

"How big a force could you take?" Zhal asked with a twinkle in his eye. Aren had seen that look before; it was the one that sent him to Opalis, put him in charge of the Army of Might, and brought Amanda to him.

"What are you thinking, Loremaster?" he said, not sure he wanted the answer.

"Does this Sulfurous Road go anywhere other than the fortress at Hilt?" Zhal asked Syenna.

"No," she said. "They built the fortress on top of the other end. If you take this road, the only place to go is the fortress."

Zhal smiled and exchanged knowing looks with Sequana. The Titan didn't respond, but raised an eyebrow tentatively. Aren was getting sick of the pair of them always being two steps ahead of him.

"You're thinking the only reason for the woman to direct us there is to lead a small force inside the fortress and take it," Aren guessed.

"How many soldiers would you need to do that?" Sequana asked.

"As many as I can take," he said, looking to Syenna.

"Fifty," she said without hesitation. "Any more and we'll risk being seen or being too spread out along the road to be effective."

Aren thought about it for a long moment. Fifty men against the fortress's garrison was likely to be suicide. They'd be outnumbered at least three to one.

Unless I can even the odds a bit.

"There's no way I can take the fortress with only fifty men," he said at last.

"Then why are you being directed there?" Sequana asked.

"There must be a way," Zhal said.

"The Empire is still building the fortress," Aren said. "The last time I was there, they had hundreds of slaves housed in the dungeons below the fortifications."

A slow smile spread across Syenna's face, and she nodded.

"If we carry weapons with us and arm the slaves—"

"That will put the odds in our favor," Aren finished.

"Will they fight?" Sequana asked.

"We'll promise them their freedom if they do," Aren said.

"And they literally have nothing to lose," Zhal added.

"So, is this what we're doing?" Aren asked.

"What do you think?" Zhal asked.

"I think it's insane," Aren admitted. "But if we can take the fortress at Hilt, and hold it, we can keep the Empire's armies bottled up in the east indefinitely." He looked around the table at each of them in turn. Zhal and Sequana looked back at him with neutral faces. Syenna glared at him coldly. She was clearly still angry with him, something that wasn't likely to change anytime soon.

"All right," Aren said at last. "Tomorrow I'll get fifty volunteers and we'll ride for the Sulfurous Road."

CHAPTER 27

The Sulfurous Road

The entrance to the Sulfurous Road was a tiny gap in an unremarkable rock face barely wide enough for an armored man to squeeze through sideways. From a distance, it looked like nothing more than a shadow among the wild grass that grew up the side of the mountain. After three days of hard riding through rough country, Aren felt underwhelmed by the sight of it.

Still, if it had been obvious, it wouldn't have remained a secret.

"You're sure that's it?" Aren asked Syenna as he handed her back her spyglass.

She accepted the instrument with a mocking look and a raised eyebrow.

"All right," he said after long moment. "You're sure. How long will it take us to reach the fortress once we're inside?"

"About a day on the road," she said. "Then we'll reach the tunnels under the fortress. From there it will take another five or six hours to climb up to the top."

Something tickled Aren's mind.

"Didn't you say the road was a narrow ledge running along a cliff?"

"Yes."

"And it takes a full day to travel it?"

Syenna nodded.

"We'll have to stop and rest at some point," Aren observed. "How will we do that?"

"Carefully," Syenna said. "There's enough room for people to sit, but I wouldn't recommend trying to sleep. Especially if you sleepwalk."

"That's going to be a very long day," Aren said.

"There are several large chambers once we reach the caves," she said. "We can sleep safely once we get there."

The sound of hoofbeats caused him to turn. Colonel Tibbs came galloping up from the rear with her red braids flying behind her. She rode with an easy grace that spoke to years spent in the saddle. Aren had thought long and hard about who to bring on this expedition. The Norgard legionnaires would have been the best choice, there weren't any better foot soldiers in the world, but he needed warriors who could ride long and hard just to get here. Norgards weren't known for their horsemanship.

Tibbs and her Resolute riders, on the other hand, made it look easy. She'd handpicked fifty of her best soldiers, experts on horseback, and the journey had gone more smoothly than he'd expected. The only real worry now was whether or not the riders would make good foot soldiers.

"Are we almost there?" Tibbs asked after saluting. "If not, we need to walk the horses for a bit."

"Right there," Syenna said, pointing in the direction of the crack.

Tibbs followed her pointing finger and nodded.

"We'll reach that in a quarter hour at most," she said. "With your permission, General, I'll get the riders ready to move."

Aren wasn't sure what they were going to do while still in the saddle, but Tibbs knew her business and he trusted her, so he nodded his approval. She started to turn her horse, but stopped and looked back over her shoulder with a grin.

"How's the saddle, General?" she asked.

Tibbs had heard about his uncomfortable Norgard saddle, probably from Syenna, and had presented him with a Resolute one. It wasn't as fancy as the Norgard, but it was far more comfortable.

"It's an excellent saddle, Colonel," he said. "Thank you."

Tibbs saluted, then galloped away. An hour later, she had her riders dismounted and lined up to pass through the narrow opening to the Sulfurous Road. A team of a dozen extra riders had come along to lead the horses back, and they had already tied their leads together for the return trip.

Aren pushed through the narrow opening in the rock and found himself in a small, dark cave. He waited for his eyes to adjust, but it was too dark inside to see into the back of the space.

"We'll need lanterns here," Syenna said, pushing in behind him.

She produced a small, hooded lantern and lit it. Golden light filled the cave, and Aren could see a passage leading away into deeper darkness.

"How far does that go?"

"A mile," Syenna said, pushing past him to take the lead. "Maybe two. Then it comes out onto the road itself."

The passage through the mountain was natural stone rather than a cut passage, so the ground was uneven and it varied in width. Some parts of it were so narrow, Aren had to turn sideways, while others were wide enough for three men to walk side by side. It made the journey slow and tedious.

The air in the tunnel was cold, and the darkness felt oppressive, but that was nothing compared to what waited for them on the far end. After almost an hour groping their way through the tunnel, natural light began to filter into the cave. A few moments later, it emptied out on a small landing of sandstone at the bottom of a narrow fissure. Above, the rock ran almost straight up a sheer cliff with a thin strip of blue sky at its top.

A narrow path ran along the cliff, angling sharply upward. It wasn't so much a walkway, but a place where the cliff face had fractured, causing the bottom to jut out a few feet. At the bottom it didn't look too bad, but the path was barely a yard wide. As it went higher, it would be much more dangerous, obliging the travelers to lean into the wall for stability.

"How did you manage to get me down this while I was drugged?" he asked Syenna.

"Carefully," she said. She took a breath, then put her foot on the path and started up. "We need to get going or the others will get bunched up here."

Aren followed as the dismounted riders exited the tunnel and began following him. He knew that Tibbs was bringing up the rear, to make sure there weren't any stragglers, so he wouldn't see her anytime soon.

Aren assumed that as they climbed, the air would get colder, but it was the reverse. As they went, the air became warm, and then hot, bringing with it the rotten egg smell that doubtless gave the path its name. Putting one foot in front of the other became all Aren thought about in an effort to ignore the sweat soaking his gambeson and the deadly drop to his left. In front of him, Syenna's tunic was dark with sweat and plastered to the chain shirt she wore under it. She'd tied her hair back into a ponytail, and it hung limp behind her dripping sweat at regular intervals.

"Where is this heat coming from?" he finally asked.

Syenna didn't turn, just gestured over the side of the cliff. Aren risked a look and saw a bright orange ribbon filling the bottom of the fissure-turned-narrow-canyon, now far below. Aren knew the area south of hilt was an open wound where magma from the world's core bubbled up to the surface, but he'd never heard of it being this far north.

A blast of heat hit Aren in the face, and he pulled his head back from the edge. The molten rock was far below, but the canyon acted like a chimney, pulling the intense heat up and past the narrow walkway.

"Well, this can't get any worse," Aren said.

"Don't tempt the fates," Syenna said over her shoulder.

† † †

What seemed like several days later, Aren could see the tops of the mountains silhouetted against a sky that was just turning pink with the light of morning. They'd stopped to rest several times already, and Aren chose to believe that this new ability to see a big chunk of the sky meant they were nearing the end of their journey.

At least he hoped it was.

His waterskin was empty and his boots felt as if they were filled with lead.

He was about to ask Syenna how much farther the path went, a question he knew she was dreading, when she suddenly pointed to a spot far above the mountaintops. Aren looked up to where a slender tower rose above the cliff wall.

"That's the fortress," Syenna said, her voice dry and raspy. "We're close to the caves."

Aren pressed his right arm against the canyon wall so he could get a better look at the tower. There weren't any lights burning in it, but he knew there must be watchmen. Fortunately, it was much too far for them to see anyone on the Sulfurous Road.

An hour or so later, Aren decided that Syenna's definition of "close" needed review. He wanted to question her about it, but his throat felt like the bottom of a sand pit, so he held his tongue.

"There," Syenna croaked.

Aren leaned around her and saw a dark spot in the side of the rock just up ahead. At that moment he was prepared to swear it was the most beautiful thing he'd ever seen.

His legs were trembling when he finally stumbled through the opening and into the shade of the tunnel. It was a wide space with a low ceiling that forced him to lean over a bit. He kept following Syenna deeper inside to make room for the exhausted men coming behind.

The air in the cave was cooler than outside, but not as cool as Aren expected. That thought was banished from his mind as he heard the unmistakable sound of water dripping. Syenna heard it, too, and she quickened her pace until they both reached a shallow pool of water collected in a depression below a short, thick stalactite.

Aren scooped up a handful of water and drank. It was bitter, with a metallic tang, but he didn't care one bit. He repeated the process several times, then stepped back so the men filing into the cave behind him could drink. He was still exhausted, but he felt reinvigorated despite the heat.

"Shouldn't it be cooler in here?" he asked.

Syenna nodded, wearily. "Yes," she said. "I don't remember it being this hot."

As the soldiers came forward to drink, Aren and Syenna had to move farther in to make room. Beyond the little pool, the ceiling rose up and the space opened out into a wide roundish chamber with more than enough room for the soldiers to rest. Aren wanted nothing more than to sink down against the wall and sleep, but Syenna headed off toward a large opening in the back of the area, so he followed. She pulled out her lantern, but before she could get it lit, orange light bloomed in the tunnel beyond the opening. A blast of heat erupted from the hole and Aren covered his face.

The light flared up into bright intensity, but faded just as quickly. The heat dulled a bit, but the passage ahead felt like an oven. Syenna lit her lantern and poked her head into the tunnel. Aren stepped up beside her, and they moved forward tentatively. After a few paces, the ground began to crunch under their feet. Hundreds of broken pieces of rock littered the floor, and Aren bent down to pick one up. It was lighter than he'd expected and full of tiny holes.

"Lava rock," he said, recognizing it from his time in Desolis.

"Some of these tunnels must be lava tubes," Syenna said, "but none of them were active last time I came through."

Aren tossed the rock away and they continued further down the passage. As they went, the temperature rose quickly until the air itself was oppressive.

"There must be an active lava tube up here somewhere," Aren said.

Syenna nodded. She started to say something, but just as she did, the wall behind her erupted in orange light. Aren could see the open lava tube in the light and the bright glow of molten rock. Grabbing Syenna bodily, he hauled her out of the way, stumbling down the hall and falling hard on the sharp bits of lava rock littering the floor.

Lava spewed out of the wall, filling the passage with light as it pooled on the floor then slid across to the far side and escaped through another opening. Intense heat started cooking Aren's feet and he scrambled back, pulling Syenna after him.

"Let me guess," he said, helping Syenna to her feet. "We need to go that way."

"I warned you not to tempt the fates," she said, running back down the passage as the lava stream began to spread out over the floor.

"What do we do if that doesn't stop?" Aren asked.

Syenna just stared at the spreading pool of lava. Aren wanted to shake her, get her mind back in the here and now, but something in her face made him stop. He'd seen Syenna in almost every situation possible from fancy dress dinners to the battlefield. He'd seen her happy, he'd seen her angry, and he'd seen her in pain, but he'd never seen her afraid.

Aren released her and spun around. The lava pool had run down the passage toward them, but it appeared to have bubbled up into a blob that was growing upward instead of flowing along the ground. As he watched, two arms emerged from the ball and a pair of glowing white eyes stared out from the top of the blob.

"What is that thing?" Syenna gasped, her voice almost a squeak.

Aren had no idea, but he wasn't about to wait to find out. He grabbed the hilt of the Avatar sword and jerked it free of the scabbard. Sight flowed over him and he could suddenly see the creature before him revealed. Its body was humanoid but consisted entirely of molten rock. Its legs were still forming out of the flowing stone around it as it surged up out of the lava.

The heat it gave off was so intense, Aren wanted to shut his eyes but he didn't dare. Stepping forward, he brought his sword down on the creature. The blade hit the shoulder, slicing a deep gash that partially severed the arm. The creature made a noise like grinding stone and lashed out with its good arm. Aren ducked back but a fat blob of magma came loose from the end of the monster's arm, splattering against his left spaulder. Unbearable heat washed over his shoulder, arm, and neck as he tried to use his sword to scrape off the blob of red hot stone.

"Get it off," Syenna yelled, pulling on the armor strap that held the spaulder in place.

"Cut it," Aren called back, catching movement in his peripheral vision just in time to avoid a clumsy swipe by the creature. He cried out as the heat burned him, slashing into the thing's arm but not enough to sever it. Yells of alarm erupted behind them, somewhere back in the pool chamber.

"Hold still," Syenna called, sawing on the leather strap with her dagger.

Aren swore as the heat from the spaulder started to cook him.

"I'm . . . busy," he gasped, avoiding another swipe. The creature's good arm seemed to flow out toward the end, and another blob of molten rock formed there. Aren slashed at its arm but it moved back far more quickly than he thought possible.

"Got it," Syenna said as her knife finally severed the armor strap.

The searing pain in Aren's shoulder abruptly ended as the spaulder came free, but he didn't have time to enjoy it. The magma monster lashed out again, and Aren threw himself to the ground, dragging Syenna with him. Heat washed over him as the lava ball flew past, ending with a wet splat.

A shriek of agony filled the passage. Several of the riders had come to help. The one in the lead hadn't seen the lava ball coming and it struck him square in the chest.

Screaming and thrashing, he fell to the floor as the molten rock burned him through his chain shirt. His fellows rushed to help him, but Aren knew they were too late. Lunging to his feet he took the Avatar sword in both hands and slashed sideways, lopping the magma creature's head clean off. Fire erupted from the wound and Aren was forced back as the remains of the monster melted down into a pool of glowing rock. As its body dissolved, the lava seemed to cool and harden far more quickly than Aren would have expected. After a minute, all that remained of the fire monster was a lump of steaming rock in the center of the passage.

By the time Aren turned back from the unearthly scene, the screaming had stopped. The young rider lay dead, his steaming, charred body filling the passage with the smell of burnt flesh. A female rider sat against the wall, weeping, cradling her burned hands to her chest. She'd tried to pull the blob of molten rock from her companion with just her gauntlets.

"Get her to the pool," Syenna shouted, breaking the spell that seemed to hang in the air. "Fill a helmet with water and soak her hands."

One of the other riders pulled the stunned woman to her feet and led her away.

"What about your shoulder?" Syenna asked.

Aren looked down at the gambison covering his exposed shoulder. It was singed, but not too badly, and his arm only stung a little when he moved it.

"I'm fine," he said.

"What was that . . . that demon?" the remaining rider demanded. He looked to Aren.

"Demon works for me," Aren said, then he nodded at the dead man. "Pick him up and move back, we need to—"

Syenna suddenly scuttled back past him, but Aren already knew what had happened as ruddy orange light flared up in the passage. He turned and found three more of the lava demons rising up from the floor as another gout of molten rock flowed out of the wall.

"Get back," Aren said, but one of the riders lunged forward and thrust a spear into the chest of the nearest demon. The spear sunk in past the lugs and the shaft began to blacken and burn. If the demon was bothered by this, it didn't show. The rider tried to jerk the spear loose, but it stuck fast. He would have been pulled off balance and into the demon had Aren not grabbed him by the back of his chain mail and hauled him away.

"Fall back," he ordered, pushing the rider down the passage.

"The spear didn't hurt it," Syenna said, staying behind him as Aren backed down the hall.

"I know," he said.

"That means you've got the only weapon that can hurt them."

That wasn't necessarily true. Aren had cut off the last one's head, but all the blows he'd delivered prior to that had only slowed the demon down.

"Pass me a spear," he ordered back over his shoulder.

As Aren sheathed his sword, one of the riders jumped forward and passed him a spear with a thick wooden shaft. Aren grabbed it as the three lava demons came shambling forward. He waited until the passage narrowed a bit, then lunged, driving the tip of the spear directly through the nearest demon's head. It reached up to grab the shaft, but Aren turned the spear, pushing the tip through the demon and into the side of the passage.

The demon thrashed for a moment, trying to dislodge the weapon, then went still. Immediately it began to turn black, oozing down the side of the passage until it hardened against the wall.

"Hit them in the head," Aren ordered as the other two demons began squeezing around their petrified brother. "Pin them to the wall," he went on. "Don't let them fall down."

"What are you doing?" Syenna demanded as two riders rushed forward, spears in hand.

"Shutting the door," Aren explained.

The tall rider in front missed the second demon's head, catching it in the shoulder as it turned. The demon tried to pull him into its deadly embrace, but the man saw that coming and jerked the spear free before the demon could grab it. Beside him, the second rider, a short, red-headed man, yelled an incoherent challenge and drove his spear right through the third demon's head.

"Look out," the tall rider called as his demon tried to grab his companion, but Aren stepped up and lopped off the demon's arm with a downward swing.

The tall man lunged again, pinning the demon this time, and it slumped forward. The spear was a loss, but now the passage was almost totally blocked by the remains of the demons.

"That ought to hold them," Aren declared.

"Unless they can ooze through the gaps," the first rider said. "Sir," he added a bit self-consciously.

Aren shrugged.

"That will take time," he said. "If any more try it, we'll kill them, too."

"That's fine," Syenna said, pointing to the blocked passage. "But what do we do now? That was the way we needed to go."

"There's bound to be another way," Aren said, not sure what else could be done. He was suddenly aware of a throbbing pain in his left arm and he winced.

"Let me see that," Syenna declared, holding her lantern up to get a look at Aren's shoulder.

In the space left by his missing spaulder, the gambeson underneath was blackened and burned. Aren could see bright pink skin showing through parts of it.

"It doesn't look too bad," Syenna declared. "But we'd better get some water on it."

Aren nodded. They headed back after leaving one of the riders to watch the makeshift barrier of demon bodies.

"You sound very sure of that we'll be able to find an alternate route to the fortress," Syenna said as they went.

Aren nodded and Syenna glanced at the Avatar sword at his side.

"How do you know?"

"Because," Aren said, "if there isn't, then General Trevan and the Army of Might are going to be in trouble."

CHAPTER
28

Trouble

General Mikas Trevan stared down the expanse of the Broken Road as if he could will it to show him what he wanted to see. Somewhere up ahead, Blackblade Fork split off to the east and ran up into Hilt Canyon, ending at the fortress at Hilt. Right now the general would give a significant sum to know exactly how far the away the turnoff was, and whether or not the raiders he pursued had reached it.

He'd been told that they would have to stop and forage, an activity that would slow them down significantly, yet somehow they had managed to stay ahead of Trevan's army, just out of reach. He could catch them with his cavalry, of course, but that would mean leaving the bulk of his army behind, forcing his cavalry to face a vastly superior force.

Trevan didn't like those odds.

He stood up in his stirrups, looking over the marching column of the Army of Might that stretched out along the Broken Road. It didn't help. There still wasn't any sign of the raiders.

"Where are they?" he said, more to himself than anyone.

"General?" Sir Llewelyn said. Trevan liked the young man, but often found him lacking in imagination. Llewelyn was a lot like his armor, rigid, strong, uncompromising, and a bit dull.

"I'm sure we'll catch up to them today," Loremaster Zhal said from Trevan's other side.

"You said that yesterday," Trevan groused. He wasn't happy about having observers in his army, especially ones who were so free with their commentary.

"And the day before that," the Lady Amanda said with a grin. She had to lean forward to see Trevan from where she rode on the far side of Sir Llewelyn and her smile vanished almost before it began.

"Are you all right?" Trevan asked as the young woman grimaced. The army had been marching hard for days, and he knew even on her horse she couldn't wear her mechanical legs for too long without pain.

"I'll be fine," she said, forcing the smile back to her face.

"We can only travel as fast as the infantry, ma'am," Llewelyn said. "We could easily stop here for half an hour and then catch up."

Amanda actually blushed at that, though Trevan couldn't tell if that was embarrassment or simple shyness at the attentions of the handsome knight.

"Really," she insisted. "I'm fine. The harness just pinches a little when I lean forward."

A blast of sound suddenly erupted from the front of the column. The noise of it was piercing, and Trevan put a hand to his temple. Aren had the army using the Resolute custom of signaling with a bugle, an instrument that turned out to be an atonal sort of trumpet. It reminded Trevan of someone attempting to strangle a goose. It gave him a headache.

"Damn the man," he cursed Aren; then he turned to Sir Llewelyn. "What's that racket mean?"

"That's the signal for an approaching rider," the knight said, trying and failing to hide a smile. Trevan's opinion of the bugle wasn't exactly a secret.

Still, he perked up at the news of a rider. It had been over a day since their scouts had reported in. If Syenna had been here, the scouts wouldn't have dared to go so long without reporting, but Aren had taken the scout captain with him.

"Damn the man," Trevan repeated, under his breath this time.

"I suspect this is the news you've been waiting for," Zhal said.

A moment later he could see a rider coming hard, galloping past the front lines and heading back along the column toward him. It was the young Aerie officer that Syenna left in charge of the scouts. He seemed solid and sensible, though Trevan was still angry at being out of contact for so long.

"I bring urgent news, General," he said, pulling his horse to a stop so quickly the animal's hooves slid on the stone of the road. "The raiders have reached Blackblade Fork and are making their way toward the canyon."

Trevan swore again. Loudly this time.

"How far is it to the fork?"

"About five miles," the man reported. "Maybe a bit more."

Trevan looked up to the sun. It was past noon, though he couldn't say how far. He'd studied the maps of the Broken Road and Blackblade Fork. For the first few miles, the fork was a wide path with a gentle slope and a few, sparse trees. After a few miles, however, it began to narrow, becoming a path only wide enough for two wagons to pass each other as it climbed up toward the pass and its occupying fortress.

"It will take them some time getting up the canyon," Zhal said.

Trevan nodded at that. The raiders wouldn't want to spend the night in the narrow switchbacks of the canyon. "They'll probably camp in the lowlands and start up toward the pass in the morning."

"You're thinking we could move in on them tonight and catch them asleep?" Zhal said.

"Not exactly," Trevan said.

"We want to use our cavalry," Sir Llewelyn explained. "And it's dangerous to try a cavalry charge in the dark."

"You aren't thinking of waiting until morning?" Zhal said, a note of disbelief in his voice.

Trevan shook his head.

"We can't risk that. If the raiders start up the canyon tonight, we'll lose them. The canyon is narrow, which means we won't be able to use the cavalry. Worse, there are switchbacks running all the way up to the fortress."

"If we try following the raiders up there, they'll be able to shoot down on top of us," Llewelyn explained.

"Or just roll rocks down on us," Trevan finished. "We have to catch them before they have a chance to move their force up into the canyon."

"What if you can't catch them?" Amanda asked, though the worried look on her face clearly communicated that she already knew the answer.

"Then the raiders will reach the fortress," Zhal said. "And General Bennis and your sister will be facing an entire army when they attack."

Amanda's face blanched and she gripped her horse's reins in white-knuckled hands.

"Don't worry," Trevan told her. "We'll make sure that doesn't happen. Go find that confounded bugler," he said, turning to Sir Llewelyn.

"Tell him to sound quick march. Then pass the word that we're going to catch the raiders before nightfall."

Sir Llewelyn saluted, then turned his horse and rode off toward the front of the column.

† † †

General Karpasic crouched in a bush on a small hill a half mile or so from the turnoff at Blackblade Fork. He didn't know how long he'd have to wait, so he'd left his armor in a heap beside his picketed horse and wore a comfortable pair of trousers and a plain, black tunic.

As he looked north along the Broken Road, a cloud of dust was plainly visible just beyond the nearest hills, growing larger by the minute.

"There they are," he said, nudging the sorcerer Evard with his elbow.

The sorcerer, who had been leaning up against a rock, sleeping, roused himself.

"Where?" he mumbled, rubbing his eyes.

"Right where they should be," Karpasic said. He didn't bother hiding his grin. Without having to forage, it was child's play to stay just ahead of Aren Bennis and his pursuing army. Now their scouts had reported that the raiders were headed up toward Hilt. Aren would see that as his chance and move to pin the raiders up against the canyon. Based on the size of that dust cloud, he was pressing his army hard in pursuit.

What he couldn't know, of course, was that Karpasic's army had doubled back as soon as the following scouts sent someone back to report. They'd killed the remaining scouts and moved the army south along the Broken Road, just far enough to be unseen by anyone making the turn at Blackblade Fork.

"Won't they be expecting their scouts to meet them?" Evard asked, shading his eyes against the late afternoon sun.

"No," Karpasic guessed. "Once they find the bodies, they'll assume the scouts got too close to us. The only shelter is up the canyon, so they won't think twice about where we've gone. Once they make the turn, we'll give them a quarter hour's head start, then follow them. They'll be trapped up against the mountain."

Karpasic allowed himself a satisfied grin at the thought. He'd sent a company of men with wagons full of firewood ahead to the bottom of the canyon the previous day. They had laid out dozens of campfires around the entrance to the canyon road. When Bennis saw them, he'd believe that his quarry was camped, an easy target. He wouldn't be in a hurry, he'd take his time, move his men into position for the attack. That delay would give Karpasic plenty of time to come up behind him.

"Won't Aren just take his men up the canyon when he realizes he's been had?" Evard said.

"He won't be able to. The road is too narrow to move that many soldiers quickly. By the time he realizes he's trapped, Bennis will have no choice but to turn and fight."

Evard regarded him with a cocked eyebrow, then nodded approvingly.

"Very well done, General," he said. Karpasic had the feeling it had cost the sorcerer to say it, which made the compliment that much sweeter. Then Evard's face darkened. "It would be a shame if something untoward happened to Captain Bennis," he warned. "Especially after all your excellent work."

Karpasic kept the smile plastered to his face.

"Not to worry," he said. "By the time we move up behind dear Aren's army, he'll know he's beaten."

"You think he'll surrender?"

"Just so," he said, confidently.

"Don't count your eggs until they're in the pudding," the sorcerer said. "Aren is being controlled by that Avatar sword. There's no telling what it will compel him do. You need to be ready to fight and your men had better take Aren alive."

"We're ready for any outcome," Karpasic said. Of course he had a few extra contingencies the sorcerer wasn't aware of. If the Lady Maradn was good to her word and made an appearance, he wouldn't have to worry about taking his *old friend* Aren Bennis alive. He hadn't heard from her again, but he had seen her little flying lizard skulking about once or twice.

It didn't really matter if she intervened or not, from Karpasic's point of view. He would be on the winning side in either case. The Avatar sword would be back in the Empire's hands—and by his hand. His restored position in the Empire would be assured. The odds were in his favor.

At the fork, the first units of Aren's army began to turn off the Broken Road.

"Let's get back," Karpasic said, moving carefully to avoid disturbing the bush. "I want to get my armor on before the festivities begin."

✝ ✝ ✝

The shadows were getting long by the time Trevan could see the mountain road rising up into the canyon toward Hilt. Down below, about a mile distant, he could see campfires, their lights winking through the trees.

He breathed a sigh of relief and waved his officers over to him.

"Get everyone in position," he said. "And make sure to keep—"

He was about to say "quiet" when the sound of thundering hoof beats rose up from somewhere behind.

"General," the scout yelled as he dragged his horse to a stop.

"Be quiet!" Trevan snapped.

"Begging the general's pardon," the scout said, ignoring the order. "We just found Harlan's horse and there's blood on the saddle."

"Who's Harlan?" Sir Llewelyn asked.

"One of the scouts we had watching the raiders," Lieutenant Hawkins of Resolute said.

Trevan turned to look at the campfires again. It was a bit strange that there were so many this early, the sun wasn't even fully down yet. One or two for the cooks, yes, but there were enough fires burning for a large camp.

"Where's that bugler?" he demanded, turning back to the grouped officers.

"Here sir," a young woman on a roan horse called.

"Count to fifty, then sound a charge," he said. "Colonel Aquila." He turned to the Norgard officer. "Lead your men straight through that camp and surround the road going up into the mountains. Form a shield wall with half your men on either side but leave room in the center for our wagons to pass. Koshiba," he turned to the Ardorin colonel. "Follow right behind, you're in charge of making sure the wagons get up into the pass. No one stops for any reason, understand?" Colonel Koshiba nodded and Trevan moved on. "Captain Hawkins, take your riders back to the supply wagons and escort them forward as fast as they'll go. Once you get them here, take your riders to the left flank and prepare to break up an enemy charge." Trevan turned to Captain Artemis. "Get your archers moving up onto the high ground and get them ready." He swept his gaze around at his commanders. "As soon as the wagons are up the canyon, I want Koshiba to follow, then the riders, and finally the infantry, any questions?"

"What about the raiders?" Colonel Koshiba said, a bit wide-eyed. "They aren't going to let us just ride through their camp."

"There aren't any," Trevan said. "The raiders are behind us." His officers gave him stunned looks. "Those fires are decoys, this is the same trap we wanted to spring. Our only chance to survive this night is if we get up on the high ground and make the raiders pay for coming after us."

Behind Trevan, the bugler started blowing the notes for the charge.

"Go!" he shouted, hoping it wasn't already too late.

CHAPTER
29

The Destiny of the Sword

*A*ren shifted his weight, trying to get comfortable as he sat, propped against the side of the cave. All around him, the men and women who'd followed him on this madcap gambit lay piled like cordwood into the available floor. As cramped as it was, no one had a problem sleeping. After the treacherous climb that must have taken at least twelve hours, they were all exhausted.

Night had fallen outside and the opening that led back out to the Sulfurous Road was a barely visible ring of darkness to Aren's right. To his left was the tall, wide passageway where they had encountered the fire demons. It was also the road they needed to take to reach the Obsidian fortress. A road that was now blocked by the cooling remains of three of the molten monsters. Aren supposed it might be possible to break through once the creatures had fully cooled, but even if they did, they'd have to risk going past an active lava tube to move forward. With no way to tell when it might decide to vomit up more lava or fire demons, it was suicide.

Aren shifted to look further left and brushed up against the rough surface of the cave wall. Pain shot through his shoulder and he grunted, clenching his jaw to keep from crying out. Moving slowly, he lifted the damp rag Syenna had used to cover his shoulder and inspected the damage. The cloth stuck to his skin and pulled painfully, but he got it off. Beneath, the skin of his shoulder was red and blistered. He'd been lucky that his shoulder plate had been there to keep the magma off him. The medic had looked at the woman who burned her hands trying to save her dying companion. She might regain the use of her left hand, but they might have to take her right. He'd given the woman some strong spirits so she could sleep, but Aren occasionally heard her whimpering from the pain as she slept.

"Go back to sleep," Syenna mumbled from his left.

Being careful this time, Aren scooted around a bit so he could see her. She sat with her back against the wall, just like he did, with her arms folded across her chest and the long curtain of her black hair falling down over her face. He was about to tell her that he couldn't sleep, when the sound of her deep, rhythmic breathing reached him.

She'd already fallen back to sleep.

With his body turned, Aren could see what he'd intended to look at in the first place. Far off to his left, past the blocked passage, there were three more openings into the low cave. Syenna said that there were entire networks of tunnels honeycombed through the mountain. Some, made by lava, were so old that they couldn't tell how just old they were. Others showed signs of human construction with cut stone, deliberate rooms and chambers, and even doors. The problem was that all of it had been disrupted by the events of the Shard Fall. Cut passages that had run straight and level when they were made became twisted, broken, and often blocked by fragments of their former grandeur and the lava tubes had a nasty habit of ending suddenly over deep fissures too wide for a man to jump across. Aren had assured her that among that fractured mess of switchbacks and dead ends, there was a way to reach the fortress far above.

Syenna hoped he was right. If Halik and his raiders managed to evade the Army of Might long enough to reach the fortress, they'd have no hope of dislodging the Obsidians. They'd be able to invade the western lands whenever they were ready.

Movement caught Aren's eye and his head snapped up as he stared intently at the three silent openings. A single lamp burned near the little pool of water, but its light reached to the back of the low cave. It wasn't much, but he could see the ragged openings well enough. As he looked, nothing moved. He held his breath, listening intently for any sign that something was amiss, but all he could hear were the sounds of sleeping soldiers and the steady drip of water into the pool.

He'd almost convinced himself that he imagined the movement when someone at the far end of the cave stood up. It was one of the soldiers, a woman by her profile, barely visible in the dim light. Walking carefully, she picked her way through her sleeping companions, heading for the centermost of the passages.

It wasn't an unusual sight, even exhausted soldiers needed to relieve themselves, but something about the woman drew him in, compelled him to watch her as she moved. When she reached the opening, she reached out to steady herself, turning to look back at the cave full of sleeping warriors. Her eyes swept around the cave until they met Aren's. Even through the darkness and the distance, he could tell she was looking directly at him.

She had dark, curly hair and blue eyes that radiated a look that was more sad than weary. When she was sure Aren saw her, that he recognized her, the ghost of a smile played over her lips and she raised her finger to them in a gesture of quiet. Before Aren could respond, she stepped out of the light and into the dark passage, disappearing from his view.

Ignoring the screaming pain in his shoulder as he moved, Aren pushed himself to his feet. She obviously wanted him to follow, but without the urgency of their previous encounters.

Moving carefully, Aren picked his way across the floor, avoiding stepping on his exhausted warriors. By the time he reached the central passage, he knew she would be long gone. Still, she wanted him to follow, and he wanted to know who she was and what danger she was here to warn him about this time.

Pitch blackness enveloped Aren as he stepped into the passage. Turning back, he saw a small lamp beside one of the slumbering soldiers. The man was probably supposed to watch this passage for signs of more fire demons, but exhaustion had overcome him. Not bothering to wake the man, Aren picked up the lantern and lit it with a flint. Dim light played out of the glass lens on the front of the lantern, revealing a roundish passage made of rough black rock. There was no sign of the blue-eyed woman, but the passage ran straight ahead with no turns or side passages, so it wasn't a mystery where she had gone.

Sweeping the lantern left and right as he went, Aren continued down the passage. After what seemed like a long time, he emerged into an octagonal chamber with a ceiling of cut stone. Molten rock had flowed across the floor and spattered onto the walls, but he could see the soot-stained remnants of painted frescos on the roof. The ceiling was divided into eight triangular shaped tiles, all radiating out from a central point. Each panel had a different scene on it. Some showed groups of men and women while others portrayed one person standing alone. There didn't seem to be any rhyme or reason to the images, but much of the artwork had been destroyed.

In the center of the room stood a stone fountain, though only its rough shape remained, encrusted with fractured lava rock. There were four exits from the chamber: three of them were marked by stone archways, while the one Aren had come down simply emerged from a break in the wall. On the keystone of each archway, an ancient symbol had been carved. Aren was surprised when he recognized them, they were old and commonly associated with the Avatars. To his right was the symbol for Truth, to his left, Love, and across from him, he found the symbol for Courage.

Playing his light around the room, Aren saw no sign of the blue-eyed woman. He tried looking for her tracks, but found only the fractured and broken lava rock, undisturbed for what looked like centuries.

"Okay," he said to the empty room. His voice wasn't loud, but it echoed off the walls and ceiling, bouncing back at him over and over until it faded away. "I'm here," he went on. "Now what?"

As the last of the echoes faded away, Aren strained to hear something, anything. It was so quiet he could hear his own heartbeat, but nothing else.

"Fine," he muttered, playing his light around the room again. Each of the three paths seemed passable, though the lava that had coated the floor so long ago clearly came from the passage marked "Love."

"I guess I'm here looking for truth," he said at last, pointing his light down the passage on the room's far side.

Like the other passages, the floor and part of the walls were coated with lava rock that crunched loudly under Aren's boots. After a few hundred feet, however, the rock gave way to smooth stone. The passage ran on like that for another dozen yards, then ended at a stone stair that spiraled around both up and down. Heat rose up from the bottom, so Aren started up, but after only a few turns, the stair was blocked by rubble.

"Down it is, then," he said, turning back.

The stair down was just as dusty and unused as the way up had been, but Aren managed to descend through several turns without finding any blockages. He also found no side paths or landings. As he descended, the air grew hotter and he began to sweat profusely. It felt like visiting a forge on a hot summer's day.

Just as he was prepared to turn back, the stair came around a turn and expanded out onto a patch of open ground. It ended there, going no lower. The air stung his eyes and began to singe his skin as he raised his arm to protect his face.

"Draw your sword, Aren," a woman's voice whispered to him.

He whirled around, jerking the Avatar blade from its scabbard, but there was nothing behind him, only the empty stair. As soon as the blade came free, however, the oppressive heat and singeing air abated. Soft blue light seemed to radiate around him, pulsing gently in time with his beating heart.

Aren reached out to where the light seemed to hang in the air like some kind of gossamer curtain, but as his hand reached the place where it was, the light receded, staying just out of his reach. Looking around, he realized that it draped over and around him, like a bubble under water.

Holding up the Avatar sword, he found the runes along the blade and the five silver symbols on the pommel and crosspiece were all emitting the same pale blue light.

"What is this?" he said, looking around. The chamber at the bottom of the spiral stair was large and at least ten feet high. He could see the roof in the shimmering light from the bubble, but even his lantern couldn't find any walls.

Sweeping the darkness with his lantern, Aren became aware of a faint, ruddy light almost straight out from the landing of the spiral stair. With nothing else to be seen in the utter darkness, he made for it. As he approached, the bubble of energy began to glow brighter.

The red glow shined up from a crack in the ground where a river of lava flowed. It was several hundred feet down but still far too close for Aren's liking. Whatever the sword was doing, he reasoned it was the only thing preventing him from being cooked by the heat that must have been rising above the molten rock.

A narrow walkway without guide or railing stretched across the red river to a nearly blank wall on the far side, clearly visible in the ruddy glow of the magma. The only feature in it was a doorway at the far end.

Aren leaned forward, looking down into the depths below. The prospect of crossing the narrow strip of stone over certain death made him shiver, but at least that would be quick.

"All a soldier can ask for," he mocked himself as he mounted the walk.

Taking his time, Aren carefully put one foot in front of the other, crossing the stone bridge without hurrying. At its center, the bridge was only about a foot wide, a fact he tried strenuously not to notice until he reached the other side.

Once he was through the opening in the wall, the air grew much cooler, though the bubble of energy around him didn't dissipate.

Holding his lantern up, he found himself in a forge. It was far larger than any he'd seen before and seemed to run off into the distance well beyond the reach of his lantern. A line of furnaces ran along a wall to his right, each with an anvil and a set of bellows that were rotted and decaying. Along the left side were rows of shelves that held rusted and corroded bits of metal, bags of twice-burnt coal, and racks of moldering tools. Workbenches were scattered along the right side as well, set with large poles for hanging lanterns.

With nowhere else to go, Aren walked forward. He moved slowly, not wanting to make noise with his boots. Something about this place inspired a sense of reverence, or maybe it was awe. At the far end of the room, past at least a dozen forges, stood a raised dais with another forge on it. This one was much larger than the others and it was surrounded by three anvils that appeared to be made of pure silver, untarnished by time. Aren knew that couldn't be, since silver was far too soft a metal to be used in forging, but he had no idea what they were actually made of.

Beyond the silver anvils a slot came out of the wall, covered with a heavy, metal door that could be raised and lowered by a metal lever. Below the door was a stone trough that ran down to the forge. Aren had the distinct impression that the forge used molten rock from the river below to do the forging.

Even cold, dark, and encrusted with dust and age it was an impressive sight.

But it wasn't the truth Aren had come to learn.

"All right," he said, raising his voice in the unnatural quiet of the forge. "I'm here. Now who are you, and what do you want?"

"I'm surprised by you, Aren," a voice said off to his right. He turned and found the blue-eyed woman standing there, on the far side of the centermost silver anvil, her hands resting on its scarred surface. She didn't move to run away as she always had before, but just stood there regarding him coolly. "Do you truly not know me? And after we have been so dear to one another."

"I don't know you," he answered, reaching for his scabbard to put the sword away. It was a reflex born of his military service, he knew that drawn weapons tended to make civilians nervous.

"Don't," the woman cautioned.

Aren's hand froze halfway through the practiced motion. She was right, the sword and the glowing bubble it created were all that kept the heat from the lava river from cooking him alive.

"You didn't answer my question," he said, lowering the sword so that the blade pointed down at the ground.

The woman's half smile shifted to a look of subtle mockery, and she raised a challenging eyebrow. Aren had seen that look on Syenna's face, usually when he'd missed something obvious.

"How come the heat doesn't affect you?" He said it out loud, but the question was directed at himself. He held the Avatar sword up so that he could see its glowing symbols. "You led me to this weapon, and you made sure it stayed out of the hands of General Karpasic and his army. Are you a ghost? The spirit of the Avatar who last owned this blade?"

She shook her head, then looked down at the silver anvil.

"No," she said, running her fingers along the tool marks that covered the anvil's top. "But I have known every Avatar who carried that sword."

The Avatar sword had been lying abandoned in an ancient tomb, forgotten for centuries when Aren found it.

"How is that possible?" he said. "Just who or what are you?"

"I was born in this very room," she replied. She closed her eyes as if remembering something from long ago. "Right here on the Anvil of Truth. My name is the Eye of Scales, but you may call me Elysia."

Aren's gaze shifted to the sword in his hand, then back to the woman. "You're . . . you're the sword?"

"In a way," Elysia said, stepping out from behind the anvil. "I'm just a shadow, a visual manifestation of the sword that only my wielder can see. I exist to make it easier to communicate my purpose to those who possess the awareness to carry me."

"And what is your purpose?" Aren asked, not sure he believed what she was saying. "You're a sword, a weapon. Most weapons only have one purpose."

Elysia laughed at that, a trilling musical sound that echoed off the stone walls of the enormous forge.

"Come now, Aren," she said in a chiding voice. "You know I'm so much more than any weapon. I do have a purpose, one for which I was specifically made. You've felt it as you've held me." She fixed him with a fiery stare. "You feel it now, don't you?"

Whenever Aren held the sword, it connected him to the people around him. At first it had been disorienting, but the more he used the sword, the easier and more natural it became. He doubted that was what Elysia meant, however.

Focusing his thoughts on the sword, he began to feel it radiating power in his hand, setting the hairs along his arm on end. It made him feel like he could accomplish anything he set his mind to. The doubt he'd felt over the Obsidians and their methods melted away. With Elysia in his hand, the world could be put right, order could be imposed, and people could finally be free from torment and fear. He *could* do it.

He looked up at Elysia. She stood a few paces away, just beyond the border of the bubble, watching him intently. Her eyes sparkled with wild intensity, with a burning desire to be wielded. To be carried into battle.

"Your purpose is to bring order to the world," Aren declared. "That's why you chose me."

She nodded, gravely.

"Not since the days of the Avatars has a mind been so aligned with me," she said. "I felt your footsteps from beyond the walls of Midras. Your soul calls out for order, it called me from my long slumber. Together, you and I can achieve our destiny."

Aren looked back to the blade in his hand. He could still feel its purpose, its desire to usher in an age of peace, but he forced his emotions back into check. Getting emotionally involved on the field of battle was a good way to get yourself killed. Aren had survived many battles by being able to sequester his feelings.

"You are a powerful weapon," he said, looking back to her. "But I'm not sure how the two of us could save the world from the state it's in."

"Really?" she asked. "You have command of an army. It's small now, but with my aid, you could easily fill it with the strong, the loyal, and the brave. No traitor could infiltrate your ranks. No coward could sully your forces." She began to walk around him, reaching through the bubble to run her hand along his arm and shoulder as she went. He was surprised that he could feel her touch. "We would sweep across the world like a brushfire," she said. "No lord, potentate, or king could deceive us. No general could conceal their strategy from us. Eventually, hordes of men and women yearning for freedom and law would flock to your banner. Nation after nation would bow to your wisdom and accept your rule."

Elysia leaned close to his back and he felt her breath against his ear.

"In less than a score of years, you will unite the world," she said, her voice full of fervor. "There will be order. There will be peace."

He knew she spoke the truth. With the sight she granted, Aren would know the deepest desires of anyone he might need. He'd know just what to offer to gain their allegiance, and if they ever decided to betray him, he'd know that, too. Elysia would make a simple man of greed the richest man in the world. In his hand, however, she could make good on her promise, Elysia would put the world at his feet.

The thought was intoxicating. No more war, no more brutal raider bosses or petty kings. People would be free to live their lives in peace.

And all you have to do to achieve that is to slaughter your way across the world.

The thought was his own, but the voice he heard in his head belonged to Syenna.

"No," he said, holding the sword out at arm's length. "I want the world to have order and peace, but your price is too high."

Aren opened his hand and the sword fell to the dusty floor of the forge. As it fell, the bubble of energy that kept the all consuming heat at bay vanished and his skin began to smoke and burn.

CHAPTER
30

Dying Ground

E vard Dirae found it hard to sit still as his horse walked slowly through the gathering darkness. Seeming to sense its rider's frustration, he animal snorted and shook its head, sending its mane flying. Ahead of him the soldiers of the new, and somewhat smaller Westreach Army marched along the road toward Hilt Canyon. Their pace was slow and deliberate and Evard wanted desperately to order them to hurry.

"Take it easy, Sorcerer," General Karpasic said, riding on Evard's right. "We've got Bennis and his forces trapped. This will all be over soon."

Evard took a breath and tried to calm his nerves. It angered him that Karpasic had been able to read his emotions so easily. He was a sorcerer of the cabal, after all; he was supposed to remain aloof, to maintain an air of mystery about himself. Still, he was eager. Months of preparation and planning were finally about to pay off. In a few short hours both Aren and the Avatar sword would be back in Obsidian hands.

His hands.

He would be the savior of the Empire, the man who went behind enemy lines to steal away their most potent and dangerous weapon, right from under their noses. His position in the circle would be assured.

Evard smiled to himself. He couldn't wait to rub Maradn Norn's smug face in that. She had given him this task believing that it was beyond his ability, that he'd return in disgrace, and now he was mere minutes from proving her wrong.

His smile faded as his sorcerer's mind began running through the possible scenarios that would soon play out. He'd done this a dozen times already, but he couldn't help it, he needed to anticipate potential problems. In magic, as in war, you only got one chance to do something right, the rest of the time was spent trying to counter the things you hadn't foreseen.

"Stop it," Karpasic said. He sat easily in his saddle, his body shifting slightly with each step of his horse. "We've been over the plan enough, all you can do now is mess it up with overthinking."

Evard narrowed his eyes as he looked at the general.

"You act as though your entire future wasn't riding on this," he observed. "If Aren Bennis is killed, or, worse, escapes, you'll be going back to Desolis in chains."

There was a time when a well-placed threat could cower the general, but those days were half a year and most of a hundred pounds ago. Now he just rode on without any sign that the threat reached him.

Apparently Karpasic's time as guest of the Norgards had stiffened his spine.

Under different circumstances, Evard might have been suspicious that his ally of convenience was planning to betray him, but Karpasic literally had no one to turn to.

"Don't worry," Karpasic said. "If we've done it right, your old friend will come with us willingly. No need to fear him being killed on the battlefield."

"And if he doesn't?"

Karpasic favored him with a stoic look.

"I make no promises," he said. "I've given my officers orders to take Bennis alive, but a lot can happen in a fight. No one's survival is assured."

Evard wanted to say something to that, but Karpasic was right. He hated it when Karpasic was right.

"How much longer?" he asked, trying to distract himself from the thoughts running through his mind.

Before Karpasic could respond, a sound erupted from somewhere ahead. I was a series of short notes played on a trumpet and it repeated over and over.

"It seems we're out of time," he said, rising up in his stirrups. He drew his sword and waved it over his head as he bellowed to his officers and men. "Forward!"

†††

Captain Lynn Artemis, commander of the archers, led her force past the slow-moving supply wagons and up onto the sloping road that would eventually reach the Obsidian fortress at Hilt. Up to this point, the canyon had been fairly wide with a good road and light forest to either side, but from here, both it and the road narrowed. Worse for the wagons, the road went through a series of switchbacks that led upward to a flatter place beyond. She'd seen a map in General Bennis's tent and, if it were accurate, the road went through seven more of these brutal elevation changes on its way to Hilt.

The good news was that for her and her archers, each switchback gave them a perfect perch from which to fire on anyone pursuing them. Each turn rose about fifty feet above its predecessor, which would give them an impressive advantage, though there was precious little cover from any return fire.

"Keep going," she said when she reached the end of the first switchback. She gestured up toward the next turn. "Go all the way to the end and form a line an arm's length apart."

As her troops moved to obey, Lynn surveyed the field below. A half-dozen wagons were already lumbering up the path toward her with a dozen more waiting on the field below. Her eyes darted to the woods beyond the clearing where the raiders had laid out their fake camp. The road back to Blackblade Fork was wide enough for two wagons to pass each other with clumps of sparse trees on either side. They had already entered Hilt Canyon and the mountains came right down on either side, not quite sheer walls, but so steep they would be difficult to climb.

The clearing itself was about four hundred yards wide with about half a mile separating the road from the switchbacks. Cleary this was a favorite stop for caravans making the journey over the mountains.

The sound of cracking wood drew Lynn's attention. On the road below her a wagon was leaning to one side over a broken wheel. The teamster driving it and one of the samurai were yelling at each other over what was to be done until the Ardorin colonel arrived. He was younger than Lynn thought a colonel should be, probably a relative of some Ardorin official, but he took charge quickly enough. The teamster grabbed his bag of personal possessions and then the Ardorin colonel and a dozen of his men, heaved the wagon over on its side and out of the road.

"Captain," the voice of Lieutenant Coulter called, urgency in her voice. Breanne Coulter was a woman of middle years from Resolute, a veteran of several wars and campaigns, and Lynn's chief lieutenant.

When Lynn turned to her, she was pointing down into the valley. Lynn knew what she'd see when she looked. Swarming out of the trees were waves of Obsidian monsters. She could see lanky goat men and some kind of short, hairy things as they raced forward, forming up in a line beyond the trees that flanked the road. Behind them came soldiers in proper armor, filling up the space behind the monstrous front rank.

Lieutenant Coulter whistled softly.

"That's a lot more Obsidians than we thought," she said under her breath.

Lynn nodded in agreement. Their best guess at the raiders' strength put them at about fifteen hundred warriors. She couldn't be sure but the force assembling in the clearing below seemed bigger than that.

"Mercer!" Lynn called the young archer at the nearest end of her line. "Go tell General Trevan that there's at least two thousand soldiers down there, and maybe a few hundred more." She pointed in the direction of the blue standard that marked the general's position. "Run."

She slapped Mercer on the back and he took off like a shot.

"Captain Artemis."

Lynn turned to find the Ardorin colonel approaching with two of his samurai.

"I'm going to position my men here," he said, gesturing to the top of the first switchback. There was a wide, flat patch of ground there where wagons could pause to make way for travelers going the opposite direction. "If the enemy breaks through, my warriors and I will meet them here. You and your archers stay up above us and harass the enemy as they come up."

"Yes sir, Colonel Koshiba," she said, finally recalling the man's name. "We'll thin them out for you."

She saluted and Koshiba turned back to his soldiers, issuing orders as he went.

"Dying ground," Lieutenant Coulter muttered beside her.

"You have something to add, Lieutenant?"

"We're on dying ground, Captain," she repeated, gesturing out at the forces arrayed against them. "They've got us pinned with nowhere to run. If we don't win, we die."

Lynn hadn't thought about it that way and a chill swept over her.

She was no coward, but she didn't relish the thought that this might be her last day of life.

"Don't worry, Captain," Coulter said, clapping her on the shoulder. "I've been here before. Nobody fights harder than a soldier with their back to a wall."

Lynn took one last look at the Obsidian army below. They weren't pouring out of the forest or up the road anymore. The front rank had formed up into neat lines five soldiers deep with a second rank getting organized right behind. It would be a few minutes before they'd be ready to attack.

"I guess we'd better get ready then," she said, more to herself than to Coulter. With a last look at the opposing force, Lynn Artemis unslung her bow from across her shoulder and headed up the hill to where her archers waited.

† † †

D on't look at them," Trevan shouted at a teamster who stood on his wagon to get a better look at the Obsidians rushing out of the trees on the far side of the clearing. "Keep that wagon moving."

The man shot him a dirty look before he saw who had shouted at him, then ducked quickly back into his seat.

"It's going to be close," Loremaster Zhal observed, shielding his eyes from the setting sun as he squinted across the field.

There were sixteen supply wagons in the Army of Might's train and eleven of them had already started up the narrow, turning road into Hilt Canyon. They'd already lost one to a broken wheel but the train was moving . . . slowly.

Trevan turned to Colonel Aquila, who stood by his side.

"Have men ready to turn the remaining wagons over if they charge," he said. "We can at least use them as barricades."

Aquila nodded, then repeated the order to one of his lieutenants.

"At least they didn't catch us with our pants down," Sir Llewelyn observed.

Trevan gave him a sour look, but before he could rebuke the young knight an archer came running up at a full sprint. He skidded to a stop and saluted as he tried to catch his breath.

"Begging the general's pardon," he said between great gasps of air. "Captain Artemis sends her regards and says that the Obsidian force is at least two thousand strong, maybe more."

Trevan looked across the field, then nodded at the archer.

"Thank Captain Artemis for me and tell her to hold half her arrows in reserve to cover our retreat up the canyon road."

The young man nodded, then saluted and dashed back toward the winding path.

"If we get to retreat," Aquila observed.

"If we fail here, the Obsidians will pour up the road," Trevan said. "If the archers still have arrows, they'll cut them down like wheat. It will give whoever's left a fighting chance."

Trevan squinted across the field. He couldn't see really well, but it looked like Artemis had been right. There were more raiders than there should be.

"They've been reinforced," he muttered.

"That would explain why we couldn't catch up with them," Zhal said. "They didn't just get soldiers, they got supplies. They didn't have to forage."

The loremaster was doubtless correct, but where had this resupply come from? As far as Trevan knew, there weren't any Obsidian forces on this side of the Blackblade range.

"Could they have come from Hilt?" Zhal asked, reading the look on Trevan's face.

"No," Colonel Aquila said. "If they had a force from Hilt, they'd have put them behind us and attacked from the rear."

"It doesn't matter where Halik got them," Trevan said. "What matters is that they're here and they've got us neatly boxed in."

"Then what are they waiting for?" Sir Llewelyn asked. "They outnumber us two, maybe even three to one. Why are they giving us time to get our wagons up the canyon? We're not set. They should attack."

"They want to parlay," Trevan said. He had no idea why the Obsidians would want to talk, but it was the only explanation for their lack of action. If he had caught an inferior foe in the open, he wouldn't have waited, he'd have sounded the charge as soon as his first ranks were formed.

"Obsidian's don't parlay," Aquila said.

"They do when they're in a bad position," Zhal said, a smile creeping across is wizened features.

"What bad position?" Sir Llewelyn said, an incredulous look sending his eyebrows up. "They've got us boxed in."

"But they're in the same box," Zhal said, turning to Trevan. "Don't you see? Our back is to their fortress, but their back is to the enemy as well."

It was true, behind Halik and his raiders was the open expanse of South Paladis with little food or shelter for a force this size. They couldn't retreat, they had nowhere to go.

"How does that help us?" Trevan asked.

"Wherever they got those soldiers and supplies, that's it," Zhal explained. "There aren't any more."

"How do you know?" Llewelyn asked.

"Because," Trevan said. "If they had more men somewhere, they'd have brought them." He nodded toward the Obsidian force. "That's everything they've got."

"Exactly," Zhal said. "If they don't break through and reach Hilt, they're doomed. It's only a matter of time before the Council of Might sends someone to hunt them down."

"Unless they get past us and reach the safety of their fortress," Colonel Aquila said.

"And how many of them will survive this fight to reach Hilt?" Zhal asked. He pointed out at the empty ground between them. "We've still got room for a cavalry charge or two and our archers have position up on the road above us."

"He's right," Trevan said. "They outnumber us, but they've put us in a no-win position with nowhere to run. If they attack, most of their force will be killed. They'll win, but there won't be more than a handful of them left."

"Imagine how they'll be received at Hilt?" Zhal said. "The survivors would be viewed as failures."

"And we know how the Empire deals with failure," Sir Llewelyn said.

"So, what?" Colonel Aquila asked. "Do they want to bargain for safe passage?"

"I guess we're about to find out," Trevan said. He nodded to where a small group of riders had disengaged from the enemy ranks and were making their way into the center of the field at a walk. The rider in front carried the flag of an Obsidian commander, signaling that whoever was in charge of the raiders wanted to talk.

"Bring my banner," Trevan said, moving toward his horse. Loremaster Zhal reached out and grabbed his breastplate, forcing him to stop.

"Remember, General," he said, his voice a conspiratorial whisper. "They aren't the only ones in a position to bargain. The knight was correct." He nodded to where Sir Llewelyn was climbing atop his charger.

"Everyone over there knows the price they'll pay for failure, even if they win this day."

The loremaster had a point. The problem was that self preservation might work on the humans in the raider force, but would it work on the monsters? Did the monsters care about this fight, or were they some bloodthirsty mob their officers wouldn't be able to contain?

"I'll see what I can manage," he told Zhal, then pulled himself up onto his horse and headed out with his honor guard onto the little field.

† † †

Here they come," Halik said, sitting easily in the saddle of his stolen horse.

General Karpasic nodded, but didn't feel the need to respond. He had eyes, after all.

"I'm surprised," Evard Dirae said from Karpasic's other side. The sorcerer sat on a donkey, which made him half a yard shorter than the general; apparently he wasn't much of a horseman.

Not that Karpasic minded, of course. The thought that he might soon be rid of this meddlesome sorcerer and his traitor friend as well almost made Karpasic smile, but he stifled that. An old saying ran through his mind about chickens and not counting them.

He was too far from the trees to see clearly, especially in the fading light, but he looked the nearest thicket over just the same. There was no sign of Lady Maradn's flying lizard.

That was the one fly in his ointment. The last time he'd communicated with her had been three days ago, and she had declared that she would arrive in Hilt Canyon in time to oversee the victory. If she arrived, and only if she arrived, Karpasic would kill Dirae and Bennis, then hand the sword over to her. Thus his own, personal victory would be assured. If Lady Maradn was late, he'd have to swallow his thirst for Bennis's blood and support Dirae. It was a riskier path, but he had no doubt that Dirae would make good on his promise if he won.

Karpasic didn't bother to hide his smile at that thought. He liked battles where his victory was assured no matter what else happened.

"I'm here, Halik," someone called from the opposite party once they were a dozen yards apart. "What did you want to talk about?"

Karpasic's smile evaporated at the sound. The voice was not that of Aren Bennis.

"That's Mikas Trevan," Halik said, keeping his voice low. "He was the captain of the Opalis Legion."

Just like Bennis, Karpasic thought. *Hiding behind others, making them his stooges*

"I'm not interested in you, Captain Trevan," Karpasic called back. "I want to speak to my former captain, Aren Bennis."

A low murmur of conversation erupted in the armed group a mere stone's throw away. Then Trevan spoke again.

"I was told that Captain Halik, formerly of the Westreach Army, was in command of the raiders. But, I know Halik. I don't know you."

"This is General Karpasic," Halik called. "You might remember him from when he tore down the walls of Opalis."

Karpasic smirked at that. The sorcerer wanted him to give the ridiculous Army of Might a chance to avoid a fight. The general wanted to think Dirae a coward for it, but a fight would cost them most of their force and Karpasic saw the wisdom in preserving as many soldiers as possible.

"I thought you were enjoying the company of Opalis still," Trevan shot back.

Karpasic growled at the memory of his incarceration.

"It seems the warriors of Norgard aren't any better at holding on to their possessions than Opalis was," he called back, not bothering to disguise the scorn in his voice. "Now I want to talk to the traitor, Aren Bennis. I know he's been put in charge of your little force. Bring him out here."

"General Bennis has appointed me to speak for him," Trevan called back. "Say your piece."

"Fine," Karpasic yelled back. "As you can see, we've got you cornered like a rat in a hole. If you give us Bennis and his cursed sword, we'll let you depart in peace. If not"—he paused for dramatic effect—"then none of you will live to see the next dawn."

A low sound drifted across the empty space, and after a second, Karpasic realized it was laughter.

"That's a generous offer, General," Trevan said. "And I'll be sure to relay it to the general. In the meantime, however, I've got an offer for you. We both know I've got the better position. You're going to lose a lot of your force if you try to take us, you might not even manage it. What will your Obsidian masters think of you then? We all know how they reward failure."

"I have no doubts about my ability to destroy you, Trevan," Karpasic yelled, a little louder than he intended.

"Don't be so sure, General," Trevan called back. "I have a counter offer for you. Any of your men who surrender will be given amnesty and parole within the lands of the Council of Might."

Now it was Karpasic's turn to laugh.

"None of my men are fool enough or coward enough to accept that offer," he growled. "Give Bennis my message and tell him he has ten minutes to surrender."

With that, Karpasic turned his horse and made his way back toward his own lines at a slow, easy pace.

W hat do we do now?" Sir Llewelyn asked as he, Trevan, and the guards made their way back toward their lines.

Trevan watched the activity at the bottom of the road that climbed into the canyon. The last of the wagons were just pushing forward and Colonel Aquila's force was forming up across the road with shield-bearing legionnaires in front and Aerie pikemen behind.

Trevan had tried to keep the Obsidians talking as long as possible to give the wagons time, and it had worked. Of course that hadn't been the only thing. The news that General Karpasic had joined the raiders and apparently brought soldiers and supplies with him gave Trevan chills. General Bennis spoke fairly poorly of Karpasic, both as a warrior and as a man, but his record of conquest stretched across both sides of the continent and Trevan would be a fool to ignore it.

"Bugler," he said to the young woman riding off to his left. "Be ready to sound the cavalry charge when I give the word. The rest of you," he raised his voice a little so his honor guard could hear. "As soon as she sounds the charge, we make a run for it."

"What are you doing, sir?" Sir Llewelyn asked, he sat straight in his saddle but his face was pale. "We can't win this fight."

"Did you see the man in the black robe, on the general's left side?"

Llewelyn shook his head.

"That was an Obsidian sorcerer," Trevan explained. "They said they want Aren, but it's really the Avatar sword that they want. It doesn't matter what it's going to cost them, they're going to attack."

"Tell them the truth," Sir Llewelyn said. "We don't have the sword."

Trevan sighed and shook his head.

"They would never believe us," he said. "There's no stopping this battle now. All we can do is strike first and hope for a miracle."

Llewelyn's face went from pale to hard and resolved and he nodded gravely back. In other circumstances, Trevan would have smiled to see the knight's bravery and dedication. Right now, however, there wasn't time.

Turning to the bugler, he said, "Sound the charge."

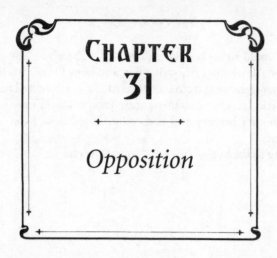

CHAPTER 31

Opposition

ren fell to the floor, trying desperately to cover his eyes as the heat from the forge burned him. It seemed to cut right through his clothing, twisting his insides and causing him to convulse in agonized spasms.

And then it was gone.

His arms and legs were still trembling, but the scorching sensation had utterly vanished. Aren risked taking his hands away from his eyes and found the blue curtain of magical energy once again surrounding him. It was larger this time, further away, and Elysia stood inside it looking down at him with her arms crossed over her chest and a demure smile on her face.

Tentatively, Aren put his hand on the ground to push himself up. He expected it to be hot, too hot for his skin, but the stone was quite cool.

"What's going on?" he asked, standing.

"The heat from the lava can't reach this far inside the forge," Elysia explained. "Not through the stone, at any rate."

Aren held up his hand and found the skin pinkish, as if he'd been sunburnt.

"What you experienced is the raw magic of this place," she went on. "Only those skilled in magic or shielded by magic can survive it."

Aren nodded, looking around. Nothing looked especially magical or powerful, the forge appeared to be exactly what it was, a large chamber cut out of the rock and used to make things out of metal.

"All right," he said, simply accepting her explanation without question. "But what are you doing? Why are you still protecting me?"

She raised an eyebrow at him, her look halfway between disdain and amusement. Aren recognized that look, he'd seen it on Syenna's face often enough.

"You ended our conversation before I was done," she said. "Rather rudely, I might add."

"You wanted me to make the world safe by killing anyone in it who might be dangerous," he said.

"With my power, you'd know for certain whether or not they were dangerous," Elysia said. Strangely there was no judgment in her tone, just a simple statement of fact.

"I'd be no better than the Empire," Aren said, keeping his growing anger in check. "I want the world to have peace and order, but I'm sorry, there must be a better way to go about it."

"Of course there is," Elysia said, as if that fact had been self evident all along.

Aren just stared at her, dumbstruck for the first time in their strange conversation.

"Then why offer me a kingdom of blood built atop a throne of bones?"

"To see if you would take it," Elysia said.

Aren struggled for words again as he tried to wrap his mind around what the transparent woman was telling him.

"This was a test?" he managed at last. "For what? I thought we knew each other so well."

Elysia looked away from him for a second, her expression one of sadness.

"You never really know what a human will do when offered power," she said. "I've seen it corrupt even the best of you. I've seen it devour not just individual lives, but whole nations." Her eyes rose to meet his, full of uncertainty and pain. "I had to be sure."

"Are you satisfied, then?" Aren asked, not bothering to hide the indignation in his voice.

"Yes," she said with no hint of shame or regret.

"Then what is this other way you mentioned?"

Elysia did not answer, but turned and walked over to a massive stone worktable. Bits of whatever its previous owner had been working on were strewn about its top, obscured under a thick layer of dust and grime. She reached down and picked up a thin, rectangular sheet of metal with her insubstantial-looking hand. Tapping its corner on the tabletop, she shook the filth of centuries off of it and held it out to Aren.

"Do you know what this is?" she said.

Aren took the sheet. It was so thin, he felt it bend slightly where he held it, and he loosened his grip. Strange symbols were cut into the metal, revealing words in some long-lost language, but they only covered half of the sheet, as if whoever had engraved them had been interrupted in their work.

"It looks like a page from a book," Aren said. "But why write on metal? It's hardly practical."

"Metal endures," Elysia answered. "And a book of prophecy needs to endure. This is a page from the *Litany of the Dark*."

Elysia said it as if Aren should know what she spoke of, but he'd never heard of such a book.

"That sounds ominous," he answered.

"Not at all. The *Litany* contains the prophecies left by the Avatars when they were driven from this world. They refer to the dark times that awaited humankind, and in them lie the hope for your redemption."

"The Obsidians have prophesies, too," Aren pointed out. He'd heard them enough during his training as a soldier, how the Empire was destined to bring order to the world.

"And where do you think those prophesies came from?" Elysia gave him an enigmatic look.

"The first Obsidian Eye divined them from the Destiny Pool," Aren repeated the answer he'd heard thousand times before.

Elysia shook her head, her dark curls bouncing with the movement. She reached out and took the metal page from Aren and held it up so he could see the marks on it.

"The First Obsidian eye used the Destiny Pool as a lens to read the words written here, in the *Litany of the Dark*. He did not understand that you cannot see clearly through a clouded lens, no matter how powerful."

"He misread the book?" It was a thought Aren had never even considered before, and it took him a minute to come to terms with the implications of it.

"And his mistake now threatens to blanket the world in blood. The Obsidians were never supposed to use their power to impose order on their fellow men."

Aren remembered what Elysia had implied earlier.

"But there's another way," he guessed, "to bring peace and order to the world."

"Of course," Elysia said. "Everything has an opposite; light and shadow, plenty and want, even life and death."

"The opposite of order is chaos," Aren said. "And we already have plenty of that."

"No," Elysia replied. She spoke quietly as if conveying a great secret. "The opposite of order that is imposed from without, is order that grows from within."

"I think that if order could grow from within we'd have seen some by now," Aren said. Certainly there were men and women who shared his goals and desires, but they were pitifully few compared to those who embraced either ordered violence or outright chaos.

"Humans are like a garden," Elysia said. "If you want something to grow, you must first plant the seeds."

Aren rubbed his temple where a headache was starting to form. Elysia's words seemed like a maze that turned inward, upon itself, and went nowhere.

"So what are these seeds of order?" he demanded, his patience beginning to fray. "And how do I plant them?"

Elysia didn't answer. She set aside the metal page and walked around the workbench to where the Avatar sword lay, shining in the dust. Picking it up, she held it in both her upturned palms and offered it to Aren. He took the weapon and as his hand closed around the hilt, the last sword symbol on the crosspiece, the one on the langet that pointed up toward the tip, turned from black to silver.

"What are these?" he asked, pointing to the silver symbols. "And why do they change color like that?"

Elysia put her hand on the crosspiece and traced the newly silver symbol with the tips of her fingers.

"These are the answer to your question," she said. "These are the seeds you must plant, if you wish for order to come, as is foretold in the prophecy." She looked up at him, across the sword, and he met her gaze. "Be warned," she cautioned. "Seeds take time to grow, and even longer to spread. Like other gardeners, you will need patience for this task. Many will embrace what you bring, others will fight it. You can only hope to start this task in your own lifetime, and it will fall to others to finish it."

As Elysia spoke, her voice changed, growing more forceful, and Aren could hear the words echoing off the stone walls and workbenches. Gooseflesh ran up his back and he could feel the hairs on his arm standing up.

"You still haven't told me what these are," Aren said once the last echoes of her words had died away.

"These represent the Virtues," she said. "The ancient code given to this world by the Avatars."

Aren had heard of the Avatars and their virtues, of course, but until quite recently he considered them nothing more than fairy stories, childish fantasies meant to give people comfort in a dark world. Which, he realized, is what they were, only based on reality rather than imagination.

"This one represents Sacrifice," Elysia continued, tracing the newly silver symbol with her finger. "You earned it when you gave up your very own empire rather than engage in the slaughter it would take to achieve."

Aren puzzled over that. He wasn't sure how not murdering people counted as a sacrifice.

"That's not the sacrifice part," Elysia said with a giggle when he asked. "The sacrifice is that you gave up being a high king, emperor of the whole world, to be a teacher instead. You chose not to impose order, but to encourage it." She put her hand on his breastplate, directly over his heart. "That's the secret of the Virtue of Sacrifice, it's giving up something good, for something better." She cocked her head and grinned. "It's just the something better is usually a lot more work."

"So what are these virtues," Aren asked. "And how am I supposed to champion them?"

Elysia opened her mouth to answer but suddenly turned as if she heard a noise.

"Our time here grows short," she said after a long pause. "You must do two things. First, you must master each of the Virtues, learn to live them and be an example of them in your own life."

"But I don't even know what they are." Aren protested.

"Ask the loremaster. He can tell you all you need to know." She gave him an amused grin. "And more, no doubt." Her face turned serious again. "Second, you must destroy the magic of the Obsidian Cabal. Its purpose is what gives them power."

"Purpose?" Aren said. "The magic has . . . purpose?"

Elysia nodded.

"I told you, Aren, everything has its opposite. As I represent the ancient Virtues, the magic of the shard represents dominion. You must destroy it or the Virtues will have no space to take hold, no room to grow."

"All right," Aren said with a sigh. "How do I destroy magic purpose?"

"By destroying the great shards," she said. "There are two, one in the place where the rivers cross, and the other in the seat of Obsidian power."

Aren had no idea where the rivers crossed, but the second location clearly referred to the city of Desolis. Elysia turned away and crossed to the shelves behind the workbench. She took a dusty lump down from one of the shelves, then brought it back and placed it on the bench. It appeared to be folded spyglass, but there were too many lenses, some on short wires and others mounted to a disk on the instrument's front.

"This is the Lens of Truth," she said with a sad look. "They used to be quite common, but now, like truth itself, they are virtually unknown."

Aren picked it up and blew the dust from it. On the back of the lens was a leather pad attached to a strap so it could be worn over the face, covering one eye.

"Only an Obsidian sorcerer can destroy the shard," she said. "Give the Lens to your friend, Evard Dirae. Bid him use it to read the *Litany of the Dark* in a place of power and he will see."

"Evard wants the sword . . . he wants you destroyed."

"Yes," Elysia said with a nod. "But there are no other sorcerers who would even consider it. Evard still trusts you. Reaching him is our only chance."

"Even if it costs both of us our lives?"

She nodded.

"Even then."

Aren looked at the lens in his hand, it didn't seem important or powerful, just a hunk of brass, leather, and crystal. He was about to ask Elysia what to tell Evard when the entire room shook and a cacophonous boom drove Aren to his knees.

"What was that?" he yelled over the ringing in his ears as he struggled back to his feet.

Before Elysia could answer a chunk of the wall split open sending rubble flying in all directions. Aren ducked behind the stone workbench as it was showered with fist sized rocks. When the avalanche subsided, he stood again. Next to the forge with the three silver anvils the crack in the wall was growing. He could see long fingered hands reaching through the gap, gripping the stone and attempting to force it open. The skin of the hands was an inky black with translucent veins of what looked like red steam flowing over the top like a mist.

As Aren watched, a glowing eye of white fire was pressed against the crack and the creature behind it shrieked. The sound was high pitched, and set Aren's teeth on edge.

"What is that thing?" he gasped, but Elysia had vanished.

"Run," her urgent voice sounded in his mind.

Aren didn't need to be told twice. Clutching the sword in his right hand and the Lens of Truth in his left, he bolted back along the hall, past the rows of cold and silent forges, and out onto the narrow bridge. He'd taken his time crossing it before, but now he didn't even look down at the magma below.

"You didn't answer my question," he yelled as he crossed the open expanse of floor, hoping he remembered where the bottom of the spiral stair was. "That's a bad habit of yours."

"Everything has its opposite," her voice said, though it sounded weaker and more distant than it had before. "While I am a force of order, that is a monster of chaos. Like all creatures of magic, it was drawn to this place of power. When it sensed me here, it came to defend its territory."

"But you can kill it, right?" Aren said as the opening to the spiral stair appeared out of the gathering darkness.

"I am too weak," Elysia said. "But the creature is big and slow. Your best chance is to outrun it. Lead your soldiers to the chamber of the virtues, then take the door of courage. It will . . . you up to the Obisid . . . tress."

As she spoke, Elysia's voice grew fainter and fainter until Aren could barely make out what she was saying.

". . . too far from the forge," he heard. "I won't be . . . talk to you again. Good luck."

Aren paused on the stairs long enough to sheathe the sword and take a better grip on the delicate-looking lens.

"I guess I'm on my own," he said, gasping for breath. He wanted to rest for a minute, but the ground shook again, this time coming up from right below. The chaos demon had reached the stair.

Chapter
32

War

Captain Hawkes watched the meeting in the middle of the clearing that separated Blackblade Fork road from the narrow path that led up Hilt Canyon. With Colonel Tibbs gone off with the general, he'd been given command of the cavalry, and he was determined not to dishonor his colonel by failing. He'd expected the Obsidian raiders to attack as soon as they arrived, but the enemy just stood there in ranks. It wasn't until their leaders called for a council and a parlay that he understood. Still, the raiders seemed to be in possession of vastly superior numbers.

"What are they doing?" he muttered, giving vent to his own frustrations.

"Don't let it throw you, sir," Lancer Tyrie said in his drawling voice. "They're just threatening General Trevan, telling him how many more men they have and how we're cornered. They want him to surrender instead of fight."

Hawkes did a quick survey of the forces arrayed on the other side of the clearing. If he had to guess, the enemy outnumbered them by a significant margin. Still, surrender wasn't really an option, either. The raiders would use their capture to gain favor with their former brethren at Hilt, and their prisoners would join the ranks of the Obsidians' monster army.

"Looks like the meeting is breaking up," Tyrie observed.

Hawkes glanced back to the knot of horses standing in the center of the field. General Trevan and his guards had turned back toward the canyon and were moving away from the enemy at a walk.

"Might as well get comfortable," Tyrie said. "The way these things usually go, they gave the general an hour or so to answer whatever terms they offered."

Hawkes had just started to relax when the brassy notes of a bugle sounded across the clearing. At the same moment the general's party leapt forward at a gallop.

"That's the charge," Hawkes gasped, recognizing the call. "Hasars, charge! Lancers at the ready!"

The horse archers hesitated for only a moment, then they leapt forward as one, thundering across the field from the extreme left of the raider lines. Hawkes didn't have to issue any more orders, his horsemen knew what to do.

As the hasars raced forward, closing the distance with the raider lines, the monsters in the front dropped to one knee. Each stood up again with a long spear they'd hidden in the tall grass. Jamming the butt of the spears into the dirt, they angled them forward, ready to break the hasars' charge.

Hawkes expected the enemy to have spears or pikes, but thought it would have taken longer to get them in position.

Still, he and his cavalry had a few surprises, too.

When the hasars were within a score of yards from the lines, they suddenly reined in hard. They unslung the bows they wore across their body as their trained horses turned around and before the enemy could react, they raked the front lines with arrow fire.

Monstrous goat men screamed and went down all along the line, yet there were many more stepping up to take the place of the fallen. The hasars fired a second volley before the enemy lines broke and, as a wave they rushed forward. They were faster than Hawkes expected, but the hasars mounts were faster. Having already turned around, they leapt away, speeding back toward friendly lines.

If any of the raider officers understood that mistake, they weren't able to stop it. The monsters pursued the hasars, stretching their lines out as they rushed forward.

Captain Hawkes drew his long, curved saber and held it aloft. As one, his men repeated the gesture, filling the air with a steely rasp that echoed over the sound of galloping horses and running monsters.

Standing in his stirrups, Hawkes waved his sword once over his head, then pointed it at the charging raiders.

"Charge!" he yelled, dropping back to his saddle and spurring his eager mount forward. All around him the lancers shouted a battle cry as the entire line moved as one. They parted briefly when they met the incoming hasars, opening spaces for the horse archers to pass through their lines, then closed up again just in time to slam into the wave of oncoming raiders.

Hawkes slashed left and right, moving his saber in a rhythmic arc over his horse's head, striking targets on either side. His horse didn't wait for him, running down many of the enemy, shattering bones and organs under her iron-shod hooves.

Arrows began to arc over their heads as the hasars came up behind them, riding in their wake and raking stragglers and the enemy's rear ranks. But they weren't the only arrows. Fully recovered, the raider archers began to shoot as well. The young lancer on Hawkes left cried out as an arrow shaft appeared in his chest and he toppled from his horse to the field below.

Another arrow struck Tyrie's horse in the flank but the animal didn't even flinch. The thick leather barding had taken most of the impact.

Hawkes felt a sharp pain as an arrow sunk into his thigh, just below where his chain tunic protected him. It hurt but he shut the pain off. Everyone knew that to stop here was to die.

The cavalry swept across the field until they reached the far end of the lines. Since the enemy was charging, Hawkes' charge had taken him closer to the canyon side of the field as they went. Now they were quite close to the steep mountains.

Holding his saber aloft, Hawkes spun the tip in a circle and turned his horse. The riders that remained followed, turning as one and galloping back, aiming for the opening in their lines right in front of the switchback path.

Another arrow slammed into Hawkes' back, and he felt it bite into his shoulder blade. The impact drove him forward over the pommel of his saddle but his chain managed to absorb some of the impact and the head didn't pierce his lung.

The infantry had taken up positions in front of the entrance to the canyon road, a passage about thirty yards wide, in a semicircle. Their long shields were braced in front and long, barbed pikes stuck out making the wall look like a porcupine. As Hawkes and his riders approached, the foremost infantry lifted their shields and stepped aside, opening a narrow channel through the wall of steel and barbs.

Captain Hawkes pushed himself off his mount's neck and put the spurs to her, urging her forward. Behind him, he knew that his riders were collapsing their wedge formation, drawing into a long line to pass trough the gap in the infantry. He hit the gap at a full gallop, turning his horse up the road and past the last few wagons, making room for his riders to reach safety as well.

When he reached the first switchback, he turned his horse aside, motioning for the rest to continue up the path to the next turn. Below on the battlefield, the infantry had already closed the gap, covering the road to Hilt Pass with an unbroken line of shields. The field beyond was littered with the bodies of the dead and dying raiders. Their numbers had been thinned, but it wouldn't be enough. Already the remaining monsters had reached the infantry, slamming against the shield wall in an effort to breach it by the press of numbers. Among the dead on the field, Hawkes could see a few stray, riderless horses.

"Give me the count," he said to Tyrie, his voice coming out in a hoarse gasp.

"Get down from your horse, sir," the lancer said in a stern voice.

"The count, man," Hawkes urged.

"Looks like we lost at least fifty," Tyrie said. "Mostly from the cavalry, but some from the hasars."

"Have the riders walk their horses," Hawkes said. He was feeling light-headed. "Have the wounded report to the surgeon."

"That's already being done," Tyrie said.

Hawkes knew that, of course. Those were the standard orders after a charge, but he needed to issue them formally. He wasn't about to let discipline slip while he was in charge.

"Those orders go for you, too, sir," Tyrie pressed.

"Nonsense," Hawkes said. "I feel . . . I . . ."

Hawkes didn't seem to be able to finish his sentence. Looking down he saw the arrow sticking out of his right leg. The saddle below was slick with blood and already a small puddle had formed on the ground. He knew this was bad, but he couldn't remember why. Before he had a chance to consider the problem, he slipped from his saddle and the world around him vanished into a dark void.

† † †

The sounds of combat up ahead drew Aren onward despite his labored breathing. Climbing the spiral stair had taken much longer than he'd anticipated as it seemed three times longer than it had been when he'd descended.

"General?!" he heard Colonel Tibbs' voice call through the darkness of the tunnel.

He remembered the passage from the octagonal room to the low cave as being more or less straight, but he couldn't see any light ahead of him, so it must have turned gradually. Holding on to his lantern with one hand and keeping his other touching the side wall to ensure his direction, Aren moved as fast as he dared.

Up ahead, someone screamed, a guttural sound of mortal agony that was cut unnaturally short. Aren began to run, heedless of the darkness. The sounds of combat grew louder until suddenly the passage turned enough that he could see to the end. A glowing lava demon stood there swinging its club-like arms wildly. Beyond it, spear-wielding soldiers slashed and stabbed, trying to drive it back.

Aren let go of the wall and drew Elysia. Without a pause, he ran the weapon right through the creature's head. The soldiers on the other side of the molten horror cried out and jumped back as the blade erupted from the demon's face.

"General," one of the soldiers gasped, relief on his young face. "Colonel, he's here," she yelled.

Aren ignored her, stepping over the cooling mound that had been the fire demon. Even that brief exposure singed him, and he moved quickly away from it. Inside the low cave, three more of the demons were raging and at least a dozen fighters were down. He spotted Tibbs, across the room, using the broken end of a spear to distract one of the demons so other soldiers could get a shot at its head.

"Colonel Tibbs," he bellowed. "Get everyone moving through here." He pointed back through the passage where he'd emerged.

Tibbs made eye contact briefly, then nodded.

"Fall back," she shouted as one of her riders managed to spear the demon through the head. "Carry the wounded."

"There you are," Syenna's voice broke over him as the soldiers began to move back. "Where have you been?"

"No time for that," he waved her rebuke away. "Where are they coming from?"

"Same place," Syenna said. "They melted their way through."

Aren looked to the passage where the lava flow had been. As he watched, another lava demon shambled into view. Syenna gripped the short spear she was carrying, turning to meet this new threat.

"I'll handle this," Aren said, passing her the lantern. "Go in front of the soldiers. This passage leads to an octagonal room with three doors. Take the one directly across from where this passage comes out. It leads up to the fortress."

"Scouting's my job," she growled, clearly angry that he'd disappeared.

"I'll explain later, go."

She didn't like it, but she withdrew, darting away down the passage to overtake the soldiers in front. Aren turned to the remaining lava demons. Tibbs and a handful of her riders were keeping them at bay while the wounded were picked up and helped toward the back passage. The newly arrived demon seemed to consider something, then turned to face Aren.

Aren didn't wait for it, he took three long strides forward and slashed at the creature's leg. With the low ceiling, he couldn't manage an overhand blow. His blade slashed partway through the demon's thigh and a blast of heat erupted from the wound. The demon bellowed a sound like grinding rocks as it stumbled. Aren brought Elysia up to meet it, slicing off the top of its head in a single cut.

More heat enveloped Aren, more intense than before. It almost reminded him of being outside the magical shield in the forge. Only this heat wasn't coming from the rapidly cooling lava demon, it came from the passage that contained the lava tube.

Aren stepped forward, expecting to meet another of the creatures. What he saw was a bright, almost white ribbon of molten rock flowing across the floor. One of the dead demons they'd used to block the hallway still stood, frozen to the spot where it had died. The ribbon of magma had encircled its feet and wound its way up, snake-like, until it disappeared into a crack in the stone demon's leg.

Almost as soon as Aren realized what he was seeing, the body of the slain demon cracked and split apart. The stone that had been its corpse moved and separated, revealing a white-hot molten core. They seemed to float, moving to cover the inner surface like plates of armor. Aren looked up at the former demon's head and the fractured stone had risen up into five spires, like a crown of dark rock, and below it, two white hot eyes opened.

Aren cursed, taking a better grip on his sword.

The new monstrosity's feet snapped off the floor and it took a step. Freed from immobility, it rose up to its full height, slightly taller than Aren himself. It lashed out at the side wall of the passage, driving its hand into the stone. As it moved, Aren could see that its form was decidedly female. With a twist of its shoulders and a might crack from the wall, the lava queen pulled out a long stone blade that began to glow white heat at the hilt where she touched it.

Deciding that discretion was the better part of valor, Aren withdrew, ducking back into the low cave. Tibbs and her riders had downed one of the lava demons, leaving only one of the shambling creatures to keep at bay. Ignoring the horror behind him, Aren dashed across the cave, crouching low, and hacked off the demon's leg. It went down like its brother had, but Aren didn't bother to finish it off.

"Hurry," he urged Tibbs. "There's a bigger one coming."

Tibbs didn't respond, but the fact that her gaze shifted over Aren's shoulder and her eyes went wide told him what he needed to know. He turned, bringing Elysia up into guard position. The lava queen approached him, crouched due to the low ceiling. Unlike her shambling brethren, she moved quickly, with precise steps.

She pulled back her sword and swept it toward Aren. It hit like a runaway cart. The shock traveled up Aren's arm, numbing it. Aren lost his footing and fell back hard on the floor.

The lava queen came in for the kill, but she hadn't accounted for the low ceiling. Attempting to raise her sword, it smashed into the stone roof and stuck there for a moment. Aren seized the opportunity and rolled to his feet, bringing the Avatar sword across the lava queen's midsection. The blade bit in, and the demon howled, but the wound wasn't deep.

Aren scrambled out of the way as she swept her stone sword at him in a wild strike. This time Aren anticipated the move, slashing across her elbow once the sword had passed.

The demon howled again and dropped her sword. Aren tried to finish the fight right there, darting in for a killing strike, but the queen slashed at him with her off hand. Each finger ended in long, bladed claws that glowed red with molten fire. She hit Aren in the chest, digging great gouges in his breastplate and hurtling him into the wall.

Gasping, and shaking his head to clear it, Aren got back to his feet. He couldn't see the queen clearly, but years of combat had given him excellent reflexes. When his vision did clear, the queen hadn't moved. She stood, hunched over in the cave, her hand extended as if she were trying to reach something.

The ground a few feet away shattered, sending shards of rock pelting in all directions. Bubbling up from beneath came another ribbon of white hot rock, much faster this time. It flowed across the floor like running water until it encountered the stone corpse of a lava demon.

"Time to go," Aren shouted behind him as a second lava queen began to rise up from the body.

Colonel Tibbs and her soldiers were way ahead of Aren, and as he turned to flee they were already disappearing into the dark passage. He heard the original lava queen move, and Aren sprinted toward the exit. Wind whipped past him as her stone claws snatched at his back, just beyond their reach, and then he was through.

Behind him, the queen screamed. Aren took a chance and skidded to a stop just inside. He turned as the monster reached in after him. The passage was taller than the low cave, and Aren had room to raise Elysia for an overhead strike. As the queen reached blindly after him, he brought the sword down with all his strength, severing the arm at the elbow.

The lava queen screeched in pain, drawing back. Aren didn't give her the chance to retreat; he stepped into the mouth of the passage and drove Elysia upward and directly into one of the monster's glowing eyes. White hot lava spilled from the wound, spattering his hand and burning him as he pulled the sword free. The queen collapsed into the mouth of the passage, convulsing and cooling, her body obscuring the opening somewhat. It wasn't much of a victory as two more lava queens were rising up behind the corpse of their sister.

The sight was unearthly, beautiful and terrifying at the same time, but Aren had no time for that. Without a backward glance, he turned and ran.

CHAPTER 33

Reversal of Fortune

The lancers in front of Aren could only move as fast as the men carrying the wounded. Aren knew that, but he didn't have to like it. From behind him, echoing up the dark passageway, came the grinding screeches of the lava queens. He couldn't see them, coming along in the dark toward him, but he knew they hadn't given up.

"I see a light ahead," Colonel Tibbs called back.

That would be the octagonal room, what Elysia had called the Chamber of the Virtues. Aren hadn't given any thought to the Virtues, but Elysia seemed to think they were the key to setting the world straight, so at some point he would have to. She, of course, had told him to enquire of Loremaster Zhal.

"Easy for you to say," he muttered in the direction of the sword in his hand.

Aren had no doubt the loremaster was a treasure trove of knowledge about the virtues, and that most of it would be entirely inconsequential. Of course, he would have to wade through all that to learn what he needed to know.

Maybe you'll get lucky and the lava queens will get you. The thought brought a sardonic smile to his face.

"Keep going," he heard Syenna's voice from up ahead. "Straight down to the big chamber with the well in the center."

A moment later, he burst from the dark passage into the octagonal room. Syenna stood there holding her lantern high and waving Tibbs and the last of the riders around the stone encrusted fountain in the center of the room and out through the far door.

"Is that everyone?" she asked when Aren entered.

He nodded, leaning heavily on the fountain for a moment to catch his breath. He felt like he'd been running for hours.

"You're bleeding," Syenna said, reaching out to touch his shoulder where the missing spaulder should be.

A shallow cut ran across his shoulder and upper arm. It was bleeding, but not too heavily. The lava queen must have done that when she raked him with her claws.

"Stop that," he said, pushing Syenna's probing fingers away from the wound. "We're not out of the woods yet." He waved back down the passage they'd all come from. "Those lava queens are still back there and they move a lot faster than the regular demons."

"Lava queens?" Syenna asked, trying again to probe his wound.

"They're women and they wear crowns," Aren said, pushing her hand away again. "What do you want me to call them?"

"Fine," Syenna said, giving him a hard look. "Call them whatever you want, just let me look at your shoulder, it wouldn't do to have you get blood poisoning."

"I'm fine," Aren insisted, stepping away from her. "We've got to get going, do you know how to get us up to the fortress?"

"I think so," she said, though her face looked dubious. "There's a big open area just ahead with a stair the wraps around the walls. It goes up to a landing that's near where the Obsidians keep their slaves."

"Good," Aren said. "We need to get up there and arm them. We need to be out of the dungeons and basements before any more demons show up."

"That might be a problem," Tibbs said, standing in the open doorway. "We left most of the spears we were bringing to arm the slaves behind. On top of that, we've got nine dead and five wounded."

It wouldn't be enough. Tibbs didn't say it, but she didn't have to. Over a quarter of his little force was out of the fight, and with no weapons to arm the slaves, the riders that were left had no chance to overpower the fortress garrison.

A sound from down the dark passage drew Aren's attention. Down at the furthest end, he could see the glowing bodies of the lava queens.

"What now?" Syenna asked.

"We pull back to the big room," he said. "There aren't that many of them, if we can keep them inside the hallway, we can deal with them one at a time."

"Okay," Tibbs said. "That should work, but what then? How are we going to get out of here? We can't go back and we can't go up."

Aren was about to answer when a chilling shriek rose up from the hall that led to the spiral stair. The chaos demon had pulled itself up onto the landing with its long-fingered hands. It stood, having to crouch in the hallway, but Aren could see it was half again as tall as he was, and broad, with thick shoulders and arms, like an ape. Its head was broad and flat in front, with eyes of red fire. A cloak of red mist fell away from its shoulders, wafting around the dark body and clinging to it like a spider's web.

"Aren," Syenna said, her voice trembling and barely a whisper. "What the hell is that?"

Aren swore, in the chaos of their flight from the lava queens, he'd quite forgotten about this monstrosity. It surged forward, but like the spiral stair, its body was too large for the hall and it got stuck. Wrenching itself free, it moved more cautiously, but it would still reach the Chamber of the Virtues in minutes.

"I've got an idea," Aren said.

"Do I want to know what it is?" Syenna asked, her voice rising toward panic.

"Nope," Aren said, pushing her toward the hallway beyond the door of Courage. "Run."

Tibbs took off like a shot and Syenna didn't have to be told twice. Aren ran after them, trying to ignore the sounds of rending rock and the chaos demon's high-pitched shrieks.

"Not to question your orders, General," Tibbs huffed, loping along in her heavy chain shirt. "But where, exactly, are we running?"

"All the way, Colonel," Aren replied. "Right up to the top of the fortress's battlements."

† † †

General Trevan stood just far enough up the canyon path to have an unobstructed view of the field below. The cavalry charge had broken up the enemy's lines and the survivors pursued the retreating horses all the way to the wall of shields at the bottom of the road. With a crash he could feel, they slammed into the wall of steel and pikes.

Normally the legionnaires would strike through the notches on the right side of their shields, but General Bennis had had a better idea. Now the job of the front rank was just to hold the shield wall. The second rank thrust their long spears through the shield gaps while a third rank behind ran their pikes over the shields of the front line. It made for an impressive wall of death, but it was not impregnable.

As Trevan watched, the hordes of Obsidian monsters pressed forward, intent on bringing down the shield wall by sheer numbers. The pikemen thrust and slashed, dropping dozens of the monsters to the field in bloody lumps. On the near side of the line, two of the massive goat men had taken hold of a shield and bodily pulled the legionnaire holding it out of the line. The monsters' fellows immediately fell on the man with axes and clubs, but before they could rush into the hole in the line, the remaining legionnaires contracted, closing the gap.

Arrows began to rain down, and soldiers in the rear of the formation held up shields to cover the line. They moved quickly, but some of the deadly shafts still found their mark and more soldiers went down.

The line contracted again.

Sir Llewelyn, standing next to Trevan, suddenly stepped in front of him and Trevan heard the clang of an arrow rebounding off the knight's shield.

"If you wish to survey the field, General," he said, stepping back. "Might I suggest you move farther up?"

Trevan was about to respond that he was wearing his armor when Loremaster Zhal grabbed his shoulder.

"Look," he said.

On the field below, the monsters were pulling back from the shield wall. A flight of arrows leapt toward them from Trevan's archers stationed farther up the hill.

"Why are they retreating?" Zhal asked.

"They're just regrouping," Trevan said. "We pulled them out of formation with that cavalry charge and that cost them." Piles of dead and dying monsters encircled the shield wall. "Their captains finally got them under control. Next time they'll be better organized, they'll try to take down the wall with arrows or break the shields with axes."

"We killed a fair number of them," Zhal observed.

Trevan looked at the shield wall. As they spoke, fresh soldiers were reinforcing it, but there were far too few of them. The wall would hold two, maybe three more charges, but then it would fail.

"The Obsidians have too many of those things," he nodded at the monsters forming up in new ranks across the field.

"Then maybe we should do something about that," Zhal said. He turned to where Amanda stood a few paces away. "I think now is your chance, my dear."

Trevan hadn't forgotten about Captain Syenna's pretty sister, but he wasn't putting much stock in her ability to turn the enemy monsters.

"Is there anything you can do?" he asked her.

She looked down at the shield wall, where soldiers were carrying away the dead and the wounded while others were taking their place. Her face had a greenish cast, but her eyes were determined.

"I can hear them," she said at last. "But I can't seem to . . . connect with any. I'm—" She hesitated. "I'm going to have to get closer."

Trevan looked back to the shield wall. It was no place for a civilian, especially one whose only means of walking was an enchanted frame. He didn't know a lot about the machines of the Titans, but he knew they weren't infallible.

Looking back at her, she met his gaze, not bothering to hide her fear nor her determination.

"All right," he said. "But stay out of the way of the soldiers."

Amanda nodded, then headed down the steep road. Trevan nodded at Sir Llewelyn.

"Go with her," he said. "If there's any chance she can turn those monsters against the Obsidians, make sure she gets it."

The young knight saluted, then moved to follow her, but Trevan caught him by the arm.

"Whatever it takes," he said.

Llewelyn nodded gravely.

"Yes, sir," he said, then continued after Amanda.

† † †

Can't you control those things?" General Karpasic growled at Evard. His Fomorians had been baited into attacking in a mob and had their teeth kicked in for it. Karpasic expected to lose the beasts—that's what they were for, after all—but he didn't get where he was by throwing troops away foolishly.

"It's not like I can will them to obey," the sorcerer said. His voice sounded dull, as if he were bored, but his body was rigid and tense.

You know how much is riding on this fight, don't you, Sorcerer?

Karpasic didn't grin at the thought, not yet anyway. His officers had finally managed to get the Fomorian soldiers back into ranks, and they still had enough manpower to overwhelm Bennis and his little army, but two things gnawed at him. First, he'd expected Bennis to play for time, or to just do the noble thing and surrender. His former captain seemed to always be doing stupidly noble things. So why did he attack?

Karpasic had no answer for that. He'd just have to break the Army of Might and find out for himself.

Then there was Lady Maradn. She promised to be here, at this battle, to take command of the field and snatch victory away from Evard Dirae. So far, however, she was nowhere to be found. This didn't bother Karpasic so much. It would have been nice to kill Aren Bennis when he finally got his hands on the man, but it was a pleasure he would have to forgo if Lady Maradn didn't arrive. He'd have to do thing's Evard's way, but he'd still get his command back.

"The sergeants report that the troops are ready to attack," Captain Halik said, jogging up to where the general and the sorcerer stood.

Karpasic nodded.

"Give the order, Captain. And see if you can't break through that blockade this time."

Halik saluted, then turned, yelling orders to his subordinates.

The Fomorian soldiers gave a ragged yell and charged. Karpasic put his hands behind his back and watched with great satisfaction. The day wasn't his yet, but it was only a matter of time.

† † †

Amanda flinched as an arrow whistled over her head. It smacked into the ground a dozen yards behind her and stuck there like a road marker.

"Are you all right?" Sir Llewelyn asked, holding his shield up so she could duck beneath it.

"Yes," she lied. All around her the sounds of battle raged. Cries of dying men, women, and monsters filled the air as the sounds of steel on steel rang out.

Amanda closed her eyes and tried to block it all out, but she simply couldn't.

"Look at me," the knight said, putting his free hand on her shoulder.

She did. He had an earnest face, calm despite everything.

"You can do this," he said with a smile and a reassuring squeeze of her shoulder.

Amanda nodded, more to convince herself than in agreement. She closed her eyes again and tried reaching out with her mind the way she did when talking to Monk. The Obsidian monsters were all around her, she could feel them there, but there weren't any conscious minds to latch onto. It was as if they were all asleep, or very distant.

Hello? She sent her thoughts into the void.

Off to her left, she felt something react. Not a response, just a twitch, like a reflex.

Are you there?

Calls? It was a strange thought, one not belonging to her, and it seemed to slither into her mind like a whisper.

I'm here.

Suddenly the battlefield snapped into sharp focus, as if Amanda were standing somewhere far above it. Below her the dark bodies of the Obsidian monsters hurled themselves against the bright shields of General Trevan's army. A dark figure appeared, standing across from her. He was tall and lank, his body covered in short, brown fur. His legs bent back, like those of a horse or a dog, and he stood upon glossy black hooves. The head atop the creature's neck wasn't human, it resembled a goat's, with their bizarre eyes, long ears, and short horns.

"Who are you?" it asked, the voice coming hesitantly as if speech were difficult for it.

"My name is Amanda. Who are you?"

"I am first," he said. "First of the Satyr."

"Is that your name?"

The creature shook its head.

"It is who I am. That is what was asked."

As he spoke, three more of the goat men appeared.

"They are second, third, and fourth," First said. "What do you want?"

"I want to free you from the yoke of your Obsidian masters," Amanda said. She wasn't sure exactly what was happening. Monk had been simple, easy to read and easy to understand. The satyrs, however, were much more guarded; she couldn't read anything of their minds.

"You speak as if we were in bondage," First said.

"Are you not?" Amanda asked.

"We serve those who created us," First said.

"It is our honor," Second added. "And our duty."

"I can free you from that," Amanda said.

"Be wary, First of the Satyr," a voice said. "She lies."

Amanda stared hard where the voice came from. Something seemed to be there, and as she gazed fixedly at it, a shorter, female monster appeared. She looked similar to the satyr, but her eyes were large and black and she had no horns.

"She seeks to separate us from our masters."

"I said that," Amanda replied, crossing her arms. "I didn't lie."

The woman looked at her, unblinking.

"You said you had the ability to free us," she said. "You cannot. It is a lie."

As she spoke, two more of the deer women appeared. They did not speak or move, just stood looking at Amanda.

"First among the Fauns is wise," First of the Satyr said. "You offer that which you do not possess, human. Our obligations are clear, we serve those who created us. We will not hear you."

"It isn't a lie," Amanda insisted as First started to turn. "Your obligation isn't to those who made you, it's to those who follow you. They are the ones who need you."

"Foolishness," First of the Satyr said, raising his head imperiously. "All of the satyr know our place. Our only service is to the creators."

With that he waved his hand and vanished. Amanda felt his presence leave her mind, along with several of the others—but not all. Third of the Satyr and First of the Fauns, along with one other, remained.

"Tell me about this new obligation," First of the Fauns said.

Amanda took a deep breath and hoped she knew what she was doing. She'd read books on philosophy that talked about such things, but she was no expert. Still, these monsters were no mere animals, they were fellow beings with minds. It had surprised her, but if she wanted their cooperation, she would have to appeal to those very minds.

"It falls to those of us with wisdom and power, to shelter and guide those with, uh, less," she said.

"Like the creators do for us?" Third of the Satyr asked. The others nodded.

"What is it your creators ask of you?" Amanda said.

"We slay their enemies," Third of the Satyr said.

"And find the pretty stones," the other Faun offered.

"So you do things for them that they won't do for themselves?"

The monsters looked at each other for a long moment, then First of Faun shrugged.

"I suppose that's why they created us," she said. "To do the things they can't."

"The Obsidians can certainly die facing their enemies," Amanda said. "But they'd rather have you do that. This is why they made you, to use you, and then discard you like so much rubbish."

This time the pause while they looked at each other was longer.

Amanda couldn't be certain, but she had the feeling they were communicating but somehow excluding her.

"You say we could be free of them with your help," First of Faun said. "What is it you propose? Are we to stop being the slaves of the Obsidians only to become yours?"

Amanda smiled. First of Faun had used the word *slave*, not servant, or creation. "No," she said. "I don't want you to be anyone's slaves."

"Then we will listen, Amanda of the Army of Might," First of Faun said. "Tell us how we might be free."

Chapter 34

Chaos and Fire

The air in Desolis had gone cold, crisp with the promise of winter. Not that Lady Maradn Norn knew that. Her suite in the old city was perfectly comfortable, warmed on cold days by large chunks of lava rock she enchanted to give off heat. It was a minor spell, almost no power at all, but Maradn found it was the little things that made life so much more worthwhile.

She thought of that as she reclined on a chaise in her library, swirling a magnificent brandy in a crystal glass. Most crystal was made with lead, but this had been made with actual fragments of the shard. There was no latent power to be extracted from such remnants, but Maradn told herself that it made the liquor taste better.

As she raised the shard glass to her lips, a rattling hiss broke the silence of the library, causing her to grimace. Her eyes flitted up to the gleaming brass cage on the library's second floor. She still expected to find Jiri there, swooping about, waiting for her to open the cage and then scratch behind its neck. The fact that Jiri was gone, used in the shaper's modifications, still caused Maradn anger and grief.

A mottled yellow head popped up above rim of the cage bottom and a long, forked tongue flicked in Maradn's direction. She shivered involuntarily.

"Filthy creature," she muttered, taking another drink from her glass. Heil was to be Jiri's replacement, a new companion to replace her dearest pet. All the stupid thing could do, however, was eat, sleep, and flick his disgusting tongue at her. If she didn't require the little beast for her plan to work, she'd have had him cooked for dinner and made another before now.

Still, it was the burden of a sorcerer to work with whatever inferior tools she could find.

Heil hissed again and launched his fat, yellow body into the air, circling the cage before exiting through the open door. He swooped around the library once, then landed on the brass stand beside the chaise. Jiri had done it a thousand times, landing like a dancer and curling its wings around itself. Heil slammed into the brass bar with enough force to make it totter, almost falling over.

Maradn checked the large clock on the mantel over the fireplace and sighed. She was excited that, at long last, her victory was at hand, but as she looked at Heil, struggling to keep his fat body perched on the stand, she was loathe to make the connection.

"Enough of this," she said, sitting up straight and setting her glass aside. "Heil, attend."

The little creature looked up at her with his dull, stupid eyes, and Maradn felt the connection snap into existence. Her mind raced over the intervening miles until she felt the all-too-familiar touch of Jiri's mind.

Or rather what was left of Jiri.

It was both Jiri and not Jiri, the same familiar feel, but changed. As the connection took hold, Jiri chirped with excitement, recognizing its master. Maradn felt a tear run down her cheek in answer. Gradually, her mind began to expand, to sense the creature's surroundings. It was flying, high above a coniferous forest stretching out below like a blue-green carpet. Mountain peaks were visible in the distance, approaching quickly. Maradn knew that the General Karpasic and dear Evard awaited her on the other side of those peaks. Soon she would have the hated Avatar sword, the thorn in her side, Evard Dirae would be dead, and her ascension to the seventh throne would be assured.

She reached out blindly and found the shard glass. Raising it to her lips, she drank deeply, feeling the warmth of the alcohol spread throughout her body. This was going to be a very good day.

† † †

Sweat ran down Aren's face, soaking his collar and stinging his eyes. The path up from beneath the Obsidian fortress wound around through dusty, forgotten rooms and debris-strewn passages. Syenna led them through holes in crumbling walls and along ledges over open pits that seemed to fall down to the center of the world. All around Aren, men and women huffed and gasped, struggling to gain their breath as they moved along without rest.

His legs burned with fatigue and his throat was parched, but they couldn't stop. They needed to stay ahead of their pursuers. The sound of the chaos demon coming along behind them was ever present as it bashed its way through walls and sundered doorways to pass. The grinding cries of the lava queens could be heard as well, though it seemed to Aren that the initial two must have been joined by several more.

"How much farther?" he asked Syenna as she stumbled over a brick of cut stone on the floor. She caught herself but not before slamming into the wall beside an ancient and rotting door. This part of the underground was made up of stone rooms that looked like they might have once been a dungeon of some kind. Occasionally there were barred cell doors or the remains of a rack, but mostly it was empty rooms and rubble.

"You smell that?" she said, reaching for the ancient-looking door.

Aren hadn't been paying attention, but now that she mentioned it he could smell a rank odor rising above the scent of dust and decay.

"We're close to the slave pens."

"What happens when we get there?" Colonel Tibbs asked, trudging wearily up behind them. "If we're going to make a stand against those creatures, I'd rather do it in here." She waved at the stone room. "The hall back there is a natural choke point. They'd only be able to come at us one or two at a time. My riders can handle that."

"I have no doubt of that Colonel," Aren said. "But to answer your question, when we reach the slave pens, you and your riders will secure it."

"But not you," Syenna said, leaning on the old door. It wasn't a question, just a statement, and she shook her head with an exasperated look. "You want to lead those things up to the fortress," she accused. "Make the Obsidians fight them."

Aren smiled at her, feeling far too clever with himself.

"Two birds with one stone," he said.

"And how am I supposed to find the slave pens?" Tibbs asked.

"They're in one of these basements," Aren said. "Syenna will show you."

"Then how will you find your way up to the fortress?" Tibbs asked. "You don't want to get lost or caught in a dead end with those things after you."

"She's right," Syenna said to Aren, then she turned to Tibbs. "Finding the slave pens is easy, just follow your nose."

"What happens if the demons don't follow you?" Tibbs asked. "Those slave pens are bound to be more open than here." She indicated the room again. "They might be able to swarm us there."

Aren drew the Avatar sword. The silver symbols running down the blade gave off a faint glow in the dim light of their lantern.

"They don't want you," Aren said, holding the sword up. "They want this. As long as I stay in sight of them and wave this around, they should follow me." He returned the sword to its scabbard and patted the hilt.

"I think I'll prepare for a fight just the same," Tibbs said with a grim look. "What do I do if you get yourself killed?"

"Take the fortress if you can," Aren said. "If you can't . . ."

"There's no going back," Tibbs pointed out. "Not with those demons blocking the way."

Aren nodded. She was right. This mission had become a do-or-die proposition. No one in his raiding party would surrender and allow themselves to be made into monsters.

Aren was about to tell Tibbs he'd do his best to cut down the demon population when the rotted door Syenna was leaning on suddenly gave way. It cracked and splintered, crumbling into pieces that fell into a deep shaft beyond. Syenna cried out as she whirled her arms in an attempt to find a handhold. Without thinking Aren grabbed her tunic and jerked her away from the gaping hole.

"Be more careful," he admonished her. "We need you to—"

The high-pitched screech of the chaos demon cut him off. The sound grated on his nerves, sending chills up his spine. Strangely, it sounded much louder and closer than it had been.

Leaning out, he looked into the gap beyond the ruined door. A large shaft went down below and he could see the lava queens moving, their glowing bodies clinging to the walls as they climbed up toward him. Much closer, however, was the chaos demon, its white eyes burning with hatred.

A narrow ledge ran along the rim of the shaft connecting the ruined door to the remains of a room a dozen yards away. Without stopping to think, Aren stepped out onto it.

"What are you doing?" Colonel Tibbs asked, peering down over the side. "Get back here, and we'll make a stand."

Aren shook his head.

"No," he said. "Stay here and wait till they've passed, then get to the slave pens and fort up."

With that, Aren started across the small ledge. Below, the chaos demon caught sight of him and shrieked, scrambling to climb faster. Aren tried not to be distracted, but he couldn't help looking at the monster. The ledge suddenly gave way beneath him. Throwing himself forward, Aren pushed off the wall with his hand and aimed for the floor of the broken room only a few yards away. He hit hard, slamming his gut into the fractured stone and getting the wind knocked out of him.

"I got you," Syenna yelled, suddenly appearing over him. She must have run across the ledge and jumped the now-broken part. She grabbed his arms as he began to slip over the edge and bore down with her weight.

Gasping, Aren tried to haul himself up onto the broken floor, but without air his muscles weren't responding well.

"Come on," Syenna yelled as Aren began to slide inexorably back into the shaft. Syenna was strong, but Aren was a full-grown man in metal armor and she wouldn't be able to hold him by herself. Finally Aren managed to force some air into his lungs, and with Syenna's aid he hauled himself up and over the side of the shaft.

"Thanks," he gasped.

Syenna shook her head, undoubtedly intending to admonish him to be careful, but before she could speak, the chaos demon's enormous clawed hand slammed down into the broken floor. The red mist that seemed to swirl and flow over its skin spread out like tentacles, searching for Aren as he scrambled to his feet.

Across the gap, Tibbs gripped her spear in white-knuckled hands as the demon's head rose up over the floor of the broken room. A stinging wave of heat washed over Aren and he jerked Elysia from her scabbard. Instantly the pain vanished and the pulsating bubble formed around him. Beside him, Syenna swore as the heat burned her. Aren reached out and grabbed her hand. The second he had her, the bubble expanded, taking her in as well.

"What?" she began, but he turned and pulled her along after him, racing through the broken room.

"You know the way up?" he shouted, realizing he had no idea where he was going.

"Straight through these rooms and take a left when we reach a broad hallway," she answered, running beside him now. Behind them, the chaos demon simply ran through the wall of the broken room, shattering it. "Turn right and there's a hidden door that opens into one of the fortress's cellars."

"You could have told me that," Aren growled. "You didn't need to come with me."

Syenna grinned at him. "Where's the fun in that?"

The hidden door turned out to be a stone slab that could be moved by a capstan attached to a counterweight with a heavy chain. Everything was covered in dust and rust, but there were signs that the mechanism had been maintained recently.

"Your work?" Aren asked as he began to turn the capstan.

She nodded.

"They built the fortress right on top of an old citadel that was here. This was part of the original foundation, so I searched it. When I found this, I oiled it and braced a few of the weaker links in the chain."

As she explained, the slab began to move back, away from the wall, pivoting on a hidden hinge. The noise of the chaos demon's approach had faded as they ran, but now it was coming closer. Aren gave the capstan a few more turns and then set the pin that kept the door from closing.

Darting through the opening, he found himself in a storage cellar packed with crates and barrels of supplies. A stone stair ran upward to a door set in the wall.

"Where does that lead?" he asked as he followed Syenna up the stairs.

"To a short hall and then out to the lower courtyard," she said. "Any plans for what we do then?"

"Put as much distance between ourselves and this cellar as we can," Aren said, pulling open the door. "If we run into anyone, just pretend like we belong here."

She stopped and gave him a level look.

"Right," he said, realizing that she knew very well how to bluff her way through an Obsidian camp. "Let's go then."

✝ ✝ ✝

Evard Dirae watched with satisfaction as Aren's shield wall got smaller and smaller. Whenever a shieldbearer went down, the wall would contract, and what had started as a semicircle was now almost a flat line across the end of the canyon road. The Fomorians had hit the wall three times already and piles of their bodies littered the field.

Beside him, General Karpasic ground his teeth loud enough for Evard to hear it. He was pacing back and forth like a nervous cat, his eyes fixed on the fight.

"Relax, General," Evard said, grinning at the man's discomfort. "Our forces are almost through. That wall won't survive another charge."

"It shouldn't have lasted this long," Karpasic spat out the words. "We've lost too many soldiers."

"Once we break through, the others will be at our mercy," Evard objected.

"They'll fight us all the way up the mountain," Karpasic muttered. "While their archers rain arrows down on us. Why didn't that fool Bennis take the deal? He's exactly the kind of sap who would surrender himself to keep his men alive."

That thought had worried Evard, too. Aren and his army were in a bad spot. They couldn't win and Aren wasn't a fool. He knew they couldn't win, so why fight?

"What's going on over there?" Karpasic bellowed at a lieutenant who stood by the soldier who was busily waving a red signal flag.

Evard's gaze shifted back to the battlefield. The knot of Fomorians attacking the shield had thinned out dramatically and many were pulling back.

"They don't need to regroup," Karpasic was shouting at the lieutenant. "That line will break if they keep hitting it."

The lieutenant yelled at the signalman, who shouted something back at her that Evard couldn't hear.

"Damn it," Karpasic yelled. "Order them to attack."

Evard wasn't sure what the signal was for attacking but he'd bet a lot that the signalman was already waving it.

"Halik," Karpasic bellowed.

Captain Halik was on the far end of their flank with their reserves and it took him a minute to cross the distance.

"The Fomorians aren't answering commands," Karpasic growled. "Get out there and take charge."

Huffing and out of breath, Halik saluted and turned to the field. He'd only gone a few steps, however, before he stopped short.

"They're deserting," he gasped.

Before Evard could sort out what the captain meant, Halik took off, running full speed to where the lieutenant and the signalman stood.

"Order them to fall back," he called. "Fall back!"

Karpasic swore and simply stood, staring at the battlefield, disbelief written plainly on his face.

"What's going on?" Evard demanded. Something was obviously very wrong, but he had no idea what it might be. He felt the mask of calm sorcerer control slipping as his heart began to race.

"The Fomorians," Karpasic said. His voice was calm, nonchalant even, and he just stood there as if he'd been brained with a mace. "They're deserting."

The ranks of the Fomorians had been thinned significantly by the assault on the shield wall and to Evard it looked as if they were all over the field. As he watched, however, he could see a knot of them in the center just beginning to pull back from the enemy in response to the signalman. There were, however, small numbers of the transformed creatures spreading out to either side of the field. As Evard watched, they melted into the trees in small groups and disappeared.

It took Evard a minute to force himself to believe what he was seeing. Fomorians didn't desert the field of battle. They couldn't desert any more than they could take their own initiative or plot against their masters. Obedience was their only rule, it was the foundation on which their bodies and minds had been built.

A Fomorian couldn't decide to disobey an Obsidian officer any more than a summoned creature could have a will of its own. They simply did what they were told and that was that. Just like . . .

"Monk," Evard gasped.

"What?" Karpasic roared, suddenly regaining control of his facilities.

"The woman," Evard said, picturing the pretty Dross girl. The one that had seemingly broken his connecting with Monk as if it were nothing. "She's here. She has to be." He turned to the general. "Pull the Fomorians back," he said. "We have to keep them away from her."

Evard didn't know just how far the blond girl could affect the Fomorians, but if it had been a long distance, she would have turned their soldiers earlier.

"What are you babbling about, Sorcerer?" Karpasic yelled. "What is going on?"

"The enemy has a weapon that can turn the Fomorians against us," Evard said. "We have to retreat."

Karpasic looked as if he wanted to argue that what he'd just heard wasn't possible, but instead he grabbed Evard by the front of his robe and dragged him bodily forward.

"We can't retreat, Sorcerer," he said, sneering the words. He pointed at the enemy force packed on the canyon switchbacks above the field. "They still have their cavalry. If we retreat now, they'll run us down and cut us to ribbons." He pushed Evard away, sending him sprawling into the dirt. "Halik!" he bellowed. "Hit them with everything. Hit them now!"

CHAPTER 35

Switchbacks

Trevan watched the wave of Obsidian monsters slam into the shield wall. His soldiers slashed and stabbed with their pikes and the wall held, but it wouldn't hold for much longer. Most of his men were wounded, even the ones still at the wall, and when they fell, there wouldn't be anyone to replace them.

"Captain Hawkes," he yelled.

"Hawkes is wounded, sir," a grizzled-looking cavalryman said, saluting. "I'm Lancer Tyrie at your service."

"Get your riders ready for a charge."

"Yes sir," Tyrie said, turning to pass the order.

Trevan noticed that Tyrie didn't ask where the cavalry would retreat to after that charge.

"Do you think the cavalry will break through?" Loremaster Zhal asked. There was no fear in the old man's voice, but Trevan could tell by the question that the loremaster's assessment of their chances was the same as his.

Before he could answer, Sir Llewelyn came jogging up with Amanda in tow.

"Give me some good news," Trevan said.

"Most of the transformed didn't listen," she said. "But I reached a few of them."

"Will they fight for us?" Zhal asked.

"No," Amanda admitted, then she pointed out to the field. "But they won't fight for the Obsidians, either."

Trevan followed the girl's pointing finger out to the periphery of the open field. On the far side of the battle a group of the monsters were beating a hasty retreat, vanishing into the trees before anyone on the Obsidian side could move to stop them. Glancing to the other side, he saw another group of the horned goat men slipping away. The Obsidians hadn't seemed to have noticed yet, but that was only a matter of time.

"Get back down to Colonel Aquila," Trevan said to Sir Llewelyn. "Tell him that the Obsidians are about to pull back. As soon as they do, he's to open the shield wall for the cavalry. Go!"

The knight didn't question, he turned and ran, his armor clanking all the way down the hill. Trevan turned to Tyrie who sat, ready in the saddle.

"I heard," he said.

"Hit them hard, then get right back here," Trevan said. "We'll hold the wall open for you."

"General, look," Zhal said, banging his hand on Trevan's armor.

On the field below, the monsters were beginning to retreat. Clearly they hadn't expected that order and they were not responding as a unit. Some were in full retreat while others were just getting the word. That meant that their lines would be strung out as they withdrew, making them much more vulnerable to the cavalry.

Apparently Lancer Tyrie was watching, too, because the moment the last monsters disengaged from the shield wall, he whistled a piercing note and clapped his spurs to his horse. As one the cavalry started down toward the turn at the bottom of the hill where the shield wall was already opening to let them pass.

"We may win the day yet, General," Zhal said, watching the charge intently.

Trevan didn't answer. There were still an awful lot of Obsidians on the field below. If the charge killed enough of them, Karpasic might disengage, but he wouldn't withdraw. Out on the plains his army would be easy pickings for the cavalry.

The Obsidians were stuck here with this fight, just like he was. The only real question is who could out last whom? The entire outcome of the battle might just rest on Lancer Tyrie and his riders. Trevan wanted to say something wise, maybe pray to whatever God might listen, but he couldn't take his eyes off the field below. The field where not just his fate, but the fate of the entire Western Alliance might very well be decided.

†††

I want to go on record as saying that this was a really bad idea," Syenna whispered as she walked beside Aren. So far they'd made it across the courtyard and up the stairs to the southern tower wall without attracting any attention. Frankly it was better than Aren expected.

"No one's noticed us," Aren said.

"That's not what I'm worried about," Syenna muttered as they passed a bored sentry. "Look around. There should be more soldiers on watch and I don't see a single archer on the wall."

Aren hadn't noticed, but now that he looked around, Syenna was right. He guessed there were only half the normal contingent on the wall. Glancing back at the courtyard, he saw that the stables appeared mostly empty. A cold chill ran through him as he realized what that meant.

"They sent the garrison out," he said under his breath. "Do you think they're trying to aid the raiders?"

"We have a more immediate problem." Syenna's voice was urgent. "What happens when that demon figures out where we went with no garrison here to fight it?"

Aren hadn't thought of that. He'd assumed the chaos demon would bash its way out of the cellars into a courtyard filled with armed soldiers. A courtyard that was now almost entirely empty.

"There have to be some soldiers still here," he said.

Before Syenna could respond, the stones under their feet trembled and the noise of shattering wood and stone rose up from below. All around the fortress, bored-looking guards snapped to attention, looking around for the source of the noise.

"Don't just stand there," Aren yelled at a young man with a broadhead spear and a confused look. "Sound the alarm."

"What?" he said, as if he hadn't heard the order.

Aren didn't respond, but he didn't really have to. The moment the young man spoke the wall of the lower courtyard exploded outward in a shower of masonry and broken stone. The chaos demon walked through the debris with one enormous stride, finally able to rise up to its full height. Aren guessed it stood at least a dozen feet high.

All around the fortress, men and women were yelling. Someone had the sense to sound the alarm and a bell began to ring. The chaos demon ignored the commotion, its head turning this way and that until at last its burning gaze came to rest on Aren.

"You just had to be right, didn't you," he said to Syenna.

† † †

Maradn closed her eyes and felt the flow of the wind on her skin. Far below, the ground slid by with every beat of her powerful wings. The connection with Jiri was complete.

Beside Maradn, Jiri's new sisters flew, one on either side. Maradn couldn't see through them as she could with Jiri, but she felt them: the simple minds of predators eager for a kill.

It was exhilarating.

As she flew, the tops of the Blackblade range came into view. She swept Jiri's head right and left until she found what she sought. The fortress at Hilt jutted up at the top of the pass, shining in the afternoon sun like a palace.

Maradn urged Jiri lower, intending to fly low over the fortress walls. As she approached, however, she could see smoke rising from the walls and broken stone littering the courtyard.

Were they under siege?

As the thought crossed her mind, an enormous creature stood up on top of the wall. It was the inky black of midnight with a cloak of red mist that clung to its form. Obsidian archers fired volleys of arrows at it as the creature lumbered along the wall, and pikemen stabbed and slashed at its legs.

For the first time in years, Maradn felt her heart race. Sweat beaded on her forehead and she had to struggle to maintain the link with Jiri. It took the effort and lives of many Obsidians to capture these beasts from the Southern Grunvald Barrens. Too much time had passed before they realized that modification of their brains to make them compliant was for naught. These beasts, much like the Kobolds, had the physical attributes and intelligence that should have made them the perfect weapon. Alas, their wills were strong and it was impossible to remove their resistance to commands without destroying their ability to fly. Jiri's brain was the answer, and finally success and total victory were at hand.

What magic did the council have that could create such beings and how did they get it into the fortress?

Telia, she sent the thought to the sister on her right. *Destroy that creature.*

She felt a surge of simple emotion from Telia, hunger and power, the desire to hunt and kill.

Maradn wanted to stay and watch, but General Karpasic had said that he would have the council's army and the Avatar sword pinned at the bottom of the canyon. That was her goal, nothing else mattered. Even if the monster tore down the fortress, she must have the sword.

Jiri sensed her urgency and her flight became swifter, diving down the back side of the mountain and skimming the tops of the trees. She could see the bottom of the canyon in the far distance and her hands began to tremble. If General Karpasic was to be believed, everything she wanted was waiting for her there. In mere minutes, her future would be assured.

† † †

Amanda watched as the cavalry swept across the battlefield leaving a trail of broken bodies in their wake. The sight was sickening and fascinating at the same time. She didn't know much about armies and battles, but she wasn't a fool. She knew her life and the lives of everyone there was riding on this charge. If the cavalry succeeded in killing enough of the enemy, they would survive, if not . . .

She didn't want to think about what might happen in that situation. Flashes of her captivity and torment at the hands of the Obsidians ran through her mind and she shuddered.

Pushing those thoughts away, Amanda focused on the battlefield. Before she could sort out who was winning, a shadow passed over her, blotting out the sun for a moment. Cries of alarm rose up around her as she looked into the sky.

Above her was a sight she simply couldn't accept. Two creatures flew over the field, rising up as they reached the trees on the far side. Each of them was long and serpentine with enormous bat-like wings and horned heads.

"What is that?" someone yelled.

"It's a dragon," Loremaster Zhal said in an awed voice.

The dragons wheeled, turning back toward the field. The green one dipped low, coming in over the combatants while the other circled high above. When the green one reached the cavalry, it opened its maw and spat bright fire down on friend and foe alike. Soldiers, monsters, and horses screamed and died as it passed overhead.

"Shoot it as it passes over," Captain Artemis yelled from the road above.

The dragon spread its wings, pulling up as it reached the steep canyon road. Amanda felt a wave of dread as it passed over her and bows and bowstrings sang in unison. The creature roared and flinched as some of the arrows pierced its hide. It reared, spinning in the air and launching another gout of flame that washed over Captain Artemis. Amanda heard her scream as she died burning.

The dragon soared past, taking another run at the battlefield. Somewhere out there, Lancer Tyrie had rallied the remaining cavalry and they were galloping across the field toward the relative safety of the trees. Frustrated, the dragon turned and headed back toward the canyon road.

Amanda didn't think, she just started running up the hill toward the spot where Captain Artemis had died.

"Where are you going?" Sir Llewelyn shouted, tearing after her.

"I have to get closer," she yelled, pointing at the dragon.

The knight put on a burst of speed Amanda wouldn't have thought him capable of in his heavy armor, catching up to her and putting his body and his shield between her and the onrushing dragon. Amanda purposely didn't look at what remained of Captain Artemis and the archers that had been next to her, instead she turned to stare down the green dragon as it approached. The blue one had remained high above the field, but she might have a chance to contact the green one as it attacked.

"Don't worry," Sir Llewelyn said, lowering his visor and raising his shield as he stood before her.

She nodded at him and closed her eyes, reaching out with her mind as the dragon drew near.

† † †

Run," Aren yelled as the chaos demon bore down on him.

Syenna didn't have to be told, she took off like a shot, running along the top of the defensive wall toward the north tower. Arrows rained down on the demon but it ignored them as it crashed after Aren. Below them, in the courtyard, a half-dozen lava queens had finally caught up and poured out of the cellar hall. The screams of the dead and dying were everywhere.

"What now?" Syenna asked as they reached the tower and turned back toward the demon.

"Inside," Aren said, pushing her toward the door that led to the tower's interior. "Head down."

Syenna grabbed the door handle and pulled, but nothing happened.

"They've barred it," she gasped, hammering on the door with her fist.

Aren turned. The chaos demon was so close he could feel the heat rolling off its body. It seemed to sense that its prey was trapped and it slowed as if it wanted to linger over the kill.

Gripping Elysia tightly, Aren faced the demon. He wanted to draw it away from Syenna but there was nowhere to go. The ramparts ended at the tower and the demon blocked the way back. He could try his luck jumping to the courtyard below, but he was sure to break a leg in the attempt.

Syenna stopped banging and drew her sword, stepping up beside him. She simply nodded when Aren looked at her. She was a proud soldier, a talented spy, a scout without peer, and she wasn't about to die cowering like a child.

Fire erupted from the demon, flowing out of it and covering the ramparts. Aren stepped in front of Syenna and willed the protective bubble to cover them. Fire washed over them, bathing them in orange light, but the heat remained outside the magical shield.

The fire died away, burning itself out along the stones of the ramparts. Aren expected the demon to charge them, but when he could finally see through the smoke and fire, the demon was looking away, over the wall and down toward the canyon below.

"Aren," Syenna said, her voice strangely calm. "What is that?"

The chaos demon roared and lunged upward as a flying lizard as big as a house passed over. It was too high for the demon to reach but it lashed out with its long tail hitting the demon in the chest and nearly knocking it off the wall to the courtyard below. The demon shrieked, forcing Aren to clap his hands over his ears to block out the sound.

The flying creature turned and raced back at the demon, raking it with fire it spat from its maw. Aren grabbed Syenna's shoulder and pulled her around the base of the tower to where it met the furthest end of the ramparts. It wasn't exactly a safe distance, but it was all he had available.

"What is that thing?" Syenna gasped.

"More tricks from the shapers at Desolis," Aren guessed.

The creature flew over the demon again, but this time when it tried to smash it with its tail, the demon grabbed it and attempted to haul the creature out of the air. The lizard lashed out with its clawed feet, tearing a deep gash in the demon's arm, and it let go.

The lizard came around again, higher this time to stay out of the demon's reach, but the demon was ready for it. Lowering its arms, the red mist that clung to the demon's body flowed like water over its skin. When it reached the demon's hands, the mist solidified into long, gossamer strands. When the lizard passed overhead again, the demon threw the strands up like a net, catching the lizard's feet and jerking it to a stop.

The lizard flapped its wings furiously, pulling at the demon, who struggled to keep hold on the creature. The lizard turned in a circle, trying to break the hold of the chaos demon who held it fast.

Aren clutched his sword until his knuckles went white.

"Stay here," he told Syenna, then he darted forward.

The flying lizard was pulling the chaos demon in circles as it tried to escape. Aren darted up behind it as the lizard flew out over the canyon. Pulling the sword back, over his shoulder, he slashed with all the force he had, cutting across the back of the demon's knee.

The demon bellowed as the Avatar sword bit into its flesh. Aren leapt away, falling onto his back as the leg buckled. Without the leg to brace itself, the demon was jerked sideways by the flying lizard. With a shriek of anger the demon toppled over the wall, plunging down into the valley far below and dragging the Obsidian creature with it.

There was a long minute where the entire world was silent, as if holding its breath, then came the sound of rocks and trees breaking, echoing up from below.

Syenna offered Aren a hand up, and he let her pull him to his feet. She wore a look of naked disbelief and she shook her head.

"You're an idiot," she said with a laugh, then she threw her arms around him and hugged him. "I can't believe that worked."

CHAPTER 36

The Price of Victory

General Karpasic stood his ground as Halik ran forward onto the battlefield. He could see the enemy cavalry gathering behind the failing shield wall. The few Formorian soldiers who remained broke, rushing back to the Obsidian lines to regroup. It was something they were trained to do in the event of a massacre, pull back to save whatever remained of the force. In this instance, however, it played right into Aren Bennis's hands.

Karpasic watched it play out like inevitable moves on a game board: The Fomorians scrambled back toward the middle of the field. The enemy commander behind the shield wall ordered his men aside, opening a gap in the center of the wall, and his cavalry charged through.

The end was inevitable now. If Halik rallied the Fomorians and the remaining troops in time, they might be able to stave off a cavalry charge, but he doubted it. He would have to disengage and wait for night. Whatever was left of his army might be able to sneak away under the cover of darkness.

The cavalry cut a swath through the rear of his retreating army, passing them as they headed into the open field where they would wheel for another pass. Halik was screaming at the soldiers, but he was too far away to be understood. Karpasic didn't need to hear him, though, Halik was ordering spears and pikes brought to bear, assuming anyone had them.

The cavalry charged again, this time slamming into the center of Halik's formation.

"Call them back," Karpasic yelled at the signalman. "Withdraw."

"Wait," the sorcerer Dirae shouted. He pointed up, above the field, where something large had risen above the trees and was sweeping down on the armies.

Karpasic grinned like a schoolboy when he saw it. An enormous dragon swept low across the field, spewing fire from its maw. The flames ripped through the cavalry, charring riders, horses, and even some of Karpasic's own men. Not that he cared about that. This was Lady Maradn's doing. He knew the sorcerers had been trying for dragons for over a year, and now it seemed, they'd done it.

He laughed as the remaining cavalry tore off for the trees on the far side of the field, the hunters suddenly becoming the hunted. Just like that, his humiliating defeat had been abated and victory was once more his.

"It's about time," he said, his overwrought muscles finally relaxing.

"What do you mean?" Dirae demanded, grabbing Karpasic by his armor and pulling him around to face him.

Karpasic's grin turned from one of relief to one of malice, and he contemptuously slapped away the sorcerer's hand.

"Don't touch me, boy," he sneered. "Your game is done."

"You made a deal with the circle," the sorcerer guessed.

"With Lady Maradn," Karpasic confirmed. "I guess when she couldn't find you, she decided to look for other, more loyal help."

The sorcerer's smug face contorted in rage and he raised his hand. As he did blue energy sparked between his fingers. Karpasic never got to see what he intended to do since at that point he shoved his dagger into the sorcerer's guts. Evard Dirae's eyes went wide and the energy vanished.

"I've been waiting to do that for a long time, Sorcerer," Karpasic said, jerking the dagger out and wiping the blood on Dirae's robe. "I'm sure Lady Maradn will reward me further for ridding her of your schemes."

The sorcerer didn't respond, he just slumped to the ground in a bloody heap. Karpasic put the dagger back into the sheath on his belt and, humming merrily to himself, strode forward to get a better view as the dragon began to burn the Army of Might's archers from their perches on the hill.

He'd been afraid all was lost just a few moments ago, but now it was turning out to be a very good day.

† † †

manda felt the dragon approaching, gliding effortlessly through the air toward her all-too-fragile body. Its mind was there, too, a thing of hunger and instinct, the need to hunt, the need to kill. There was no vestige of reason, such as she found in Monk or the Fomorians; this was an animal, nothing more.

Still, its mind was simple, uncomplicated with schemes or hidden motives. While it couldn't be reasoned with, it might be influenced.

Stop, she thought, pushing out toward the dragon's mind.

It didn't stop, but she felt it flinch, turning aside.

Amanda opened her eyes and saw the dragon bank hard, turning back toward the battlefield. As it went the archers on the road above her shot at it. Some of their arrows bounced off or stuck in the membrane of the creature's wings, but other stuck deep, biting into the monster's flesh. It roared as it turned away.

"Did you do that?" Sir Llewelyn asked.

"Maybe," Amanda said, not sure herself. "It's just an animal, not like the others. It can't be persuaded."

"Well, whatever you did worked," he said, pointing to where the dragon was circling back toward them. "Try again."

This time the dragon's mind was full of anger. It didn't know what Amanda had done, all it knew is that it had been hurt when she told it to stop. Now it wanted her to die and it bore down on her with fire rising in its throat.

Go back, Amanda projected at it. *There are easier meals that won't hurt you.*

The words might have worked on a rational mind, but while the dragon flinched again it kept coming this time.

To her credit, Amanda didn't panic. She could feel the dragon getting closer, its jaws opening to burn her as it had done to the unfortunate archer officer. She pushed that thought from her mind, forcing only on the dragon. If it couldn't be convinced, maybe it could be spooked.

STOP!

She pushed the thought out with all the force she could muster and it hit the dragon's mind like a physical blow. The dragon roared and thrashed above her, the wind from its wings buffeting her.

Amanda opened her eyes. The dragon was close and she could see its reptilian body and the dark blood that ran from its many arrow wounds. Beside her, Sir Llewelyn hefted a metal javelin, then hurled it up into the dragon's side. It roared in pain, flapping its wings more furiously to gain height. As it did, another volley from the archers slammed into it.

Stricken, the dragon turned back toward the field. It flapped its wings but then faltered, dropping heavily down to the ground below. It thrashed and struggled to rise, but then Lancer Tyrie and his remaining cavalry erupted from the trees. Unsheathing their short lances, they charged the downed beast, impaling it as they rode by.

With a long, ragged cry of pain, the dragon flopped down on the ground at last, dead.

Amanda gasped and would have fallen had not Sir Llewelyn been there to support her.

"You did great," he said with a grin.

"I'm not the one that stabbed it."

He shrugged, modestly.

"It seemed like the thing to do."

Amanda turned back to the field, intending to ask what was happening now that the dragon was dead, but suddenly a splitting headache washed over her and she felt herself being drawn inward to the place in her mind where she had first met Monk.

† † †

Maradn watched in horror as the dragon Neshla fell out of the sky to the bloodstained field below. She felt its pain and rage as the enemy horsemen rode her down and delivered their killing blows. It wasn't possible. How could this little band of soldiers have defeated a dragon?

And yet, there was something. She had felt it, some magic at work that had tried to overcome Neshla. Perhaps it had.

Maradn brought Jiri lower, being careful to stay away from the cursed archers. She reached out with her mind, seeking magic, but there wasn't any. There was, however, a faint echo of something. Focusing on that, Maradn willed her mind to find it. A moment later she found herself standing in the sitting room of a modest cottage. A young woman was there, holding her head as if it hurt. After a moment, she straightened up.

The girl's hair had been pulled back in a ponytail, revealing ears that were pointed. Maradn gasped; this was one of their own creations, an elf. No, she corrected herself, not an elf. The woman's legs were withered and she was supported by a metal frame of some kind. She was a Dross.

"Who are you?" the woman asked.

She spoke as if she didn't understand her place, that she was speaking with a sorcerer of the Obsidian Cabal and a member of the Central Circle.

"I am Maradn Norn," she introduced herself. "Who are you?"

"I am called Amanda," she said. "Are you are a sorcerer?"

Maradn nodded. The woman spoke after a long pause, as if picking her words carefully, perhaps she did realize her place after all.

"How is it that we are here?" Maradn asked.

"This is my home," she said. "Though I didn't choose it, I suspect you brought us here."

"And how can you sense my mind at all?"

The woman smiled and shrugged. Maradn was beginning to become annoyed with her. She hardly seemed to be listening.

Jiri wheeled in the sky and began descending down toward the archers. Maradn almost didn't recognize her peril in time. Her mind disengaged from the blond woman and focused on Jiri, urging her back into the sky.

That shouldn't have happened. Maradn had left Jiri flying high above the fight, so why had she—?

The girl.

Maradn sent her mind out again, this time seeking anyone trying to contact Jiri. She found the connection almost immediately. The woman, Amanda, was trying to get Jiri to come closer, into the deadly range of the archers.

Back in her library in Desolis, Maradn chewed her lip. This wasn't possible. Fomorians had no connection to magic, and Dross were less than useless. It had to be the Avatar sword. Somehow the council had used it, found a way to awaken some ancient Avatar power. Fear rose in Maradn's breast but she willed herself to be calm.

With Neshla gone and Telia battling that monster at the fortress, her chances of recovering the sword were rapidly slipping away. That was a blow, but it wasn't, necessarily, a total loss. The failure to reclaim the sword could be blamed on dear Evard, of course, but several members of the circle knew she'd planned to intervene here. If she came home with nothing, she would weaken her position.

A smile crossed her face and she pushed her mind back outward, taking full control of Jiri. As soon as she did, Maradn could feel Amanda's mind, probing around the edges of the dragon's consciousness. It was easy to follow those probing thoughts back, to find them on the narrow canyon road.

Maradn loathed the idea of subjecting Jiri to the archers, but she had no choice. She turned and sent Jiri into a steep dive, plummeting down toward the ground at incredible speed. She could see the blond woman clearly and the metal-armored knight who stood beside her, sword and shield in hand.

At the last possible moment, Jiri threw out her wings and arrested the fall, gliding in mere feet off the ground as the archers pelted her with arrows. The knight rushed forward, hacking at Jiri's foot with his sword. Maradn screamed as she felt the blow in her own body and lashed out. The injured foot hit the knight square on his shield, sending him flying across the road to slam into a wagon. He fell heavily to the ground and lay, unmoving.

The girl didn't scream or try to run, though Maradn wasn't sure she could given her support frame. She simply stood there as Jiri grasped her with her good foot and swept her upward into the air.

✝ ✝ ✝

Syenna blocked the sword blow, deflecting it off her own. She reversed the stroke and slashed the man across the face. The wound wasn't deep but the blood ran into his eyes, forcing him to retreat. Syenna followed but the man lashed out blindly with his sword, trying to keep her at a distance. It worked, but he took one step too many and fell backward off the rampart, landing with a bone crunching thud on the flagstones below.

Looking down over the edge, Syenna leaned on her knees, trying to catch her breath. Since the big demon had gone over the wall, dragging the flying lizard with it, she hadn't had a moment's rest. First the lava queens and then Colonel Tibbs and her riders had invaded the courtyard. It had been a running fight since then, especially for Aren and her up on the wall.

Behind her, Aren slashed at one the two remaining queens, chopping off its hand as it attempted to rake him with its bladed fingers. Syenna forced herself to stand and brought her sword up, advancing on the demon from Aren's right side.

She should have warned him, told him she was there, but in her exhaustion it simply didn't occur to her. As she advanced, Aren caught her movement out of the corner of his eye and started to turn, bringing his guard around to block any potential attack.

Syenna recognized her mistake too late. The lava queen saw the opening and lunged forward, raising her maimed hand like a club.

Without thinking, Syenna rushed Aren, slamming painfully into his breastplate and pushing him aside. Her action worked as Aren was driven out of the path of the blow. Unfortunately, Syenna was not so lucky.

Pain exploded through her back as the lava queen's arm came down. She heard something snap and smelled the acrid odor of burning flesh as she collapsed to the stone walkway. The impact of her fall sent new waves of pain coursing through her side and back and she cried out.

Aren was somewhere above her, driving the lava queen back with furious blows. He was gone for what seemed like a long time. All around her she could hear the clash of arms and the cries of the wounded and dying. One ragged noise seemed closer than all the rest. Eventually she realized it was her own ragged breathing.

"Careful with her." Aren's voice came from somewhere above.

The pockmarked face of a young man Syenna didn't know swam into her vision, then she closed her eyes tight as pain racked her body again.

"Sorry," the young man said. He looked up at Aren. "I think she's got a couple of broken ribs and there's a pretty good burn on her back."

With Aren's help, the young man managed to get Syenna into a sitting position with her right arm bound across her chest to keep it from moving. Her back hurt, but now that she couldn't move her arm, it didn't hurt to breathe anymore.

"That was stupid," Aren said once the pockmarked medic had gone.

"Sorry," she said. "Did we win?"

Aren looked around and then nodded.

"The fortress is ours. Colonel Tibbs is okay and we still have about half her riders."

Syenna nodded. It had been a costly victory.

"Come on," Aren said, offering her his hand. "Let's get you somewhere you can rest."

She took his hand, but he let her pull herself up at her own speed. Doing it without torturing her broken ribs took longer than she thought it would.

"Do you think General Trevan made out okay?" she asked as Aren helped her toward the stairs.

Aren shrugged and was about to answer when a cry of alarm came from off to their left.

"Dragon!" a young rider was shouting as he pointed over parapet.

Syenna had never seen a dragon before today. The guard looked terrified. She turned in time to see another of the monstrous flying lizards pass over the walls. It was blue and the black shafts of arrows stuck out from its body. One of its clawed feet was mangled and bleeding and the other carried something.

It was a person.

Syenna recognized the flowing golden hair and the metallic walking frame.

It was Amanda.

She took a deep breath to scream her sister's name, but pain tore through her and she crumpled to her knees.

"Amanda," she gasped as the dragon flew off over the mountaintops, dropping down toward the far side and carrying Amanda out of sight.